THE THING . . .

was enclosed in a metal cage, restrained behind sturdy bars. Three scientists, all wearing white smocks, stood outside the cage. One of the scientists, a young slim woman, held out a plate of raw steak. She moved closer to the bars.

"Here, boy," she said in a high, tense tone. "Here, try this."

The thing was squatting in the middle of the cage, growling.

"Nice boy. Try this." The scientist reached the bars and touched them with the plate.

The thing was on her before she could react.

Snarling, it bounded to the bars, its right hand flicking out and grabbing the woman by her wrist. She shrieked and attempted to pull away, but it was much stronger. It yanked her arm, forcing her to drop the plate, then pulled her arm between the bars. Before the other two scientists could stop it, the thing buried its teeth in her wrist. Blood sprayed everywhere.

Other Leisure Books by David Robbins:

BLOOD CULT
THE WERELING
ENDWORLD SERIES

DAVID ROBBINS

The Wraith

LEISURE BOOKS NEW YORK CITY

A LEISURE BOOK

Published by

Dorchester Publishing Co., Inc.
6 East 39th Street
New York, NY 10016

Printed in the United States of America

PROLOGUE

Plagues have periodically ravaged the human race since antiquity, possibly for as long as mankind itself has existed on this planet.

The Holy Bible relates the story of Moses and the Pharaoh of Egypt. When Pharaoh hardened his heart and refused to permit Moses and the Israelites to depart Egypt, the Egyptians suffered from plagues of frogs, lice, flies, the death of their cattle, an outbreak of boils, devastating hail, locusts, darkness, and the death of their firstborn.

During the Middle Ages everyone feared the scourge of the Black Death; during the 1300's, it wiped out a fourth of the population of Europe.

In recent times, some have referred to a plague of "social diseases", everything from herpes to AIDS.

Some say more plagues are in the offing.

From Revelation, Chapter 18, Verses 2 thru 4: "And he cried mightily with a strong voice, saying, Babylon the great is fallen, is fallen, and is become the habitation of devils, and the hold of every foul spirit, and a cage of every unclean and hateful bird. For all nations have drunk of the wine of the wrath of her fornication, and the kings of the earth have committed fornication with her, and the merchants of the earth are waxed rich through the abundance of her delicacies. And I heard another voice from heaven, saying, Come out of her, my people, that ye be not partakers of her sins, and that ye receive not of her plagues."

And from Zechariah, Chapter 14, Verse 13: "And it shall come to pass in that day, that a great tumult from the Lord shall be among them; and they shall lay hold every one on the hand of his neighbor, and his hand shall rise up against the hand of his neighbor."

Some say the worst is yet to come.

Some say we have yet to feel the full fury of . . .

THE WRATH

PART 1

EXPOSURE

1

Simon Darr thought he was still dreaming. At least, he hoped he was still dozing on the Pan American 747 as the huge jet glided to a smooth landing at the Cairo airport after an overnight flight from New York City. One moment he was thinking of his fiancée, idly recalling her lovely features and the enjoyable sensation of her lips upon his, and the next instant his train of thought was rudely derailed by a clamor within the 747.

People shouting.

Screams.

Loud reports.

Simon opened his blue eyes and gazed around, not fully awake yet, his senses sluggish from the extended overseas flight. His dark blue pants and light blue shirt felt slightly clammy on his lean frame. As he twisted in his seat to glance behind the first class section, a strand of his long brown hair dropped over his right eye, and he brushed it back with his right hand.

The commotion was coming from the rear of the aircraft. White smoke filled the aisles, restricting visibility. Even as he watched, a stewardess emerged through the smoke, running, her face fearful, her dark tresses flying.

Simon started to rise, when he saw a swarthy, stocky man in a brown uniform step from the smoke and raise an automatic pistol.

The fleeing stewardess was abreast of Simon's seat when the gunman fired, his pistol surprisingly quiet in the confines of the 747, making a half dozen burping noises in rapid succession.

Horrified, Simon saw the heavy slugs penetrate her back and erupt from the front of her blouse, spraying blood in every direction. She managed to utter a solitary shriek, then toppled onto the floor, her head turning to the right and her wide, lifeless eyes locking on Simon.

The man in brown raced up the aisle, bellowing orders in Arabic to the terrified passengers in first class. He brushed past another stewardess, a young redhead gaping at her fallen friend, and reached the door leading to the cockpit. He didn't bother to pause and open the door; he simply slammed into it and crashed on through. His abrupt entry was followed by cries of alarm and the popping of the automatic pistol.

The 747 lurched violently.

Simon frantically clutched at the seat in front of him, striving to retain his precarious footing as the aircraft swerved to the left. An image of the giant jet spiraling into the hard ground and bursting into flames filled his mind. He gripped the top of the seat and steadied himself as the 747 straightened and gathered speed.

Someone was tugging on Simon's right elbow.

He glanced down, trying to remember the name of the portly Egyptian doctor in the next seat. They had chatted briefly during the long flight. The doctor's name was . . . what?

"You must sit down," the doctor urged in clipped, precise English. "Make haste!"

Simon, stunned by the violent turn of events, couldn't seem to get his mind in gear. "What?" he asked absently, uncomprehending. "What did you say?"

"Sit down!" The doctor yanked, displaying considerable strength, pulling Simon into his seat.

Simon stared at the dead stewardess. "I don't believe it," he mumbled. "This can't be happening."

"But it is," the Egyptian countered, sweat glistening on his bald forehead, his green suit rumpled from protracted sitting.

"I don't understand . . ." Simon began slowly.

The doctor extended his left hand and gently slapped Simon on his right cheek. "You must come out of it, Mr. Darr. Now!"

Simon nodded, concentrating, focusing his attention as his brother had taught him, shutting everything else from his consciousness except the here and now. Here and now. He repeated the phrase to himself over and over, regaining his composure.

"Are you all right, Mr. Darr?" the Egyptian asked solicitously.

"I'm fine," Simon replied, suddenly recollecting the doctor's name. "Thank you, Dr. Ibrahim."

Dr. Ibrahim pointed toward the cockpit. "We are in much serious trouble here, Mr. Darr."

"Call me Simon."

Dr. Ibrahim eyed him quizzically. He was about to say more, but the stocky gunman emerged from the cockpit and began yelling in Arabic.

"What's he saying?" Simon asked.

"Shhhh!" Dr. Ibrahim motioned for silence as he listened to the gunman.

Simon noticed the other passengers were staring at the man in brown with various expressions, ranging from anger to abject fear. An elderly woman across the aisle was praying, her bony fingers clasped together so tightly that her knuckles were white. One man in particular caught Simon's attention; he seemed to be the only completely calm individual on the entire aircraft. This man wore a gray suit and red tie. His hair was blond and cropped in a crew cut. Penetrating green eyes were surveying the first class section, as if analyzing and calculating probabilities. Simon knew that look. He'd seen it often enough on his own brother to recognize the characteristics. It was the look of a born fighter, of a professional, someone trained to handle dangerous situations—the look of a military man, perhaps, or a security agent. Simon knew that agents were common on overseas flights because of increased terrorist activity.

The gunman had finished his spiel and returned to the cockpit.

"Oh, this is very bad," Dr. Ibrahim exclaimed nervously. "Very bad, indeed!"

"What did he say?" Simon asked, keeping his voice low.

"He and two of his fellows have taken over the plane. He claimed they are revolutionaries fighting for the freedom of the people from imperialistic domination. They call themselves the Glory of Light Brigade. They want some of their friends released from prison or they will kill everyone aboard."

"They planning to shoot all of us?"

"No, no, nothing like that. They want my government to release their comrades, or they will keep this plane circling over the airport until it runs out of fuel. He's killed the pilot, and the copilot now is flying the plane." Dr. Ibrahim wiped his left palm across his perspiring brow.

"What are we going to do?" Simon asked.

"Not a thing," Dr. Ibrahim cautioned. "He told us to stay in our seats or we will be shot."

"Do you think your government will give in to their demands?" Simon asked.

Dr. Ibrahim shrugged. "Who can say? My government has been—how do you say it?—getting tough with terrorists, just like all the other governments."

"So all we can do is wait?"

"What else?" Dr. Ibrahim retorted. "They will shoot us if we try anything foolish."

"We can't just sit here," Simon said, wondering what his brother would do at a time like this? Attack the terrorists with his feet and fists flying? No. Jay would patiently wait for the proper moment before making his move. What was it Jay had said once? "Knowing when to strike is equally as important as knowing where and how to strike. The three are mutually interdependent."

"What are you thinking about?" Dr. Ibrahim asked anxiously.

"My brother," Simon said.

"What is his name?"

"Jay. He's thirty-two, six years older than me, and lives in Philadelphia now. That's in Pennsylvania."

"I know," Dr. Ibrahim said. "I attended a seminar once at the University of Pennsylvania. What is your brother's vocation?"

"He teaches," Simon said. He scanned the first class section, looking at the other passengers huddled together, whispering to one another.

"Oh? What does he teach? History? Mathematics? Physics?"

Simon shook his head. "None of those. Jay teaches martial arts."

Dr. Ibrahim appeared puzzled. "What?"

Before Simon could reply, the gunman stepped into view and shouted at the passengers. While the terrorist barked orders, Simon glanced at the man with the red tie. The blond man was leaning casually against a window, his right arm draped across his lap, his fingers only inches from his belt. His grey jacket was open. Was he carrying a gun?

The terrorist disappeared inside the cockpit.

"What was it this time?" Simon asked the doctor.

"He told us to stay in our seats at all times," Dr.

Ibrahim translated. "He said he is in radio contact with the authorities and has presented his demands."

Dr. Ibrahim removed a white handkerchief from an inside coat pocket and mopped his sweaty forehead. "I don't believe I will ever fly again."

"What if you need to visit another country on business?" Simon asked. "Didn't you tell me earlier that you make a lot of trips to the States?"

"The next time I must go," Dr. Ibrahim vowed, "I will swim."

Simon looked over his left shoulder and saw the aisle was almost clear of smoke. In the middle of the next section, straddling the center of the aisle, was another terrorist in brown. How had they managed to get on board undetected? Why had they waited until now to hijack the 747? Did it even matter?

"What line of work did you say your brother is in?" Dr. Ibrahim asked.

Although he considered their conversation ridiculous, given the circumstances, Simon decided it was better than silence. "He teaches martial arts. Specifically, *Hung Gar*."

"*Hung Gar*?" Dr. Ibrahim repeated. "I've never heard of it. What is this *Hung Gar*?"

"Have you ever seen a Bruce Lee movie?"

"Bruce who?"

"Tell me," Simon said, leaning closer to the doctor, "what do you do in your spare time? Have any hobbies?"

Dr. Ibrahim seemed surprised by the change in subject. "I like to read medical journals, and I devote much time to the Koran. Why?"

"Oh, no reason," Simon said. He gazed at the cockpit, wishing there was some way he could wrestle the pistol from the terrorist and pay him back for shooting the stewardess.

"Do you teach this *Hung Gar*, too?" Dr. Ibrahim asked.

"No. I'm a reporter with a small newspaper in Colorado called the *Lyons Bugle*. It's a weekly. Not exactly an exciting life, but I like it."

"Are you here on an assignment?"

Simon smiled. "The *Bugle* doesn't have the money to send me to Denver, let alone Egypt. I'm on vacation." He stared at the stewardess. "Some vacation this turned out to be."

"Why did you pick my country?" Dr. Ibrahim inquired, genuinely curious.

"I didn't," Simon replied. "My fiancée is here working with her professor on a dig. We thought it would be a great idea to spend two weeks together here, then fly to Chicago for the wedding."

Dr. Ibrahim brightened. "You are getting married soon?"

"In sixteen days," Simon said. "Initially, we wanted to get married first, and then take a nice honeymoon. But our schedules won't allow it. The dig she is on is entering a crucial phase. She has to be back at the site four days after we're married." Simon sighed. "Oh, well, we'll get that honeymoon someday. At least my boss was kind enough to give me an extra week off," he said, frowning, "although without pay."

"It is good for a man to take a wife," Dr. Ibrahim stated. "May Allah smile on your union."

"Thank you," Simon responded.

They lapsed into an uncomfortable silence, strained by the thick tension, the impending danger.

Simon kept his eyes trained on the cockpit doorway. What was happening in there? He doubted the Egyptian government would capitulate to the terrorists. Would the fanatics carry through with their threat to allow the 747 simply to run out of fuel and plunge to the earth? Probably. He thought of Amy and speculated on whether or not he would be alive to participate at their wedding.

There were loud voices coming from the cockpit.

Simon unsuccessfully tried to relax. It figured that this would happen to him! Murphy strikes again! His first vacation in two years, and his very first trip overseas. Three weeks off, two of them to be spent reveling in the sights and sounds of Egypt with Amy, and then the trip to Chicago and their wedding. And now it looked like all of their meticulous preparations were for nothing.

The swarthy gunman abruptly appeared in the cockpit door and, judging from his livid countenance, wasn't any too happy. He began spouting in Arabic again.

''Allah preserve us!'' Dr. Ibrahim declared when the terrorist stopped.

''What is it?'' Simon demanded.

''He said the government has refused to grant his request to release his comrades unless the plane lands first. He says he won't let us land because he distrusts the authorities and suspects a trap.''

''So we're right back where we started,'' Simon said.

Dr. Ibrahim vigorously shook his head, his jowly cheeks shaking. ''No, my friend, you have not heard it all. He says he must convince the authorities that he means business.''

''How does he intend doing that?'' Simon inquired, watching the terroist. The man had moved forward several steps and was glaring at the passengers.

''He says they will show they are serious by killing an American.''

''An American?''

''To be exact,'' Dr. Ibrahim quoted, ''an American pig.''

''Uh-oh.''

A second terrorist from the back section joined his companion and started jabbering away.

So two of the three terrorists were now in first class.

Simon glanced at the man with the red tie. The man's face was averted, as if he were looking out the window, but Simon knew he wasn't missing a thing. His right hand was out of sight, under his jacket. If the man was a security agent, what was he waiting for? This was his big chance, with two of the terrorists only a few yards away.

The two terrorists, both of them unshaven, with curly dark hair, looking enough alike to be twins, advanced along the aisle, studying the passengers.

Simon knew what they were doing.

They were selecting their victim.

What should he do if they picked him? Simon debated whether he should flee or fight. But where could he go? Running to the rear of the aircraft would be useless. The third terrorist was back there somewhere and would undoubtedly shoot him down mercilessly. Resisting wasn't too practical, either. What could he do against two armed killers? He mentally lambasted himself for failing to take more lessons from his brother when he had the opportunity. There had been a six month stretch, about a year and a half ago, before Jay left Lyons for Philadelphia, when he had diligently strived to learn *Hung Gar* and understand his brother's keen interest in the martial arts. But after six months of painful effort, despite Jay's promptings to continue, he gave up and stopped practicing his sets and techniques, throwing in the towel. He told his brother he was too busy at work to devote sufficient time to *Hung Gar*, but he had lied. He was unwilling to divulge the real reason he quit for fear of offending his brother, but the truth of the matter was more mundane than being overworked—he was bored to tears. At first, he found the prescribed movements and techniques interesting, even relaxing and fascinating in their simplicity and fluid flow of movement, but after a while his fascination turned to weariness. He grew to dislike the necessary repetition so it became an automatic response and attained the level of an ingrained, almost instinctive reflex.

If only he'd kept with it.

The two terrorists had stopped next to his seat, and the one from the cockpit was leering maliciously down at him.

The one from the cockpit, the apparent leader, spoke several sentences in Arabic, directing his remarks at Dr. Ibrahim. He finished and pointed his finger at Simon.

Dr. Ibrahim's voice quavered as he translated the message. "I am so very sorry, my friend. He says that it is obvious you are an American. He told me to tell you . . ." Ibrahim paused, his tone conveying the depth of his regret and sorrow, ". . . to tell you that you will be the first one they execute."

Simon stared up into the baleful eyes of the leader and felt his mouth suddenly go dry.

2

There were two of them, a beautiful young woman and an elderly gentleman, seated in filmsy folding chairs on either side of a metal collapsible table. The table was positioned in front of a large green tent situated at the base of a steep cliff.

The woman gazed overhead at the starry sky and smiled contentedly. Her shoulder length blonde hair glistened in the light from a nearby campfire. "I'm almost reluctant to leave," she said, stretching, her deep blue eyes seeming to twinkle in the firelight. "It's so beautiful here, especially now. So quiet and peaceful. And look at all those stars! I never saw this many back home."

Her colleague, a tall man in his fifties who wore his age well, ran his left hand through his short gray hair and snickered. "Of course, you didn't. You're from Chicago, Amy," he reminded her. "In the cities you see fewer stars due to light refraction and atmospheric opacity. Out here, hundreds of miles from any sprawling metropolis, the stars are crystal clear." He paused. "Besides, in some of the larger cities back in the States, you have to cut the air with a hacksaw just to catch a glimpse of the sun."

"Is that one of the reasons you took up archaeology, Professor?'' Amy asked him. ''To get away from so-called civilization?''

''Civilization!'' He snorted derisively. ''Is that what they have the gall to call it? Well, I'll tell you a thing or two about civilization, Ms. Brant,'' he declared, adopting the formal style of speech he invariably used when about to embark on one of his notorious impromptu lectures.

''Fire away, Professor Crenshaw,'' she replied, grinning.

Professor Artemas Crenshaw was her teacher, her mentor, and one of the best friends she'd ever had. The two of them were a mutual admiration society. She respected his decades of experience and expertise in archaeology, and had grown to admire his integral honesty and humor; he was fond of her bubbling enthusiasm and frequently envious of her decidedly perceptive insights and her alert, analytical mind. If all of his students could be as industrious and dedicated as Amy Brant, he often told himself, major archaeological discoveries would be unearthed every week. He sincerely believed she was the best student he'd ever taught in a long and distinguished academic career.

''Civilization, Amy,'' he began, pulling his black cardigan sweater closer to his body, ''is in a state of decay, not on a progressive upswing as the social liberals would have us believe. Look at what our current culture has done to our planet. We have pollution on an unprecedented scale, despite our feeble efforts to curtail it. Literacy rates, particularly in the inner cities, are a disgrace. Drug use in the industrial nations is epidemic, and so is governmental corruption. Wars are as common as they ever were, but with one big difference. Now we can destroy entire societies with the flick of a switch. Crime is rampant. In many cities a person can't walk on the streets at night for fear of being mugged or worse.

Citizen apathy is at an all time high. Do our children grow up to become creative, caring, responsible individuals? I should say not! Instead, they become spoiled materialistic hypocrites, mired in deceptions of their own devising. Or they become paranoid clones, subservient to their society, unable to think for themselves and unwilling to try. Is this civilization?"

"That's what they call it," Amy replied, idly toying with a button on her yellow blouse.

"Well, they're wrong," Professor Crenshaw snapped, aroused by one of his many pet peeves. "Compare our civilization to that attained by the ancient Egyptians. They were magnificent. For thousands of years they dominated the Middle East. Look at the contributions they made. They virtually were pioneers in astronomy. They developed a 365-day calendar. Their architectural achievements rank as some of the greatest the world has ever seen. Just look at the pyramids and the Great Sphinx! I could go on and on, but you know Egyptian history as well as I."

"What about the crime rate in ancient Egypt?" Amy inquired, eager to keep Crenshaw talking. Their camp was located almost 40 miles west of Idfu in a rugged, desolate area, notable for steep ravines and gorges, sparse vegetation and a remarkable lack of wildlife. Idfu was about 370 miles south of Cairo on the west bank of Egypt's life line, the Nile River. There wasn't very much in the way of entertaining diversion way out in the middle of nowhere, which was precisely the reason she wanted to sustain their conversation as long as possible.

"From what we've learned," Crenshaw stated, "their crime rate was minimal."

"Why do you suppose that was?"

"Two reasons, basically," he answered. "First, if someone committed a crime, they weren't sent to a comfortable prison for a few years and then released to perpetuate their criminal activities. The Egyptians made certain that the punishment fitted the crime."

"What was the other reason for their low crime rate?" Amy asked.

"The family."

"The family?"

"Absolutely," he said, nodding. "The ancient Egyptians revered the family. They were extremely family-oriented, and the family is the basic institution of civilization. I've studied the matter extensively, and I'm convinced that if any society or country, no matter what type of political organization they may have, ignore or belittle the family or render it difficult to maintain, then that society or country is doomed to extinction."

"You're serious?" Amy asked, grinning. "I mean, there's more to civilization than the family."

"Is there?" he promptly countered. "Well, yes, in a sense you're right. There is one more primary factor contributing to the stabilization of civilization, and that is religion. As you know, the Egyptians were exceedingly religious people."

Amy stared up at the dark cliff looming above them. "Do you think *these* people were religious?"

Crenshaw thoughtfully chewed on his lower lip. "Yes, I'd say they were," he said at last, "although these people seem to be an exceptional anomaly in Egyptian history."

"How so?" Amy pressed him, leaning forward and resting her elbows on the table.

"The Valley of the Dog People," Crenshaw said slowly. "It just doesn't make any sense."

"Tell me."

"What?" Crenshaw looked at her. "You've already heard the story umpteen times. Now you want to hear it again?"

"It excites me," Amy admitted. "When you called and told me about it, I couldn't wait to get on the first available flight over here. My parents objected, at first, but when they realized what a tremendous chance this was for me, they even chipped in part of the air fare. Dean Wassell at the University was a lot easier to convince. He let me cut short my classes so I could get over here as fast as possible." She smiled at him in gratitude. "This is my first dig, Professor, and it may turn out to be somewhat historic. I owe it all to you."

"Nonsense, Amy," Crenshaw stated affectionately. "I chose you because you're competent and hard working and . . . you are one of the few people I know who can tolerate my idiosyncrasies."

"So tell me," Amy badgered. "I know you like to talk about it."

"Well, if you insist." Crenshaw leaned back in his chair and placed his hands behind his head. His brown eyes narrowed as he reflected on the sequence of events.

"It was in November, right?"

"November 15th, I believe," Crenshaw began. "I received a call from my friend, Hassan Kheir, who is a high official with the Egyptian Department of Antiquities. Hassan told me about the scroll."

"The leather scroll?"

"Yes, the leather scroll. Contrary to popular belief, the ancient Egyptians didn't do all of their writing on papyrus. Some of it was done on leather. According to Hassan, the proprietor of a curio shop purchased this scroll from a scruffy desert wanderer. This fellow walked into the shop and offered to sell it, claiming it had been in his family for generations and the only reason he was selling it was because he was destitute. The proprietor examined the scroll, and realizing it was authentic and unique, he contacted Hassan. You'd be surprised at how many artifacts are stumbled upon in this fashion," Crenshaw said, digressing. "Fortunately, the Egyptian government has impressed upon the dealers the necessity of preserving these historical treasures, and they receive outstanding coopration most of the time."

"So Hassan called you," Amy interjected, hoping to get him back on track.

"Yes. Hassan and I go way back," Crenshaw stated. "He knew I'd be interested in investigating this scroll, and he also knew I might be able to arrange a grant to cover some of the expenses. Since Egypt has to devote a considerable portion of her revenue to the military and to social ills, they don't have quite as much money as they'd like to spend on archaeological expeditions."

"So Hassan called you," Amy said again, then added, "because you could find some grant money and you also happen to be one of the leading Egyptologists on the face of the planet."

"Exactly," Crenshaw affirmed. "I set my affairs in order and came over. As soon as I saw the leather scroll, I knew we were on to something special. The hieroglyphics predated any known so far, and it took several months for me to decipher their meaning. Once I had, and Hassan had confirmed my results, we were confronted by a perplexing enigma. The scroll relates a strange and astonishing tale." He stopped and gazed at the cliff. "It told us where we could find the Valley of the Dog People, the very first mention of this valley ever found in Egyptian literature. Once, according to the scroll, this area was a lush paradise with ample water and a great city. This city was conquered by a tribe referred to as the Dog People. Who these Dog People were, and where they came from, is anyone's guess at this point. A nobleman, a prince, was sent from the capital and fought the Dog People. He was killed in the battle, and the scroll tells us he was entombed near this very spot, but not until a mighty magician appeared and destroyed the Dog People, eradicating every last one. And that wasn't all. The city was put to the torch and razed to the ground, and all of the surrounding countryside was likewise burned. An edict from the king mandated this area as totally unfit for habitation, and anyone caught defying the decree was immediately put to death."

"How bizarre," Amy commented.

"That's an understatement," Crenshaw remarked, his brow furrowed in comtemplation. "The scroll leaves so many unanswered questions, so many mysteries begging resolution. For instance, why is this the only mention of the Valley of the Dog People we've ever discovered? If our estimate of the scroll's origin is correct, then it is at least five thousand years old. It's quite remarkable that it survived this long, although we do have other artifacts from even earlier periods."

"Why do you think they were called Dog People?" Amy asked.

Crenshaw shrugged and scratched his narrow chin. "That's another puzzle. At first, I speculated it might be an intentional insult. Dogs weren't held in very high esteem in ancient Egypt. Oh, they owned some. We know that farmers used dogs to assist in tending their flocks, and very wealthy families usually owned greyhounds. But as just about everybody knows, the Egyptians considered cats sacred. Cats held a special niche in Egyptian culture. They built temples for them and even buried some in gold coffins. But dogs were generally looked down upon as lowly beasts, unworthy of exalted honors. That's why I initially supposed the term was used as a slur."

"But something changed your mind?"

"Yes. The more I read, the more convinced I became that the writer of the scroll was literally referring to these strange people as Dog People. Quite inexplicable. One phrase, in particular, was extremely troubling."

"Which phrase was that?" Amy asked.

"It's found in the part where the writer describes

the city being conquered by the Dog People. If I didn't know better, if the very idea wasn't patently ridiculous, I'd swear the writer states the residents of the city actually *became* Dog People. Not subjugated by the Dog People, you understand, but transformed into Dog People. Amazing!"

"Could you have misinterpreted the hieroglyphics?" Amy suggested.

"No," Crenshaw responded emphatically. "The rendering of the hieratic was quite accurate, making it all the more confusing."

"When we find the tomb of the prince we should learn more," Amy said optimistically.

"*If* we locate the tomb," Crenshaw said.

"You don't think we will?"

"I hope we do," Crenshaw admitted, "but who can say? Let's face facts. It's been around five thousand years. The tomb could have been washed away by a flood. It could have been desecrated by graverobbers, just like so many of the other great tombs were looted. And even if we do find it, there's no guarantee it will clear up the mystery of the Dog People."

"But you think we're very close to finding it, don't you?" Amy asked excitedly.

"Truth to tell, yes, I do," Crenshaw said, staring at the cliff. "If my calculations are correct, then it should be somewhere in that cliff. At the rate my men are digging, it shouldn't be long now."

"I can hardly wait," Amy exclaimed.

"As soon as we do locate the tomb," Crenshaw stated, "I must contact Hassan. He will assist us in taking inventory. It's required by law."

"I know," Amy said. "The government wants to insure its artifacts are all accounted for, that none of them wind up on the black market."

"I can't blame them," Crenshaw said. "They've lost so many of their priceless treasures in the past."

He began rubbing the back of his neck. ''Seems to be a bit of a chill in the air tonight. My muscles are stiffening up on me.''

''It can get down to around fifty at night,'' Amy noted, ''even this late in April.''

''April 29th,'' Crenshaw clarified. ''You've been here two weeks so far.'' He paused and grinned. ''But I should think you will find the next two weeks even more stimulating than the past two.''

''What's that supposed to mean?'' Amy demanded, as if she had to ask.

''Your young man, Simon, should be here in a day or so. I just hope you can concentrate on your work with him around.''

''Don't you worry about me,'' Amy told him.

Professor Crenshaw laughed. ''Tell me, how does Simon feel about disrupting your honeymoon schedule, just so you can dig up some old bones?''

''Simon appreciates how important this is to me,'' Amy replied. ''It's a once in a lifetime opportunity. I want to be here for the inventory, when we catalogue everything, and I'd miss it if we took our honeymoon as originally planned.''

''So how have you worked it out?''

''Simon was able to get three weeks off from his employer,'' Amy explained. ''We'll spend two weeks here, then fly to Chicago for our wedding. We'll have a few days together before I have to fly back here.''

''I'm sorry,'' Crenshaw apologized. ''I didn't mean to mess up your wedding.''

''You didn't know we'd set the date. Actually, if it'd been just up to me, I would have postponed the wedding, but our families were already so involved with the preparations, I didn't want to hurt anyone's feelings.''

''Where did you meet your young man, anyway?''

''I met him about a year ago,'' Amy replied, ''when I went to Colorado to attend a summer course at the University of Colorado in Boulder. I went there to get away from Chicago for a while, to enjoy the outdoors. I met Simon at a party a friend was throwing."

"Let me guess. It was love at first sight." Crenshaw grinned.

Amy smiled as she reminisced. "Not quite, but close. We spent every spare minute together during the summer, and it was murder when I had to return to Chicago in the fall. Simon came to Chicago over Thanksgiving, and I went to Colorado over Christmas vacation. That's when he proposed."

"And the rest, as they say, is history." Professor Crenshaw gazed at the campfire and the dozen tents housing the workers employed on the dig. "I hope Simon won't be expecting plush accomodations."

"He has a good idea of what to expect," Amy said. "I explained everything in my last letter. In fact, he should be in his hotel room in Cairo by now."

"Yes," Professor Crenshaw said. "Those overnight flights from New York usually arrive in Cairo by midafternoon. Sometimes, though, they're delayed until late afternoon or even early evening. In any event, by tomorrow morning your young man will be on his way to Idfu. I've already dispatched Naan to meet him and escort him to this site. If all goes well, by the night after next you won't have to fret over the chilly conditions. You'll be able to keep warm without any problem." He winked at her and chuckled.

Amy rose and stepped toward the green tent. "In the meantime, how about a beer to keep our insides warm?"

"Fine by me, but I hope Simon won't become annoyed with me."

Amy paused at the tent flap. "Annoyed? Why?"

Crenshaw smiled impishly. "At the rate you've been chugging that Stella beer, he's liable to think I've turned you into a drunkard."

3

Thank the Lord Amy wasn't with him!

Simon Darr was standing against the wall, his arms at his sides, facing the passengers as ordered by the leader of the terrorists. He was thinking of Amy and their many happy times, while he waited to die. Earlier, the gruff leader had put him against the wall, intending to carry out his threat to kill an American passenger, when suddenly the navigator had poked his head out and said a few words. The second terrorist maintained a careful watch over the pasengers while the leader went into the cockpit.

Simon waited apprehensively, as the minutes slowly ticked by.

Finally, the leader came out and addressed Dr. Ibrahim, then stood next to Simon while the doctor translated.

"He says you are a fortunate man," Ibrahim said. "The government has agreed to his demands, provided he does not hurt any of the passengers."

Simon suddenly found he could breathe a bit easier.

The navigator appeared again and spoke to the leader in Arabic, then both men returned to the cockpit.

The second terrorist walked up to Simon and sneered.

Over the terrorist's left shoulder, Simon saw the man with the red tie shift in his seat so that his body was now facing the aisle.

The second terrorist jabbed his right hand into Simon's abdomen and said something in Arabic.

Simon froze, sensing the man was attempting to provoke him, but what else could he do? The bastard was holding an automatic pistol on him.

Dr. Ibrahim was observing the tableau with concern.

The second terrorist prodded Simon again and laughed, while Simon resisted an impulse to knee the son of a bitch in the groin.

The leader walked from the cockpit, and right away the two terrorists became embroiled in a vociferous argument.

Simon wondered what they were arguing about.

The leader moved down the aisle, stopped near Dr. Ibrahim and spoke to the doctor while pointing at Simon.

Dr. Ibrahim nodded when the leader concluded his speech. "I am sorry, Simon," he said. "You are not out of the woods yet, I'm afraid."

"But you said they weren't going to kill me."

"That one," Dr. Ibrahim stated, pointing at the second terrorist, "wants to kill you anyway, just to show the government they are not to be trifled with. This man here," and Ibrahim indicated the leader, "doesn't agree. He doesn't want to do anything to jeopardize the release of his comrades from prison."

"So what are they going to do?" Simon asked, and was promptly slapped across the face by the second terrorist. The man growled a few words in Arabic.

"He says if you open your mouth again, he will kill you," Dr. Ibrahim informed Simon.

Simon could feel blood trickling out of the right

corner of his mouth. He could see the leader over the second terrorist's right shoulder, and it was plainly evident that the man wasn't any too pleased by this turn of events.

The leader talked to Ibrahim again.

"He says that you must not take any of this personally, that there must be casualties in their holy war," the doctor interpreted. "His fight is against imperialism, not innocent dupes like yourself. You are just in the wrong place at the wrong time. They have decided to hold a vote on your fate."

The leader walked to the back of the first class section and shouted a name several times.

The second terrorist was eyeing Simon gleefully, fingering the trigger on his pistol.

Simon watched that finger, afraid the man would pull the trigger for the sheer fun of killing an "American pig."

Not quite a minute later, the third terrorist joined his companions in the first class section. This man was dressed exactly like the other two, but instead of carrying an automatic pistol he toted a machine gun in his right hand and a hand grenade in his left.

The leader and the third terrorist engaged in an animated discussion, both repeatedly glancing in Simon's direction.

Eventually, the leader wheeled and stalked into the cockpit.

Fifteen minutes dragged by, and with each passing minute Simon became uneasier. What was the leader doing in there? Talking on the radio to the authorities? Why was he taking so long?

The leader finally stepped from the cockpit and said something to the second terrorist, who looked at Simon and grinned, displaying his crooked front teeth.

Simon didn't need a mind reader or a translator to know what the leader had said.

He was going to be shot!

The second terrorist jammed the barrel of his pistol into Simon's nose.

Dr. Ibrahim courageously intervened, speaking to the leader, and although Simon couldn't comprehend a word of Arabic, he knew the doctor was trying to persuade the leader not to go through with the execution.

Ibrahim was not successful.

The leader angrily snapped at the doctor, silencing him.

Meanwhile, the third terrorist had advanced a little ways down the aisle while constantly looking toward the rear of the aircraft to be sure everyone was remaining in their seats.

Simon could feel the terrorist's hot breath on his face. The fanatic was relishing this, his angular features reflecting his open contempt and hatred. Without warning, he spit into Simon's face.

Simon inadvertently recoiled in revulsion and almost raised his right hand to wipe his face, but the pressure of the pistol barrel against his nose dissuaded him.

The second terrorist laughed sadistically.

Simon abruptly felt a wave of rage sweep over him. Realizing he had absolutely nothing to lose, that his death was mere moments away, he was moved to action. From somewhere deep within himself, from the very core of his being, surged an instinctive reaction to the abuse, to the spittle and the pistol and the taunting visage of the terrorist only inches from his own face. He exploded.

His right knee swept upward, even as he brought his left hand up and around. Simon connected with his knee, catching the second terrorist completely by surprise, and at the instant of impact, Simon deflected the pistol barrel to one side.

The terrorist fired, the shot plowing into the wall of the 747.

And all hell broke loose.

Some of the passengers screamed and shrieked, while a bearded man made a lunge at the third terrorist, wrapping his arms around the gunman's legs.

The leader was shouting as he began to level his pistol at the passengers.

Simon locked his hands on the second terrorist's wrists, and they fell to the floor, wrestling for control of the pistol.

The blond man with the red tie entered the fray, his right hand sweeping up, a sophisticated plastic automatic with a silencer on the barrel aimed at the terrorist leader. The gun coughed, and the leader was jerked backwards as the slug penetrated his forehead. He toppled against one of the seats, his arms waving wildly then falling limp.

The third terrorist, about to blast the bearded man holding onto his legs, tried to bring his machine gun to bear on the blond man.

But the blond man was faster. He pivoted and fired, striking the third terrorist between the eyes, then scrambled from his seat to the aisle.

Simon found himself pinned to the floor as his fanatic opponent attempted to direct the pistol barrel at his head. Simon strained, his arms shaking from the exertion, holding the terrorist's arms at bay. He caught a flash of black out of the corner of his right eye as something was pressed against the terroist's temple. There was a muffled retort and a spray of crimson, and the terrorist abruptly went completely limp, slumping onto Simon.

"Are you all right?" someone was asking.

The body was hauled to one side, and Simon looked up to find the blond man towering over him.

"Are you all right?" the blond man repeated.

Simon nodded and started to rise. Dr. Ibrahim was suddenly at his side, supporting him.

"That was a brave thing you did," Dr. Ibrahim said.

"I didn't have much choice," Simon said. "It was him or me."

"Will you make sure none of the other passengers are hurt?" the blond man asked the doctor.

"Of course," Dr. Ibrahim said, immediately starting down the aisle.

Simon studied the blond man. He had been right, after all—a professional, if ever there was one. "Thank you for saving my life."

"It's my job, kid," the blond man responded, his green eyes scanning the first class section.

Simon grinned, guessing the blond man wasn't more than 35. "Are you with security?"

"Interpol," the man replied.

"Interpol? I didn't know you guys flew airline security."

"We don't, but we received a tip from a reliable informant. We knew the New York to Cairo flight had been targeted, but we didn't know which day or how they would do it. So we decided to tighten terminal security and place an agent on every trip. It paid off."

"What's your name?" Simon inquired.

"Name's Lanning. James Lanning."

Simon extended his right hand. "I can never repay you for what you've done. I'm Simon Darr."

Lanning was holding his pistol in his right hand. Instead of shifting it to shake, he reached out with his left and awkardly shook Simon's hand. "Pleased to meet you, kid." He glanced at each of the dead men, then headed for the cockpit. "We'll talk later," he said over his left shoulder. "First, we've got to land this big bird and tidy up this mess. See ya."

Simon leaned against the wall, feeling oddly light-headed and weak. His legs were quivering, and his knees were on the verge of buckling.

Dr. Ibrahim came toward him. "Are you all right,

my friend? You look ill."

"I don't feel so hot," Simon admitted.

The doctor took Simon by the shoulder and led him to an empty seat. "Here. Be seated. You are having a reaction to what just occurred. The adrenaline, you know, pumps and pumps as you get all excited, and it is still in the blood after the excitement passes. You understand?"

"Yes." Simon smiled weakly. "Thank you, Dr. Ibrahim, I'll be okay."

"Good. I must continue checking on the others." The good doctor moved down the aisle.

The Interpol agent strolled from the cockpit and approached Simon. "Got the shakes, huh, kid?"

"I wish you'd stop calling me kid," Simon said. "You don't look much older than me."

Lanning chuckled. "It's not how old you look, Simon, that counts. It's how old you feel—and sometimes I feel very, very old."

"How long have you been with Interpol?"

Lanning leaned against a nearby seat, folded his arms over his chest, and watched the passengers expressing their relief and dismay. He grinned, radiating an air of amused detachment. "I've been with Interpol about ten years, now. I worked for the F.B.I. for a few years after I graduated from college, but they assigned me to a desk job." Lanning frowned. "Lord, how I hated it! I applied at Interpol and they made me one of their special troubleshooters. I like this work. It keeps me on my toes."

Simon gazed at the dead terrorist leader. "I'll bet." He scrutinized Lanning. "Why'd you select Interpol, James?"

Lanning faced Simon. "Nobody calls me James. It's Lanning. Got that?"

Simon nodded, wondering why the agent was so touchy about his first name.

"Interpol is a topnotch outfit," Lanning went on.

"I work out of the Paris Bureau, which is the major reason I wanted to join them. You see, I was born in France."

"Oh?"

"Yeah. My dad was a diplomat, attached to the American Embassy at the time I was born. I spent the first seven years of my life in France, and they tell me I speak French like a native. I had this urge to go back, which is why I picked Interpol over the Foreign Legion." Lanning laughed at his own joke. "Besides, I was real tired of Chicago."

"Chicago?"

"Yeah. Are you from there?"

"No," Simon replied. "I'm from Colorado, but my fiancee is from Chicago. We're going to be married there in a couple of weeks."

"I haven't been there in years," Lanning stated wistfully. "My mother settled there after my dad kicked the bucket. She keeps writing to me, begging me to visit."

"Why don't you?"

Lanning ignored the question, glancing at the dead leader, his thin lips tightening. "We were lucky, Simon. Those idiots could have caused an implosion if one of their shots pierced the pressurized cabin."

"What about that one shot that was fired by the guy trying to kill me?" Simon asked.

"It lodged in the wall between the cockpit and this section."

"What about your shots?" Simon thought to ask. "What if one of them had gone through the wall of the aircraft?"

"Not very likely." Lanning patted the shoulder holster under his left arm. "This baby is specifically designed for missions like this one. Do you know much about guns and ammunition?"

"No," Simon confessed, "I don't."

Lanning leaned toward Simon. "Let me try and

explain it to you. Do you know what a .357 Magnum is?"

"I've heard of them. Didn't Clint Eastwood use one in his *Dirty Harry* movies?"

"Nope. That was a .44 Magnum, but you're on the right track. You see, what makes one revolver pack more punch than another, when you get right down to the basics, is the cartridge the revolver fires. A .44 Magnum cartridge is more powerful than a .357 Magnum cartridge because the .44 Magnum cartridge can hold more grains of gunpowder. Take just the .357 Magnum. You can get cartridges with 158 grains of gunpowder, or you could get cartridges with, say, 120 grains. The cartridge with the 158 grains, although it will fit in the same revolver as the cartridge with 120 grains, will be more powerful. Do you follow me so far?"

"Yes." Simon was secretly tickled by Lanning's obvious zeal for firearms.

"Good. Then you can understand the principle behind my pistol. By reducing the number of grains in the cartridges, our experts produce a gun with a limited effective range. They also added hollow points, which flatten upon impact, reducing the degree of penetration. Sure, if I were to fire my pistol at point-blank range at one of the windows, we'd have an implosion. But if my bullet strikes something else first, it's highly unlikely it would have enough force left to puncture the windows or a wall."

Simon nodded at the dead terrorist leader. "They sure do a number on the human body, though."

Lanning beamed in satisfaction. "That they do."

A stewardess came down the aisle and stopped next to Lanning. "Excuse me, sir, but we've been cleared to land. Please strap yourself in."

"Will do," Lanning promised, squeezing into the seat next to Simon.

"Say, Lanning," Simon inquired, "why'd you

wait so long before making your move?"

"Had to." Lanning secured his seat belt. "In addition to French, I also speak Arabic. I knew there were three of them on board. If I had blown away the one here, the other two would have blown a lot of passengers to kingdom come. I was hoping all three of them would group together. Thanks to you, they did."

"As I recall," Simon quibbled, "the third terrorist was up here for a good twenty minutes before you opened up."

"I know it was rough on you," Lanning said, "but I had to check out the grenade first without being noticed."

"What about the grenade?"

"The pin, dummy. I had to make sure the pin was still in the grenade. I didn't want him to drop it with the pin out. None of us would be alive right now if he had. Once I was certain the pin was still in the grenade, I could take him out with relative confidence." He paused. "You're not very observant, are you? What do you do for a living?"

"I'm a reporter," Simon answered indignantly.

"Oh." Lanning nodded knowingly. "That explains it."

4

Amy Brant, wearing grubby jeans and a checkered blouse, was seated at the table in front of the large green tent savoring her lunch when the runner brought them the good news. Professor Crenshaw was sitting across from her, wearing his inevitable khakis and black boots. Both of them were in the middle of a meal consisting of a falafel sandwich and Stella beer.

The runner raced around the southwest corner of the tent and stopped, gasping for breath. His wide forehead glistened with sweat, and his white shirt, under the armpits, was drenched. His brown trousers were ragged and dirty.

Crenshaw paused in mid-bite as the runner appeared. "What is it, Abdel?" he demanded.

"Come quick," Abdel panted. He was Crenshaw's right-hand man; 40 years old, married, his wife and nine children living in Cairo; he had worked with the Professor on several previous digs. "Think this is it. Found big wall."

Professor Crenshaw and Amy exchanged grins.

"Let's go!" Crenshaw directed, and led the way around the tent toward the cliff.

The 24 men in the excavation crew had been

diligently toiling at their task for almost two months, ever since Crenshaw ascertained the probable location of the royal tomb. An earthen ramp had been formed from the base of the cliff to the top, running from the northern base to the southern escarpment. Two-thirds of the way up the cliff a tunnel had been dug, the workers boring directly into the cliff. And now, 60 feet in, they'd discovered a stone wall.

Amy marveled at the speed Professor Crenshaw displayed in ascending the ramp. The prospect of finding the tomb had filled her mentor with youthful exuberance.

And he wasn't the only one.

Amy felt her blood pounding as they reached the tunnel entrance. Her emotional state was euphoric; she had never imagined that she would be this thrilled over an impending archaeological find. The feeling gave her an even better idea of why Professor Crenshaw loved archaeology so much. This kind of natural high could become habit forming.

The tunnel was illuminated by a succession of lanterns placed at regular intervals. Large wooden beams, trucked in for the purpose, provided support for the tunnel walls and ceiling. All of the workers had ceased digging and were awaiting the Professor's arrival.

As they reached the wall, Abdel stepped in front of the Professor, holding a lantern aloft.

"Wow!" Amy exclaimed.

The excavation crew had unearthed a section of wall about ten feet wide by ten feet high. The stones in the wall were actually large blocks, fitted together with astonishing skill and precision so that the seams between the blocks were almost invisible.

Professor Crenshaw put his hands on the wall, examining its smooth surface. "From here on in," he warned, "we must be very careful."

"Afraid of a cave-in?" Amy asked.

"No. Booby traps."

"Really?" Amy studied the wall with renewed interest.

"It's happened before," Professor Crenshaw elaborated. "The ancients didn't want their tombs ransacked. It was a common practice for a ruler, after the tomb had been constructed, to kill every worker on the project to insure its secrecy. The Egyptians took their afterlife very seriously. They believed that a person who had led a good life in this world would awaken in the next. That's why they furnished their tombs with everything they thought they would need in the next world, everything from clothing to food to jewelry. They also believed that a person should be preserved exactly as they were in life, which is why they developed embalming into such an art. It's easy to see why they didn't want their tombs violated, and some of the wealthy ones who could afford the luxury of a private tomb took extraordinary measures to protect their resting place. We must be very careful," he reiterated. "Instruct the men to remove a block at a time," he told Abdel, "starting here." He touched a block in the center of the wall. "When we've opened a hole large enough for me to squeeze through, stop."

"Maybe an hour, at most," Abdel predicted, surveying the wall and estimating its thickness from prior experience.

"We'll be outside," Crenshaw said, walking from the tunnel with Amy in tow. Once outside, he stopped and leaned against the cliff.

"Do you think we'll find a mummy in there?" Amy asked.

"Most likely," Professor Crenshaw replied. "Although there's no telling what condition it will be in after five thousand years. There are precedents, however. Back in 1880, the mummy of King Mer-en-re was discovered in a pyramid at Saqqara. It was estimated to be about 4500 years old. The very next year, the body of Ramses II was found perfectly preserved after 3200 years. So there is an outside chance we'll find a mummy in there."

"I read an article not too long ago," Amy said, "about some mummies they found in South America—in Peru, I believe. They didn't use the same embalming techniques as the Egyptians, did they?"

"Definitely not," Crenshaw said. "The Peruvians were not as advanced as the Egyptians, who were quite thorough and methodical."

Amy stepped back out of the sun and sat down just inside the tunnel entrance with her back to the north wall.

"We have discovered some texts detailing the process they employed in their embalming," the Professor said. "We know it took about seventy days for completion. The embalmers would remove the internal organs, all of them except for the kidneys and the heart, via a surgical incision. The brain would be extracted through a nostril. After the abdomen was empty, they would fill it with sawdust or maybe linen pads, and the whole body would be submerged in sodium carbonate. After the tissues had all dried out, they would wrap the body in layer after layer of linen bandages. Finally, the body was placed in a coffin. The richer the deceased, the more elaborate the coffin. Sometimes the coffins were inlaid with gold. In later years, after they acquired silver from the Hittites, they used that, too. Quite often the coffins were shaped like the body of the mummy and might even be painted in the exact likeness of the deceased. The tombs themselves might have carved inscriptions on the walls, and frequently a copy of *The Book Of The Dead* was put in the tomb to safeguard the spirits of the departed. All in all," he concluded, "a fascinating accomplishment."

"I hope we find one," Amy declared.

Crenshaw glanced at her and winked. "So do I,

Amy. I never tire of the rush I get every time I first enter a new tomb."

"Isn't it dangerous, though? What with the threat of booby traps and all?"

"Crossing a street in rush hour traffic can be dangerous," the Professor countered. "People who live in constant fear never really know what living is all about. The more of life you experience, the more alive you feel. Do you agree?"

"Of course."

"I can't help but feel pity for all the people who spend their day in a cramped office, and then go home at night and do nothing but sit in front of a television set. What a waste! Life is meant for living. If the good Lord had intended for us to spend our lives in our butts, then He wouldn't have given us legs."

Amy laughed.

"Do you think I'm joking?" he asked.

"Not at all," she responded, "and I do agree with you, one hundred percent. That's why I'm here, isn't it? I didn't want to miss this experience, even though it meant blowing my honeymoon plans."

"Too bad your young man hasn't arrived yet," Crenshaw said. "He's missing out on all the fun."

"By tomorrow night he'll be here," Amy said, "and I'll do my best to make up for all the boredom he had on his long flight over. I know how dull it can be."

"What I hate most about those flights," Professor Crenshaw admitted, "is the icky sensation you feel all over your body. Give me good, clean dirt any day of the week. At least dirt doesn't make you feel like a clam."

Amy grinned and rested the back of her head on the tunnel wall. Memories washed over her—pleasant recollections of Simon, cherished moments engraved in her heart, like the first time he'd kissed her, and how boyish and insecure he had been. And there was the time they went dancing, and Simon accidentally trod on her toes. The pitiful, puppy dog expression on his face when he thought he had hurt her was both profoundly touching and blatantly ridiculous. She fondly recalled their visit to a small carnival in Colorado, one of those two-bit, fly-by-night operations where the carnies milked the rubes for all they're worth. Simon had decided he was going to win her a giant stuffed dog, so he tried his hand at knocking over wooden pins with a ball. And he tried and tried. Seventy-five dollars later he did qualify for a consolation prize, a small stuffed dog so crudely constructed it would simply fall apart if you sneezed on it. He'd been so embarrassed by his stupidity, but she treasured that little stuffed dog above all her others.

"Maybe we'll find some seeds," Professor Crenshaw said, intruding on her reverie.

"Some what?" Amy asked, not sure if she had heard him correctly.

"Some seeds," he repeated.

"What type of seeds?"

"Didn't you hear about what happened in China?"

"No," she admitted. "What?"

Crenshaw walked into the tunnel and sat down next to her. "In 1983," he informed her, "in Chengdu, which is in Sichuan province in China, some Chinese archaeologists were examining a tomb from the Han Dynasty."

"I didn't know you were so knowledgeable concerning Chinese archaeology."

"Any archaeology interests me," Professor Crenshaw replied. "Anyway, they came across some carbonized objects which turned out to be two thousand year old seeds."

"Two thousand years old?"

"That's right. They covered these seeds with sterilized blankets after boiling them in water. About a month or so later, they received a big surprise.''

''The seeds sprouted,'' Amy deduced.

''That they did.'' Crenshaw smiled at his protege. ''The seeds germinated and produced around forty plants. On the plants grew a most peculiar fruit. Initially, from the shape and color, they thought they had a date. But then it changed, and they ended up with an oval shaped tomato about as large as an egg. Do you realize the implications of this?''

''I guess it means,'' Amy said grinning, ''that if we find some seeds in this tomb we can plant them and start a little garden.''

Crenshaw gave her a serious, paternal glance. ''Not quite, Ms. Brant,'' he said, ''but finds like the Chinese one could have startling implications. We already know that a number of fruit and vegetable strains have been lost to the world. What if some seeds belonging to one of these lost strains are recovered and successfully propagated? The rediscovered strain could turn out to be inexpensive to produce, highly nutritious, and climatically flexible. It's highly feasible a new staple of the human diet could be found buried in a long forgotten tomb somewhere on our planet. Such a find would be tremendously significant.''

''I hadn't thought of it that way,'' Amy confessed.

''There are other ramifications of the Chinese find,'' Professor Crenshaw said. ''Disturbing ramifications, especially for biologists.''

''Biologists? What do they have to do with tombs and mummies? I can see where they might be involved in the reproduction of a new plant strain, but what else?''

Crenshaw bent over and began wiping the dust from his boots. ''Biology has many divisions, remember. Some top scientists in the field have raised a pertinent, troubling question.''

''What question?''

Professor Crenshaw looked at her. "We already know, and have known ever since the very first mummy was discovered, how perfectly preserved the human body can be after being buried thousands and thousands of years. Now we know that seeds can still germinate after two thousand years. The questions is—what else might survive as well?"

"Like what?"

"Like bacteria or a virus," he answered.

"After thousands of years?" Amy said skeptically. "Is it really possible?"

"We don't know. The odds against it would seem to be overwhelming, and it hasn't happened yet. Scientists are extremely doubtful that it could occur, but then scientists as a whole tend to take a conservative approach to any new idea or different concept. I only mention all of this in light of what we're about to do."

"So what do we do?" Amy asked. "Wear masks inside the tomb? We might scare the mummy."

Professor Crenshaw chuckled. "No, we won't be wearing masks. I've participated on almost two dozen digs over the course of my career. Nothing out of the ordinary has ever transpired. We'll conduct this dig like we would any other. Just be very careful."

5

"So what did you think of the movie?"

"It was as realistic as anything else Hollywood produces."

"You didn't like it?"

"I didn't say that."

They stopped on the street corner, waiting for the light to change. Marcy Wiliams stared at her date, her intuition telling her something was bothering him. But what? A storm was approaching Philadelphia from the west, and the wind was whipping her long black hair across her face and covering her brown eyes. She brushed her hair aside, revealing her full cheeks, thin, arched eyebrows, and oval chin. She wore a beige sweater, a white blouse, and dark brown pants. "What's eating you, Jay?"

Jay Darr glanced at her. He was lean, almost to the point of being skinny, without so much as an ounce of fat anywhere on his muscular, wiry physique. His sandy hair and blue eyes enhanced his exceptionally handsome features. He wore a black T-shirt and grey corduroy trousers, the visage of a snarling tiger highlighting the front of the T-shirt. "Is it that obvious?" he asked.

When the light changed to green, they crossed the

street to the other side. Near the intersection, parked alongside the curb, was Jay's fully restored, bright red '69 Corvette, one of the few extravagant luxuries he allowed himself. Jay unlocked the passenger door so she could slip into the mohair covered bucket seat, one of many customized touches that reflected his personal taste.

''Yes, it's obvious,'' Marcy finally answered as she sat down.

Jay stared at her thoughtfully for a moment, then closed her door, moved around to the driver's side and sat down behind the steering wheel.

''Would you like to talk about it?'' she prompted him.

''Not right now,'' he responded, starting the engine. The powerful motor rumbled and growled as he eased away from the curb and headed north, switching the headlights on.

Marcy knew better than to press the issue. Jay Darr wasn't the type of man you could coax or nag into doing or saying anything. He would open up to her in his own sweet time. She should know. They'd been going together for the better part of eight months. Until about the beginning of the year everything had been fine, but then Jay changed, his character undergoing a subtle transformation. She didn't have any idea why. Or did she? Marcy recalled the change in Jay took place shortly after he received a phone call from his younger brother, Simon, who had called to say he was getting married. Normally, such information would be considered good news. So why had it seemed to affect Jay adversely?

The Corvette swerved left as Jay turned onto Lehigh Avenue.

Once again Marcy asked herself why she was sticking with Jay Darr. His moody disposition wasn't much to her liking. She preferred the carefree life. Except for her classes at Temple, where she was majoring in music, there wasn't very much she took seriously. While still a teenager she had learned an important lesson. Her first "true love" had ended tragically, so to speak, when her boyfriend had left her for another girl. The experience was romantically traumatic and also highly educational. She realized that she didn't have any control whatsoever over others; even a loving relationship could turn topsy-turvy in a minute. So if she had no control over others, she decided it would be foolish to allow herself to become upset over anything they did. Personal relationships were a lot like the weather; periodic storms were inevitable. Was a person supposed to cry every time it rained, every time it thundered and lightninged? Of course not. You accepted the storm as a matter of course and went on with your life. Such was her philosophy of life. Unfortunately, Jay Darr didn't share it. In a way, it was ironic. Here was a man with superb control over his own body, but a man lacking any control over his emotional swings. During the past month he'd become almost unbearable, somewhat surly and decidedly taciturn, the antithesis of what she liked. So the question still remained—why was she sticking with Jay Darr?

He took a right, and she knew they were going to his apartment.

They had gone to a restaurant the evening before and returned to her place. She had fallen asleep in Jay's lap, on the couch, while watching television. Only 20 minutes ago, about 5:00 A.M., she had awakened to find him viewing a martial arts movie on cable. What with Jay's devotion to the martial arts, she had assumed such a movie would perk up his listless nature. Evidently, she was wrong again. She glanced at him, at his rugged, jutting jaw and those striking blue eyes, promising so much and displaying so little. She felt the old, familiar craving wash over her again. Damn it, what was it about him? Why couldn't she get enough of him?

Jay had suggested going out for breakfast, but instead they were headed for his place. What was up?

Jay pulled up to the curb in front of a three story brick house, converted into six apartments by the current landlord. Jay's apartment was on the third floor, fronting the street. As they climbed the stairs with Jay in the lead, Marcy grinned, watching the cute swing of his compact posterior.

Jay's apartment contained only three rooms—a spacious living room which Jay had decorated in a martial arts theme, complete with a kicking bag and floor mats in the middle of the room; a bedroom with an attached bath; and a tiny kitchenette to the rear of the living room. A huge picture window with red curtains on either side faced the street.

Upon entering, Jay tossed his car keys onto the television set located to the right of the door. He sighed and crossed to the picture window, gazing down at the street below.

Marcy removed her sweater and threw it onto one of the floor mats.

"I'm sorry for the way I've been acting," Jay said to her, still watching the scene below.

"I wish you'd let me know what's bugging you," Marcy told him. "I don't mind telling you, Jay, I'm growing a bit tired of it. I thought we said we wouldn't keep any secrets from each other."

Jay sighed again. "You sure you want to hear it?"

Marcy moved up behind him. "I'd rather hear about what's bothering you than silently watch your mood swings. Maybe I can help."

"You might think it's stupid," he said.

"You let me be the judge of that."

Jay faced her. "Are you happy with me?"

The unexpected query caught her off guard. She hesitated and immediately detected a hurt look in his eyes.

"Ahhh," Jay said and turned to the window.

Marcy placed her right hand on his shoulder. "You didn't give me a chance to answer."

"You didn't need to," Jay stated. "I saw how you reacted."

"I like you, Jay," Marcy said hastily, afraid she had hurt his feelings. "I really do. Hell, I may even love you, but I don't know for sure. I've never been in love before, not really in love. How do I tell if this is the real thing? As to whether I'm happy with you or not, I can tell you I was until you changed. It wouldn't be so bad if you'd only tell me what it is."

Jay looked at her, his brow furrowed, then moved around her and over to his stereo. Kneeling, he searched through the dozens of records in a wooden rack until he found the one he wanted.

Marcy recognized he was stalling, buying time to organize his thoughts. Whatever was bugging him must be important.

Jay placed a record on the turntable and switched on the machine. The apartment was filled with the superb voice of Frank Sinatra.

Jay rose and came over to her. "Do you recognize the song?"

She listened to the melody and the words until she identified the title. *I've Got You Under My Skin*. She studied Jay, surprised. Was he trying to say something?

"Do you remember when we first met?" Jay asked.

"Of course. I walked into your school looking for someone to teach me the martial arts. One of my girlfriends, Irene, had been raped right in our dorm, and I decided I was going to do something to insure it never happened to me. When I was going through the yellow pages I saw your advertisement offering special discounts on self-defense classes for women. Why?"

Jay stepped to the window. "When we first met, I never expected we would become as involved as we have. You may not believe this, but I'm a lot like you. I've had girlfriends in the past, but never a serious love. I never wanted to commit myself fully to another person." He paused. "And then you came along."

Marcy remained silent, reluctant to interrupt.

"Just when I was getting to the point where I could admit how I felt about you to myself, to acknowledge how deeply I cared, my brother called and told me he was getting married," Jay said in a husky voice.

"Yeah. Around Christmas. I remember," Marcy volunteered. "So what does your brother getting married have to do with us?"

"Did you know Simon is six years younger than me?"

"Yeah. So what?"

Jay frowned. "I'm thirty-two and I've never been married."

"What difference does that make? According to the Census Bureau, more and more marriages are taking place at a later age than ever before. That's what I heard on the news. Is that what's been bugging you?" Marcy demanded. Why all this talk about marriage? Surely he wasn't going to propose!

"Simon's phone call started me thinking about my own life," Jay said, continuing. "I got to thinking about all of the years I've dedicated to the martial arts, to *Hung Gar*. It's been twelve years, Marcy. Twelve years! Ever since I was twenty, when I was assigned to the U.S. Naval Supply Depot in California. It was in Berkeley where I met the man who would change my life, the sifu who would teach me the rudiments of *Hung Gar* kung fu. I wish you could see him in action. He still teaches in California. His name is Lum Wong, and before he came to the U.S. he was renowned as a famous instructor in Hong Kong. After I was discharged from the Navy, I returned to

Berkeley and studied under Lum Wong for five years. He qualified me as an instructor, and I returned to Colorado to be near my family. About a year ago, an old Navy buddy wanted me to come to Philadelphia and pay him a visit. I did. Fell in love with the city. Opened my own school. Met you. I thought I was on top of the world."

"You're not?"

"I thought I was," he reiterated. "But after Simon called, I took a good luck at myself, at my life, at my so-called accomplishments, at what I've got to show for twelve years of applying myself to *Hung Gar*. Look around you. What do I have to show? One fancy car and a place to live I can't even call my own. What else?"

"You have your school," Marcy answered.

"The school? A few dozen students, half of whom don't have the inner discipline necessary to stick with *Hung Gar* long enough for it to really benefit them. Oh, they'll learn a few basic techniques and get some exercise, but that's about it. Only a relative handful of students will incorporate the teachings into their life and make it an essential part of their very existence. So what's the use in teaching them?"

Marcy crossed her arms and stared at the red carpet. What should she say to him? His problem was more than mere moodiness; it was a spiritual crisis. He was questioning his basic values and doubting his ideals and goals.

"My brother is going to get married," Jay resumed before she could reply, "and buy a house and raise a family. He works in a respectable profession, as a newsman. He has a normal job. You should see the looks I get when I tell people what I do for a living. Simon is doing something with his life. What am I doing? What do I have to offer any woman?"

Marcy moved over to him and placed her arms around his neck. He kept gazing at the sidewalk below. "I think you're making a mountain out of a molehill," she told him. "You still have your whole life ahead of you."

"If I live to an average old age," Jay corrected her, "then I only have about half of my life ahead of me."

Marcy decided to try another tack. "So what if your brother is a newsman and you teach kung fu? That doesn't make one of you better than the other. It only makes you different. You aren't weird because you like kung fu. Remember, not many people could do what you're doing, would have the guts to stick with it, just like you said. It all boils down to this—different strokes for different folks."

Jay glanced at her, and she read an intense inner turmoil in his eyes. "What woman in her right mind would marry a kung fu instructor?"

Before she could stop herself or give herself time to ponder the question, she answered, "I would."

Jay's face brightened, and he encircled her narrow waist with his arms. "You would? Really?"

"Don't misunderstand me," she quickly elaborated. "I would if I met Mr. Right. I don't think it would matter what the man I love does for a living. It's the love that's important, not his vocation."

"Which brings us right back to square one," Jay said. "Are you happy with me?"

"Generally speaking, yes," Marcy responded.

"Then would you . . ."

Marcy cut him short by placing her right hand over his lips. "Don't ask me that question now, Jay. I don't think I'm ready for it. Give me some more time. Okay?"

His expression showed his disappointment, but he nodded.

Marcy removed her hand from his lips. "I had no idea you were that serious about us. Marriage is a heavy subject, a big responsibility. I've still got a year of college left before I graduate." She paused and traced her finger under his chin. "I do care for you, Jay. Don't ruin what we have by trying to pressure me into anything prematurely. I need to give this a lot of consideration. Do you see my point?"

Jay slowly nodded. He leaned over and gently kissed her on the lips.

Marcy returned the kiss. She felt his tongue flick across her lips, and she opened her mouth. Their tongues entwined as he ran his hands up her back. Unbidden and unwanted, a question filled her mind—what was her real motive for hedging on marriage? Was it because she sensed their relationship was based more on the sexual stirrings he created inside her than on any profound affection?

Jay broke the kiss and lifted her into his arms. He effortlessly carried her to the mats and deposited her on the nearest one. He lay next to her, on his right side, and caressed her face with his left hand.

Marcy took hold of his hand and kissed his palm. She pulled him down and over her, and their lips locked. His left hand began unbuttoning her blouse. When the blouse parted and fell open, he cupped her right breast and tenderly pinched the nipple under her brassiere. She raised herself up, and he deftly undid the clasp on her bra, then pulled it off of her and tossed it aside. His lips descended on her breasts and went from one to the other, licking and sucking.

She moaned when he slowly ran his right hand up her thighs. His left hand removed her belt and undid her zipper. She elevated her hips so he could strip off her brown pants. Her socks and sneakers followed in quick order.

"I hope you'll never leave me," he said, and kissed her on the lips.

Jay's right hand lightly touched the wet lips of her sex, and she groaned.

"Oh, Jay!"

He inserted his right index finger into her and felt

the heat she was generating. She squirmed under him as he worked his finger in and out. He kissed her chin, then her throat, then between her breasts as he moved down her body until he reached her mound. Her eyes, narrowed in passion, followed him. He smiled and extended his tongue, registering the exquisite scent of her and the tangy taste of her nether lips.

Marcy gasped and gripped his head by the hair, pulling his face toward her so that his mouth was buried in her womanhood.

Jay drove his tongue inside her, his hands on her hips, holding her in place as she bucked and writhed. He kept it up until she yanked on his hair, tugging him out of her, raising his face to her own. Their hot lips meshed once more.

Marcy could feel his hardness tight against her mound. She wanted him then, wanted him to fill her with his manhood, wanted him more than she had ever wanted any man.

Jay kissed her eyelids and licked her eyebrows, his hands busy kneading her breasts, her nipples hard and pointed.

"Now," she whispered. "Now, Jay. Please."

His right hand parted her legs and his hips moved, thrusting down and in.

Marcy arched her back as he entered her, her entire body consumed by passion.

Jay stroked her and her body reciprocated, the two of them moving in a smooth rhythm.

The heat and the urgency built and built until they exploded together.

And as her orgasm engulfed her in a joyous ecstasy, Marcy was dimly aware of one thought running through her mind, over and over and over again.

I do love him! It's not just physical!

I do! It's not!

I do!

6

"We have two out," Abdel announced as he reached the tunnel entrance.

Amy and Professor Crenshaw instantly rose and moved through the tunnel to the wall of the tomb.

Abdel and his men had removed two of the stone blocks. The opening wasn't large, but one person at a time would be able to squeeze inside.

"Want I go first?" Abdel asked the Professor.

"Not on your life!" Professor Crenshaw exclaimed. He took a lantern from the wall and stooped over near the opening.

Amy gripped his left arm. "Shouldn't someone else go in first?"

Crenshaw snorted. "I'm perfectly capable of entering a tomb, Ms. Brant."

"But it might be dangerous," she protested.

"We've already discussed that," Crenshaw reminded her. "This comes with the territory."

"Please, be careful!"

Professor Crenshaw winked at her. "You needn't worry on that score. I didn't become the delightful old codger I am by being careless."

"Any problems," Abdel interjected, "you yell quick."

The Professor held the lantern in front of his face as he slowly eased into the opening. When he was inside up to his waist, Abdel and another worker grabbed his legs and held them steady while Crenshaw completed his entry.

Amy leaned down and peered inside. She could see Crenshaw standing about two feet away, the lantern over his head as he surveyed his surroundings. "It's a small chamber," he called back. "It's not the tomb. Very odd," he commented, moving left to one side.

"What'd odd?" Amy asked, fearful they would lose sight of him and something would happen. All that talk of booby traps had made her extremely apprehensive.

"It's empty," Professor Crenshaw shouted. "Nothing but the dust of the ages."

"Maybe the tomb was ransacked," Amy suggested.

"This isn't large enough for a tomb," Crenshaw replied. "It's more like an antechamber. Abdel, assist Ms. Brant in getting in here, then come in with another man and two lanterns."

Amy slid into the opening before Abdel could help, her leaner frame permitting her to slip through without any difficulty.

Abdel and another worker were on her heels.

"Search the walls," Professor Crenshaw instructed. "The tomb has to be nearby. I think this room was put here to throw graverobbers off the scent."

Amy stayed by the opening.

Professor Crenshaw was examining the north wall of the small chamber, while Abdel was running his hands over the south wall.

The other worker crossed to the east wall, the one directly across from the opening they'd made, and raised his lantern over his head, scanning the blocks and the seams for telltale signs of a way out.

"There must be a clue," Professor Crenshaw insisted.

"Not see thing," Abdel informed them.

Amy saw the worker take a step to his right.

There was a sudden grating sound and a loud snapping noise. The worker screamed as the floor under him collapsed. The stone tile he was standing on buckled and crumpled, and he began to drop.

Abdel, who was closest, dropped his lantern and leaped, diving across the floor, his arms extended to their utmost. The worker was down to his shoulders when Abdel reached the hapless man and managed to grab him by the fabric of his green shirt. It wasn't much of a grip, and in another moment the worker would have plunged from sight.

The Professor, in a rush of speed belying his age, ran to their aid. He knelt and slid his hands under the worker's armpits. "Heave!" he yelled to Abdel.

Amy joined them, as they struggled to lift the worker from the hole, raising his waist to floor level. She took hold of his belt and added her strength to theirs.

When the worker finally was hauled from the hole, he was trembling, his dark eyes wide with terror.

"Whew, that was close," Professor Crenshaw gasped.

Abdel nodded in agreement. "Too much close," he agreed in his broken English.

The worker abruptly shrieked and jumped to his feet. He spun, raced to the opening in the antechamber wall, and was through it in a flash.

"I think we've seen the last of him," Professor Crenshaw remarked.

"What happened?" Amy asked.

"One of those booby traps I was telling you about," Crenshaw replied. He reached out and tugged on a jagged edge of the crumpled stone tile. It broke off easily, and he handed it to her.

"It's light," Amy commented as she hefted the piece in her right hand. "This isn't stone."

"It certainly isn't," Professor Crenshaw affirmed. "It's an old trick. It was a fake tile, constructed of a plaster-like substance and painted to resemble the real thing. Very clever. The fake tile wouldn't support the weight of either man or woman. All someone had to do, as you just saw, was step on it and it would give out."

Amy stared at the hole in the floor. "Where do you suppose that goes?"

"My guess would be it's a deep hole with sharp stakes imbedded in the bottom to impale whoever fell in," Professor Crenshaw explained. "I've seen them before."

"What now?" Amy asked.

Crenshaw looked at Abdel. "Go get another worker and a hammer. From now on, before we step on any of the floor tiles, you'll give it a whack with the hammer. If it's fake, we'll know right away. Your government wouldn't be too pleased with me if I inadvertently was responsible for the death of one of its citizens."

Abdel departed.

"You seem slightly pale," Professor Crenshaw said to Amy.

"That man was almost killed. It could happen to any of us."

"No one ever claimed archaeology was a dull vocation," Crenshaw said, then grinned. "Actually, Amy, this is a good sign."

"What?"

"It tells us two things. First, the makers of this tomb went to great pains to insure it remained inviolate. It could indicate items of great wealth are buried inside."

"What's the other thing?"

Professor Crenshaw pointed at the hole in the floor. "It tells us that no one else has been in here. If they had, if someone had broken in to rob the tomb, that hole would have been there when we came in."

"It also tells us something else," Amy added.

"What's that?"

Amy gazed at the walls. "If they went to all the trouble to build one booby trap, odds are we'll find another one."

"Just so we find it before it finds us," Professor Crenshaw stated.

Abdel returned with the hammer and another worker, a man in his sixties with a patchwork of wrinkles creasing his weathered features.

"Where do we go from here?" Amy asked.

Professor Crenshaw indicated the section of wall above the hole in the floor. "We'll go through that wall."

"Why that one?"

"Because if they located the trick tile next to that wall, it stands to reason they were hiding something behind it."

"Makes sense," Amy admitted.

Professor Crenshaw turned to Abdel. "Give each and every floor tile in this antechamber a pounding with the hammer. We don't need any more deadly surprises."

Abdel went from one floor tile to the next, smashing the hammer against each until he made a complete sweep of the chamber, finding the rest of the floor solid.

"Fine," Professor Crenshaw said when Abdel had finished. "Now get four more men in here and remove several of the stone blocks from the wall above the hole."

"Right away," Abdel responded.

Amy and the Professor waited patiently while

Abdel and the others cautiously chipped away at the seams using large chisels specifically designed for slicing into solid stone, the same type of chisels professional geologists and paleontologists used in their line of work.

Over an hour later, three of the stone blocks had been extracted and lined up at the base of the north wall.

"Let me have a lantern," Professor Crenshaw requested, as the third block was deposited with the other two. One of the workers offered him a lantern, which Crenshaw took. He leaned into the new opening in the wall. "Now this is more like it," he commented.

"What is it?"

"See for yourself." Professor Crenshaw moved aside so Amy could stand next to him and peer inside.

Amy grabbed a lantern from Abdel and joined the Professor. She used her left hand to balance herself while she extended her right arm and the lantern into the cavity. It required but a moment for her eyes to adjust and recognize the sight in front of her. "It's a tunnel," she exclaimed.

It was a stone tunnel, angling down into the bowels of the earth. The walls were constructed of the large stone blocks, while the floor and ceiling were composed of the smaller stone tiles. The air was musty, and the light from her lantern showed the air was filled with minute dust particles.

"You wait here," Professor Crenshaw instructed. He started to climb into the tunnel.

Amy clasped his right elbow. "Wait a minute," she protested. "I'm going with you."

Professor Crenshaw glanced over his shoulder. "You are not. Stay here with Abdel until I signal you to enter."

"I'm not going to wait here," Amy declared defensively. "I didn't come all the way over here to cool my heels on the sidelines. You sent for me because you thought I was competent enough to handle this job. If you make me stay here, it will seem like you don't trust me. I thought you knew me better than that."

Professor Crenshaw frowned. "You and your darned logic! I don't like it, but I'll let you come along on one condition."

"What's that?"

"That you let me lead the way, and at the first hint of danger you will turn tail and run. Your safety must be our paramount concern."

Amy nodded. "Sounds fair to me. Lead on, Professor."

Crenshaw scrambled into the tunnel and stood, waiting for her to catch up. "Remember what I just told you," he said when she stood by his side.

"I will," she vowed.

Holding their lanterns above their heads, the Professor a few steps ahead, they moved forward down the tunnel. The floor sloped gradually underfoot.

"How far down do you think this will go?"

"There's no telling," Professor Crenshaw answered.

The tunnel continued downward for about 100 yards and then abruptly turned to the right. Up to the point where the tunnel turned, the walls and the ceiling were plain and smooth, devoid of any markings of any kind. But as they rounded the corner and their lanterns illuminated the stretch of tunnel ahead, they discovered brilliantly painted hieroglyphics on both walls and ceiling.

Amy gasped in delight. "Look at it!"

Professor Crenshaw chuckled. "I never tire of a sight like this," he remarked.

The hieroglyphics consisted of the two dozen characters used for consonants and semi-consonants, as well as the ideograms and the phonograms inevitably present in hieroglyphic writing. On the wall next to Amy's right arm was the image of an Egyptian man wearing a conical hat and the traditional dain, a white loincloth made from linen or cloth. This figure carried a spear in his right hand.

Professor Crenshaw was examining the other wall. "This is outstanding," he said, excited. "These are some of the earliest hieroglyphics we've found to date, and look at how well preserved they are."

"They're beautiful," Amy enthused. "Can you read them?"

"I'll try."

They continued following the tunnel as the Professor read the writing on his side.

"I can't claim to know everything it says," he informed her, "but here goes." He paused for a moment, then began reading. " 'Here lies the noble prince, the valiant Hiros, third to the throne of the mighty king of Upper Egypt.' "

"Upper Egypt?" Amy interrupted, striving to recall her Egyptian history. "Of course! Prior to about 3000 B.C., Egypt was divided into two large states called Upper Egypt and Lower Egypt."

"Exactly," Professor Crenshaw said. "It was King Menes who rose to power in Upper Egypt and conquered Lower Egypt, forming one country for the first time."

"Keep reading!" Amy goaded him on.

Crenshaw grinned and resumed his deciphering, moving down the tunnel as he followed the flow of the writing.

" 'Prince Hiros died in battle with the Dog People and . . .' " He suddenly stopped.

"What's the matter?" Amy stepped closer to him and studied the wall. "Why, look at that. Those people are down on all fours like dogs."

Some of the hieroglyphics depicted men and women running or squatting on their hands and knees.

"I've never seen anything like it," Professor Crenshaw mumbled.

"Don't stop!" she urged.

"Yes, of course. Where was I?" He picked up where he had left off. " 'Prince Hiros died in battle with the Dog People and is interred within. The Dog People have been . . .' " He hesitated, uncertain of the next word, deciding to guess as best he could. " '. . . eradicated by the fire dust . . .' "

"What's fire dust?" Amy interjected.

"I have no idea," Crenshaw said. They reached the next section of the wall, and he drew up short.

"What is it?"

"It's a warning," he told her.

"Read it." Amy stared at the hieroglyphics in fascination as the Professor continued.

" 'Beware! No one may enter under penalty of death! For the safety of mankind, the Dog People must not be allowed to live again.' "

"What do you make of it?" Amy asked.

"Apparently, the Dog People were to be denied an afterlife," Professor Crenshaw speculated. He walked several feet further. " 'If you will not heed the threat of death,' " he said, " 'then heed our plea. Do not disturb this resting place of Hiros. Leave now before it is too late.' "

Amy stopped. "Professor . . ."

"Yes?" Crenshaw faced her.

"Maybe we shouldn't go any further," she suggested.

"What?"

Amy indicated the wall. "They were obviously sincere about their warning. Maybe we should leave this tomb undisturbed."

Professor Crenshaw grinned. "Have they gotten to you?"

"I guess so," Amy confessed. "I have the same feeling I had when I was thirteen and a bunch of us turned some tombstones over in a cemetery. It's like what we're doing isn't right, and the dead are better off left alone."

Crenshaw laughed. "That's a fine attitude for an aspiring archaeologist to have." He reached out and squeezed her right shoulder. "Amy, when you get right down to it, we're in the bones business. No bones, no business. Many of the tombs I've seen have had cryptic warnings and outright threats near the entrance or inside the tomb itself. Remember, they didn't want their tombs violated, and they went to great lengths to insure they weren't, even going so far as to employ some basic superstitious psychology. When all else failed, they would try to scare you to death."

"Are you sure we should go through with this?" Amy inquired.

Professor Crenshaw eyed her critically. "What's the matter with you? I credited you with considerably more gumption than this."

Amy gazed at the walls and ceiling. "I don't know what it is," she said, "but I have this feeling we should leave right now."

Crenshaw shook his head. "We're not leaving at this stage of the game. What you're experiencing is perfectly natural. This is your first dig, your first tomb. It's understandable you would be apprehensive. I can vividly recall what I went through on my first dig. I was thrilled to death and scared to death at the same time. You'll get over it. Trust me."

"I trust you," Amy assured him.

"Then let's get on with it." He resumed their exploration of the tunnel.

Amy shrugged her slim shoulders in resignation and followed him.

Crenshaw began translating another section of the wall. " 'You have not listened to us. You have disobeyed an official edict. You have ignored our plea.

You leave us no choice. Stop now or suffer the consequences.' "

"Professor . . ."

Professor Crenshaw took two more steps and was startled when the stone tile under his right foot unexpectedly shifted.

Amy screamed, thinking he was about to suffer the same fate as the worker in the antechamber.

Instead, there was a loud clicking noise and the tile resettled into the floor.

"What was that?" Amy asked nervously.

"I'm not certain," Professor Crenshaw answered uneasily.

A tremendous, thunderous crash, from somewhere behind them, shook the walls of the tunnel.

Both of them turned and held up their lanterns.

"I don't see anything," Crenshaw observed. "Do you?"

"No. What could it have been?"

A peculiar rumbling filled the tunnel and stirred the dusty air.

"What is that?" Amy asked.

The rumbling was getting louder.

"I don't like this," Professor Crenshaw commented. "Maybe I should have followed your advice," he added.

The rumbling grew, sounding like an express train barreling down the tunnel toward them.

"Have you ever heard anything like this before?"

"Never," Crenshaw replied.

Amy clutched her lantern, her skin tingling with expectation. What could it be?

She received her answer a mere moment later.

With a clattering roar, a huge cylindrical object, resembling for all the world a giant stone rolling pin, came rushing down the tunnel toward them. It completely filled the tunnel with no way around it on either side.

"Run!" Professor Crenshaw shouted.

Amy didn't need to be told twice. She spun and fled down the tunnel in stark fear.

Professor Crenshaw was a yard in front of her.

Behind them, the stone cylinder roared down the tunnel.

7

Simon Darr wearily rested his forehead on his forearms. He was seated at a table in the corner of a large room at police headquarters in Cairo. Many of the other passengers were scattered at other tables. He closed his eyes, wishing he could sleep. How much longer would the Egyptian authorities question them about the hijacking attempt? The debriefing had already taken hours and hours. How many was it now? 16? 18? Amy would be worried sick when he failed to show up on time.

"Hey, kid, wake up," someone said. "How do you expect to develop stamina for your wedding night if you can't handle a little inconvenience like this?"

Simon looked up. Lanning, appearing as fresh and invigorated as ever, stood on the other side of the table. "What did I tell you about calling me a kid?"

"Ooohhh, touchy! Mind if I sit?" Lanning sat down before Simon could respond. "How you holding up?"

"Just great! Can't you tell?" Simon snapped.

"Boy, you lose some sleep, and you get crabby as all get out. I hope your wife is fond of quickies," Lanning remarked.

Simon glared at the Interpol agent. "Keep your

mouth off of Amy."

Lanning leaned back in his chair and held up his hands, palms outward. "I didn't mean to hurt your feelings. I saw you sitting here all by your lonesome and thought you might like some company."

Simon placed his elbows on the table and perched his chin in his hands.

"Where's your friend?" Lanning inquired. "Dr. Ibrahim?"

"He's being questioned by the police," Simon answered, "for the third time."

"Don't be too rough on the police," Lanning said. "Hijacking isn't something you can take lightly, you know. They have a couple of hundred passengers to interview, not to mention all the paperwork they've got to complete. It takes a lot of time."

"But how much longer will we be here?" Simon asked, annoyed. "I was supposed to leave Cairo this morning for Idfu." He gazed at his watch, reset for Egyptian time. "It's already about three in the afternoon."

"Relax," Lanning advised. "You'll be out of here within the hour."

"Sure I will."

"I'll see to it personally," Lanning promised.

"Why would you do that for me?"

"I like ya, kid."

Simon couldn't help but grin. "For a linguist," he mentioned, "you sure have one hell of a vocabulary."

Lanning chuckled. "Isn't that what a linguist does? Speaks the native lingo? Thanks for the compliment."

"You can really get me out of here?" Simon asked anxiously.

"I'll try," Lanning offered. "I have some clout with the local boys. I'll tell them that you're a good friend of mine."

"I'd really appreciate it," Simon said sincerely. "I can't wait to see Amy again."

"I'll bet. In a way, I envy you," Lanning stated pensively.

"What?" Simon laughed. "You envy me? What for? You're the one who gets to travel all over the globe for Interpol. You live a life of adventure, of thrills. You live the life every man who's seen a James Bond movie would like to live. Why would you envy me?"

Lanning studied Simon. "So you think I've got a great life, huh?"

"Of course. Don't you?"

Lanning slowly shook his head in disbelief. "You know, kid, most Europeans I've met believe that Americans are extremely naive, and I'd have to say I go along with them. I don't know if it's all the movies Americans watch, or what, but many Americans seem to subscribe to what I call the Gunfighter Syndrome. Ever seen any old cowboy pictures? The ones where the gunman beats the baddie and gets the girl in the final reel?"

"Sure."

"And haven't you noticed how many Americans think that blowing away the baddies is a lot of fun? It's great sport, kind of like shooting a rabid dog or skunk. One big adventure." Lanning stared morosely at the table. "Idiots."

"I don't get you," Simon remarked. "You're the last person I would expect to talk that way."

"Why?"

"I don't know, really," Simon replied. "It doesn't seem to fit your image."

"My image?" Lanning snorted derisively. "I can see I have some explaining to do. I'm not in this business for the glory. Just because I told you I hate desk work doesn't mean I like killing people. I enjoy police work, true, and sitting behind a desk all day is sheer torture. But there are several reasons why I decided to join the elite new Counter-Terrorist Unit at

Interpol, and none of them have anything to do with my assumed blood lust. I do like to travel, and this job entails a lot of traveling. I get to spend as little time as possible pushing a pencil, and, believe it or not, I happen to believe in traditional, old-fashioned values like law and order. What with the upsurge in terrorism in recent years, I saw this as my chance to do something constructive, to make a positive contribution to society, as it were. Does all of this surprise you?"

"Yeah," Simon confessed. "It goes."

"I don't enjoy killing," Lanning elaborated. "It comes with the territory. I do like firearms and I'm an expert marksman, but Interpol would never have accepted me for this position if I weren't. I killed those three hijackers because they had to be killed. There was no way to bargain with them. They'd already shot one stewardess and were on the verge of perforating you. I simply didn't have any other option. There. Are you satisfied?"

"You don't need to be telling me all of this," Simon said.

"Yes, I do," Lanning countered. "I don't want you going through life thinking James Lanning is a trigger-happy nut."

"I won't," Simon assured him.

"Good."

"But none of this explains why you envy me," Simon noted.

"I envy you because you're getting married."

"And you're not?"

"Nope. Never was, and probably never will be."

"That's pretty negative," Simon observed. "Why say something like that?"

"Because it's true," Lanning said. "I have this gut feeling I'll never be married."

"Everybody says that," Simon stated, "until Cupid strikes. There must be someone, somewhere, you're fond of."

"Well, there *is* one woman," Lanning divulged. "Her name is Monique. She and I have been seeing each other for about six months now."

"What does she do for a living?"

"Monique is a hairdresser. I met her through one of the secretaries at Interpol. She and I have been sharing the same apartment for about two months."

"You see?" Simon commented. "What did I tell you? It sounds like Monique and you are a heavy item, if you know what I mean."

Lanning grinned. "It does, doesn't it? She hasn't complained once about my long absences, just takes them in stride."

Simon nodded knowingly. "See? Monique could be the one for you."

"About time, if it's true."

"How do you mean?" Simon asked.

"I'm thirty-six," Lanning answered. "If I don't tie the knot, soon, I might as well forget it."

"That's ridiculous," Simon declared. "You're never too old to marry."

"Let's hope you're right," Lanning said.

Simon looked up and spotted Dr. Ibrahim walking toward the table. The doctor looked very fatigued.

Dr. Ibrahim greeted him, sat down on Simon's right and nodded at the Interpol agent. "I remember you from the plane, but I don't believe we were introduced."

"Lanning," Lanning said, offering his right hand.

Dr. Ibrahim shook it. "It is good to see you again. On behalf of the other passengers I want to thank you for what you did."

"No need. It's my job."

"What is your job, Mr. Lanning?" Ibrahim inquired.

"I'm with Interpol," Lanning replied.

"My name is Abbas Ibrahim," the doctor disclosed. "I am a physician. But then, you already know all of this, yes?"

"How would he know that?" Simon interjected.

Dr. Ibrahim was eyeing Lanning. "Don't you recall, my young friend? On the aircraft, right after the radicals were shot, this man asked me to check on the other passengers. I think he knew I was a physician, and yet I never talked to this man before."

"Is he right?" Simon asked the Interpol agent. "Did you know he was a doctor?"

Lanning nodded.

"How?" Simon demanded.

"I was provided with the passenger list and passport information before I boarded the 747 in Paris," Lanning detailed. "My assignment was the Paris to Cairo leg of your trip, then back again. Most bookings were made at least several weeks in advance, so it was possible for Interpol, with the cooperation of law enforcement agencies in the native countries, to assemble background information on a majority of the passengers."

"And yet those three terrorists got on board anyway," Simon added.

"We suspect it was an inside job," Lanning revealed.

"Why do you say that?" Simon asked.

"Do you remember that stewardess they shot?"

Simon vividly recalled the horrible sight of the stewardess being shot, of the six bullets striking her body. "How can I forget her?"

"Don't feel too sorry for her," Lanning suggested. "We suspect she was in on it."

"What?"

"We think she was romantically involved with the guy who shot her," Lanning explained. "She probably smuggled those idiots onto the 747 in Paris. She was French, and an ardent leftist during her university days. Being a revolutionary, in case you hadn't heard, is considered to be quite chic in some social circles.''

''But why did she shoot her?'' Simon asked, confused. ''Didn't he love her?''

''The only thing a communist loves is The Communist Manifesto,'' Lanning said dryly. ''They just used her, that's all. She may have had a last minute change of heart and was trying to warn the pilot. Or maybe she saw something in the bastard's eyes and knew they were going to execute her. Who knows? Either way, she got what she deserved.''

''Weren't you trying to convince me a few minutes ago that you aren't the bloodthirsty type?'' Simon said, ribbing him.

''I'm not,'' Lanning reiterated. ''But I happen to believe in justice.''

''Say,'' Simon suddenly thought to ask, ''why didn't any of those shots cause an implosion? I know for a fact he shot her at least six times.''

''Because,'' Lanning explained, ''like the shot that almost got you, they lodged in the wall between first class and the cockpit. I told you once and I'll say it again—we were very lucky.''

''Thank Allah we are alive!'' Dr. Ibrahim exclaimed.

An Egyptian policeman walked up to their table, smiled at Simon and Dr. Ibrahim, and addressed the Interpol agent. ''Pardon, Monsieur . . .''

Lanning glanced up. ''Qu'est-ce que vous désirez?''

''Téléphone,'' the policeman said.

''Ou est le téléphone?'' Lanning inquired.

''Venez avec moi,'' the policeman directed.

''C'est bien,'' Lanning responded, rising. He looked at Simon. ''Hang in there, kid. I'll be back in a jiffy, and you'll be on your way in no time.'' He strolled off after the policeman.

Simon and Dr. Ibrahim spent five minutes discussing the doctor's nine children and three grandchildren, Ibrahim producing his wallet and proudly displaying photographs of each one. He was relating the difficulties encountered in toilet training young children when Lanning returned, all smiles.

"You're out of here, kid," the Interpol agent told Simon. "In about fifteen minutes." He glanced at the physician. "You too, doc. The other passengers will need to hang around here for a couple more hours."

"You arranged for me to leave?" Dr. Ibrahim asked the agent.

"Sure did."

"Why would you do such a thing?"

"Any pal of Simon's is a pal of mine," Lanning replied. "I promised the kid I'd spring him and threw you in for free."

"You are most kind, Mr. Lanning," Dr. Ibrahim said. "I would like to invite you to my house for our evening meal."

Lanning smiled and responded in Arabic. To Simon, the words sounded like "Shokran gazilan." Then the agent averted to English. "You honor me, doctor, but I just received a phone call from my superior in Paris. I'm going back earlier than expected. I thought I would be here at least another day, maybe two, but I'll be leaving this evening. Maybe another time."

Simon was watching the other passengers and noting their fatigue. "You know," he observed, "I always assumed the authorities let you go as soon as a hijacking incident was over. I never expected to be detained this long."

"In some countries you're detained longer than in others," Lanning explained. "What with the crack-down on terrorist activity, most governments are now conducting very thorough investigations into each and every case, interviewing all of the witnesses and the like. Just like I told you before."

Simon saw the police officer who had told Lanning

about his phone call enter the room and speak to one of the passengers. He pointed at the officer. "I didn't know Egyptian policemen spoke French."

Lanning looked at the officer and chuckled. "You mean Deram? He spent a year at a university in Paris when he was younger, and he likes to practice his French every chance he gets. He's one of their liaison officers with Interpol. The last time I was in Cairo, about four months ago, we went out on the town and got just a bit smashed on Aswan beer." Lanning paused and concentrated. "I seem to remember some belly dancers . . ." He let the sentence trail off and shrugged.

"Mr. Lanning," Dr. Ibrahim ventured, "you are a most colorful character."

Lanning glanced at Simon and smirked. "Not another one."

"What?" Dr. Ibrahim asked.

"Nothing important," Lanning replied.

Simon suddenly sat straight up in his chair. "Hey!" he exclaimed.

"Something bite you?"

"Why'd you do it?" Simon asked the agent.

"Do what?" Lanning appeared puzzled. "What are you babbling about, kid?"

"When we were on the 747," Simon said, "you asked me if I was from Chicago. Why'd you do it? If you had access to all of that background information on us, then you must have known I wasn't from Chicago. Why?"

Lanning grinned. "I was wrong about you, Simon. You are the observant type. It just takes a while to sink in." He gazed around the room. "Do you know how many passengers were on that flight? Two hundred and seventy-one. My memory is good, but it isn't what you would call outstanding. Sure, I did read a one page report on many of the passengers and crew, but do you really think I would remember every small detail?''

''I guess not,'' Simon answered.

''I'll be back in a minute,'' Lanning said, starting to leave. ''Nature calls.''

''There is something about that man I like, Dr. Ibrahim remarked.

''Me, too,'' Simon admitted.

The Egyptian police officer, Deram, came up to their table. ''I understand you will be leaving soon,'' he said to them. ''I want to apologize for any inconvenience as I know many of you are impatient to leave. We have tried to handle this matter as quickly as possible. My name, by the way, is Captain Deram.''

''We know,'' Simon informed him. ''And may I compliment you on your excellent English? James Lanning was telling us that you also studied French in Paris. It must be gratifying to know three languages. I wish I knew more than just English.''

Deram smiled and bowed. ''Thank you, sir. It is gratifying. Although, compared to Mr. Lanning, my accomplishments are nothing.''

''Why do you say that?'' Simon asked. ''Mr. Lanning knows three languages, too.''

Deram shook his head. ''You are wrong, sir. Mr. Lanning knows nine languages.''

''Nine?''

''Yes. He knows them well. He is also somewhat conversant with four more. A most exceptional man.''

Simon gazed at the door through which Lanning had departed. ''I had no idea.''

Deram chuckled. ''Of course. Mr. Lanning does not brag about it. But then, I imagine it is easy for him to learn so many languages.''

''Why?''

''Didn't you know?'' Deram asked. ''He has a photographic memory.''

''He does?''

"Yes, sir. He is one of Interpol's top agents. They tell me that he never forgets something once he has committed it to memory. Isn't it amazing?"

"You'd never know it to look at him," Simon noted.

Deram grinned. "It is funny, sometimes, the lengths he will go to, the things he does, to hide it. For some reason, he doesn't want anyone to know. He even pretends to forget things at times. I don't know why he does it, but it's quite comical. I could tell you some stories you wouldn't believe."

"Oh, I'd believe them," Simon assured the officer.

Deram checked his watch. "Well, I must be off. It is unfortunate we could not have met under better circumstances. Perhaps another time?" He strolled off.

Simon found himself wondering about Lanning. Why would he disguise the fact he had a photographic memory? Why play silly games with other people? What motivated Lanning to act the way he did?

The Interpol agent wandered into the room and walked directly to Simon's table. "Let's go find your bags and we can split this place."

Dr. Ibrahim rose. "I must thank you again for your kindness. Should you ever return to Cairo, I insist you share the hospitality my humble home has to offer."

"If I'm ever in the neighborhood," Lanning promised, "I'll look you up."

"Please do. I reside at number 15 Banha Avenue. My door is always open to you."

"Thank you," Lanning said, then added, "I just hope I can remember your address."

Inexplicably, to Lanning at least, Dr. Ibrahim and Simon both burst out laughing.

8

"Run!" Professor Crenshaw yelled again. "Hurry!"

Hurry? To where? Amy was staying a few feet behind the Professor. She could have passed him any time she wanted, but she refused to abandon him to save her own skin.

The stone cylinder was still after them, rolling down the tunnel at a sustained, moderate speed.

How long had they been running? Her left side was hurting terribly and her leg muscles felt tight. The lantern was bobbing and bouncing in her hand, causing their shadows to flutter and sway eerily. The hieroglyphics flashed past as they sprinted down the tunnel. Amy fervently hoped the tunnel would branch off in either direction, since there was no way the stone cylinder could turn corners.

Professor Crenshaw stumbled, but instantly recovered.

Amy drew alongside him. "Are you all right?"

Crenshaw nodded. He was breathing heavily, his face flushed from the exertion.

The cylinder rumbled behind them.

Amy risked a quick glance over her right shoulder and saw the massive object about fifteen yards to their rear. The thing must weigh tons! It would literally crush them to a pulp if it rolled over them.

Professor Crenshaw abruptly tripped and fell, sprawling onto his stomach.

"No!" Amy screamed. She grabbed him by his right elbow and hauled him up. "Move!" she directed, shoving him forward.

Crenshaw had managed to retain his grip on his lantern. He lurched into a shuffling run, his body unaccustomed to such strenuous activity.

The stone cylinder had gained five yards.

Amy stayed near the Professor, ready to assist him if he should fall again. If he did, she might not be able to get him up again before the cylinder reached them.

Professor Crenshaw was wheezing.

Amy suddenly noticed the hieroglyphics had ended; the walls and the ceiling were bare stone again. Was it her imagination or were the walls wider apart than before? It could be the light playing tricks on her, but it definitely appeared like there was more space between the walls.

"Leave me!" Professor Crenshaw ordered as he started to slow down. "I can't go on!"

Amy shot a look over her left shoulder.

The walls *had* widened! There was about a foot of clearance between the sides of the cylinder and the walls of the tunnel. Not much, but it was their only chance!

Amy lunged, clutching the Professor and shoving him against the far wall. "Don't move," she instructed him. "Do like I do." She sprinted to her side of the tunnel and flattened, pressing her back against the hard wall, striving to make herself as thin as she could.

None too soon.

The very walls of the tunnel vibrated as, with a deafening din, the gargantuan stone cylinder streaked by her trembling body.

Amy held her breath. The surface of the cylinder was only inches from her face. She could clearly see the smooth, rotating stone and its grey, grainy texture. Her bangs stirred in the breeze the cylinder's passage created. Dust choked her lungs, filled her nostrils, and stung her eyes.

In the space of a heartbeat, in the flutter of an eyelid, it was over. The stone cylinder rolled past them and disappeared into the darkness ahead.

Amy's eyes locked on the Professor's.

Crenshaw was as pale as a sheet. He was motionless, his body flattened against the fall wall.

Amy exhaled and eased away from the wall. "We made it," she said in stunned disbelief.

Professor Crenshaw was about to comment when the entire tunnel shook from the impact of the enormous cylinder colliding with something further down the passageway.

A cloud of dust billowed up from below.

"What was that?" Amy asked.

Professor Crenshaw joined her, his composure slightly restored. "Let's go see," he suggested.

"Shouldn't we get out while the getting is good?" Amy proposed.

"After what we've just been through," Crenshaw stated adamantly, "nothing is going to stop me from seeing what's down there."

Amy swallowed hard. "Okay, I'm with you," she said. Mentally, she chided herself for being a fool. After all, she told herself, if this was what archaeology had to offer, she'd be better off becoming an accountant.

Professor Crenshaw moved slowly along the corridor.

"Do you think there will be any more booby traps?"

"There could be," Crenshaw answered. "Stay alert."

"I wasn't planning to take a nap," she cracked.

A few yards down the tunnel they found the cause of the crash. The huge stone cylinder had collided with a wall which had collapsed, forming a pile of jagged rock and other debris on top of the cylinder.

Amy and Professor Crenshaw paused at the rubble and lifted their lanterns high overhead.

"Dear Lord!" Amy said in awe.

"Indeed," the Professor concurred.

They had discovered the burial chamber, the tomb of Prince Hiros, amazingly intact after 5000 years. Except for the brown dust covering everything within the tomb, it was exactly as the priests had left it on the day they had sealed the chamber.

Professor Crenshaw stepped to their left. There was a two foot space between the left side of the stone cylinder and the wall. He bypassed the debris and entered the tomb, Amy at his elbow.

"I had no idea . . ." Amy began, then stopped, unable to find any adequate words to convey her astonishment.

The walls and the ceiling were completely covered with hieroglyphics, both painted and carved bas-relief figures and symbols. The burial chamber was huge. It was packed with artifacts of varying shapes and sizes, some of which Amy recognized. There were rows upon rows of stone ushabti, carved images of the workers the prince would need in the next life, each one meticulously painted. According to tradition, these workers, including slaves and artisans, were frequently slaughtered when a royal personage was entombed so they could accompany the deceased dignitary to the other side.

"Look at all those ushabti," Amy marveled. "There must be hundreds."

"The tomb of Seti I contained seven hundred," Professor Crenshaw mentioned absent-mindedly.

The ushabti were lined up directly in front of them.

Just to the right of the ushabti was a long cedar boat, at least 50 feet in length, the sun boat built to carry Prince Hiros on his trip to the afterlife. The boat was complete with oars and life-size oarsmen.

"This is incredible," Professor Crenshaw remarked. "We had no idea they used sun boats this early."

The right side of the tomb was filled with glistening jewels and wooden furniture, as well as piles of fine clothing and even some paintings, all representative of the wealth of Prince Hiros whose coffin reposed in the center of the room.

"What in the world!" Professor Crenshaw ejaculated when he spied the gold coffin of the prince.

Amy, too, was astounded by the sight.

They walked toward the coffin, circumventing any obstacles in their path.

Amy noticed a cluster of pottery vessels, the type used to hold food for the departed. The vessels, like the ushabti and everything else in the burial chamber, were covered with inscriptions.

The early Egyptians strongly believed that certain words and amulets conferred special powers on the user. These words, or groups of words, if uttered properly and in the correct sequence, could exert a compelling force. They were called words of power, and the Egyptians believed these words could be transferred to amulets, rendering the amulets as powerful as the words themselves. Consequently, the Egyptians buried amulets and scrolls containing words of power with the dead to protect them and serve as magic charms.

Amy speculated on whether they would find any charms or amulets in the coffin of Prince Hiros. She recalled reading about Tutankhamen, whose tomb was found in 1922 by a man named Howard Carter. This was the very first tomb of an Egyptian king ever found intact, unmolested by graverobbers. There were several rooms in Tutankhamen's tomb, each one piled high with priceless treasures. On the body of Tutankhamen himself, placed in the mummy wrappings, were about 150 amulets.

Professor Crenshaw had reached the gold coffin and was staring at it in transparent confusion. "I don't understand . . ."

"Have you ever seen one like this before?" Amy asked.

Crenshaw gazed at her, plainly baffled. "No. This is utterly incredible. Coffins have been found lying on the floor of tombs, or leaning against a wall, or even standing straight up. But always, without exception, the occupant of the coffin has been laid out in a prone position, sometimes with their arms folded across their chest. Never, never have I heard of one like this!"

Amy studied the coffin at her feet. Like the other items in the tomb, it was coated with a layer of dust, but the gold still gleamed in the light from their lanterns. As with other Egyptian coffins, it had been formed in the image of the departed. Unlike other coffins, it was not in a vertical or horizontal position. The coffin had been formed into the shape of a man down on his hands and knees, squatting on all fours like some animal.

"It sort of reminds me of the Great Sphinx," Amy observed, picturing that famous stone figure with the head of a man and the body of a lion.

"Yes, doesn't it?" Professor Crenshaw said thoughtfully. He knelt next to the coffin and placed his right hand on top of it.

Amy did likewise. The gold felt cool to the touch. "Will we open it now?"

"No," Professor Crenshaw replied. "I must contact Hassan. We are not allowed to touch a thing until we have notified the Department of Antiquities."

"How soon do you think we can start the

inventory?''

''Hassan could arrive within forty-eight hours,'' the Professor speculated. ''I know he'll want to begin as soon as he arrives.''

''I can hardly wait.''

Professor Crenshaw stood. ''Did you hear something?''

Amy rose and cocked her head. ''Like what?''

''Like someone moaning,'' Crenshaw said.

Amy glanced at her mentor, thinking he was kidding. ''You're not very funny,'' she told him, watching the shadows on the walls.

''I'm serious,'' he stated. ''Listen.''

It took a minute, but then she heard the sound, like a faint, soft groaning, coming from somewhere in the dark depths of the tomb.

''What is it?'' Amy whispered.

''I don't know,'' Professor Crenshaw answered.

There was an abrupt pounding of feet on stone from behind them, and they whirled around.

Abdel and two of the workers were running down the tunnel. At the sight of the stone cylinder and the collapsed wall, they stopped.

''Abdel!'' Professor Crenshaw yelled. ''In here.''

The three men entered the tomb. The combined light from five lanterns was almost sufficient to illuminate the entire area.

''I am most sorry,'' Abdel apologized as he reached the Professor's side.

''For what?'' Crenshaw asked.

''We heard big noise,'' Abdel said. ''Sound much like thunder. Then come loud blast and dust. I try and have men come, but many too afraid. So come with these two. Brave men.''

Professor Crenshaw put his right hand on Abdel's left shoulder. ''Thank you, my friend.''

The two workers were gawking at the contents of

the tomb with an expression of commingled fright and stupefaction reflected on their faces.

"What must we do?" Abdel inquired of the Professor.

"We heard something," Crenshaw told him. "Listen and tell me what you think it might be."

In the subsequent silence, the moaning was clearly audible.

With cries of dismay, the two workers bolted from the tomb and disappeared up the tunnel.

"I don't blame them," Professor Crenshaw commented.

"Are we going to leave?" Amy asked, hopefully.

Professor Crenshaw turned and stared in the direction of the unusual sound. "In a bit. First, though, we'll investigate and ascertain the source of that groaning."

"That's what I was afraid you'd say," Amy quipped.

Professor Crenshaw moved through the burial chamber, weaving between pile after pile and row after row of valuable treasures.

The closer they grew to the southeast corner of the tomb, the louder the sound became.

"It's coming from here," Amy stated.

Professor Crenshaw raised his lantern and examined the wall. "Ahhhh! There it is!"

"There what is?" Amy couldn't see anything.

Crenshaw reached up and touched a hairline crack in the wall. "The wind is blowing through this crack. Do you see it?"

"I see it," Amy confirmed.

Professor Crenshaw scratched his chin. "The shock of the impact of that cylinder against the north wall of the tomb undoubtedly shook the very foundation of the tomb itself. I would guess it caused this crack, and the sound we hear is the equalization of air pressure. This corner must be very close to the southern face of the cliff.'' He grinned at Amy. ''What did you think it was?''

''Passionate ghosts.''

9

Harold "Buddy" Synder was awakened by the buzzer on his electric alarm clock. He groaned, reluctant to open his eyes and begin a new day. Was it that time already? He didn't feel like going to work today. Maybe he'd call in sick and spend the day viewing sports on the tube.

The sounds of his wife's raucous snoring suddenly drowned out the buzzer.

The last thing Buddy wanted to do was wake up Gladys. It was way too early to have to put up with her constant nagging.

Buddy opened his brown eyes and stared at the alarm clock on the nightstand on his side of the bed. Whoever was responsible for inventing alarm clocks should have been shot as soon as word of the invention got around. It was inhuman to wake someone up before their own body told them it was time to roll out of the sack.

Gladys was sawing logs in her sleep, petrified logs.

Buddy reached out and switched the alarm clock off. He threw the white sheet from his bulky body and staggered from bed, his mouth tasting like he had swallowed a handful of dead grass and his bladder telling him to take a leak, quick, before he put Niagara

Falls to shame. He stumbled into the pink bathroom and glared at the walls. He hated pink. It was a sissy color. Every time he was in the bathroom it depressed him, reminding him of Gladys and her domineering nature. The same with the family of five pink flamingos, plastic replicas on a metal rod, Gladys had planted in the front lawn. One of these days, Buddy promised himself, when Gladys was off visiting her mother, he was going to take his shotgun and bag five flamingos. He could always blame it on vandals.

Buddy stood in front of the mirror and critically scrutinized his pitiful imitation of a human being. His short black hair was tinged with grey, especially around the temples and the ears. His bulbous nose looked like it once belonged to a walrus. In fact, more than one acquaintance over the years had remarked on Buddy's uncanny facial resemblance to a male walrus. Just the kind of thing a person needed to hear to build their confidence.

Buddy glanced down at his sagging abdomen, the end result of one beer too many. Who was he kidding? The end result of one million beers too many.

He'd better hurry or he'd be late for work.

After relieving himself, Buddy brushed his teeth, and shaved. He quietly dressed in the bedroom, watching Gladys snore and toying with the notion of dropping an anvil into her gaping mouth to see if it would wake her up.

Probably not.

Attired in a conservative blue suit with a pink and orange polka dot tie Gladys had given him as a Christmas gift, he walked downstairs to the kitchen. He could never decide what to do with the damn tie—burn it, or use it to strangle Gladys? He was saving it for the day he finally made up his mind. Buddy made some fresh coffee and consumed two pieces of toast—plain, no butter, no jam. His doctor had ordered him to lose 15 pounds, and if he wouldn't or couldn't lose them, the doctor had threatened to tell Gladys he was overweight again. And here Buddy had always entertained the mistaken notion that physicians were supposed to *save* lives! The last time his doctor ratted to Gladys, she made Buddy eat a steady diet of cottage cheese, yogurt, and, horror of all horrors, liver. Buddy shivered at the mere memory. He'd much rather hack the excess baggage from his frame with an axe than eat liver again.

Buddy washed his mug and plate, then left the house. The birds were singing in the trees, but what did birds know? Did birds pay taxes or have a mortgage every month? Were birds married to Gladys?

The sun was rising in the eastern sky and the temperature was typically mild for Atlanta this time of year.

Buddy climbed into their station wagon, turned it over, and a minute later was driving toward McDonough Boulevard. It was a bit of a drive from his home in Lakewood Heights to the Centers for Disease Control, where he was employed in the Office of the Director as a coordinator for the Center for Infectious Diseases. It was a position he really enjoyed, one of the few bright spots in his otherwise dreary life.

Another bright spot in his life was bowling night.

Tonight!

Buddy arrived at the Centers for Disease Control in a cheerful mood, prompting one of his co-workers to sarcastically inquire if he was on drugs. He ignored her barb and went about his current assignment, a routine evaluation of a new immunizing agent. With the prospect of his bowling night ahead of him, Buddy cruised through the day. Unfortunately, paperwork delayed his departure and he didn't arrive home until after six.

Gladys was in the living room, her large feet

propped up on the arm of the sofa while her thin form was sprawled out in all its magnificent ugliness. Her tiny brown eyes and hooked beak of a nose, which would have done justice to a mature bald eagle, swung around to face him as he walked in the front door.

"You're late," Gladys noted in her high, raspy voice.

"Yes, dear." Buddy started up the stairs to change his clothes for bowling.

"Your liver is in the microwave," Gladys informed him.

Buddy froze in midstride and looked at her. "My liver?"

"Yes. I've seen how you've been cutting back on your portions at mealtime, so I took the liberty of calling Dr. Fisk."

"You did what?" Buddy had to consciously suppress his rising anger. Nothing made Gladys madder than seeing him mad.

"Dr. Fisk told me you must lose more weight," Gladys said. "So I'm putting you on a diet, effective immediately."

"Yes, dear." Buddy continued up the stairs.

"Hold it!"

Buddy stopped. "What?"

"Where do you think you're going?" Gladys demanded.

"It's my bowling night," he reminded her.

Gladys sat up, adjusting her pink dress so the hem covered her knobby knees. "You're not going bowling tonight," she stated.

"I am so," Buddy retorted.

"And *I* say you're not!"

"Why not? Why can't I go?"

"I know you." Gladys frowned. "You'll spend all your time guzzling beer and feeding your face with junk food. Dr. Fisk says all that weight you're carrying around is bad for your heart.''

That settled it. Buddy mentally vowed to replace Dr. Fisk with a new physician as soon as possible.

''I think you should stay home with me tonight,'' Gladys finally suggested.

Buddy adopted an appropriately sheepish, meek expression. ''I would much rather go bowling, if you don't mind. I give you my word I'll behave myself and stay away from the junk food and the beer.''

''Do you expect me to believe you?''

''Have I ever lied to you?'' Buddy asked innocently. The line always worked. He never had lied to her; he just never told her the whole truth. When it came to women and marriage, he firmly believed in one basic motto—what they didn't know couldn't hurt the husband.

''You promise me?'' Gladys pressed him.

''Cross my heart,'' Buddy said, crossing his heart.

''All right,'' Gladys agreed grudgingly.

''Thanks,'' Buddy said and went upstairs.

''Don't forget to eat your liver,'' Gladys shouted up after him.

Buddy hastily showered and dressed in his black pants and his bowling shirt. He was the best player on his team, the Rejects. The team shirt was dark blue, depicting two large cantaloupes on the back, which everyone else considered stupid. They couldn't see the connection between the cantaloupes and the team name, the Rejects, which was fine by the Rejects, because the cantaloupes weren't really cantaloupes. They were actually an artistic reproduction of a well endowed woman, cleverly camouflaged to resemble cantaloupes. But if you looked real, real close . . .

Buddy hurried downstairs to the kitchen. Gladys was immersed in one of her favorite game shows, trying to solve a phrase before the contestants. Buddy never could comprehend what she saw in the program. The phrases were insipid, and the host of the show was as funny as a visit to the dentist. The only redeeming element in the program was the woman who assisted the host. She rarely said a word, but she didn't need to. Her cantaloupes spoke eloquently for her.

The lousy liver was on a plate in the microwave. Gladys had already cooked it; all he had to do was heat it up. He pressed the buttons necessary to warm the liver and waited while the microwave did its stuff. When the microwave beeped, he removed the liver and sat at the kitchen table.

How long would it take to eat a piece of liver?

Buddy waited five minutes, then folded the liver into a paper napkin and stuck the napkin down his underwear, adjusting the band of his boxer shorts so it held the napkin in place. He emerged from the kitchen with a smile on his face.

"Did you eat your liver?" Gladys immediately demanded.

Buddy patted his stomach, smacking his right palm against his shirt and feeling the small bulge of the napkin. "It's right where it should be," he replied.

Gladys nodded, satisfied. "If you'd listen to me more often, you wouldn't be overweight in the first place," she said with an air of smug superiority.

"Yes, dear." Buddy pecked her on the left cheek and left.

The evening was cool and refreshing, with a slight breeze blowing in from the northwest.

Buddy hopped into the station wagon and took off, eager to reach the Happy Lanes bowling alley.

But first he had a stop to make.

He took a sharp left, then a right, and braked in front of a home belonging to a close pal, Dean Vaughn, who already would be at the bowling alley. Luckily for Buddy, Dean's dog didn't bowl.

Buddy saw the Great Dane come loping toward his station wagon. Alexander, as the canine was called, was at least 32 inches high at the shoulder and must have weighed a ton. About a year ago, Buddy had pulled the liver trick on Gladys on his way over to pay Dean a visit. The liver was still in his underwear when he arrived and started up the front walk. Inspiration struck when Alexander appeared from around the corner of the house. No one was looking, so Buddy tossed the liver to the dog. Ever since, every time he came over, the Great Dane expected to receive another treat. Dean had commented on how much the dog liked Buddy since normally the animal was cool toward strangers. Over the past year, Buddy had fed the dog about a dozen times. Alexander now recognized his station wagon and came running at the sight of it.

Buddy glanced at the Vaughn home, but no one appeared to be in. Dean's car was gone, and there was no sign of the kids.

Alexander trotted around to Buddy's window, his thick tongue lolling out the corner of his mouth, his imposing teeth exposed.

Buddy pulled the napkin from his pants and removed the liver, while the Great Dane slobbered all over the glass.

Buddy rolled the window open and gingerly handed the liver to the dog.

Alexander took two bites and swallowed.

Presto! No more liver.

"Good dog," Buddy muttered, patting Alexander on the head and hoping the Great Dane wasn't in the mood for dessert.

Alexander belched, then turned and returned to the Vaughn property.

Buddy chuckled as he drove off. Maybe he was in the wrong line of work. With a devious mind like his, he should have become a secret agent.

The drive to Happy Lanes took about 15 minutes. Buddy grabbed his shoes and ball from the back seat and hurried into the building. Dean and the rest of the Rejects were already practicing in lane four.

"About time," Dean yelled as Buddy approached. Dean, a lean man with grey hair and glasses, was employed at the Fernbank Science Center. He was 48, two years older than Buddy. "I didn't think you were going to make it."

"Why not?" Buddy sat down and began changing his shoes.

"Gladys called Milly earlier," Dean said. "Gladys told my old lady you were going on a diet. She also said there was no way you would be bowling tonight."

"Well, I'm here, aren't I?" Buddy retorted. "I guess it shows you who's the boss in my house."

"Can I get you anything?" Dean asked, moving toward the snack bar.

Buddy fished in his right pocket and extracted a five. "Here." He tossed it to Dean. "Get me a six-pack of the usual and four bags of nuts."

"You got it, pal."

Buddy finished putting on his bowling shoes and stood. He stretched, watching a lovely blonde two lanes away. She jiggled more than a tree in a hurricane when she bowled.

"Here you go." Dean gave Buddy the six-pack and the nuts.

"Thanks," Buddy said.

"Say, I've been meaning to ask you a question," Dean said.

"Shoot."

"You've been on a lot of diets," Dean began.

"Thanks," Buddy snapped.

"Don't take me wrong. I just need some of your expertise."

Buddy stared at Dean. "Expertise?"

"Yeah. My brother says that Alexander, my dog, is way overweight. I don't want to spend a lot of bucks taking Alex to the vet, just to find out the mutt is fat. I was hoping you might be able to give me some advice on what kind of food to feed Alex so he'll lose a little weight," Dean said hopefully.

"I don't think that dogs and humans have the same nutritional requirements," Buddy stated, slightly miffed.

"I know that," Dean commented, "but there must be something we eat that would be good for dogs, too. Do you have any idea how much that dietary dog food costs?"

"No," Buddy admitted.

"Come on." Dean goaded him. "There must be something you can think of."

Buddy pretended to give the matter serious consideration.

"Well?" Dean said impatiently.

"How about liver?" Buddy recommended.

"Liver? Are you nuts?"

"No. Why?"

"No one likes liver and that includes dogs. There's no way Alexander would go for it."

"Why don't you try it?" Buddy advised.

"No way."

"You'll never know unless you give it a shot," Buddy said.

"It would be a waste of my money," Dean stated emphatically.

Buddy unzipped his bowling bag and withdrew his ball.

"Any other bright ideas?" Dean asked cynically.

"Tell you what I'll do," Buddy offered. "I'll bet you ten bucks Alexander will accept the liver."

Dean was an inveterate gambler, but he still hedged. "I can't do that to you. It would be like taking money from a baby. No contest."

"Then put your money where your big mouth is," Buddy declared, challenging him.

''Dean's eyes narrowed. ''If you're going to be that way about it, then fine, let's do it. Only make it fifteen bucks instead of ten. I want to teach you a lesson.''

''Okay,'' Buddy agreed. ''Fifteen it is.''

Dean laughed. ''It'll be the easiest fifteen bucks I've ever made!''

Buddy raised his bowling bowl, pretending to examine the holes and hiding his smirk.

Fifteen dollars would buy a lot of beer.

10

The afternoon sun felt hot on his face, and the dry desert air caused his skin to feel tight.

Simon Darr gazed at the barren countryside on either side of the dirt road, if you could call the faint impression of tire tracks a road. The jeep bounced continuously over the unavoidable ruts and depressions.

"Not long," the driver, Naan, appraised his passenger. "Good me wait, yes? You very late."

Simon looked at the driver dispatched by Professor Crenshaw to bring him to the excavation site. Naan, in his thirties, wore a white turban and a blue galabiyah, a one piece cotton garment reaching from his neck to his ankles. Naan had told Simon this was the second dig he had worked on with Professor Crenshaw. According to Naan, only one man, someone named Abdel, had worked more times with the Professor. When Naan talked about Abdel, Simon noticed, he sounded envious of Abdel's superior position, especially monetarily. Naan was a chronic chatterbox, but the twisting, curving road demanded all of his concentration for the moment.

Simon used the respite to reflect on his departure from Cairo and his farewell to James Lanning. The

Interpol agent had escorted him outside to hail a taxi. As they stood on the cement steps in front of police headquarters, Lanning had eyed Simon quizzically.

"What were you two laughing about back there?" the agent asked.

Simon grinned, debating whether he should reveal he knew Lanning's secret. He scanned the crowded street below, searching for Dr. Ibrahim. The kindly physician had already left, eager to see his wife and family again. The authorities had permitted the passengers to phone their loved ones upon landing, to assure their families they were safe and sound.

"I asked you a question," Lanning had stated.

Simon stared at him. "What year was Napoleon defeated at Waterloo?"

"What the hell does Napoleon have to do with anything?" Lanning demanded, annoyed.

"You answer my question," Simon had told him, "and I'll answer yours."

Lanning studied Simon suspiciously.

"I'm waiting."

"I think it was 1815," Lanning answered, "but I could be mistaken."

Simon thoughtfully stroked his chin, absently gazing at the two brown suitcases at his feet. What else would Lanning be interested in? The agent had an abiding fondness for France and the French people, so the question concerning Napoleon was a safe bet. But what else? He knew Lanning lived in Paris. "Have you ever been to the Eiffel Tower?" he asked.

"Yes, but I don't . . ." Lanning began.

"Ever taken a tour or read its history?"

"I may have," Lanning replied, "but what . . ."

"So how many rivets are there in the Eiffel Tower?" Simon had cut him off again.

"What?"

"You heard me. How many rivets are there in the Eiffel Tower?"

"What kind of stupid question is that?" Lanning demanded angrily. He opened his mouth to speak again, then froze as something seemed to dawn on him. The agent frowned and glared at Simon. "If I recall correctly," he said stiffly, "when the Eiffel Tower was built for the World's Fair in 1889 there were two million, five hundred thousand rivets in the structure." He paused. "So! Who told you? Deram?"

Simon nodded.

"The damn blabbermouth!"

"I don't get it," Simon admitted. "Why try to keep your talent a secret from everybody? Why do you try to hide the fact you have a photographic memory?"

"To avoid situations like this," Lanning said, frowning.

"I still don't get it."

"You would if you were in my shoes," Lanning said, his bitter tone conveying both frustration and irritation.

"But a photographic memory is something you should be proud of," Simon insisted.

"Oh, yeah?" Lanning snapped. "Says who? You don't have the slightest idea of what you're talking about."

"Why don't you enlighten me?" Simon proposed.

Lanning hesitated for a moment, inner turmoil registering on his features. "You can't have any idea of what it was like when I was a kid," he said resentfully. "Everyone, even my own family, looked at me as if I were some kind of freak."

"Surely you're exaggerating," Simon suggested.

"Exaggerating!" Lanning exploded. "I'll tell you what it was like, Mr. Know-It-All. I was eight when my folks and the D.C. school administrators figured it out. Once they had determined I had a photographic memory, once all the tests were completed, I found myself being treated like a completely different person. I wasn't little James Lanning anymore; I wasn't just a normal kid like all the others on my block. Oh, no, I was something special. I was the brain, the kid who could remember practically everything. And that's the way I was treated, like I was some kind of child prodigy."

"What's wrong with that?" Simon asked when the agent paused for breath.

"What's wrong with that?" Lanning repeated sarcastically. "I told you that you wouldn't understand. You see, everyone expected me to be a mental whiz. I was expected to get straight A's in school, and if a grade slipped to a B my father had a fit. My classmates expected me to remember every word said in class and everything I read in a textbook. They were constantly coming up to me and asking me for answers to ridiculous questions, just like you did a minute ago. And the jocks! You should have seen them! When I went out for sports I was treated like I didn't belong, like I should be home with my nose buried in a book instead of playing football or baseball. Do you know what the kids called me?"

Simon shook his head.

"I wasn't called Jim or Lanning," the agent disclosed. "I was always referred to as 'James the Brain', or just 'The Brain'. I got so I hated that nickname. Everywhere we went it was the same, because my school transcript would follow me, and the whole cycle would repeat over again. It wasn't until I reached college, until I was away from home and living on my own, that the stigma disappeared."

"I'm sorry," Simon apologized. "I didn't know . . ."

"The worst was my parents." Lanning went on, as if he hadn't heard Simon. "My parents, particularly my dad, just knew I was destined for great things. My father wanted me to follow in his footsteps and enter the diplomatic corps or become a politician. A damn politician! When I let them know I was interested in law enforcement instead, they hit the roof. My father told me he didn't want me setting foot in his house again until I came to my senses. I was banned from my parents' home because I wanted to live my own life." Lanning's voice lowered. "I never did go home again, and my father died with that chip on his shoulder. Cancer took him," Lanning said sadly. "He lingered on his deathbed for weeks. I called to talk to him, but he wouldn't accept the call. The old fart kicked the bucket still hating his only son because I wouldn't make full use of my wonderful potential, as he called it. That was a decade ago. My mother began writing to me about five years ago, saying how sorry she was and how much she wants to see me. Ha!" Lanning snapped angrily. "I'll bet!"

Simon had been silent after Lanning's revelation, unsure of what he should say.

"So there you have it, kid. The story of my life, so to speak, and the reason why I keep my photographic memory to myself as much as possible. I will not allow myself to be treated like I'm something special, like I'm a freak, when I'm not. I want to be treated the same as everybody else. Got it?"

Simon nodded. Eager to direct the conversation away from Lanning's parents, he decided to ask a question. "What's it like, having a photographic memory?"

"A pain in the ass."

"No, really. I'm curious. I've never met anyone with a photographic memory before. How does it work? Do you remember everything in explicit detail?"

"It doesn't work that way," Lanning answered, elaborating. "I don't remember everything. For instance, I wouldn't have the slightest idea what I had for supper exactly three weeks ago today. On the other hand, if I read something, say a page out of a book, I can recall what that page looked like word for word. I actually see the page in my mind's eye. That's why they call it a photographic memory, because it functions a lot like a camera by vividly recording the image in front of it. That's why I can read a book on the history of France and know what year Napoleon fought Waterloo. That's why I can read a brochure describing the history of the Eiffel Tower and recall the bit about the rivets."

"And that's why you're so good at languages," Simon deduced.

"You got it."

"I'm really sorry," Simon said, apologizing again. "I had no idea. You were right. I just couldn't see why you'd be so touchy about it."

"So now that you do understand," Lanning said, "you won't bring the subject up again?"

"Nope."

"And you won't ask me any more dumb-ass questions?"

"I promise."

"Good." Lanning nodded, satisfied. "If you need to know something, look it up at the library like everybody else." He smiled. "It's time for me to go, kid." He offered his right hand. "You take care of yourself."

Simon shook Lanning's hand. "I hope we meet again someday."

"Yeah, sure." Lanning turned to leave.

"Hey," Simon said.

Lanning glanced over his right shoulder. "Yeah?"

"Just in case you decide to visit your mother soon, or happen to be in the Chicago area, my wedding is set for May 15th. You have a standing invitation to drop in if you'd like."

"You're inviting me to your wedding?" Lanning asked, surprised.

"Yep. Try and make it, if you can. I want to show

off the man who saved my life."

"No one has invited me to a wedding in ages," Lanning remarked.

Simon stooped and opened the side flap on one of his suitcases. He withdrew a pen and a red notepad, then scribbled on a blank sheet of paper. "This is my home address and my phone number. This other one is the name of the church, the address, and the time. Here." He handed the sheet to the agent.

Lanning took the paper, scrutinizing Simon intently. "Are you sure about this?"

"Of course."

Lanning folded the sheet and placed it in his pocket. "I can't guarantee you I'll be there," he said. "I don't know what my schedule will be like."

"No problem. I'll understand if you don't show up."

Lanning nodded and raised his right hand to his forehead in a snappy salute. "Vous etes tres aimable. A bientôt."

Simon had waved as Lanning walked up the steps and into the building, wondering what the agent had said.

Bouncing through the desert, he still wondered what the French words meant.

Simon was jolted from his reverie when the jeep struck a deep rut. He looked at Naan.

"Am very sorry," Naan stated. "Very wild place, yes?"

The jeep was climbing a steep rise. As it reached the crest, Simon was afforded a panoramic view of the stark vista below. He saw a cluster of a dozen or so tents about 500 yards from the base of the rise. Beyond the tents rose a rocky cliff. A ramp had been constructed from the base of the cliff to its top, and there was a gaping tunnel about a third of the way down from the summit. Simon realized Naan had circled to approach the site from the west.

"There it is," Naan exclaimed.

Simon scanned the tents as the jeep descended toward the excavation camp. He could see some workers on the ramp, but there was no sign of Amy.

Naan braked the jeep below the ramp and directed a question at another worker. After the man responded, Naan faced Simon. "He says Miss Brant in hole." He pointed at the tunnel.

"I'll unpack later," Simon stated. "Can you take me to her?"

Naan nodded and climbed from the jeep. "Follow me."

Simon stayed beside Naan as they ascended the ramp and entered the tunnel.

Another man stopped and conversed with Naan in Arabic. Naan replied, then stepped aside, deferring to the newcomer. Simon noticed Naan could scarcely conceal a frown.

"I am Abdel," announced the man. "Please to follow me."

"Thank you," Simon said to Naan, then hastened after Abdel. Why did Naan seem to resent Abdel so much? Naan had glared maliciously at Abdel for just an instant when Abdel turned his back. He pushed the matter from his mind as they neared a stone wall. A number of large stone blocks lay to one side, apparently removed from the wall to permit passage.

"Professor Crenshaw and Amy in tomb," Abdel said over his shoulder, smiling at Simon. "Miss Brant tell Abdel to call always Amy. Say we friends."

Simon nodded, wishing they would hurry.

They crossed a small chamber and walked through another wall into a tunnel, sloping downward. The tunnel air was cool, a welcome relief from the heat of the afternoon sun.

Abdel pointed down the tunnel. "We walk some."

The walk seemed interminable, and Simon chafed

at the delay in reaching Amy. When the tunnel branched to the right and the hieroglyphics appeared on the walls and ceiling, he gaped in amazement and inadvertently slowed a bit to observe the writing. After another lengthy spell, they reached the tomb. A huge pile of rubble was stacked to one side of a wide opening in the wall, and a peculiar stone cylinder had been angled against the left wall of the tomb. Lanterns were hung at ten foot intervals.

Abdel moved to the right, allowing Simon to pass him.

Simon paused on the threshold of the tomb and scanned the interior. He spotted Amy, wearing dirty jeans and a blue sweatshirt, standing 20 yards to his right, engaged in a discussion with an older man in khakis. Amy's back was toward him.

The older man, evidently Professor Crenshaw, caught sight of Simon over Amy's shoulder and said something to her.

Simon saw Amy whirl, her face bathed in relief as she saw him.

"Simon," Amy shouted, and flew into his arms.

Simon met her halfway, hugging her and clasping her tight. "God, I've missed you," he said when he eventually found his voice.

Amy's eyes, pressed against his neck, felt moist. "I've missed you too, you big dummy," she stated huskily. "Where have you been? You were supposed to get here yesterday."

Simon drew back and gazed into her lovely blue eyes. "We'll talk about it later. Right now, I just want to look at you."

Amy impulsively kissed him on the mouth, her lips soft and warm against his.

Someone nearby was making a show of clearing his throat.

Amy twisted and indicated the man in the khakis. "Oh, this is Professor Crenshaw."

Professor Crenshaw offered his right hand. "I have heard a lot about you, Mr. Darr."

Simon shook. "You can call me Simon, Professor Crenshaw."

"Will do. Why don't we go down to the tents and enjoy a beer or two while you tell us about your trip and Amy makes goo-goo eyes at you? We were about done up here for the day anyway."

"I don't want to interfere with your work," Simon said.

"Nonsense!" Crenshaw scoffed. "We can't commence the inventory until a friend of mine shows up sometime tomorrow or the next day, and there's really not much we can do until then."

Simon idly gazed at the artifacts surrounding them. His eyes alighted on a bizarre gold object occupying the middle of the tomb. "What in the world is that?"

Professor Crenshaw followed the direction of Simon's glance. "It's the coffin of an Egyptian nobleman."

"But why is it shaped like that?"

"I wish I knew," Crenshaw responded.

"It looks like he's imitating a dog," Simon casually commented.

Crenshaw's brow furrowed. "Yes, it does, doesn't it?"

"Is there a mummy inside?" Simon asked.

"We don't know yet," the Professor stated. "We are not permitted to open it until a representative of the Department of Antiquities is present."

"Enough of this shop talk," Amy interrupted. "Simon's arrival calls for a celebration. Let's go!"

"You go ahead," Professor Crenshaw directed. He watched the young pair exit the tomb arm-in-arm.

Abdel walked up to the Professor and pointed at the gold coffin. "My men say that bad sign, bad omen."

''That's silly superstition, Abdel, and you know it,'' Crenshaw stated. ''It's nothing but a coffin, just like the others we have found.''

Abdel shook his head. ''Not like others, Professor. Very much different. What does it mean?''

Crenshaw put his right hand on Abdel's shoulder. ''It means, good friend, it's time for us to call it quits for the day.''

''You still want no guard for tonight?'' Abdel asked.

''No, I don't believe a guard will be necessary,'' Professor Crenshaw replied. ''We didn't use one last night, and I don't see why we should tonight. The men are too scared to come down here.''

''But what about graverobbers?'' Abdel reminded him.

''Professionals?'' Crenshaw surveyed the contents of the tomb. ''Not very likely. They couldn't have heard about our discovery already.''

''Never know for sure,'' Abdel replied.

Professor Crenshaw realized Abdel had a valid point. One could not afford to underestimate the desert grapevine. If professional graverobbers were aware of this unique find, they would stop at nothing to loot the tomb.

''All right,'' Crenshaw agreed. ''Post a man on the ledge at the tunnel entrance. Tell him to keep a fire lit all night and to holler if he spots anything suspicious.''

''Will do,'' Abdel stated.

Professor Crenshaw rubbed his hands together in anticipation of a relaxing evening. ''It's been a busy day. I could use a couple of Stella beers right about now. Let's go.''

11

At 9:00 A.M. Buddy Snyder was at his desk, his horn-rimmed reading glasses perched on his prominent nose, immersed in a special report, one with staggering implications.

There had been another outbreak of Lassa fever.

One of the many responsibilities of the Centers for Disease Control, including the Center for Infectious Diseases, was to serve as an epidemiological consultant to State and local health departments, federal agencies, and certain national and even international health organizations. In this instance, the Peace Corps had officially requested assistance in dealing with the latest Lassa fever outbreak.

Buddy was thoroughly acquainted with the history of Lassa fever.

Lassa fever first showed up in Nigeria in 1969. It was a totally new disease; consequently, no one knew how to treat its victims and over two-thirds of them died. As Buddy recalled, the very first victim was a nurse who lasted ten days after contracting the fever. The second victim was another nurse who had treated the first one. Shortly thereafter, another nurse died from this startling new malady, then some of the staff at the hospital. Doctors and visitors who had had contact with the victims also perished.

The smart thing to do at that point would have been to isolate the affected facility and quarantine the entire hospital, but someone decided to send one of the victims to New York so researchers could properly study the disease. Sure enough, two researchers came down with the fever. After one of them died, the scientists determined Lassa fever was simply too dangerous to study; all work on it was stopped.

No one else contracted the fever, and for about seven years everyone thought they'd seen the last of the mysterious disease. They were wrong.

It was in March of 1976 when Lassa fever put in another appearance.

A passenger on a flight through Dulles airport in Washington, D.C., developed Lassa fever. There were about 300 other passengers who had flown across the Atlantic Ocean with the Lassa fever victim. Authorities located and examined all of them to be certain they weren't carrying the disease.

Then in August of 1976 another case of Lassa fever was reported from Toronto. The Canadian authorities acted promptly, closing the hospital and placing it under quarantine until they were positive the contagion had been contained.

Lassa fever put in its fourth appearance in May of 1977. This time, someone from England returned to London after taking a trip to Africa. Fortunately, not many victims were recorded in this instance.

And now it had shown up again in, of all places, Toledo, Ohio. A young man, a Peace Corps worker, had recently returned from a tour in Africa, in Cameroon to be exact, and was now in a hospital in Toledo with Lassa fever. The Peace Corps had requested help from the Centers for Disease Control, wanting to know how they could effectively minimize the risk to their workers. The hospital needed to know what techniques, equipment and medication could be utilized in their efforts to save the young man's life.

Buddy dreaded the prospect of notifying the hospital in Toledo that there was little they could do. About one-third of the Lassa fever patients had survived, but only after lengthy recuperations and the use of extremely sophisticated medical equipment, the type many hospitals did not have because it was too specialized and expensive for their ordinary needs. One woman who did survive lost close to 30 pounds in about three weeks before she pulled out of it. So the hospital in Toledo could well be fighting a losing battle. The authorities were not about to allow the patient to be flown to another facility because of the threat to the general population.

As far as the Peace Corps was concerned, Buddy wouldn't be able to help them much, either. The cause of Lassa fever was unknown. Scientists did know, or thought they knew, that Lassa fever was not easy to catch. They maintained it had to be spread through body fluids like urine or blood, although they hedged and also claimed some victims might contaminate others by coughing up viral drops of mucus.

Buddy leaned back in his chair and absently gazed out his window, distressed by the cavalier attitude of some of his colleagues. Because Lassa fever was infrequently reported, and since the outbreaks were somewhat controlled by a diligent quarantine, they believed there was nothing to worry about. As one of them had said to Buddy, "Sooner or later we'll get a cap on it, so why sweat it?"

The clowns missed the point.

In ancient times, when the means of travel were agonizingly slow and the time required to reach a distant destination exceedingly lengthy, it was relatively easy for health officials to isolate a contaminated area or intercept an infected individual.

But now everything was different.

With the advent of the industrial revolution,

especially with the astonishing advances made in the realm of transportation, the potential for spreading a lethal disease was enormous. Air travel in particular posed a major problem. It would be too easy for a severe epidemic of an unknown disease in one country to speed around the world in mere days or weeks if an infected carrier flew to another part of the globe.

Buddy watched some pigeons wing past his window.

The way he saw it, mankind was toying with fire. So far, humanity had been lucky. New diseases arose regularly, but most of them were held in check.

What would happen, Buddy asked himself, if an unknown deadly disease should arise and envelop the world like an uncontrolled forest fire destroying dry timber?

There would be hell to pay.

The intercom buzzed.

"Yes?"

"It's your wife," his secretary warned him, "on line three."

Buddy depressed the button for line three on his phone. "Yes, Gladys?"

"Buddy, when you get home you're going to get it."

"What did I do now?" Buddy wearily inquired.

"Don't act innocent with me," Gladys snapped.

"I'm really busy, Gladys," Buddy told her. "Can you get to the point, please?"

"You . . . you murderer!" Gladys screamed.

"Murderer?" Buddy knew what was coming, but if he confessed she wouldn't give him a moment's peace for a year. "What are you talking about?"

"You know damn well what I'm talking about," Gladys exploded.

"I really am busy, Gladys."

"How could you do it?"

"Do what?"

"Run over the poor thing like you did," Gladys said angrily.

"Gladys, please . . ."

"You ran over one of my adorable flamingos," Gladys accusingly said. "Why?"

"Slow down. Are you telling me one of your flamingos was run over?"

"Don't play innocent with me, mister. Yesterday evening, when you went out and cut the grass, you ran over one of my flamingos with the lawnmower."

"I did not," Buddy lied.

"You did so," Gladys retorted. "I have a witness."

"Who?"

"Eddy Minor," Gladys informed him.

"The little kid who lives across the street?"

"He's not a kid," Gladys corrected. "Eddy's twelve. He told me he saw you deliberately run over my baby flamingo, and he said you were smiling when you did it."

Buddy grinned at the memory. "I did not."

"Eddy saw you!"

Buddy never had liked the Minor brat. How could you like someone who constantly referred to you as "fatso"?

"Eddy saw you with his own eyes," Gladys repeated when Buddy didn't comment.

"Eddy is mistaken," Buddy said.

"You admit you ran over my flamingo?" Gladys demanded.

"Yes," Buddy replied, "but it was an accident. I didn't mean to do it. I just wasn't watching where I was going."

"Why didn't you tell me about it when it happened?"

"I knew how much those birds mean to you, Gladys, and I didn't want to upset you, that's all. I figured I could find a replacement before you found out and avoid hurting your feelings."

There was silence at the other end.

"Is that the truth?" Gladys finally asked.

"Cross my heart and hope to die," Buddy said.

"You wouldn't lie to me, would you?"

"Gladys," Buddy stated with conviction, "may God strike me dead if I'm lying to you."

"Okay, I guess I believe you," Gladys said, not sounding at all convinced.

"Thank you, dearest."

"I'm sorry I accused you," Gladys added, apologetically.

"No problem," Buddy responded condescendingly.

"I'll tell you what I'm going to do," Gladys proposed.

"What's that?"

"To make up for it," he offered in her sweetest tone of voice, "I'll have a plate of hot liver and cottage cheese all set on the table for you when you walk in the door tonight."

"Gee, Gladys, you don't have to go to all that trouble for me."

"It's no trouble. Ta-ta!" She hung up.

Buddy sighed and replaced the receiver. Not liver and cottage cheese again! He stabbed the intercom. "Ms. Krepps?"

"Yes?" the secretary answered.

"Are you going out for lunch today?" Buddy asked her.

"Yes, I am."

"Would you do me a favor?"

"What is it?"

"Now you know I don't ordinarily make requests like this, but I'm going to be tied up all day preparing this consulting report. Could you possibly pick up something for me if I call ahead and order it? You could get it on your way back from lunch.''

''Sure, I don't mind. Just don't make a habit of it.''

Womens' lib! Who needed it? ''Could you stop at Dante's for me?'' Buddy asked politely.

''The Italian food place? Sure. What will I be picking up?'' Ms. Krepps asked.

Buddy almost drooled in anticipation. ''A large pizza with the works.''

''Aren't you on a diet?''

''Not any more. I'm celebrating,'' Buddy explained.

''Celebrating what?''

''A death in the family.''

There was a protracted pause.

''Mr. Snyder,'' Ms. Krepps said tentatively, ''do you mind if I tell you something?''

''No, go ahead.''

''You won't be offended?''

''Of course not,'' Buddy assured her. ''What is it?''

''Sometimes you are *really* weird!''

12

Jay Darr was teaching an evening class at his school on Girad Avenue. The students were all women, 14 in all, who had responded to his ad in the yellow pages offering a self-defense class at a discount, a special two week course geared for those who wanted to protect themselves against rape or domestic abuse. He stood at the front of the large room, wearing the Chinese uniform bestowed on him by his sifu in California. Except for its wide white cuffs on the sleeves and white buttons up the front, the shirt and pants were black. He had on a pair of black Chinese Gong Fu shoes actually made in China, and they were without a doubt the most comfortable shoes he had ever worn.

The women were variously attired in jeans or slacks or sweat suits, whatever they wanted.

"Good evening, ladies," Jay greeted them. "Welcome to what I hope will be a rewarding and beneficial experience. First off, I'd like to talk a little bit about why all of you are here. According to the latest statistics, there is a violent crime committed in America about once every twenty seconds, a murder once every twenty minutes, a forcible rape every five to ten minutes. Five to ten minutes! Think about that for a moment."

Jay paused for effect.

"There is an aggravated assault about every fifty seconds," he continued. "A burglary every ten seconds. It boggles the mind when you think about how serious crime is in this country. We had about one hundred thousand reported cases of rape last year, and the experts say that's only the tip of the iceberg because most rapes aren't reported to the police. Around sixty-five of every one hundred thousand women will be raped this year. Even if these women do report the rape, there's less than a fifty percent chance the suspect or suspects will be apprehended. That means if you were to be raped tonight, there's a good chance whoever does it to you will get away scot-free."

He stopped and scanned the group, pleased to note all of them were paying attention.

"I assume you're here because you want to do something about those appalling statistics," Jay resumed. "You want to make sure you can defend yourself if someone tries to harm or rape you. You may be wondering if *Hung Gar* will help you in this respect. So let me enlighten you concerning *Hung Gar*, and then we'll move on to some practical applications. *Hung Gar* kung-fu is an ancient martial art from southern China. The founder is believed to have been a man named Hung Hei Gune. Be sure and memorize that name because I'm giving a quiz at the end of our class tonight."

Some of the women chuckled or grinned.

"*Hung Gar* is a very popular system," Jay detailed. "It's so popular, I suppose, because any type of body, tall or short, lean or heavy . . ."

One woman, who was grossly overweight, giggled nervously.

". . . can adapt to the techniques. It's also good

for all age brackets because it's slower than some other systems, but that doesn't mean it is less effective. Far from it. *Hung Gar* kung fu uses strong stances and very powerful hand techniques. If you apply yourself, if you take the time necessary to learn all the moves until they become a conditioned reflex, you will be able to defend yourself against a rapist. You will have confidence in your ability. *Hung Gar* can instill in you a new sense of self-reliance. Any questions so far?"

A blonde raised her hand. "Mr. Darr . . ."

"Yes?"

"Where can we get cute outfits like yours? They look so nifty."

Several of the women laughed.

"Yeah," threw in another woman, "it looks real comfortable. I could wear it around the house when I'm doing the laundry and vacuuming."

More laughter.

Jay grinned, pleased the ice had been broken. New students were invariably somewhat tense and nervous at the beginning of a class, and now they would relax and banter among themselves. He disliked those occasional classes where every student was deathly serious. *Hung Gar* kung fu was a strict discipline to those who adhered to it, but it was also, as his sifu Lum Wong had said, a lot of fun, even more fun than sex. Well, Jay wouldn't go that far, but he did agree a sense of humor was essential in any endeavor.

Funny, wasn't it, how until the other night, when Marcy and he had clarified their relationship, his life had been devoid of humor and play?

Jay shut Marcy from his mind and concentrated on his class. Slated to last an hour, the class ran 20 minutes overtime. He showed them some basic exercises and stances designed to tone their muscles and invigorate their bodies. He explained the basic principles behind Tan Tien, how the abdominal area should be the primary source of their inner strength through concentration and proper breathing.

"I want to thank you all for coming," he said at the end of the session. "I hope you'll return for our next class. Next time we're going to look at vital pressure points on the human body, knowledge you can use to dissuade or subdue any attacker. See you then."

The women thanked him as they went out the door, and the blonde mentioned she would like to try on a uniform sometime, perferably at his place if he had a spare that might fit. Not wanting to offend a paying customer, he smiled and told her he would think about it. She was the last to leave. He closed the door behind her, reflecting on how aggressive women were nowadays. Perhaps women had always been sexually assertive, or maybe he was simply old-fashioned. Whatever the case might be, he became oddly uncomfortable when a woman came on to him.

Jay turned and stopped in surprise.

Marcy was standing behind him, her arms crossed, eyeing him critically. "So you'll think about it, huh, bozo?"

"Where'd you come from?"

"Don't evade the issue," Marcy stated, grinning. "For your information, I arrived a half hour ago. You were still involved with the class, so I waited in your office. Now what about that blonde?"

Jay moved closer and placed his hands on her shoulders. "I only have eyes for you," he assured her.

"How do I know that?" she demanded mischievously.

"Would you like me to prove it?"

Marcy gazed around the room at the floor mats, the kicking bags, and the other apparatus. "Right here and now?"

"Why not?"

Marcy glanced at the front windows. "Someone could see us."

Jay smirked and drew the shades. He locked the door and flicked off the overhead lights.

"Oh, you kinky, kinky thing!" Marcy said as he walked over to her.

Marcy was wearing a yellow skirt and a light blue pullover. The short skirt displayed her shapely thighs and legs, and the pullover did little to conceal her ample bosom. She licked her full lips in anticipation as she affectionately looked up into Jay's eyes, detecting that certain gleam in his stare as he studied her. Usually Jay was tender and gentle during their love-making, but occasionally he became extremely aggressive and forceful. She didn't know the reason; he just did. Marcy wouldn't admit it to Jay, but she eagerly awaited these passionate interludes in their otherwise normal sex life. They drew her out of her conventional shell, kindling her sexual fires.

Jay placed his right hand in the small of her back and jammed her body against his. His left hand slid under the blue pullover and cupped her left breast, his fingers plying her flesh and pinching her nipple until it hurt. His lips descended on hers, mashing them, as his tongue darted into her open mouth.

The intensity and the abruptness of his longing aroused her. Marcy enjoyed being wanted this much by a man. It confirmed her sensuality and satiated her amorous appetite.

Jay dispensed with any prolonged foreplay. His right hand came around and plunged up her skirt. His hand cupped her mound, and his fingers slid her white panties aside and caressed the lips of her sex.

Marcy moaned and leaned on him.

Jay suddenly bore her to the nearest mat. He

quickly moved behind her and bent her over. "I want you," he stated huskily.

Marcy felt her skirt being lifted, and then he was penetrating her from the rear while massaging her breasts with his hands.

Jay grunted as he drew back and then lunged, filling her with his throbbing organ.

Marcy quivered and sagged to her knees.

Most of the time, Jay delighted in sustaining their coupling for as long as he could, but at moments like this, when his primal urges dominated his behavior, his lust was uncontrollable. He pounded into her again and again, his body vibrant, on the verge of his release.

"Ohhh, Jay!" Marcy moaned, lost in her own rapture.

They bucked and heaved, strained and cried, and collapsed in a trembling heap on the mat.

Jay, lying on his right side, pressed flush against her back and kissed her on the ear. "Thank you."

Marcy snickered. "For what? You did most of the work."

"But I couldn't have done it without you," he reminded her.

"Yes, you could," Marcy teased, "but it wouldn't have been as much fun."

They cuddled together, savoring the quiet aftermath.

Jay eventually broke the silence. "I need to ask you a question," he informed her.

Marcy twisted and glanced over her left shoulder. "You're not going to propose again, are you?"

"No. Nothing like that."

Marcy breathed a sigh of relief. "Good. Then what is it?"

"It's about Chicago," Jay told her.

"The Windy City? What about it?"

Jay playfully bit her earlobe.

"Ouch!" Marcy squirmed and giggled.

"You know what I'm getting at," Jay said. "I want you to come with me to Chicago for Simon's wedding."

"I don't know . . ." she hedged.

"What's the big deal?" Jay demanded. "If you're worried about missing some classes, or you're concerned your boss at the jewelry store will get bent out of shape, we'll fly out on the fourteenth, stay overnight, attend the wedding on the fifteenth, then fly back that same evening. This way you won't miss too many classes and only two nights of work."

"I don't know . . ." she reiterated doubtfully.

"Come on," Jay prompted her. "What's the big deal?"

Marcy contemplated the repercussions. It was close to the end of the semester, and she didn't have any finals on the fourteenth and fifteenth, so skipping classes wouldn't pose a problem. From 4:30 until 7:30, Tuesday through Saturday, she supported herself by working as a sales clerk at a jewelers in a large downtown mall. She could trade off nights with one of the other workers if need be, and her employer would be understanding enough to allow her the rest of the time off.

"Well?" Jay inquired.

Marcy glanced at him and grinned. "Okay, lover. But you'd best remember we're going there for your brother's wedding. I don't want you getting any idea about keeping me in the sack the whole trip. I've never been to Chicago before, and I intend to do some sightseeing."

Jay roguishly pinched her fanny. "I'm hoping to see some sights, myself," he stated, leering.

"You've been warned," she advised him, and then rubbed her bottom against his erection.

"And just what do you think you're doing?" Jay asked.

Marcy imitated the purring of a cat. "Anyone for seconds?"

13

James Lanning liked Paris best in the early morning hours, especially taking a leisurely stroll along the Seine river. He liked to idly walk between the Pont Sully, which was at the eastern end of the Ile Saint-Louis, and the Pont de la Concorde. It was peaceful and restful, particularly near the two islands, the Ile Saint-Louis itself and the larger Ile de la Cite. He would gaze at the poplars and meditate on his existence, on his purpose in life. He often came to this spot when troubled, and he was troubled now.

Monique was missing.

He had returned from Egypt much earlier than expected, submitted his report at Interpol headquarters, and returned to the apartment he shared with Monique on the Left Bank in the Latin Quarter. After purchasing some flowers, he had hastened to the apartment, anxious to see her.

The talk with Simon Darr had unsettled Lanning, and he found himself giving serious consideration to marriage and a family. When he had told Darr he envied his impending matrimony, he wasn't kidding. The possibility of a family, of buying a home and rearing children, seemed inconceivable to him. His erratic work hours precluded any prospect of stability, and what woman would relish never knowing when her husband might be called out on the spur of the moment, or not knowing if her husband would return from his latest assignment.

Lanning had to face facts. His profession was highly dangerous. If he stayed with it, sooner or later some fanatical psycho was going to get in a lucky shot or detonate an explosive device within his immediate proximity, and that would be that.

So long, Mrs. Lanning! Sorry to leave you a widow with four mouths to feed!

Still, the idea of a wife and kids appealed to him.

On the flight from Cairo to Paris Lanning had ample opportunity to reflect on married life, and he speculated on whether Monique was the woman for him.

They had hit it off right from the start. He'd attended a party thrown by one of the Interpol secretaries, and no sooner was he in the door than he noticed Monique; her radiant red hair stood out in the crowd, as did her naturally stately bearing and voluptuous figure. He'd come on to her, expecting her to tell him to take a hike. Instead, to his pleasant surprise, she responded and invited him to her place after the party was over. One thing led to another, and within two weeks he had moved in with her. She accepted his lengthy absences without griping or criticizing him for neglecting her.

But maybe the last trip had been one too many.

Lanning looked at his watch and saw it was almost six. Paris was beginning to come to life, to confront another day with the typical hustle and bustle of any huge metropolitan center. The number of cars and other vehicles was increasing as commuters headed for work.

The day promised to be sunny and clear.

His stomach growled, reminding him he hadn't eaten since noon the day before. Spotting a sidewalk cafe he decided to eat a hearty breakfast, then return to the apartment and see if Monique had shown up.

The restaurant was one of those clean, comfortable establishments Paris was noted for. No sooner was Lanning in the door than the smiling headwaiter approached.

"Bonjour, Monsieur."

"Bonjour," Lanning replied. "Avez-vous une table?"

The headwaiter, a heavy man in his forties, scanned Lanning from head to toe, noting the expensive cut of his brown suit and his costly leather shoes. "Oui, Monsieur," the headwaiter responded, motioning toward a table to the right of the entrance. He stepped back so Lanning could pass him. "Asseyez-vous, s'il vous plaît."

"Merci." Lanning took a seat. He unbuttoned his jacket and looked up as a waiter appeared, bearing a menu.

"Bonjour, Monsieur," the waiter said. He was a young man in his twenties with a thick moustache and a hooked nose.

Lanning was too famished to bother with the menu. He already knew what he wanted—a breakfast of soft-boiled eggs, some toast, bacon, a banana or two, and some cocoa. "Bonjour," he addressed the waiter. "Je veux le petit dejeuner, s'il vous plaît." He rattled off his list. "Des oeufs a la coque, des toasts, du bacon, des bananas, et du chocolat."

The waiter seemed surprised by Lanning's grasp of French. "Certainement, Monsieur." He started to turn, then paused, his curiosity getting the better of him. "Pardon, Monsieur. Êtes-vous américain?"

"Oui," Lanning confirmed. Why was it always so obvious?

"Mais vous avez un bon accent," the waiter said, complimenting him.

Lanning nodded. "Merci. Vous êtes très aimable,"

he said, thanking the waiter. The man left for the kitchen, and Lanning stared at the table top, musing about Monique. Where the hell could she have gone? He knew she was an avid skier, but surely she would have left a note before departing? It was out of character for her to just take off unannounced. He was still brooding over her abrupt departure when his breakfast arrived.

Since he had the day off, Lanning dawdled over his meal. He was torn between his intense eagerness to return to the apartment and see if she was back and his fear he might find a letter explaining she wanted him out. Pronto! When the last lingering morsel was gone, he felt pleasantly satiated.

"Garcon! L'addition, s'il vous plaît," Lanning called out, requesting the check. After it came, he thanked the waiter for an excellent repast and left a hefty tip.

The morning sun was well up in the eastern sky when he walked from the restaurant.

Lanning saw a taxi stand down the avenue and headed for it. He knew he couldn't delay any longer; it was time to confront the situation head-on. If Monique still wasn't home, he'd make the rounds of her friends and try to track her down.

Enough was enough.

His resolve began to dissipate a short while later as the lift carried him to their fourth floor apartment. He had an uneasy feeling in his gut, like he had right before he opened fire on those terrorists in the 747 over Cairo.

Lanning reached their apartment and surprisingly found the door unlocked.

Easing the door open, he had visions of one of his old enemies waiting for him inside with a drawn pistol.

Was that it? Had someone gotten to Monique? Was that the reason she'd been absent for three days, maybe longer?

Lanning wasn't armed, but he knew there were some knives in the kitchen that could be used in an emergency.

There were loud voices emanting from inside the apartment.

Lanning stepped inside and closed the door behind him. To his left was a coat closet and to his right a hallway leading to the kitchen. In front of him was an elaborate maple partition, separating the living room from the foyer.

There were two people arguing in the living room. One of the voices belonged to Monique. The other was also a woman's, but who?

Monique was talking, berating the other woman for being too impatient and promising the situation would be resolved soon.

The second woman spoke up, demanding to know how Monique could do "it" to her. She maintained she could not endure the strain much longer. Monique must act or else.

What in the world were they talking about? Lanning was totally perplexed.

Monique was comforting the other woman, telling her everything would be all right. Then she paused and said something in a low, soft voice.

Lanning strained to hear.

Monique repeated herself. "Je vous aime."

I love you? Lanning wasn't sure he'd heard correctly. He inched to the edge of the opening in the partition and peered around the edge.

Monique and the second woman, an attractive brunette, were seated on the sofa. Monique was wearing a red dress, the brunette green slacks and a black blouse.

They were kissing.

Lanning froze, unable to take his eyes from the tableau in front of him.

Monique put her hands under the brunette's blouse and began massaging her breasts. Lanning could see their mouths moving as their tongues entwined. The brunette hiked Monique's red dress up her thighs, then slid her fingers under Monique's panties. Monique sighed and moaned as the brunette inserted her middle finger into her sex while easing her down onto the sofa.

Lanning stepped back, out of sight. His mind seemed to be stuck in neutral; he couldn't bring himself to concentrate, to think coherently. He actually felt slightly dizzy, and suddenly he wanted fresh air, desperately needed fresh air and the outdoors. He quietly opened the front door and slipped from the apartment.

An elderly woman looked at him strangely as he moved to the lift.

So that was it!

Monique had been off with . . . with another woman. No wonder she had never objected to his trips abroad.

Lanning got off the elevator and walked, as if in a dream, to the street. The bright sunlight and a cool breeze somewhat revitalized his shattered senses.

Dear God, tell him it wasn't so!

The woman he cared for was a . . . a . . . damn dyke! He began walking, still emotionally dazed, utterly oblivious to his surroundings.

What should he do?

He could storm back into the apartment and angrily confront Monique, but what good would that accomplish except for interrupting their tête-à-tête? Monique must love this other woman. She would be on the defensive as soon as he walked in the room, and there might be a loud, potentially violent scene. What if one of the neighbors called the police? He could see it now. When his superior at Interpol demanded to know the reason he was arrested for disturbing the peace, what could he say? "Well, you see, sir, I'm afraid I lost my cool when I found the woman I was going to ask to marry me in the sack with another woman."

Nope. That scenario was definitely out.

He could wait outside the apartment building, and when the other woman came out, he could trail her and find out where she lived—or drag her into an alley and break her neck.

Lanning stopped and shook his head. He was behaving stupidly and entertaining childish thoughts.

But what *could* he do?

Was he still willing to consider Monique as a wife after what he'd just witnessed? For all he knew, Monique sincerely liked him. Maybe Monique was torn both ways—between him and the other woman—but could he bring himself to marry her, knowing what he now knew?

No, he realized, he honestly couldn't.

Maybe he wasn't with it and behind the times, but he believed loyalty was a fundamental ingredient in any successful marriage. Somehow he no longer could see Monique remaining exclusively loyal to him and him alone.

Lanning glanced around, only vaguely aware of his surroundings. He spied a bench to his left, near a small fountain, and he strolled over and sat down.

The wisest move would be to put some distance between Monique and himself. He needed to be all alone, to try and get a perspective on the situation. His accumulated vacation time was at least two weeks, and he could use it by getting away from it all to some exotic locale.

It sounded like a good idea!

His clothing and other personal effects were all at Monique's. If he waited for Monique and the brunette to leave the apartment, he should have ample opportunity to pack up and get out before they returned. All of the furniture and most of the utensils belonged to Monique. He always traveled light; a man in his vocation couldn't afford to accumulate too many personal items.

Lanning sighed and absently-mindedly watched a pigeon land on the rim of the fountain.

Where should he go?

Tahiti? He'd always entertained the notion of visiting an island in the south Pacific. All that sunshine and palm trees and beautiful women!

Lanning frowned. No, that wouldn't do. The last thing he needed right now was to become involved with another woman.

What about Chicago?

He felt an odd yearning to visit his mother, to seek her out after ten years of estrangement. He didn't have any brothers or sisters, only an uncle in Detroit and an aunt somewhere in Oregon, whom he hadn't seen since childhood. His mother, for all intents and purposes, was his only close relative, and he wanted to be near someone close to him. It wasn't his mom's fault he'd been branded a pariah, the black sheep of the Lanning family. In her many letters, his mother swore she still cared for him. If she truly did, then she was the exception, the one constant in his life, the only one who hadn't betrayed his affection and trust.

Unlike Monique.

Or his own father.

Lanning stood and stretched. Funny. The idea of bidding au revoir to Paris for a spell didn't bother him in the least. Maybe he was really homesick for America and was only using Monique as a pretext. After all, if he really loved Monique, if he genuinely was as fond of her as, say, Simon Darr had been toward his betrothed, Amy, then he wouldn't be standing near this fountain concocting excuses for leaving Monique and Paris. He would be in her apartment, pleading his devotion, striving to convince her to dump the other woman and stick with him.

But he wasn't.

Lanning headed for the apartment, determined to wait in the vicinity until the women departed. Once the coast was clear, he could gather his belongings.

He thought again of Simon Darr. Wouldn't the kid be shocked if he showed up at the wedding? One thing was for sure. The circumstances of their second encounter would be infinitely more pleasant than their first meeting.

At the wedding, at least, no one would be trying to kill them.

14

There were four of them seated around the metal folding table in front of the large green tent. They were taking an afternoon break from the inventory in the tomb, quenching their thirst with a tall glass of Sehha, a popular bottled mineral water from Lebanon. Professor Crenshaw sat nearest the tent opening, attired in his usual khakis. Amy was to his left, wearing jeans and a white cotton blouse, with Simon to the Professor's right, his lean form covered by brown trousers and a matching brown shirt, both obtained at a discount store before he left Colorado.

The fourth person at the table was a newcomer. Hassan Kheir sat quietly, listening to the others converse. Hassan was a short man, only five feet in height, but what he lacked in stature he more than compensated for in his impressive appearance. His outstanding feature was his white halo of hair, his hairline beginning parallel with his elongated ears and forming a striking mane extending to the collar of his grey shirt. In stark contrast to his white hair, Hassan sported a full black moustache. His brown eyes were alert, yet tranquil. At the moment, he was observing Crenshaw's comical reaction to Amy Brant's last declaration.

The Professor's mouth had fallen open for a second, his eyes widening in surprise. "What did you say?"

"I said," Amy patiently repeated herself, "I'd like to leave earlier than we intended, if it's okay with you."

Crenshaw glanced at Simon. "Is this your idea, young man?"

"Don't blame Simon," Amy said, defending her fiancé. "It was my idea, not his."

"But I thought you planned to stay here until the twelth or thirteenth, then fly to Chicago for the wedding?" Crenshaw reminded her.

"That was our original intention," Amy conceded.

"It's only May fifth," the Professor noted. "Why do you want to leave so early?"

Amy reached out and placed her right hand on Crenshaw's left wrist. "I don't want to hurt your feelings," she assured him, "but please try and see it my way. I want to be fair to Simon. You know that I canceled our honeymoon plans so I could get back here sooner. That hasn't changed. We'll be married on the fifteenth, and I'll be back here at the site by the nineteenth or the twentieth at the very latest." She gazed at Simon and smiled. "I just figured I'd make up the lost honeymoon time by spending more time with Simon before our wedding day. You won't hold it against me, will you?"

"Of course not," Professor Crenshaw stated curtly, feeling offended, "but I was under the impression you two would spend your time together here."

Amy snickered. "We wanted to," she admitted, "but it isn't working out."

"Why not?" Crenshaw inquired testily.

Hassan Kheir laughed.

Professor Crenshaw looked at his friend. "And what's so funny, may I ask?"

''You are showing your years,'' Hassan stated in his deep, cultivated voice. ''You have forgotten what it is like to be young and in love.''

''I have not,'' Crenshaw sputtered.

''You have, Artemas. Look around you.'' Hassan swept his right arm in a circle. ''What do you see? I'll tell you what you see. Nothing! Rocks and dirt and sand and a few scruffy shrubs here and there. That is all. Hardly the setting one would select for romance, is it?''

Crenshaw gazed at the barren landscape. ''I see your point,'' he acknowledged.

''Then you can understand why I don't think its fair to Simon to stay here,'' Amy interjected.

''I hadn't thought of it that way,'' Crenshaw confessed.

''Besides,'' Amy pressed on while she had the advantage, ''you don't need me right now. You're still in the organizing stage, getting a general overview of the tomb and its contents. Yesterday, Hassan said the actual inventory might not begin for a week or more. Right?''

''That's true,'' Professor Crenshaw grudgingly concurred.

''Hassan also said the coffin won't be opened here,'' Amy stated.

''That is correct,'' Hassan said. ''The Department of Antiquities has decided to ship the coffin, intact, to Cairo where we can open it under controlled conditions.''

''You're taking all the fun out of archaeology,'' Professor Crenshaw told Hassan.

''It is not my doing,'' Hassan stressed. ''The Egyptian government has simply grown tired of being misled and abused by foreign interests. Our future and our past must be regulated by us.''

''Are you saying I would mislead you?'' Professor

Crenshaw asked in a hurt tone.

"Not at all." Hassan smiled. "I know you better than that, but my government must be impartial in cases like this. If we permitted you to open this coffin here, then other, later expeditions would demand the same right." He paused and lowered his voice. "Had it ony been my decision, Artemas, we would have opened the coffin of Prince Hiros two days ago when I arrived."

"The world is changing," Crenshaw remarked, "and I can't say it's for the better." He glanced at Amy. "So when did you want to leave?"

"Would thirty minutes be okay?"

"What?" Crenshaw rose from his seat. "Thirty minutes?"

"If it's okay with you," Amy said, "Abdel said he will drive us. If we leave in half an hour, we should roll into Idfu about an hour after dark. If we make all the right connections, we'll make Chicago by the eighth or ninth, and it'll give us six days together before the wedding. What do you say?"

"What can I say?" Professor Crenshaw extended his palms in defeat. "You have it all worked out. I wish you a safe and speedy journey and a happy wedding."

Amy rose and hugged Crenshaw. "Thank you. This means a lot to me."

Simon stood and offered his hand to Hassan. "It's been nice meeting you."

Hassan shook hands, grinning. "You are getting a marvelous woman for your wife."

"I know," Simon said.

"I am most sorry you had so much trouble in Cairo," Hassan commented.

Simon had related his adventure to Amy and Crenshaw his first day at the site and to Hassan upon his arrival.

"I'd like to forget all about it," Simon stated. "I'd never want to go through something like that again."

"Most understandable," Hassan agreed. "But remember, not all Middle Eastern people are like those on the plane. Most of us want to use constructive, peaceful methods to bring about change. Those advocating violent revolution are in the minority."

"Thank goodness," Simon said. "Can you imagine what the world would be like if everyone was like those three hijackers?"

"It would be terrible," Hassan opined.

"We'll help you pack," Professor Crenshaw said to Amy.

"No need. We're already packed," she replied, beaming.

"You were pretty sure of yourself," Crenshaw declared.

"No. I was sure of you," Amy replied.

"Then we'll lend you a hand carrying your luggage to the jeep."

"There's no need for you to do that."

"Be serious," Professor Crenshaw said.

The four of them walked off.

No sooner were they out of sight around the corner of the tent, than Naan appeared from the opposite side and began clearing the glasses and Sehha from the table.

Allah be praised! Events were proceeding better than expected!

Abdel would undoubtedly stay the night in Idfu rather than risk driving all the way back to the camp in the dark. The distance was only 40 miles, but the last thirty were treacherous and difficult to navigate even in daylight. With Abdel absent, Naan would be in charge of the excavation crew, which meant Naan could pick the man for guard duty at the tunnel entrance.

He already knew which worker he would select.
The one who had the most to gain.
Himself.

15

Buddy stifled a yawn and concentrated on the file lying in front of him. It was close to ten in the morning, but he couldn't seem to shake a lingering sensation of fatigue. He propped his elbows on the desk top and cupped his chin in his hands. This report was interesting, but he couldn't see where the practical applications would be too significant. He focused on the words.

"Researchers at the Stoner Institute have discovered an intriguing relationship between certain sexually transmitted viruses and an agent that triggers brain disease in animals. This agent has already been detected in AIDS patients, explaining why about 75% of all patients who develop AIDS will have brain disease by the time they die. The researchers are concentrating their work on an infectious agent called a prion. This highly unusual agent is a baffling mystery to scientists who have studied it. It is known that in sheep the prion can cause a brain disorder called scrapie. This is a progressive, degenerative disease of the central nervous system and the brain. What has drawn the attention of researchers at the Stoner Institute is the astonishing similarities between scrapie and the brain disorder in humans caused by

AIDS. Both the AIDS virus and the scrapie virus produce severe abnormalities in the brain. The researchers note that the similarities between the two do not mean that they both share the same biological properties. Homologies between viruses is not a rare occurrence. The researchers claim it is peculiar that portions of the genetic code in an AIDS virus gene should so closely resemble portions of the genetic code for a prion."

Buddy leaned back in his swivel chair. A virus that affects the brain and the central nervous system! The versatility of viruses never ceased to amaze him. They could strike any part of the human anatomy with devastating results—the brain, the nervous system, the muscles, the lungs, the digestive system. The multiplicity of tiny microbes capable of invading the human form was astonishing.

Over the years, Buddy had contemplated the diversity of viruses and their origin and thought he detected a disturbing pattern. It started with the array of sex-related diseases in the seventies and the eighties. No sooner did one come along and an antibiotic was developed to check its spread, than another would appear, a new strain more resistant to medication and capable of ravaging the body even worse than the preceding virus.

It was almost as if it was deliberately planned.

Gonorrhea, syphilis, nonspecific urethritis, chlamydia, lymphogranuloma venereum, chancroid, granuloma inguinale, genital herpes, AIDS; on and on and on it went. Some of the diseases had been with humanity since recorded history began. Others, so far as was known, were recent developments.

Where did they come from?

Why did they first appear when they did?

Some prominent scientists speculated the sixties were to blame—the decade of "free love" and sexual promiscuity. The sixties and early seventies saw the most sexually active younger generation the world had ever known.

Were they now reaping the consequences?

Only the fundamentalists seemed to know for sure.

Gladys had been viewing a religious program on cable the other night and he happened to catch part of it.

A well-known TV evangelist was talking about punishment for sin. He told his listeners that every man and woman was going to be judged, their souls weighed in the balance, and while the righteous would reap a magnificent reward beyond the ken of their imagination, the wicked would suffer a dire fate for the evil they had perpetrated. The evangelist discoursed on Armageddon, the final battle between good and evil. He claimed one of the signs of the end would be the pouring out of God's wrath in the form of a series of plagues. He read from The Holy Bible, from Revelation, Chapters 15 and 16. And then he paused and looked directly into the camera, and Buddy found his next words extremely interesting. The evangelist mentioned the staggering increase in the types of sexually transmitted diseases, and he asked his audience if they knew the reason for the upsurge. Buddy could remember his next words clearly: "For every cause there is an effect. For every action there is a reaction. For every violation of the divine will there is an inevitable repercussion. Do you think we can mock our Maker and get away with it? No! No! As surely as night follows day, as a thunderstorm disrupts the tranquil firmament, there will be hell to pay for the Godlessness we have wrought. Repent! Repent before it is too late or you, too, shall feel the wrath!"

Buddy shook his head and grinned. Some of those fire and brimstone types could sure get a person worked up, couldn't they? If Buddy didn't know better, he might be inclined to believe the evangelist, but his logical mind prevented him from accepting such a doctrine. There had to be a scientific explanation for the proliferation of viruses and the marked increase in social diseases.

There had to be!

16

It was time.

The moonless sky was dark, the stars twinkling in the firmament. All signs of activity in the camp below the tunnel entrance had long since ceased. Abdel had not yet returned, which definitely meant he was spending the night in Idfu.

Naan smiled, delighted with his own deviousness. He threw some more brush onto the fire, insuring it would remain bright while he attended to other business. He stood and stretched, then removed the crowbar from the folds of his blue galabiyah. He had taken the crowbar from one of the jeeps earlier, before assuming his post on the ledge.

Everything was working out splendidly.

Although the very idea bordered on the sacrilegious, Naan speculated Allah might even want him to succeed.

Why else would it be this easy?

Naan hurried down the tunnel. The sooner he accomplished his objective, the better. One of the other workers might decide to enjoy a midnight stroll and find the fire unattended. Naan hastened through the antechamber and into the tunnel beyond. The lanterns were all lit, providing excellent illumination.

He was able to race at full speed, and within minutes he reached his destination—the tomb.

His heart pounding, Naan slowly walked past the stone cylinder and over to the coffin of Prince Hiros. He ignored the jewels and other valuables scattered throughout the tomb. What he wanted would be on the Prince.

Naan knelt and examined the strange coffin. He was unable to locate a seal anywhere on its surface, which was very unusual. On most such coffins there would be a lid or the top could be swiveled open.

Naan placed his right cheek on the cool floor and, studying the bottom of the gold coffin, detected traces of a seal around its base.

Why would the ancients have put it there?

Naan applied the thin edge of the crowbar to the bottom edge of the coffin and heaved.

Nothing.

He tried again, straining until his face turned red and his veins bulged.

Still nothing.

Naan carefully worked his way around the coffin, using the crowbar to apply leverage every few centimeters. When he was two-thirds of the way along the base, he felt the coffin give slightly. With renewed vigor, he wedged the crowbar under the coffin and lifted.

A second time.

And a third.

On the final try, the coffin abruptly shifted, and Naan nearly lost his balance. He grinned, knowing he was on the verge of victory. He was so close to having the wealth he'd always dreamed of. The ancients always buried royal personages with their favorite articles of jewelry on the body, whether it might be a ring, a necklace, a braclet, or whatever, and such items always carried an intrinsically higher value than any other artifacts. So although there were other historical treasures in the tomb, Naan desired an object from the mummy itself. One piece of jewelry from Prince Hiros—a ring, an amulet, anything—could set Naan up for a lifetime.

Naan snickered. He rose and walked out to the tunnel, to the pile of rubble from the collapsed wall. After sorting through the debris, he found a large chunk to his liking. Returning to the coffin, he placed the jagged section of stone near the front of the gold figure. Quickly, he rammed the edge of the crowbar under the lip and hoisted the coffin from the floor. When it had raised to the height of his knees, he used his left foot to push the stone under the lid, supporting the top of the coffin.

Allah smiled on him!

Naan dropped the crowbar and instantly regretted the move. The tomb was filled with a loud metallic clang, and he nervously waited, listening for any response from outside the tomb.

All was quiet.

Naan went to the wall and removed a lantern. As he walked back to the coffin, an idea occurred to him. Originally, he had decided to steal one of the jeeps and head for Idfu. His contact in the black market was waiting for him there. But now he reconsidered. A better course of action presented itself.

All he had to do was take whatever he wanted from the mummy, then replace the bizarre coffin and no one would be the wiser. He knew they were in the preliminary stages of their inventory, so it was unlikely Crenshaw or Kheir knew what the coffin contained. They certainly wouldn't be able to prove he'd stolen anything if they didn't know what had been stolen.

Naan chuckled. It would be good riddance to this menial existence, to barely scraping by with never enough money to provide for his wife and eight children. At long last, he would be getting what he deserved.

He reached the coffin and lowered himself to the floor, lying prone in front of the elevated portion. Anxious to see the contents, he brought the lantern near the opening.

Allah save him!

Naan recoiled in shock, startled by the grisly sight before him.

The light from the lantern clearly revealed the interior of the gold coffin. Inside was Prince Hiros, or what was left of him after 5000 years. Unlike any other mummy Naan had ever seen or heard of, Prince Hiros had not been embalmed and wrapped in linen bandages. From the condition of the remains, it appeared the ancients had simply placed the body on the floor in a squatting position, then deposited the gold coffin on top of him. The lack of moisture in the tomb and the airtight seal on the coffin had combined to insure the preservation of the Prince. His discolored, yellowish-brown skin had shrunken, flattening and tightening around the bone beneath it. The skull seemed to glare at Naan in reproach for violating the coffin. Its teeth were exposed, the lips all but gone, and it was as if the mouth was about to take a bite out of him. The eyes had long since disintegrated, leaving two black cavities in their place. Incredibly, the body was still in the same position it had been in when rigor mortis developed, that peculiar squatting pose.

Naan knew he couldn't afford to dawdle. He noticed the vestige of a white cotton dain clinging to the hip bones and tattered shreds of a shirt or cloak hanging from the spine.

Why hadn't the body caved in?

Why didn't the ancients adhere to custom and embalm and wrap Prince Hiros in bandages?

Naah had the impression this burial had been a rush job, that the priests had wanted to complete their task as quickly as possible. Why else would they neglect tradition? And for a Prince, no less!

That was when Naan noticed the ring.

There was a large gold ring on the index finger of the left hand. Because there was scant skin or withered flesh on the finger, the ring had toppled forward. Plainly visible, inset in the face of the ring, beautifully resplendent in the light from the lantern, was a large gem, a transparent green emerald.

Naan gawked at the precious stone. It was easily as big as a hen's egg, with a fine velvety appearance and an even distribution of color.

It was the key to his future, a gift from Allah.

Naan impulsively grabbed for the ring, gripping it by the emerald and tugging to free it. He wasn't prepared for what transpired next.

The skeleton of Prince Hiros collapsed.

One moment Naan was jerking on the ring, frustrated because it wouldn't come loose, and the next instant the whole body dropped to the stone floor, the gruesome skull listing to one side, some of the bones rattling as they struck the floor. A spray of dust and other particles spread from under the coffin and engulfed Naan, choking him, causing him to cough and wheeze as he gasped for fresh air. He cupped his hands over his mouth, an acrid taste on his lips, his eyes watering, and resisted an impulse to vomit. Within seconds the small cloud dissipated, falling to the floor and covering Naan with a fine layer of reddish dust.

Naan rose to his hands and knees, still hacking, his mouth intensely dry. He quickly slipped the ring from the index finger and stood.

He had the ring!

Elated, he slid the emerald ring under his white turban for temporary safekeeping and hurried now, anxious to vacate the tomb. He stooped and retrieved the crowbar, then used it to prop the coffin up while he kicked the stone support aside. Gently, he eased the coffin to the ground. Next he carried the section of stone to the pile of debris in the tunnel. Finally, he collected several handfuls of dust from the piles of clothing and other artifacts and sprinkled dust over the gold coffin to eradicate any evidence of tampering. When he was satisfied no one would be able to determine he had opened the coffin, not even Crenshaw or Kheir, he replaced the lantern on its hook and dashed from the tomb to his post at the fire.

The stars still twinkled overhead.

The camp was still quiet, the men in repose.

Naan sat next to the dwindling flames, incredulous at his good fortune. He hid the crowbar in the folds of his galabiyah again, then relaxed.

He had done it. He would be a rich man. A palatial home and fine clothes, even a car of his very own, would be his for the asking. In the blinking of an eye his whole social status had changed from that of a servile laborer on an excavation crew to a member of the wealthy elite.

Naan cackled, unable to suppress his overwhelming joy. Tomorrow he would ask Crenshaw for permission to drive to Idfu for some needed supplies, supplies he had conveniently hidden after Abdel departed. Once in Idfu, he would negotiate with his black market contact. He wasn't worried about being cheated; the man he was dealing with had a solid reputation. After the deal was concluded, to forestall arousing suspicion, he would return to the site and work for another week or two. Only then would he announce he must leave for home, pleading an illness in his family. Crenshaw would pay him and wish him well.

Naan grinned. He felt like he was in control of his life for the very first time. He was in charge of his destiny.

He reached up and gingerly touched the ring, insuring it was still under his turban. It was unfortunate, he reflected, that he could never relate his achievement to anyone else. The crime of the year, maybe the century, and he could not confide in a soul.

Only one other person would ever know what he had done—Prince Hiros—and, Naan chuckled, Prince Hiros wasn't about to tell anyone.

PART II

INFECTION

17

It was after midnight on May 8th when Artemas Crenshaw was awakened from a deep slumber. He opened his eyes, uncertain of what had aroused him, and listened. All he could hear was the muted howling of the wind.

Howling?

Professor Crenshaw rose on one elbow, puzzled. If the wind was gusting that strongly, his tent should be billowing with the breeze, but his tent wasn't even rustling.

Crenshaw clambered from his cot, wearing only his white boxer shorts, and walked to the tent opening. He pushed the flap aside and stepped outside.

There it was again!

The mysterious howling was coming from somewhere in the desert.

What could it be? A dog? Not very likely. There wasn't a settlement within miles. A jackal, perhaps? He didn't believe they ranged in his area.

There was a noise to his left, and Crenshaw spun around.

"Did I frighten you, Artemas?" Hassan Kheir was standing five feet away, grinning, his legs covered by brown trousers but his chest and feet bare. "It's good I didn't tap you on your shoulder, or we'd be rushing you to the hospital right now."

Crenshaw laughed. "Did you hear that howling?"

Hassan moved closer. "Something woke me up, but I don't know what it was."

"I heard something," Crenshaw said and pointed at the desert. "Out there."

"Really? Undoubtedly an animal."

"You think so?"

"What else could it be?" Hassan retorted. "We don't have werewolves in Egypt." He chuckled.

"It must have been a dog," Crenshaw declared. "I think I'll turn in. We have a hectic schedule tomorrow."

"Do you miss Amy?" Hassan asked.

Professor Crenshaw sighed and nodded. "She lit up the place, if you know what I mean. When she was here my work was fun. Now it's just . . . work."

"She will return," Hassan reminded him.

"I can't wait," Crenshaw said, turning toward his tent.

The night was rent by another howl, only this time the sound was much closer.

"Allah!" Hassan exclaimed. "What was that?"

"Your animal," Professor Crenshaw said.

"I have never heard an animal like that," Hassan stated, "and I was born in the desert. It was not any animal I know."

"What about a jackal?" Professor Crenshaw suggested.

"That was no jackal," Hassan responded emphatically.

They waited in the dark, listening.

"Whatever it was," Hassan commented after a while, "it has gone."

The howl sounded again, not more than a hundred yards away.

"It's getting very close to our camp," Professor Crenshaw commented.

"I wonder why none of the others have heard it?" Hassan asked.

"Yes," Crenshaw said thoughtfully. "That last howl was loud enough to wake the dead."

Hassan was scanning the area. There wasn't any moon, and it was difficult to perceive distinct shapes beyond a range of 15 to 20 feet. He happened to glance up at the tunnel in the cliff. "Look!" he pointed. "Didn't you tell the men to keep a fire lit all night?"

Professor Crenshaw faced the cliff. There was no sign of the fire, not even the faint flicker of a smoldering ember. The entire cliff was plunged into blackness. "Yes, I did," he confirmed.

"Possibly the watchman fell asleep." Hassan speculated.

"I won't tolerate dereliction of duty," Professor Crenshaw snapped, annoyed. "I'm going up there."

"I will wake Abdel and have a fire started down here," Hassan offered.

"A good idea," Crenshaw agreed. "It will discourage the dogs or jackals or whatever is out there."

Hassan walked off. His own tent had been pitched immediately next to Crenshaw's, while Abdel shared a tent with Naan just beyond Hassan's.

Crenshaw entered his tent and donned his khakis. Searching in one of his backpacks, he found his flashlight. Once outside, he looked for Hassan and Abdel who should have appeared by now.

They hadn't shown up.

Professor Crenshaw opened his mouth to shout to them, and then reconsidered. He didn't want to needlessly awaken the men. Hassan and Abdel were probably gathering brush and wood for the fire. The vegetation around the site was sparse, and they might have to travel far afield to collect sufficient tinder. He walked around his tent, making for the cliff.

Whoever was on guard duty would regret falling asleep on the job! Without a fire, it would be easy for professional graverobbers to sneak into the tomb, plunder it, and depart without anyone in the base camp being aware of the raid.

Crenshaw switched on his flashlight as he neared the ramp.

There was a sudden sound to his right, like the pattering of feet on the ground, and Professor Crenshaw swung around, beaming his light in the direction of the noise.

Nothing. Just a few small desert shrubs and boulders.

Crenshaw wasn't too concerned about the dogs or jackals. Wild, feral dogs could pose a threat, but reported attacks on humans were rare. Jackals, cunning creatures that they were, avoided people like the plague.

He slowly climbed the ramp. There was a slight breeze coming from the desert beyond the camp, and it was cool and refreshing on his face.

The camp was still dark and silent.

Professor Crenshaw was almost to the tunnel entrance when a veritable chorus of howls erupted below him. He moved to the edge of the ramp and aimed his flashlight at the base of the cliff. Shadowy figures darted for cover, at least a half-dozen or so. Crenshaw observed an odd, shuffling gait to the way they moved, but was unable to discern much before they vanished from sight.

Awfully audacious for a pack of dogs!

He completed his climb to the tunnel and paused on the ledge, startled to discover the tunnel lanterns had been extinguished. The charred remains of the fire was to his left, while to his right, lying on his stomach near the tunnel wall, was the watchman.

Asleep!

Professor Crenshaw stepped toward the man. "Wake up," he demanded in Arabic. "Come on, I said to wake up!" He reached the worker and nudged him with his right foot.

The man didn't budge.

"Wake up!" Crenshaw shouted. He knelt, grabbed the worker by the back of his white shirt, and flipped him over.

Crenshaw instinctively recoiled in shock and horror. He couldn't believe the sight in front of him.

The worker's throat had been ripped out, literally torn open, and there was a bloody gap where his Adam's apple had been. Strands of flesh hung down his neck, and the front of his shirt was a dark crimson. His eyes were wide open, and his features conveyed the impression of absolute terror.

Professor Crenshaw staggered to his feet.

Graverobbers! It had to be graverobbers!

Crenshaw backed toward the ramp, alarmed the graverobbers might still be in the tunnel. He would sneak down the ramp to the camp and alert Hassan, Abdel and the others, then they could investigate the tunnel en masse. After all, there was greater strength in numbers.

Something growled behind him.

Professor Crenshaw whirled, his flashlight sweeping over the ramp. To his right there was a flash of movement as something scurried down the ramp.

The wild dogs had followed him up the ramp!

Crenshaw froze. He was trapped—graverobbers in the tunnel and wild dogs in front of him!

A bloodcurdling howl arose from the base of the cliff, and as its last notes wafted away on the breeze, eerily drifting into the desert, a horrifying thought occurred to the Professor.

What if graverobbers hadn't killed the watchman?

What if it had been the dogs?

But if the wild dogs were the culprits, why hadn't

they consumed the body?

There was another guttural growl from the ramp, from just below the tunnel entrance and beyond the area illuminated by his flashlight.

With dreadful certainty, Professor Crenshaw realized the wild dogs were coming after him.

He turned and ran into the tunnel. Possibly the canines would be wary of the close confines of the tunnel. Even if they weren't, he might be able to block one of the openings in the antechamber walls and prevent the dogs from reaching him.

There was yet another howl, this time sounding as if it came from the tunnel entrance.

Crenshaw ran faster, his fear pumping vitality into his limbs. He was almost to the antechamber when a question leaped into his mind, ghastly in its implications.

If the wild dogs had indeed killed the watchman, then who was responsible for turning out the lanterns? It was inconceivable the watchman would have turned them out himself? Why would he do such a thing? And it was positively ludicrous to think the wild dogs had done it!

He reached the antechamber and darted through the expanded opening in the wall. Initially, Abdel and his crew had removed two blocks, but subsequently the workers had taken eight blocks from each antechamber wall to better accomodate the traffic in the tunnel.

Professor Crenshaw leaned against the antechamber wall, catching his breath. It would take an hour or longer to block off the antechamber. Even though the stone blocks had been lined up along the tunnel wall within easy reach, they were large, cumbersome, and very heavy. He might be able to erect a partial barricade, but only if the dogs remained outside the tunnel long enough for him to complete the task.

The dogs weren't about to let him to do that.

An ominous snarl filled the tunnel, followed by the stealthy pad of something coming toward the antechamber.

Crenshaw eased to the opening in the wall and flooded the tunnel with the bright glare from his flashlight. It took a moment for what the flashlight exposed to register, and when it did dawn on his stunned senses, when he clearly saw his pursuers for the first time, it was as if someone poured ice-cold water over his body; he gasped as his entire body trembled and shook, goose pimples breaking out over every inch of his skin. Almost paralyzed from the shock, he staggered backward, keeping his flashlight on the things approaching the antechamber.

One of them hissed at him.

Professor Crenshaw struggled to control his composure. He now knew what had slain the watchman, and why Hassan and Abdel had not appeared earlier.

He understood it all—the meaning of the hieroglyphics, the tomb, the coffin of Prince Hiros.

What a damn fool he'd been!

Crenshaw rushed to the opening in the other wall and raced down the stone tunnel.

To his rear, a cacophony of howls reverberated in the antechamber.

Professor Crenshaw forced his lungs to overexert themselves as he fled for his very life. His sides ached and his chest heaved, as he struggled to maintain his fastest pace. He reached the point where the tunnel abruptly angled to the right, and he nearly collided with the wall as he negotiated the turn.

He had one chance.

If he could reach the tomb, he might be able to find a hiding place before the pack arrived. The tomb was spacious, and there were plenty of places where he could conceal himself—in the sun boat, under one of the piles of clothing, in one of the large wooden chests mixed in with the collection of furniture.

Anywhere!

His flashlight was bouncing off the walls and the ceiling as he ran, seeming to lend animated life to the hieroglyphics. The combination of light and shadows conspired to present the illusion of movement in the figures, adding a macabre element to his flight.

More howling behind him served to remind the Professor that the pack hadn't given up.

Crenshaw was nearly on his last legs when he finally reached the tomb. He wheezed, sucking in the air, and propped his body against the stone cylinder, striving to collect his wits and focus his energy.

Where should he hide?

The sun boat wasn't a viable option. They would be able to scamper aboard and locate him.

Hiding under a pile of clothing wasn't very sensible, since clothing would be extremely flimsy protection against . . . them.

Professor Crenshaw lurched into the tomb, frantically seeking his salvation. He tripped over one of the ushabti and stumbled several yards before he recovered his balance.

Crenshaw scanned the burial chamber, beaming his flashlight on the far side as he sought one of the wooden chests he'd seen before. His body unexpectedly slammed into a hard object, his knees bearing the brunt of the impact, and he felt something heavy shift as he fell. His left hand contacted a cool, smooth surface, and he twisted the flashlight in his right hand so he could ascertain what he'd hit.

It was the gold coffin of Prince Hiros.

Crenshaw glanced down, surprised to note that the whole coffin had been jarred several inches by his collision with it. Given the shape of the coffin, and the past practice of the Egyptians, he would have expected the coffin to be sealed to the floor.

The coffin!

Inspiration struck, and Crenshaw, placing the flashlight on the floor, attempted to insert his fingers under the bottom edge of the coffin. There wasn't sufficient space, however, between the cofin and the floor. Frustrated, he looked around for any implement he could use.

His eyes alighted on a pile of jewelry to his right. In a frenzy, he rummaged through the pile, tossing rings and bracelets and other useless artifacts aside. He spotted a metallic amulet, about six inches in diameter, with a narrow edge.

Professor Crenshaw scooped up the amulet and returned to the gold coffin. He could hear the pack baying in the stone tunnel as he applied the edge of the amulet to the bottom of the coffin. He strained his muscles to the utmost until his fingers hurt. Stark fear served as a biologic catalyst, inspiring a brute force he ordinarily lacked. Grunting from his exertion, he managed to lift the coffin an inch or two off the floor. He slid his left hand under the lower edge of the coffin, and then his right, dropping the amulet. Sweat poured from his pores as he tried to lift the coffin.

Slowly, laboriously, he was able to raise the coffin a foot off the floor. Then two feet. He angled his body and slid his legs and hips underneath the coffin. Carefully, using his right shoulder as a temporary support under the lower edge, he turned himself entirely around. In this position, he could rest the coffin on his shoulders while he crouched on his hands and knees. The coffin was relatively easy to uphold this way. He used his right hand to pull the flashlight underneath the coffin, followed by the amulet.

Crenshaw abruptly realized he'd forgotten something important. He would be able to lower his body under the coffin without any problem, and he could use the amulet to free himself when the time came, but what if the pack lingered in the tomb? There wouldn't be enough air in the coffin to support him for long.

The tomb echoed with the sound of a rumbling growl, emanating from the vicinity of the stone cylinder.

Damn his stupidity!

He was about to emerge from under the coffin when he spied one of the rings he'd tossed away from the pile a few moments ago. It was a large gold ring with a turquoise stone in the center, and it was lying only a foot or so from his left hand. Wobbling, he used his right hand and back to support the coffin as he lunged for the ring with his left hand. He nearly toppled forward and would have had his neck broken by the falling weight of the gold coffin, but he grabbed the ring and righted his body in the nick of time.

The ring would have to do!

The pack was in the tomb now. He could detect the soft smack of their feet on the stone floor.

Crenshaw gripped the coffin with both hands and eased under it, lowering it until the lower edge made contact with the ring. For a horrified moment he thought the ring would buckle, but it held, keeping the forward portion of the coffin from reaching the floor. The space wasn't much, not more than half an inch, but it would suffice to permit a flow of air.

The fit inside the coffin was tight, but not as constricting as Crenshaw had been afraid it would be. Prince Hiros must have been a very big man, because there were at least two inches all around between the sides of the coffin and Crenshaw's body. He was able to slide his right hand back until he touched the flashlight. With a sigh of relief, he switched the flashlight off, enveloping the interior of the coffin in an inky blackness.

There was no way they could get at him now.

Professor Crenshaw held his breath, his ears cocked for the slightest sound. He could feel some hard objects under his arms and legs and assumed they were bones. When he'd lifted the coffin, he had anticipated finding the mummy of Prince Hiros inside. Instead, he beheld a skull and a pile of bones, which worked in his favor because he didn't need to waste precious seconds dragging the mummy from the coffin.

Something thumped on the outside of the coffin.

Crenshaw stayed immobile, wondering if they had seen him slip inside the coffin. If they knew where he was, what would they do? Wait around for a while, until hunger drove them from the tomb in search of prey? Or post a guard near the coffin, waiting for him to emerge? What level of intelligence did the pack retain?

There was the sound of heavy breathing near the ring. One of them was sniffing at the crack.

Professor Crenshaw closed his eyes and wearily rested his chin on his hands. Thank the Lord that Amy and Simon had departed before this occurred. The very idea of the pack getting to Amy was more than he could bear.

From the volume of breathing near the crack and the scuffing noises as their bodies passed by, it was evident the whole pack had surrounded the coffin.

Crenshaw opened his eyes and found they were adjusted to the lack of light. He could just distinguish the ring and the crack, and he saw them pawing at the opening in a vain attempt to break in. The gold coffin would adequately shield him for as long as he stayed put, but eventually his sanctuary could prove his undoing.

It all depended on the patience of the pack. Would they loiter out there for hours or days? If they left the tomb in a couple of hours, he could leave the safety of the coffin and try to escape. The jeeps and trucks were still at the camp, and if he could reach one of those he knew the pack would never catch him. If the pack dallied for days, it would put him in grave jeopardy. Lacking food and water, he would lose his vitality, and there would be no way he could extricate himself from the coffin. He would weaken and die, and the world would never know what had happened here.

The royal coffin of Prince Hiros would become his own coffin.

And, worst of all, the pack might still be lurking in the area when Amy returned from the States.

Professor Artemas Crenshaw watched the pack pawing at the air space and shivered as a frigid chill racked his very soul.

18

This was an historic occasion, so he accordingly noted the time as he paused on the sidewalk fronting his mother's home. It was almost seven in the evening as he set his suitcase on the ground.

James Lanning was wearing his best blue suit and stylish maroon tie. He wanted to make a decent impression on the woman he hadn't seen in a decade. His mother resided in southwest Chicago, not far from Marquette Park and the Chicago Midway Airport, on South Komensky Avenue.

The house was a two story brick affair with the front lawn neatly maintained and two flower gardens, one on either side of the front door.

Nervously, Lanning rechecked his tie for the tenth time since leaving the airport. He advanced along the walk leading to the front door, his stomach turning over.

What if she had changed her mind?

What if she tossed him out on his ear?

Lanning took a deep breath, hoping to calm his frayed nerves. He wasn't about to back down now; he'd come too far to turn chicken on her very doorstep.

One of the front curtains moved, and he realized

someone inside had seen him.

Lanning swallowed hard and reached for the doorbell, then froze as the front door was flung wide open.

The years hadn't changed her much.

Gloria Lanning was still a petite woman, her trim figure youthful despite her 68 years. She wore a yellow dress which served to accent her light brown hair and green eyes. Her cheekbones were high and rounded, her chin oval, her lips thin and curved in a wide smile.

"Jimmy!" she exclaimed. "Is it really you?"

No one else on the face of the planet could call him "Jimmy" and get away with it.

"It's me, Mom," Lanning confirmed. "The prodigal has returned."

Gloria Lanning embraced her son, holding him close, as tears of joy flowed from her eyes. "Jimmy, I can't believe it! After all these years!"

Lanning returned her hug, slightly uncomfortable, unprepared for her outpouring of emotion. He'd expected her to be on the reserved side after their ten year separation.

Gloria drew back and affectionately gazed into his eyes. "I was so surprised when you called the other night and said you were coming for a visit. I've been watching out the window all day, afraid you would decide against the trip or something delayed you at work. Oh, Jimmy!" She impulsively kissed him on the lips. "Come inside," she urged. "I have some refreshments all made. You must be famished after your long flight."

Lanning allowed her to pull him into her house and close the door. The interior was tastefully decorated with plush carpeting and comfortable furniture.

"Say," his mother exclaimed, "where's your suitcase?"

Lanning turned toward the door. "I almost forgot. I sat it down on the sidewalk when I adjusted my tie."

Gloria moved past him and opened the door. "You stay put. I'll be right back."

"Mom, you don't . . ." Lanning began, then stopped. She was already hurrying down the walk to retrieve his brown suitcase. He chided himself for being so edgy to utterly forget the suitcase. It was funny, in a way. He was more jittery around his mom than he was on a plane commandeered by terrorists.

Gloria returned, bearing the valise. "I'll show you to your room later. Right now, why don't we have some refreshments and chat?"

Lanning nodded. "Sounds fine to me."

She led him to her kitchen, a spotless, cheery room with a tiled floor and several appliances lining the shelves—a microwave, a blender, a can opener, a mixer and others. A Formica table and four chairs were situated in the middle of the kitchen.

Gloria indicated one of the chairs. "Why don't you have a seat?" She moved to the refrigerator and took out a tray containing a pile of sandwiches. "I didn't know what to make. Had I cooked something, the whole meal might have been ruined if your flight was held up, so I decided these would be best. Tomorrow I'll show you just how good a cook I am," she promised.

"I remember," Lanning assured her. "You don't need to prove anything to me."

"Yes, I do," she countered, setting the tray on the table. "It's been ten years, Jimmy."

"I told you on the phone not to make a fuss over me. I don't want you going out of your way just because I'm here."

Gloria ignored his statement, changing the subject. "What would you like to drink? I have juice, milk, beer, some wine, and several soft drinks. There's also some of the hard stuff downstairs behind the bar, in what the real estate agent who sold me this house called the family room." She spoke the last words with a trace of sadness in her tone.

"I'd really appreciate a glass of water," Lanning told her.

Gloria busied herself getting a glass from a cupboard, filling it from the tap, and adding ice cubes.

Lanning watched her, wondering what he should say. How did a person go about mending a ten year rift?

"Here you go." She placed the water next to him and took the chair to his left.

"Thank you."

"You haven't touched your sandwiches. Would you rather have something hot? I can always whip something up for you."

Lanning picked up one of the sandwiches, a ham and cheese, and took a bite. "This is dandy," he said, the food bulging his right cheek. "Thanks."

"You still talk with your mouth full, I see," his mother remarked, grinning.

Lanning gulped the food. "Sorry. Some habits are hard to break."

Gloria reached across and took his hands in hers. "I was beginning to think I might never see you again. You seldom answered any of my letters, and when you did write they were short notes which didn't tell me very much."

"I'm not much of a writer," Lanning lamely explained.

"I'm just so tickled you could make it," Gloria said excitedly. "I couldn't sleep last night, just thinking about you coming."

Lanning took another bite from his sandwich.

"We'll do whatever you want to do," his mother offered. "I'm at your disposal."

He was about to thank her, but he still had some of the sandwich in his mouth.

"Do you have anything specific in mind?" Gloria asked.

Lanning swallowed, shaking his head. "I thought we'd play it by ear. My plans aren't firmly set. My coming here was sort of a spur of the moment idea. I just wanted to see you again," he admitted.

Her eyes lit up. "We have so much to talk about." She paused and frowned. "It's too bad your father . . ."

"I don't want to talk about him," Lanning interrupted.

"But . . ."

"I don't want to talk about Dad," Lanning stressed. "I came here to see you."

Gloria sat back in her chair and studied him. "Maybe it would be best if we cleared the air right now."

"It isn't necessary," Lanning stated.

"I think it is," Gloria disagreed. "I think we should get some things straight."

"Like what?"

"Like what took place between your father and you," she replied.

"It's all water under the bridge," he commented.

"Is it? I doubt it."

"Let's drop the subject!" Lanning snapped defensively.

Gloria reached up and touched his cheek. "Jimmy, I saw the expression on your face when I mentioned your father. Has it been eating at you all this time?"

Lanning didn't respond.

"I never agreed with him," his mother said. "You know I didn't. I thought the whole quarrel was stupid, just a clash of two mule-headed men, a contest of egos. I tried to get him to change his mind, to welcome you back into our house, but he was too stubborn. You know what he was like . . ."

"I remember vividly," Lanning interjected acidly.

". . . and you're just like him."

"I am not!" Lanning retorted.

Gloria smiled at her son. "Yes, you are. Whether you'll admit it or not, you take after your father. Both of you could be as hard as a rock when you wanted, and once you made up your minds nothing was going to change them. I suspect that's why you two fought so often."

Lanning concentrated on his sandwich, avoiding her gaze.

"After your father passed on," Gloria said, "I was sure you would come home, at least to visit me. But when you never showed up, I began to believe you might not care for me anymore, that you held me as much to blame as your father."

"I never blamed you," Lanning said.

"How was I to know? You never called or wrote for five years. Five years! I finally decided I would have to break the ice." She stopped, her eyes misty. "You really should have called."

Lanning looked at her, accurately reading the years of anguish she had suffered, and felt a constricting sensation in his throat. He hadn't cried in years, and he knew he was on the verge of bawling his brains out. To protect himself, he grabbed another sandwich and started stuffing it into his mouth.

"Well, now that we have that out of the way," Gloria said happily, "you still haven't told me what you would like to do while you're here."

"Like I said," Lanning replied, "I don't have any definite plans except for maybe attending a wedding."

"A wedding?"

"Yeah. I met this guy in Egypt. He invited me to his wedding," Lanning explained.

"Oh. For a moment there, I thought it might be yours," Gloria stated hopefully.

"Not quite," Lanning said.

"Do you have someone of your own?" his mother asked tentatively.

"Not at the moment," he confessed. "There was someone for a while . . ."

"Oh? Who is she?" Gloria pried.

"Her name's Monique, but she and I broke up."

"Too bad. A man should have a wife, you know," Gloria declared. "What does Monique do for a living?"

Lanning hesitated. He really didn't want his mother knowing anything about Monique. "She's an engineer," he fibbed.

"What type of engineer?"

Lanning suppressed a laugh. He'd forgotten exactly how nosy his mother could be. "Oh, Monique is a construction engineer. Her company works on a lot of big construction projects."

"A career woman. I like that," Gloria declared. "What kind of projects was she involved with?"

"Monique specialized in dykes," Lanning said with a straight face.

"Oh? Is she from Holland?"

19

How long had it been?

According to his best estimate, at least 24 hours had elapsed since the pack trapped him in the coffin.

Professor Crenshaw didn't know how much longer he could hold out. He was extremely hungry, and there was a sharp pain in his abdominal region. His mouth and throat were dry. Even harder to take than the hunger and the thirst, though, were the cramps. His lower back and leg muscles were aflame with agony, incessantly demanding relief.

But what could he do?

If the sounds outside the gold coffin were any indication, then most of the pack had already departed the tomb in search of other food, but at least one die-hard was persistently lingering near the coffin. It would sniff at the coffin every now and then or paw at the air space.

Professor Crenshaw felt the urge to sneeze again. Every now and then some dust would settle in his nostrils, and he would pinch his nose as hard as he could, desperately striving to prevent any noise. If he kept silent, if he didn't do anything to remind the pack he was still inside the coffin, he hoped they would lose interest and leave. With one notable exception, his idea had worked. He clamped the fingers of his right hand on his nose until the impulse to sneeze passed.

One of the creatures was whining.

Crenshaw listened attentively. He heard the thing move away from the coffin in the direction of the tunnel. A few seconds later it howled, and from the distance and volume it appeared the creature was heading up the tunnel toward the surface.

Was it the last one?

Professor Crenshaw pressed his right ear to the air space and couldn't hear a thing—no growling, no heavy breathing, no infernal howling.

They were finally gone!

Or were they?

Crenshaw was torn by indecision. On the one hand, he had to get out from under the coffin while he still had the strength to do so. He required sustenance, and his back was killing him. But, on the other hand, what if some of them were out there, lying in wait for him? Even if there was only one of them, he wouldn't stand much of a chance without a gun.

What a choice to make!

He could either stay in the coffin and die, or he could emerge and die.

Crenshaw's lower back made his decision for him. He tried to move, to ease some of the torment, but his lower back protested by jarring him with an incredibly acute spasm. He almost cried out, but gritting his teeth, he rode out the torture until it subsided.

Enough was enough!

Professor Crenshaw placed his hands on the floor and heaved, using his shoulders and back as a fulcrum. The gold coffin rose easier than anticipated. He nearly lost his balance when he attempted to apply any weight to his legs. They reacted like they were made of jello, shaking and tottering, and his entire body swayed before he regained control and steadied himself. He was able to slide the coffin down his back, gripping it with both hands to stop it from crashing to the floor. Carefully, as quietly as he could, he lowered the coffin to the stone floor behind him. Elated to be free at last, he stood up straight.

And instantly regretted his stupidity.

A lancing cramp racked his lower back, doubling him over, and his vision spun. It took the better part of a minute before the twinge disappeared and he could see clearly again.

The pack was gone.

Professor Crenshaw picked up his flashlight and walked toward the tunnel, shuffling forward, feeling his way in the dark, afraid the flashlight might attract unwanted attention. He reached the stone cylinder without incident and peered up the tunnel.

It was empty.

Crenshaw edged around the stone cylinder and into the tunnel. Keeping his back pressed against the wall, he proceeded toward the surface, stopping frequently to listen. His stomach was goading him to hurry, and his throat craved water desperately, but his reason advised him to go slowly, not to take any chances.

One mistake could cost him his life.

Professor Crenshaw smiled when he spotted the vague outline of the antechamber directly ahead. He slowly stepped to the opening in the wall, peeked inside and found it deserted.

He couldn't believe his luck. The pack must be outside, having given up on him.

Crenshaw was about to slip into the antechamber when he heard the low growl. He ducked back and froze, panic-stricken.

One of them was still in the tunnel!

He gingerly moved into the dark corner formed by the junction of the tunnel and antechamber wall.

The thing was coming his way!

Professor Crenshaw detected the patter of its feet on the antechamber floor, and then it appeared, coming through the opening in the wall and going down the tunnel. Crenshaw could feel his neck hairs standing on end, and his skin was crawling as if covered with ants.

The thing didn't bother to glance to the right or left; it simply kept going, intent on its destination.

With a start, Crenshaw realized the creature was going to check up on him.

How long before the thing discovered he had escaped? Five minutes? Possibly ten?

Professor Crenshaw waited, counting to 60, wanting to be sure the rest of the pack wasn't trailing behind the first creature. When none materalized, he rushed into the antechamber where the light was brighter than he expected. He crossed to the other side and searched the tunnel beyond.

Nothing.

At the far end was a glimmer of sunshine. Apparently, he had miscalculated. More than 24 hours had elapsed, probably closer to 36.

Daylight!

Crenshaw forgot all about his hunger and thirst as he ran along the tunnel and paused just shy of the entrance. He could see the dead watchman lying near the wall, only the man seemed different, somehow. It took a moment to register. The creatures had been at the body again. The face had been ripped off and his shirt torn open. His chest and stomach were gone, except for his rib cage jutting upward amid a spreading pool of blood. Crenshaw wrested his eyes from the horrid sight and crouched, treading lightly as he moved to the ramp and risked a quick glance to the right and the left, then over the side.

The ramp was clear, and the base camp appeared to be deserted.

He guessed the time at close to six in the morning and hoped the creatures were primarily nocturnal. If there were any lurking in the camp below, they would be on him before he could reach one of the vehicles.

And what about the one in the tunnel?

The recollection sparked action. Crenshaw hurried down the ramp, constantly scanning the sparse vegetation, the boulders, and the tents, anything they could utilize as cover. At the bottom of the ramp he discarded the flashlight and picked up a large rock. It wasn't much of a weapon, but it would have to suffice.

He seriously toyed with the notion of fleeing into the desert and making for Idfu on foot. A vehicle would be safer and speedier, but using one meant he would have to enter the camp for the keys. He had to face the fact that the forty mile trip to Idfu on foot would be impossible, especially in his weakened condition.

A plaintive howl wailed in the tunnel above him.

Professor Crenshaw jogged to the tents, his nerves frayed, on the verge of exhaustion. He arrived at his tent and paused to regain his breath.

Something was moving on the ramp.

Crenshaw lurched into his tent and stumbled over to a small folding table holding his key ring. He leaned on the table as he recovered the keys, his gaze resting on a bottle of Sehha in the corner.

Water!

Professor Crenshaw propelled himself to the corner and dropped to his knees. He released his rock and clutched the bottle in his trembling hands.

His fingers were awkward and ungainly as he opened the Sehha and raised the bottle to his parched lips. The water was on the tepid side, but it was unquestionably the tastiest, most refreshing water he'd ever had. He gulped the liquid down, some of it spilling out the corners of his mouth and splattering over his khakis. With a supreme effort, he finally forced the bottle aside and rose to his feet. The water had a revitalizing affect on him, and his legs were steadier as he walked to the tent flap and pushed it aside.

They were waiting for him.

Nine of them encircled his tent, their tongues lolling in their mouths, their eyes glazed, white froth flecking their lips.

Crenshaw dropped the Sehha and gripped the tent for support. His legs abruptly went weak, his knees ready to buckle.

They hadn't moved yet. As if they sensed there was no rush, they simply watched and waited.

Professor Artemas Crenshaw felt light-headed and knew he was about to faint. Instead of fighting it, he willingly succumbed. He would be better off if he were unconscious when they charged. Fondly, he thought of his wife, now dead some 12 years, killed by a drunk in a car wreck. Then he thought of Amy Brant, who was like the daughter he'd never had. He hoped the pack would be gone by the time she returned. His consciousness was fading. As his eyes closed and his legs collapsed, he blamed himself for everything.

Abdel.

Hassan.

All of the others.

His stupidity and pride had been his downfall.

Dear God!

He was only dimly aware of falling forward and smacking into the hard ground.

They were on him in a flash.

20

''Are you getting antsy yet?'' she asked him.

''What do I have to be antsy about?''

''I just assumed you'd be worried about keeping up with me on our wedding night.''

Amy Brant and Simon Darr were enjoying a relaxing afternoon strolling along Lake Shore Drive. They were bearing south with the waters of Lake Michigan on their left.

''Let's see,'' Simon said. ''Today is May 10th. Not counting today and the fifteenth, which is our wedding day, I'll have four days. Perfect!''

Amy glanced at him, puzzled. ''Perfect for what? I don't get it.''

''I'll have four days to cram as many oysters down my throat as I can,'' Simon told her and leered lecherously.

Amy snickered. ''You big dummy, that's nothing but a silly superstition.''

''Oh, yeah? Let's see if you still feel it's silly the morning after we're married.''

Amy playfully pinched his fanny. ''Promises, promises!''

Simon pulled her close and kissed her on the lips.

"Our wedding day will be the happiest day of my life," he predicted.

"It will definitely be the busiest," Amy promised, winking seductively. She nibbled on his chin. "Do you know wht I would like to do right now?" she asked huskily.

Simon laughed. "I think I can guess, you vixen."

"You've got it. I'd like to go the zoo."

"The zoo?"

"Of course." Amy grinned impishly. "What did you think I meant?"

"I knew you meant the zoo," Simon lied.

"Sure you did."

They took a right at West Fullerton Parkway, then cut across to North John C. Cannon Drive and ambled south, toward the Lincoln Park Zoo. The weather was breezy and mild, with the temperature in the upper seventies. Both of them wore shorts, Simon a brown pair and Amy's gold colored. She wore a green halter top, Simon a blue T-shirt.

Amy linked her arm through his and leaned her head against his shoulder. "It's really been nice, this time we've had together."

"It certainly has," he concurred.

"Just think. After we're married, every day will be like this one," Amy said. "Together, forever." She sighed happily.

"Let's hope so," Simon remarked.

"What's that supposed to mean?" Amy demanded.

"I get kind of concerned, sometimes," Simon confessed.

"About what?"

"That maybe you won't love me as much five years down the road as you do today."

Amy looked up at him and chuckled. "I knew it. I knew you were becoming antsy."

"It's not that," Simon said, correcting her. "I saw a show this morning while you were taking your shower and putting on your war paint. It was about divorce. The program showed how marriage in America has changed from the good old days. Now, with so many parents being forced to work because of the economic situation, both fathers and mothers, it's putting a severe strain on the marriage institution. At no point in our history have we experienced as many divorces as we're seeing nowadays. It's hard to keep a family together with Mom and Dad gone all day and the kids left to their own devices. This talk show cited some statistics claiming many couples only see each other for ninety minutes a day, if that. They noted it's difficult to grow together when you spend so much time apart."

"And you're afraid we'll grow apart someday?" Amy asked.

"Aren't you?"

"Nope," she replied confidently.

"Why not?"

"Because I love you, lunkhead."

"And I love you." He kissed her again.

"Speaking of talk shows," Amy said after their embrace, "I've been meaning to ask you. Why did you reject that invitation to appear on that talk show?"

Simon snorted derisively. "The guy on the phone said they'd been trying to reach me for a week. I was lucky that I got out of Cairo when I did. I guess the news media swarmed all over the passengers from my flight, wanting to know the details of the hijacking. The reporters from our major networks, in particular, wanted the reactions of the Americans aboard to beam to their affiliates back home. For some ridiculous reason, they thought I was some kind of hero. I understand they wanted to interview me on *Nightline*, but they couldn't find me and it drove 'em nuts.'' Simon laughed.

''You still haven't told me why you declined.''

''Because I'm a reporter,'' Simon stated harshly.

''I don't get it.''

''Amy, how many times have you been watching the news and you see a story about a plane crash or a train wreck or some other disaster?''

''Tons of times.''

''Right. And how many times have you seen some asshole of a reporter shove a microphone in the face of a relative of one of the victims and stupidly ask them how they feel?''

''Tons of times,'' Amy repeated.

''Exactly. In their competition for the highest ratings, and in their single-minded pursuit of a story with visual or emotional drama, our newspeople have become insensitive, asinine, arrogant clods with no respect for the privacy of others. The news organizations rightfully maintain we have a free press in this country, but then in the next breath they assert that people have the right to know what is going on in their world at all costs. I don't subscribe to that sophist philosophy. A reporter has to exercise some basic common sense when dealing with the public and deciding which stories should be aired. Who in their right mind wants to sit in front of their television set and watch some poor mother cry her heart out because her little child has just been crushed to death in an accident? That's not news. It's cheap sensationalism. And that's why I told them I wouldn't do an interview. I won't be a party to it.'' Simon stopped, aware of Amy staring at him strangely. ''What's the matter?''

''Oh, nothing,'' Amy replied. ''I just didn't know you felt this way.''

''You don't agree?''

Amy took hold of his hand and squeezed. ''I do agree, my handsome hunk. It shows you have character. I knew there had to be a sound reason why I'm marrying you."

A few minutes later they were touring the zoo where Amy expressed her dismay at the limited areas some of the animals were forced to live in. They each ate a hot dog and then decided to head on back to Amy's parents place.

They were driving in heavy traffic, Amy at the wheel of her dad's car, when Simon reached over and turned on the radio.

". . . is Malcom Dutton with our hourly update. the top story involves the reports of widespread violence coming out of Egypt."

"Egypt?" Amy interrupted. "Did he say Egypt?"

"Yes. Shhhh. Listen."

". . . correspondent Sally Nash in Cairo." After a pause and some static, the reporter came on the air. "The Egyptian government today declared a state of emergency and imposed martial law in an effort to suppress what has been described as growing civil unrest in Upper Egypt. Details have been difficult to obtain, but it is known the outbreak began in the town of Idfu where hundreds were reportedly killed. The violence has spread as far north as Asyut and as far south as Aswan. A news blackout is in effect, and the Egyptian government will not allow anyone to enter the area. From Cairo, this is Sally Nash reporting."

"Dear God!" Amy exclaimed. "That's right where the Professor is."

Simon saw how upset she was and tried to calm her fears. "No, it isn't. Professor Crenshaw is way to the west of Idfu, out in the middle of nowhere. He won't be affected by it."

"You really think so?"

"Of course."

"I hope he's okay."

"He will be."

Amy's jaw suddenly dropped in dismay. "Oh, no!"

"What is it?"

"I just hope my parents haven't been listening to the news or seen it on TV. They'll never let me return to the excavation site," Amy said with some alarm.

"They would be right," Simon stated.

"What?" Amy glanced at him.

"You just heard the news. They're not letting anyone into the affected area. There's no way you could reach the site until they get everything under control. If your parents object to your going, I'd have to side with them."

"Traitor!"

The voice of the announcer filled the car again. ". . . and finally, we have this story out of Paris, France. French police arrested a man who ran amok among a group of people at Roissy-Charles de Gaulle airport today. Police report the man attacked over a dozen persons at one of the terminals. Four were severely injured. Police would neither comment on the man's motive nor release the identities of the victims. According to witnesses, the suspect assaulted his victims with his bare hands and teeth . . ."

Simon turned off the radio.

"This world is getting sicker and sicker," Amy said.

"Ain't it the truth," Simon agreed.

They drove in silence to West Grace Street. Amy's father was a prosperous lawyer, her mother an accountant, and their home, by Simon's humble standards, was quite luxurious. Amy parked in the driveway and led him into the house where Simon was staying in a guest room until the wedding. His own parents and his brother, Jay, would also be lodging at the Brant home during their visit to the Windy City.

"Amy? Is that you?" a loud feminine voice shouted from off to the right.

Amy looked at Simon and apprehensively bit her lower lip. "Uh-oh, they know."

Amy's parents were waiting for her in the living room. Her father, Frederick Brant, was a tall man with a commanding presence. He always wore immaculate business suits. His dark brown hair was neatly parted on one side and greying at the temples. His wife, Louise, was as meticulous in appearance as Frederick. Her blonde hair was inevitably stylishly coiffured, and her clothing expensive and elegant.

"Have you heard the news?" Frederick asked as soon as he saw them.

Amy walked up to his chair. "We heard."

"I guess you know what it means," Louise said.

"You're not going to let me fly back, are you?"

"Is that so difficult to accept?" her mother asked.

"Simon doesn't think I should go back, either."

"Oh?" Frederick Brant stared at Simon, his narrow lips forming a reserved smile.

Why was it, Simon asked himself, he felt so uncomfortable around Frederick and Louise Brant? Was it because he suspected they weren't too pleased with their daughter's choice of a bridegroom?

"Simon is correct in this matter," Louise stated. "It would be too dangerous to travel in that region until conditions stabilize."

"But what about Professor Crenshaw?" Amy asked.

"Professor Crenshaw is a grown man," Frederick said. "He can take care of himself."

"But I don't want him to think I'd abandon him."

"Crenshaw wouldn't think that of you," Frederick declared authoritatively. "Besides, I'm sure he would rather have you safe and sound than caught in that mess over there."

Simon noticed how Amy's father had stressed the

word "there." He received the distinct impression Amy's parents were more than a bit on the snobbish side.

"Maybe the Professor will call," Amy said hopefully.

"I'm sure he's fine," Louise stated optimistically. "So . . ." She gazed at Simon. "How was your day today?"

"We walked out by the lake and visited the zoo," Simon said.

"I wish I could have went," Louise said. "I don't get out of the house enough as it is, except for work and shopping and other errands."

"Have a seat." Frederick vaguely motioned toward the furniture.

Simon and Amy sat on a nearby couch.

"Tell me, Simon," Frederick started right in, "I'm still a little unclear about your plans after the wedding. I know Amy wants to pursue her archaeological career, but what about yourself? Do you intend to remain at that small newspaper in Colorado? What is the thing called?"

Simon had already mentioned the name at least a dozen times, and he didn't appreciate having the paper referred to as a "thing." "It's the *Lyons Bugle*," he reminded Amy's father.

"And do you plan to stay on there?"

"I don't see why not," Simon answered.

Frederick and Louise exchanged glances.

Louise stood. "Come along, Amy," she ordered. "I want you to lend a hand getting supper ready."

Amy pecked Simon on the cheek and left the room on her mother's heels.

Frederick locked his gaze on Simon. "Can we talk frankly, Simon? Man-to-man, as it were?"

Simon braced himself. "Sure."

"I don't believe staying at the *Bugle* is a good idea," Frederick said bluntly.

"Oh? Why not?" Simon opted to play the innocent to minimize the risk of offending Amy's father. He had seen this coming months ago, even as far back as last Thanksgiving.

Frederick folded his hands in his lap and pursed his lips. "Don't misunderstand what I'm about to say. I think the newspaper business is a respectable profession, but I fail to see why a young man of your talent should waste his time at a small paper in Colorado when you could work at a prestigious paper right here in Chicago."

"I don't think a Chicago paper would hire someone like me," Simon remarked. "Chicago is the big time. I'm just small potatoes. I'm not qualified. They'd toss my resumé in the trash."

"You underestimate your abilities," Frederick said politely.

"I can apply," Simon offered, knowing his chances of landing a job at one of the Chicago papers were nil, "but don't get your hopes up."

Frederick Brant grinned, and for some reason it reminded Simon of the grin of a leopard about to pounce on an unsuspecting gazelle. "What if you could be guaranteed a position here in Chicago?" he asked.

"Guaranteed? I don't see how . . ."

"Never mind how." Frederick cut him short. "Would you move to Chicago if you had a job here?"

"I wouldn't come unless I obtained the job honestly."

Amy's father frowned. "Let's be realistic about this. On your salary, and whatever Amy makes digging up old relics, it's going to be hard to make ends meet. Think about it. Money doesn't grow on trees, you know. Coming to Chicago would be a big step for you, I'm certain. Think of all the advantages. You'd be making a higher income, no doubt about that. You'd have all the cultural and social benefits of living in a major city. Amy would be near the University and Professor Crenshaw . . ."

"And Amy would be closer to Mrs. Brant and you," Simon inerjected.

Frederick's brown eyes narrowed. "You saw right through me, didn't you? You knew what I was about before I started this spiel, right?"

"Yes," Simon admitted.

Frederick actually smiled. "Bottom line, then. Louise and I would be grateful if you would consider moving to Chicago. We are very close to our daughter, as you know. Some might say we've spoiled her by giving her everything we could, even allowing her to traipse off to some godforsaken backwards country to indulge her interest in archaeology. We can't bear the thought of being separated from her on a long term basis. Will you do it?"

"And what about *my* family?" Simon asked. "I'm close to my parents, too."

"I can symphathize," Frederick stated.

"I like it where I am," Simon said.

"Look at it from Amy's point of view," Frederick suggested.

"Amy's?"

"Do you think it will be easy on her, moving away from us?"

"No, I guess not."

"It would be hard on both of you." Frederick pressed his argument. "The question you must answer is this—do you want it to be hard on Amy or yourself? Which one of you should have to suffer the pangs of separation? Should it be Amy, or should it be you? If you truly love her, there can be only one answer."

Simon studied Frederick appreciatively. "You fight dirty, Mr. Brant."

Amy's father grinned again. "I didn't get where I am today by fighting fair."

"I'll think over what you've said," Simon promised.

"That's all I can ask."

"When would you like my answer?"

"There's no rush," Frederick replied.

"Thank you."

"Of course," Frederick added, "we'd appreciate knowing by your wedding day, just so we can plan accordingly, you understand."

"I understand completely."

There was the grin again. "I thought you would."

21

Jay Darr wasn't teaching any early classes on the morning of May 11th, so he slept in late. It was shortly after nine when he opened his eyes and caught sight of Marcy, still asleep beside him in his waterbed. She looked so beautiful, so very vulnerable, lying there with her black hair askew and her lips slightly parted. He wanted to take her in his arms and smother her body with kisses, but since she had been up late the night before, studying for one of her finals, he decided to let her sleep for as long as she wanted.

He quietly slid from under the sheet and padded across the floor to the bathroom, stark naked. After relieving himself, he donned a pair of red briefs and walked to the living room. Bright sunlight was streaming in the picture window. He went over to his stereo unit and switched on the radio; mellow music from the thirties and forties filled the room. Jay wasn't a big fan of hard rock or pop music; he much preferred older tunes with a less frenetic rhythm and beat.

It was time for his daily ritual, his morning workout.

Jay moved to the floor mats and began. First, he performed his stretching exercises, unlimbering his muscles for the day ahead. Next, he executed the basic *Hung Gar* stances, holding each one for at least two minutes. In his usual order, he squatted in the Horse Riding stance, then moved into the Bow and Arrow stance, followed by the Cat stance, the Scissors stance, and the Hanging Horse stance. There were other stances in *Hung Gar*, but Jay believed these five distributed his body weight more efficiently, thus providing a firmer foundation for his varied techniques. After the stances came his basic sets, a combination of the different stances and techniques. He went over them again and again, as he had done for years, mastering them until they became a reflex action on his part. Throughout all of his movements, as his hands and feet flowed in a balletic sequence of motions, he breathed as his sifu had taught him. Proper breathing, for a martial artist, was as critically important as the stances and the forms. In order to maximize his strength and striking force, he must inhale through his nose, expanding his abdomen. Then, at the moment of impact, when he used an arm or leg blow against a foe, real or imaginary, he must exhale the air in his abdomen, allowing the tension thus produced to flow up from his abdominal region and along his limb to his opponent.

Ten minutes into his workout, the music ended and the news came on.

Though wishing they would play music again, one portion of the newscast did catch his attention.

". . . international news. From Egypt, word that the government there has temporarily enacted a ban on all travel into and out of the country. Flights are not being permitted to land or take off, and all Egyptian ports have been closed. The government has not released an official explanation as yet, but the ban and the martial law announced previously are believed connected to several days of civil unrest."

Jay was glad that Simon and Amy were safely out of Egypt. Simon had called him the night they arrived in Chicago.

". . . were several reported incidents of unexplained violence in Paris, France. French authorities have issued a statement warning of a new wave of terrorist activity. In national news at this hour, a terminal at John F. Kennedy International Airport was closed for four hours early this morning when an unidentified man went on a killing spree. Five people were reported killed, seven others injured. Police have not indicated a motive, nor revealed the type of weapon used."

Jay paused, wiping the sweat from his brow. It sounded like the damn terrorists were at it again. Too bad he hadn't been on that 747 instead of Simon.

". . . this note from San Francisco. Last night a twenty-nine year old man was arrested on Fisherman's Wharf. According to witnesses, the young man walked onto the Wharf, stripped off his clothes, and spent fifteen minutes howling like a wolf before police arrived on the scene. The man, identified as Peter Winchell, is undergoing a psychiatric examination . . ."

Sounds like Mr. Winchell had one too many, Jay told himself. He walked to the kitchen and began preparing breakfast, thinking all the while of his brother. Jay was looking forward to seeing Simon again. He often missed his younger brother and wished they could be closer than they were. He almost couldn't believe his brother was getting married before him.

Jay grabbed a tray from a cabinet and loaded it with toast, scrambled eggs, crisp bacon, and a glass of orange juice, Marcy's favorite. He crossed the living room and tiptoed down the hallway to the bedroom, pausing at the door to peek inside. Marcy was still sound asleep and snoring lightly.

Jay entered the room and positioned the tray of food on the waterbed alongside Marcy. He leaned over her face and flicked his tongue over the tip of her nose.

Marcy mumbled something unintelligible, but otherwise didn't budge.

Grinning, Jay bent lower and blew in her ear.

Marcy made a swatting motion, as if shooing flies away from her face.

Jay suppressed a laugh and eased the white sheet lower on the bed.

Marcy was wearing an old blue T-shirt and her red undies.

Jay slowly pulled her T-shirt up until her breasts were exposed. She moved toward him, but did not awaken. He brought his lips down on her left nipple and tongued it softly.

"Ummmm," Marcy moaned in her sleep.

Jay switched to her right breast.

After a minute, her hands, which had been at her side, came up and entwined in his hair. "You sure know how to start the day right," she remarked throatily.

Jay pulled back, then kissed her on the lips.

Marcy's eyes opened and she broke their kiss. "What did I do to deserve this?"

"I needed to do something to stop your snoring," Jay quipped.

"Beast!" She grinned and punched him on the left arm.

"If you're going to be this way," he said, pretending to be offended, "I'll take it back."

"Take what back?"

Jay nodded toward the tray of food.

Marcy's eyes widened in surprise, and she sat up in bed. "I don't believe it. Now I definitely know you're up to something. What is it?"

Jay placed the tray on her lap and sat beside her. "I'm not up to anything," he informed her.

Marcy gazed in much astonishment at the tray. "It looks real inviting. You sure it isn't poisoned?"

Jay chuckled. "Does her highness want the royal food taster to test it for her?"

"That won't be necessary," Marcy replied, grinning, "but I still don't see what you're trying to prove."

"I'm just demonstrating a point," Jay explained.

"What point?"

"That I can be a good little boy if I try. You told me you wouldn't go to Chicago unless I promised to behave myself. Well, look at this. I'm serving you breakfast in bed, and I didn't even try to molest you."

"Oh, yeah?" Marcy pointed at her exposed breasts. "What do you call this action?"

"I was experimenting with a new style alarm clock I hope to patent," Jay said. "It's called the Jay Darr sensory alarm clock, batteries not included."

"Sensory alarm clock? Don't you mean sexual alarm clock?"

"Whatever." He started to rise. "Enjoy your breakfast."

Marcy gripped his wrist and yanked him back to the bed. "And just where do you think you're going?"

"To let you eat your breakfast in peace," Jay informed her.

Marcy pulled his face close to hers. "Not after what you've started, you're not. You stoke the fire, lover, you've got to put out the flames."

"But I don't want you getting the wrong idea," Jay objected half-heartedly. "I don't want you to think I'm only interested in you for your body."

"You mean you're interested in me for my mind?" she asked, snickering.

"Among other attributes," Jay said, smiling.

"Well, right this moment my mind says it wants you," Marcy stated seductively.

"I don't know . . ." Jay hedged. "You won't have second thoughts about coming to Chicago with me, will you?"

"I said I'd come, didn't I?" she retorted.

"I still don't know . . ."

"Kiss me, you fool!" Marcy planted a passionate kiss on his lips.

"What about your breakfast?" Jay asked when they came up for air.

"What about it? We won't hurt it."

"I slave over a hot stove, and this is what happens!" Jay groused in jest. "It's true what they say. Women do take men for granted."

"Forget the stupid food." Marcy pressed against him. "Which would you rather have—I eat the food, or you eat me?"

Jay tenderly kissed her forehead. "Not much of a choice, is it?"

"Besides," she added, "I could tell the eggs weren't scrambled enough, anyway."

"Then let's get to scrambling."

They embraced and kissed, the tray of food scrunched between their bodies.

"Just remember," Marcy said softly a few minutes later, "you clean up the mess."

There was a moment of profound silence, then Jay mumbled, "Yep. Definitely taken for granted!"

22

The ringing of the phone was like the detonation of dynamite in his skull. Buddy Snyder, flat on his back in bed, rose up as if he were shot from a cannon and lunged for the telephone on the nightstand. He glanced at the digital display on the clock—10:02 A.M., May 12th.

"Hello?" Buddy said, his voice sounding like he'd swallowed a mouthful of gravel.

"Buddy? Is that you?" inquired an anxious male voice.

Buddy recognized the voice of his boss, Kramer. "Yeah, it's me, all right." He coughed, his chest aching terribly from all the congestion in his lungs.

"You sound lousy," Kramer declared.

"You called to tell me something I already know?" Buddy asked.

"I just heard that you called in sick today."

"Are you checking up on me?" Buddy demanded.

"No, nothing like that," Kramer assured him. "I want to know how serious it is."

"Not very," Buddy replied. "The doc says I have a super-duper case of the flu. I spend half of my time in bed, the other half on the john."

"How long before you'll be in to work?" Kramer asked.

"I don't know," Buddy responded. "The doc said the runs and the vomiting may take two to three days to clear up. Why all of this sudden interest in my health? Don't I have enough sick days accumulated?"

"I couldn't care less about your sick days."

"Then what's going on?" Buddy demanded.

"We need you."

Buddy tried to laugh, but the resultant noise sounded more like a goose being strangled. "Need me? What's with you? All the qualified people we have working in the Division, and you say you need me? What is this, a gag?"

"No gag."

Buddy abruptly realized that Kramer's voice had a tense edge to it. "Hey, Tom, what's going on?"

"I just called to see if you'd be in," Kramer explained. "We need everybody we can find today."

"Why? What's going on?"

"The shit has hit the fan."

"What are you talking about?" Buddy asked, intensely curious.

"I can't say over the phone," Kramer replied cryptically.

Buddy speculated that something big had broken. "Listen," he offered, "if you need me this bad, I'll come in. Since when have I ever listened to a doctor?"

"No, you wouldn't do us much good in your condition. We need you at peak performance. Do what the doctor told you and don't come in until you're feeling better."

"If you insist . . ."

"I insist," Kramer stressed.

"Okay. But can you at least give me a hint?"

Kramer sighed. "Have you caught the news lately?"

"The news?"

"Buddy, that's all I can say. I've got to scoot. Report to my office when you get in. So long." Kramer hung up before Buddy could reply.

Confused, Buddy replaced the receiver. What the hell was going on? Kramer wouldn't call unless it was something major. He rose, his knees shaky, and walked to the portable television at the foot of the bed, perched on a movable stand. He was thankful Gladys had gone to the store. Otherwise, she'd be nagging him to death to find out what Kramer had wanted.

Buddy turned on the set and switched to the all-news cable channel. He staggered back to the bed and collapsed, hoping the exertion wouldn't trigger another attack of diarrhea. A big case comes along and he contracts the flu!

The weather was on the news channel, the weatherman assuring the audience that the entire nation would enjoy predominantly seasonal conditions except for a few snow showers in northern Montana and sweltering heat in the desert southwest.

Buddy impatiently waited for the weather to end.

Finally, the news anchor, a blonde woman with the reddest lips Buddy had ever seen, came on.

"In the news today, the mystery continues over what is happening in Egypt. A news blackout has been put in effect and the Egyptian government has refused to comment. Some reports are being received from unsubstantiated sources, and they would seem to indicate a full-fledged civil war is in progress. The U.S. State Department claims it does not know what is going on."

The anchor paused and shifted her copy.

"Equally baffling is the closure of the two main airports serving Paris, France. Both Orly and the Roissy-Charles de Gaulle have been shut down with no explanation given. Only two days ago, Roissy-Charles de Gaulle was where an unidentified man went berserk, injuring over a dozen people. Last night there were reports of widespread rioting in the streets of Paris, and one unofficial estimate is that over three hundred people may have been killed. It is believed Paris has become the focal point of heightened terrorist atrocities."

Again she paused.

"The mayor of New York City is blaming street gangs for the rioting and looting there last night. Every available police officer was required to report for duty. Some sections of the city have been cordoned off. There has been talk of calling in the National Guard, but the mayor says the Guard would be an over-reaction to a localized problem. The Police Commissioner has vowed to clamp down a lid on the city tonight to prevent a repeat of last night's violence. At least three dozen people were killed in the rioting."

Buddy shook his head to clear it of some drowsiness brought on by both the flu and his medication.

"Then there is this item out of California," the anchor said. "Health officials have placed a hospital in San Francisco under temporary quarantine. They say the move is necessary to curtail the spread of a contagious disease. At last report, three patients and four staff members have come down with it. They have not identified the disease in question, but reliable sources indicate it may be Legionnaire's Disease."

She started reading the political news, but Buddy mentally shut her out. Exactly what the hell was going on?

First, Kramer calls and says the shit has hit the fan.

There's a news blackout in Egypt.

The airports serving Paris are closed.

Portions of New York City have been cordoned off.

And there's a hospital quarantined in San Francisco.

How did all this add up? What connection, if any,

did it have with the Centers for Disease Control and the Center for Infectious Diseases? How many of the divisions at the Center for Infectious Diseases were involved in whatever was transpiring?

Kramer had told him to watch the news, and what had he picked up?

Egypt. France. New York City. San Francisco.

Were they tied together? If they were, and the Centers for Disease Control was conducting an investigation, it could only mean one thing—plague! The Centers for Disease Control only took part in disease related cases, and only an epidemic disease of massive proportions could span entire continents.

A plague was the thing that fit the bill.

But what type of plague? A new one, previously unknown to medical science? Something like Lassa fever? What?

Buddy longed to be at work. He might be missing a chance to conduct research on an exotic new disease because he was bedridden with the common flu. And it was all Gladys' fault! The doctor had said Buddy caught the flu because his resistance was so low due to his strict diet. So the blame rested squarely on Gladys and her damn liver!

Too late, Buddy recalled the doctor's admonition not to become excited or exert himself. As he ran into the bathroom, his abdomen cramping so badly he wanted to double over, he made a silent vow. The next time he mowed the lawn, another flamingo was going to die!

23

"That's odd. I still can't get through to Interpol."

"Maybe all of the overseas lines are tied up. It happens, you know."

James Lanning glanced at his mother and shook his head. She was on the sofa in her living room, viewing the evening news on television. "It doesn't matter if the overseas lines are tied up," he explained. "I placed a priority call and they should have broken one of the other connections to get me through. It's very odd," he reiterated.

"Try again tomorrow," Gloria suggested.

"I've been trying for twelve hours," Lanning noted. "I can't believe I didn't get through. Something really strange is going on."

Gloria pointed at her television set. "You heard the reports. Yesterday they closed Paris down. It must be because of all those horrible terrorists."

"No," Lanning explained. "They might declare martial law because of terrorists, but they wouldn't shut down the entire city."

"New York City is under martial law," Gloria said and then stared at him with concern in her eyes. "Don't you fly through there on your way back to France?"

"I go through JFK," Lanning confirmed.

"Maybe they'll close JFK like they did those airports near Paris," Gloria said hopefully.

"That's another thing," Lanning stated. "I can't believe they would impose martial law in New York City because of a gang problem."

"What else could it be?" Gloria asked.

Lanning shrugged. "Beats me, Mom." He noticed how she smiled when he called her "Mom."

"Maybe you shouldn't try to return to Interpol until you hear from them," Gloria recommended. "Didn't you say they have my number and address?"

"Yes. I'm required to let them know where I'll be at all times, but I'm surprised I haven't heard from them by now."

Gloria frowned. "I take it you still intend to cut your vacation short?"

Lanning walked over to her and placed his hand on her shoulder, gazing fondly into her eyes. "I have a duty, Mom, a responsibility I must fulfill. If things are so bad in Paris that I can't get through to Interpol on the phone, then I've got to make an effort to get back there and find out what's going on. Don't you see?"

Gloria averted her eyes. "I still think you should wait for them to contact you."

Lanning sighed, frustrated. They had been arguing over the issue for the better part of two hours.

"I only wish you didn't need to interrupt our time together," Gloria said sadly.

"I'm really sorry about that," Lanning apologized. "I've had a great time, really. At least today is the fourteenth. I've already agreed to stay until tomorrow, so we can attend Simon's wedding."

Gloria fidgeted with her blouse. "I don't understand why I should go to this wedding. I don't even know the man."

"Simon invited you, too. At least I was able to track *him* down. After not getting any answer at his home phone in Colorado, I had to call the number of the church he gave me, and they were able to supply the number of his fiancee, Amy Brant. I phoned her and found out Simon is staying at her house. I was going to tell Simon I couldn't make it, but he sounded so tickled I was in Chicago, he made me give him my word I'd be there." Lanning chuckled. "I kind of like that kid."

"At least we'll have one more day together," Gloria said stiffly.

"We'll have more than that," Lanning vowed. "Next year, I'm coming back on my vacation."

Gloria faced him, her features lighting up. "Really?"

"Really," he affirmed. He could see the promise of a return trip pleased her immensely.

"I'll be counting the days," Gloria said.

Lanning opted to change the subject. "That was a fantastic supper you cooked tonight."

"It was nothing," Gloria stated happily.

"If that was nothing," Lanning cracked, "I'd hate to see a meal you prepare when you're serious about cooking. I'd gain ten pounds."

Gloria laughed.

"Tell you what I'll do," Lanning volunteered. "You sit here and take it easy while I take out the trash and then bring you a dish of ice cream. How's that sound?"

"Don't bother."

"It's no bother, Mom." Lanning started toward the kitchen.

"Be careful out there," Gloria called. "Remember what they said on the news last night about the dog packs loose in the city."

"I'll be careful," Lanning replied. "Don't worry. I'm only taking out the trash."

Lanning walked to the yellow trash can in the far corner of the kitchen, lifted the white lid and pulled out the full garbage bag. After twirling the bag to tighten the open end, he took a plastic tie from a cabinet and secured the bag. He opened the backdoor and headed across the backyard toward the two metal cans positioned at one end of a tall hedge. The sun was almost touching the western horizon.

What the hell was going on?

Lanning's inexplicable sixth sense was bothering him again. Whenever something was wrong or he was about to be confronted by danger, he experienced this nagging feeling, a vague, indistinct awareness that some element was out of place. He didn't know what caused it, but he didn't much like it when this uneasiness came over him. Sometimes, this premonition was weak, like when he boarded that 747 that was almost hijacked. At other times, he became so subliminally agitated, so filled by a bizarre foreboding, he found sleep difficult and his concentration suffered.

Like right now.

His anxiety was compounded by the mysterious situation in Paris. Why in the world couldn't he get through to Interpol? Why would the authorities close Paris down? None of it made any sense whatsoever.

Lanning had contacted several U.S. agencies in the hope they could provide some answers, calling friends at both the F.B.I. and the C.I.A., but none of them knew anything. At least, they *claimed* they couldn't help, but Lanning received the impression they were deliberately holding back on him.

Why?

Lanning was five yards from the hedge and the metal cans when something growled.

The sound came from behind the hedge.

Lanning stopped and listened. Maybe his mother had been right. On the late news last night, the newsman had gravely relayed a warning from the Chicago Police Department to the general public. There had been several people in Chicago, mainly in the inner city area although there was one report from near the Chicago Midway Airport, attacked by dogs. Two of the victims were seriously injured. Police speculated a pack of abandoned pets was roaming the city and foraging for food. They urged everyone to take appropriate precautions and to avoid unlit areas after dark.

The thing behind the hedge growled again.

Lanning grinned. This was just what he needed. A little action to take his mind off Paris and Interpol. If one of those dogs was lurking behind the hedge, he'd kick its face in and notify the Police Department or Animal Control.

The hedge rustled as if a large animal were shaking the bushes.

Lanning quietly set the garbage bag on the grass and eased toward the metal cans.

The hedge ceased its rustling.

Lanning crouched and tried to peer under the hedge, but the bushes were too dense to allow him to catch a glimpse of whatever was on the other side. He stood and moved to the metal cans.

All was quiet on the other side of the hedge.

Lanning slid past the cans to an opening in the hedge, a space between the end of the hedge and a row of shrubs to his right. Cautiously, he peeked around the edge.

Nothing.

Behind the hedge was a vacant lot overgrown with weeds and dotted with trees and bushes. There was no sign of any living creature either behind the hedge or in the vacant lot.

Curious over what it may have been, Lanning walked along the rear of the hedge, examining the ground for clues. The earth was soft and would easily retain an impression. He was a third of the way down the hedge when he spotted a set of tracks on a bare patch of dirt. The impressions were readily recognizable; they were footprints—naked human footprints.

Lanning stared at them, perplexed. The tracks were those of an adult, not a child. Why would an adult be waltzing around barefoot behind his mother's hedge? The recent daytime temperatures had been very mild, but who in their right mind would be walking in a vacant lot cluttered with stones and prickly weeds in their bare feet?

It was puzzling but no more so than whatever was transpiring in Paris. Lanning decided he would try to reach Interpol again. Returning to the backyard, he finished dumping the garbage bag into one of the metal cans.

Lanning strolled across the lawn, but as he was reaching for the doorknob, a sound made him turn.

The hedge was rustling again.

Was someone playing games?

Lanning debated whether he should run to the hedge and attempt to nab the culprit in the act, but discarded the notion. Whoever was out there would run away again. They were probably hiding in the vacant lot.

He had more important things to do.

Lanning opened the back door, paused in the doorway, and flipped the middle finger on his right hand in the direction of the hedge. He hoped whoever was having fun at his expense would step on a piece of glass. It would serve them right.

"Is that you?" Gloria yelled as he closed the door.

"No," Lanning replied, "it's not me. It's a being from Mars."

"Come in here," Gloria called out. "Quick."

Lanning hurried through the kitchen to the living room. "What is it?" he asked as he entered.

"Look!" She pointed at the television.

Lanning could see a line of soldiers in the foreground of the television screen, and in the background loomed the Eiffel Tower.

"It's a special report," Gloria explained.

Lanning crossed to the TV and increased the volume.

". . . order has been given to shoot to kill on sight. Absolutely no one is permitted to enter or leave the city of Paris. Only an hour ago, Army units and the National Guard were deployed around New York City."

The scene on the TV switched to the military forces establishing their perimeter.

"Reliable sources indicate the situation in Paris and the latest developments in New York are connected. The governor of New York has refused to comment at this time. It has been learned that the mayor of New York City left that metropolis yesterday, flying by helicopter to Albany. He has been in seclusion since his arrival at the state capital."

A newsman appeared on the screen.

"When Paris was first placed under martial law, authorities cited terrorist activity as the reason. When New York City was first put under martial law, street gangs were blamed. Although the governments of France and the U.S. have yet to announce anything to the contrary, it is widely believed that the terrorism and street gang rampages cited earlier were largely fabrications. Congress sent a special bipartisan delegation to the White House just a short while ago, demanding to know what is going on. So far, there has been no response from the Administration, but not ten minutes ago all networks were asked to relinquish an hour of prime time tomorrow night, beginning at 7:00 P.M., Eastern Time, for an important Presidential address to the nation. We will cover the President's speech live, of course, and provide updates as more news becomes available."

"What do you think is going on?" Gloria asked in amazement.

"I wish I knew," Lanning answered.

"I know you'll be mad at me for saying this," Gloria forewarned him, "but one good thing will come out of all of this."

"What's that?"

Gloria smiled sheepishly. "It doesn't appear you'll be returning to Paris in the near future."

Lanning chuckled. The world might be coming to an end, and his mother was happy about it because it meant her son wouldn't be cutting his vacation short. "I'm glad someone is benefiting from this mess."

"Don't get me wrong," Gloria said hastily. "I feel sorry for those poor folks in New York City and Paris, but I can't help it if I'm happy you'll be around for a spell. Do you blame me?"

Lanning walked over and kissed her on her forehead. "Of course not, silly."

"If only we knew what was going on," Gloria muttered.

Lanning glanced at the television. For the hundredth time that day he asked himself the same question: What *was* going on?

24

The big day had finally arrived.

Simon Darr critically examined himself in the full-length mirror, insuring his tuxedo was perfect for the occasion. He aligned his tie and took a deep breath, striving to relax his tense muscles.

"If it wasn't for the face," said someone behind him, "you might almost be handsome."

Simon glanced over his shoulder at Jay, grinning. "I'm really glad you could make it."

Jay Darr was wearing a rented grey tux. He came up next to his younger brother and began picking lint from Simon's black jacket. "There's no way I'd miss your wedding," Jay informed him. "You're setting a precedent, and I could use the incentive."

"Incentive for what?" Simon asked.

"You'll find out, soon enough," Jay promised.

Simon looked in the mirror again. "I hope Mom and Dad make it. I'm surprised they haven't shown up already. Did you have much difficulty getting to Chicago?"

"There seemed to be more confusion than normal at the Philadelphia International Airport," Jay said, "and our flight was delayed about thirty minutes, but beyond that there weren't any major hassles."

"I'm glad you don't live in New York City," Simon said, straightening his tie again. "You never would have made it."

"Yeah. That's all everybody has been talking about," Jay remarked. "New York City and Paris. I wonder what the President will have to say tonight?"

They were standing in a small room to the right of the altar. With only 15 minutes until the ceremony was scheduled to commence, Simon was becoming increasingly worried about his parents.

"I like this old church," Jay commented. "What's it called, again?"

"It's called The Holy Temple Of God. The building was constructed almost a century ago."

"We're not far from Lake Michigan here, are we?"

"No, we're not," Simon replied. "This church is on Diversey Parkway."

"That doesn't tell me much," Jay said. "I'm not familiar with Chicago. I saw the highway signs on the way here from Amy's house, but I might as well be in Tokyo for all the good they did me."

"I won't letyou get lost, kiddo," Simon stated. "I need the ring you're carrying for the ceremony."

Jay snickered. "I'm the oldest here. I should be calling you kiddo."

"It's impolite to refer to a married man as a kid," Simon informed him.

"Is that right? Then why does that blond guy keep calling you 'kid' all the time? You know. The guy you were talking to out front about twenty minutes ago?"

"Lanning? He's harmless. That's just the way he talks," Simon explained.

"Lanning? Isn't he the one from your flight? The Interpol agent you were telling me about?"

"That's him," Simon confirmed.

The minister entered the room. Reverend Treece was a short, stocky man with a prominent forehead and large ears.

"There's a phone call for you in my office," Reverend Treece told Simon. "It's your parents."

"Thank you." Simon hurried from the room, proceeding down a long hallway until he came to the minister's office. He had tried to phone his folks from the office an hour ago, speculating they might have been detained at home for some reason, but there wasn't any answer. He scooped up the phone, nearly dropping the receiver in his haste. "Hello?"

"Simon? Is that you?" It was his mother, Rebecca.

"Yes. Where are you? Why aren't you here yet?" he asked.

"I'm afraid we have some bad news."

"You can't make it?"

"No."

"Where are you?"

"At Stapleton Airport," she replied.

"You're still in Denver?"

"I'm afraid so," she said sadly.

"Why?"

"I'll let your father explain. He wants to talk to you."

There was a momentary commotion on the other end of the line, then the booming voice of Richard Darr came on the phone. "Simon! It must be getting close to the time, isn't it?"

"There's about ten minutes," Simon answered, "but if you guys aren't going to make it, I'll postpone it."

"Nonsense," his dad scoffed. "Go on with your wedding."

"I want Mom and you here," Simon protested.

"We can't make it," Richard Darr stated.

"So Mom said. Why?"

"They've temporarily grounded all flights out of Stapleton," his father elaborated. "We were at the terminal, waiting for our flight, when there was a lot of shouting and screaming about fifty yards from where we stood. Police and airport security people were all over the place. Apparently, they've arrested a woman for something, although no one knows what it is. We did see three people carried out of here on stretchers."

"How long before they get the flights going again?"

"The lady at the ticket counter said four hours."

"We could delay the wedding four hours," Simon suggested.

"Don't be ridiculous," Richard Darr responded. "You have a church full of guests waiting for the ceremony, not to mention all the time and expense Amy's parents have invested in it." He paused. "I only wish Amy's parents had allowed us to help out with some of the expenses. It wasn't fair for them to shoulder the cost."

"They thought it was the least they could do," Simon told him, "especially after you two consented to having the wedding in Chicago instead of Colorado."

"Well, you go ahead with it. We won't have you postponing your wedding on our account. Some things just can't be helped."

"I still don't like it," Simon objected.

"Is Jay there?" his father asked.

"Yeah. Marcy and him got in last night," Simon replied.

"Marcy?"

Simon realized his brother had not mentioned Marcy to their parents. The prospect of Jay having a serious "lady friend," as his mom invariably referred to their dates, would elate them. His father worked as a machinist in Denver and was only seven years away from retirement. His mother was employed as a secretary. Neither of them accepted Jay's vocation, viewing the martial arts as "so much nonsense."

They had also repeatedly criticized Jay's extended bachelorhood. Simon decided to put in a good word for his brother. "You mean Jay hasn't told you about Marcy?"

"No," his father responded. "Who is she?"

"A woman he's been seeing for about eight months," Simon explained. "I get the impression they're really tight."

"Tight? Do you mean close?"

"Close as can be," Simon informed his dad.

"Well, that's good news," Richard Darr said happily. "Maybe we'll have another wedding to attend before too long, eh?"

"What about my wedding?" Simon pressed him. "I won't feel right without you two here."

"Baloney! You've gone this far, you can't stop now. Give our apologies to the Brants."

"Will do," Simon said, feeling depressed.

"Just be sure your photographer takes a lot of pictures."

"Okay," Simon promised listlessly.

"And cheer up," his father ordered. "Do you want everyone to think you're a grouch on your wedding day?"

"No," Simon answered. "They'd never let me hear the end of it."

"All right, then. Now get going. And remember, even if we can't be there in person, we're there right beside you in spirit. God bless you, son, and grant you as happy a marriage as I've had to your mother," his father said.

"Thanks."

"We've got to go. Take care."

"I will."

"Bye." His father hung up.

Simon slowly replaced the receiver, dejected.

"Are you coming, or what? This may be the first time that the bride shows up at the altar before the groom," quipped someone behind him.

Jay was standing in the doorway.

"Why didn't you talk to them?" Simon asked.

"I was helping usher in some last minute guests," Jay replied. "I take it they're not going to make it, are they?"

Simon shook his head.

"Don't let it get you down," Jay advised.

"I can't help it," Simon retorted.

"If it'll make you feel any better," Jay suggested, "I won't invite them to my wedding. That way, we'll be even."

"You know," Simon observed, "you've been in an awfully good mood since you arrived. How come?"

"What's that crack supposed to mean?"

"The last couple of times I talked to you on the phone, you sounded down in the dumps. Now you show up here acting on top of the world. What gives?" Simon asked.

"Things are looking up, is all," Jay answered.

"Things? You mean Marcy?"

"We've finally got our act together," Jay admitted. "It's been real nice."

Simon chuckled. "Maybe we should make this a double wedding?"

"I can't rush her. She'll take her own sweet time about coming to a decision."

From in back of Jay, someone else joined their conversation. "So here you bozos are."

James Lanning appeared, nodded at Jay and grinned at Simon. "How are you holding up, kid?"

Simon smiled. "Just fine, thanks. What are you doing back here?"

"My mother and I are sitting in one of the rear pews," Lanning explained, "near the front doors. A lovely woman dressed in a weird white dress is standing outside on the steps, waiting to make her grand entrance. She poked her head inside and asked me if I would track you down and relay a message."

Simon glanced at his watch. It was three minutes till four! He looked at Lanning. "What's the message?"

"Tell him if he doesn't get his butt where it belongs by the time she counts to one hundred," Lanning quoted, "she will kick it from here to Tahiti and back again. By 'it', I believe she means the aforementioned butt." Lanning laughed.

"I'd better get out there," Simon declared.

Jay and Lanning stood aside so Simon could pass.

"We're right behind you," Jay said to Simon as he hurried along the hallway.

"Name's Lanning," Lanning said, offering his hand.

"Jay Darr."

"I figured you were Simon's brother."

"And you're the hero Simon has told me about."

"The kid thinks I'm a hero?" Lanning asked, his brows arching.

They were moving down the hallway after Simon.

"Sure does," Jay confirmed. "He said he would have been killed if it weren't for you."

"I was just doing my job," Lanning said.

"Are you coming to the reception at the Brant home after the wedding?"

"I might," Lanning responded, shrugging. "It depends on my mother."

"Why do you call Simon 'kid' all the time?" Jay asked.

Lanning snickered. "It's that puppy dog look he gets on his puss every now and then."

They reached the small room from which Simon and Jay as best man would enter the chapel.

"I'm going to get back to my seat," Lanning said and departed.

Directly ahead was the curtained entrance to the

altar area. Simon was peeking past the curtain at the packed pews.

"See anything interesting?" Jay asked him.

"The Brants sure know a lot of people," Simon replied. "There must be two hundred out there."

"And not one of them from Colorado," Jay noted dryly.

"My friends would come if they could," Simon said. "They would have needed to take a day or two off from work and would have had to spend a lot of money on transportation and accomodations. I couldn't impose on them like that."

"Not even Ralph showed up," Jay mentioned. Ralph Meeker was one of Simon's closest friends from the newspaper where he worked.

"Ralph is filling in for me while I'm gone," Simon said, scanning the pews and spotting an elderly woman with a mink stole. "Wow! Have you taken a look at the people out here?"

"Yeah. Why?"

"Did you see their clothes?" Simon asked. "The Brants certainly travel in affluent circles."

"You'll be traveling in those circles before too long," Jay predicted.

"What? You're crazy."

"Don't tell me! Marcy and I stayed at the Brant house last night, remember? I've seen the spread they've got. And I caught on to Frederick and Louise real quick. They're money, bro, pure and simple. I'm surprised they didn't raise a stink over their daughter marrying a podunk like you," Jay observed.

Simon glanced over at his brother. "To tell you the truth, I don't think either of her parents are too keen on the idea. They're sort of . . . resigned to it."

They heard Reverend Treece commence his address to those gathered for the occasion.

Simon peered around the brown curtain, waiting for his cue. "You still have the ring, don't you?" he whispered.

Jay didn't answer.

Simon turned and found Jay frantically going through all of his pockets, searching for the ring.

"You didn't!" Simon exclaimed in disbelief.

Jay looked up, frowning. "I think I did."

Simon took a step toward his brother. "Why, you dimwit, I ought to . . ."

Jay abruptly smirked and held up his left hand with the ring in his palm. "I had it the whole time," he revealed. "I just wanted to see how you'd react."

Simon shook his head and moved to the curtain. He peeped out and realized they had missed their cue. "Come on," he urgently whispered to Jay, and together they moved out and stood to the left of the minister, their backs to the pews.

Reverend Treece smiled and continued with the ceremony, thanking everyone for attending and discoursing on the joys and responsibilities of matrimony.

Simon was nervous, the sweat running down his legs and arms. He thought of Amy, waiting outside the front doors for the wedding march, her cue to enter the church.

Before long, Reverend Treece reached the appropriate juncture in the proceedings and nodded toward the organist. As the music filled the church, all eyes focused on the massive wooden doors.

Seconds passed, but the doors didn't open as anticipated.

"What's holding them up?" Jay whispered to Simon.

In addition to Amy, her mother and father and three bridesmaids were to have filed inside on hearing the first notes from the organ.

A few of the guests were muttering among themselves.

"What's holding them up?" Jay repeated.

Simon shrugged.

"Want me to go see what the holdup is?" Jay asked.

Simon was about to say yes, when he saw Lanning stand up near the rear of the pews. Lanning pointed at his own chest, then at the doors. Simon nodded.

"I hope it's nothing serious," Reverend Treece casually commented.

Lanning was almost to the front doors when a piercing scream erupted from outside.

25

Everyone was working late at the Centers for Disease Control.

Buddy couldn't recall ever seeing so many employees on the premises at one time, and he speculated on whether the higher-ups had imported some additional help from other agencies. He spotted Tom Kramer approaching from the other end of the crowded hallway.

"Glad you could make it in on such short notice," Kramer said as he neared Buddy.

"No sweat," Buddy replied. "The doc cleared me to come in tomorrow morning, anyway. So what if I'm a bit early. I haven't worked a swing shift in quite a while," he noted.

They shook hands.

"You may be here all night," Kramer stated. "Follow me."

They retraced Kramer's path until they reached his office. Once they were inside, Kramer closed the door. "Have a seat," he directed.

Buddy sank into a comfortable leather chair in front of Kramer's desk. He noticed a projector on the desk top, and lined up along the wall was a portable screen on a tripod.

Kramer closed the door, then moved around the desk and collapsed in his swivel chair. His features appeared drawn and haggard; there were bags under his brown eyes, his dark brown hair was uncharacteristically disheveled, and the lines in his face seemed deeper. Even his beige suit was rumpled. "Thank you for coming in," he said.

"When you called at one you sounded so somber. How could I refuse? I got here at quick as I could."

Kramer wearily rubbed his eyes. "Was Gladys upset about you working an afternoon shift instead of your usual day?"

"Not at all. I suspect she was delighted to get me out of the house so she could watch her soaps in peace," Buddy replied.

"And you're positive you're better?"

"It finally tapered off late last night. I'm a bit weak, but otherwise I'm fine. At least I've stopped running to the john every two minutes." Buddy smiled, but Kramer didn't appear to see the humor.

"Okay. Glad to hear it," Kramer stated. "Enough small talk. Do you have any idea what's been going on?"

"I've followed the news closely," Buddy said as Kramer adjusted the reels on the projector. "No contact with Egypt for two days. Israel has closed her borders. Massive violence in the Middle East. Martial law declared in Athens, Rome, Bonn. Paris has been closed down. New York City is encircled by the military, and the President is going to give a speech to the nation this evening. I think that about sums it up."

Kramer glanced up from the projector. "You're not even close. Any idea why all of this is happening?"

"I'd put my money on a plague," Buddy answered.

Kramer nodded. "We have experts in every field here, from all over the country, all over the world."

He stared into Buddy's eyes. "There hasn't been anything like this that we know of in the course of human history."

"Like what?"

Kramer stood and walked to the light switch. "You'll see in just a moment. Brace yourself. After we're through here, take your brilliant and devious mind to your desk. You'll find all the files and relevant data you need to get started, all the technical information we have on this thing, which isn't much. All divisions are working on this one, exclusively, until further notice. Everything else has been placed on the back burner until we solve this baby or . . . it wipes us out."

Buddy glanced at Kramer as he stepped to the projector and activated the machine.

An image formed on the screen.

Buddy gaped, aghast, at the sight before him.

"This is from Egypt," Kramer divulged.

A ragged line of troops were retreating toward the camera, struggling to maintain formation as they were attacked again and again. There were buildings all around, and the conflict was taking place in a large square. A chorus of howls filled the air.

"Where was this?" Buddy asked, leaning forward for a better view.

"Cairo," Kramer replied.

Buddy suppressed an impulse to pinch himself to ascertain if he were dreaming.

The troopers were firing at their adversaries as rapidly as they could, to no avail. Their foes poured over them, darting out from darkened alleys or pouncing from walls and windows, in a surging tide of ferocity. One of the attackers came bounding toward the camera, howling at the top of his lungs.

Kramer pressed a button on the projector, freezing the frame in place. "Take a good look," he advised.

Buddy rose and walked closer to the screen, his

eyes widening in disbelief.

The thing was a man, or had once been a man, although it was loping on all fours instead of walking upright. Its clothes were gone, its body coated with cuts and bruises. All of these aspects were shocking, but the most disturbing feature was its face.

The face was a livid mask of bestial flury, contorted almost beyond human recognition. The skin was flushed, the eyes distended and crazed, the teeth exposed in a feral snarl, and there was a foamy white ring around the mouth, coating the lips.

Buddy sat down in his chair, shaking his head. "I never expected this," he remarked.

"Keep watching," Kramer said. He set the reels in motion again.

The troopers broke and fled. Those caught by the charging horde were pulled to the ground and literally ripped apart. One of the creatures took hold of a trooper's throat, gripping the flesh with its teeth and savagely tearing the neck open.

A few seconds later the screen went blank.

"The cameraman had to take off to save his own skin," Kramer explained. "There's more."

This time it was Paris. Buddy recognized the Arc de Triomphe in the background. French police were frantically battling dozens of the things. The police outnumbered their opponents and were winning, but at a frightful price.

The scene shifted again.

"This is New York City," Kramer said.

About a dozen creatures were at one end of an alley, trapped because the alley was a dead end with walls too high for them to scale. Advancing down the alley, automatic rifles at the ready, were soldiers who fanned out and waited.

They didn't wait long.

The things came on a run, directly at the soldiers, howling like banshees. A hail of automatic rifle fire plowed into them, stopping them dead, their bodies twitching and jerking as they were struck again and again.

The screen became white again.

"I had no idea," Buddy mumbled, dazed.

"Hang in there," Kramer urged. "There's one more segment."

The setting was a laboratory. One of the things was enclosed in a metal cage, restrained behind sturdy bars. Three scientists, all wearing white smocks, stood outside the cage. One of the scientists, a young slim woman, held out a plate of raw steak. She moved closer to the bars.

"Here, boy," she said in a high, tense tone. "Here, try this."

The thing was squatting in the middle of the cage, growling.

"Nice boy. Try this." The scientist reached the bars and touched them with the plate.

The thing was on her before she could react.

Snarling, it bounded to the bars, its right hand flicking out and grabbing the woman by her wrist. She shrieked and attempted to pull away, but the thing was much stronger. It yanked her arm, forcing her to drop the plate, then pulled her arm between the bars. Before the other two scientists could stop it, the thing buried its teeth in her wrist. Blood sprayed everywhere.

Kramer turned off the projector, then switched on the lights. As he turned to his desk, he noticed a pallid tint to Buddy's complexion. "It got to me the first time, too," he said, commiserating.

"I wouldn't want to see that a second time," Buddy said slowly, striving to compose his emotions.

"We have our work cut out for us," Kramer admitted pensively.

"Where did it originate?" Buddy asked. "How did it spread? Is it a bacteria or a virus?"

"The information is in the files on your desk," Kramer reiterated, "but I have a few spare minutes, so I'll encapsulate some of the crucial details." Kramer paused. "We don't know what it is yet. If we can pinpoint whether it's a bacteria or a virus, it would be an important first step. The damn thing has been incredibly elusive. We've seen the results of its handiwork in the Canines—"

"Canines?" Buddy interrupted.

"One of the lab boys coined the term, and that's what everyone here is calling them," Kramer elaborated. "Offically, we've assigned identification code number C-666 to the disease."

"C-666," Buddy dutifully repeated.

"As far as the medium of contagion is concerned," Kramer continued, "we don't know that, either. We suspect simple respiratory spread, but it hasn't been confirmed. For all we know, it could be close contact or through the water or food. We have eliminated insect transmission as a possibility."

"Do we know where it originated?"

Kramer nodded. "We are ninety percent certain on that, at least. Egypt reported it first, and we believe the entire country was overrun in a seven day span."

"The entire country in a week? It spreads that fast?"

"We're still in the process of timing the symptoms," Kramer stated. "They seem to be variable." He sighed. "And we do have a major problem in this respect."

"Which is?"

Kramer jerked his right thumb in the direction of the screen. "Those three researchers you just saw . . ."

"What about them?"

"Within forty-eight hours of beginning their work with the Canine, they became Canines themselves. One of them transformed within twenty-four hours."

"Dear God!" Buddy exclaimed.

"We've captured some of them," Kramer said. "Unfortunately, every single time we've initiated a laboratory study, those conducting it became infected. It has us stymied."

"How was it spread from Egypt?" Buddy thought to ask.

Kramer sat back in his chair. "That's the only concrete information we have. Early on, we detected a pattern. There were scattered reports from some of the major cities in Europe. Athens, Rome, Bonn, Paris and the like. Next it showed up at JFK, and from there spread into New York City. We've also had reports from Chicago, Denver, and San Francisco."

"I knew it," Buddy interjected. "It's what I've always dreaded. An infected carrier of a disease hopping from country to country aboard the airlines."

"Exactly," Kramer confirmed. "We ran a computer check on all the passengers on all the airlines flying out of Egypt back to the first of the month. We discovered one man who left Egypt and then visited all the cities where infection was later reported. His name was Philippe Talon. According to the authorities, he was a dealer in rare artifacts, and he evidently conducted most of his business in the black market. He flew from Cairo to Athens, then to Rome, Bonn, and Paris, making one of his monthly swings through Europe to obtain items and cultivate his contacts. His home was in Paris."

"I've noticed you're using the past tense," Buddy commented.

"Talon was one of the first victims of the plague outside of Egypt, and he transmitted the disease to all of those cities before he himself contracted it in Paris."

"So how did it get to America?"

"Through one of Talon's business associates, a man named Quincy Pritchett. Pritchett met Talon in

Paris for only a few hours on the day before Talon developed the symptoms. Afterward, Pritchett returned to the States, stopping at JFK to meet a crony, then traveled on to Chicago, Denver, and San Francisco. That's where he transformed, as we call it. The F.B.I. determined that Pritchett was Talon's American distributor for the illegal treasures Talon purchased in Europe and the Middle East."

"So we do know a little bit," Buddy said encouragingly.

"Big deal!" Kramer said angrily. "It hasn't helped us at all. Talon and Pritchett are both dead. We're still awaiting an autopsy report on a Canine." He sadly shook his head. "We're running out of time, Buddy."

"Have we performed a computer projection?" Buddy asked.

Kramer nodded.

"What did it tell us?"

Kramer locked his eyes on Buddy's. "The computers calculated an approximate rate of transmission, based on what we've seen in Egypt and the European cities and what meager data we have on the disease."

"And?" Buddy prompted him.

"And if we haven't produced an antidote within six to seven weeks," Kramer gravely intoned, "there won't be enough left of the United States worth saving."

Buddy glanced at the blank screen and shuddered.

PART III

EPIDEMIC

26

James Lanning ran to the front doors of the church, threw them open, and reached the first concrete step outside of the building before he paused, momentarily shocked by the sight below him.

Amy Brant, her father, Frederick, and her mother, Louise, along with the rest of the bridal party, were standing on the steps below him. All except for one of the bridesmaids. She was lying on the bottom step, her beautiful gown splattered with blood, her neck torn open. Crouched on top of her body was a man. At least, he somewhat resembled a man. He was stark naked, his chin and chest coated with crimson. His face was drawn back in a hideous snarl, and a ragged chunk of flesh was hanging from his mouth.

Lanning had been scrupulously trained to control his emotions, to function rationally even when confronted by extreme adversity. His reflexes and instincts were honed to a fine edge. So although he was stunned by what he saw, he consciously repressed his loathing and astonishment and reacted automatically.

As the thing growled and bounded up the steps toward Amy Brant, Lanning moved to intercept it. He covered three steps at a leap, reaching Amy's side just as the creature launched himself through the air.

"Move!" Lanning shouted as he shoved Amy to one side.

The thing attempted to twist in midair, going for Lanning, but it missed and landed on all fours on the steps between Lanning and Amy.

Lanning didn't give it a chance. He had no idea where this thing came from, but he wasn't about to let it do to him what it had done to the poor bridesmaid. He drew back his right foot and brutally kicked it in the neck.

The crazed thing lurched away from Lanning, gasping and gurgling, scrambling to recover its equilibrium.

Lanning followed it, kicking once, twice, three more times, each blow planted on the chin, staggering the thing, and finally dropping it to the concrete, barely conscious, drooling blood and spittle from its frothing lips.

Amy Brant raced down the steps. "Sue! Sue!" She reached the side of the bridesmaid and knelt beside her friend.

Lanning kicked once more to insure unconsciousness, and then ran down the steps to check on the bridesmaid.

Amy was shaking her head in disbelief, tears flowing from the corners of her eyes. "God, please let her be alright! Please!" she wailed.

Lanning gripped the bridesmaid's wrist and felt for a pulse.

There wasn't one.

Amy grabbed Lanning's shoulder. "Is she alive?"

Lanning looked at her and sadly shook his head.

Amy rose unsteadily and put a hand to her forehead. "I feel faint."

Lanning caught her before she could topple to the cement. He glanced up at the front doors and saw Simon and Jay Darr emerge from the church. They hesitated, surveying the scene. Simon came down the steps and took Amy from Lanning's arms.

"What the hell happened?" Simon demanded, staring in horror at the bridesmaid.

"Beats me," Lanning replied. He scanned the steps.

Frederick Brant was holding Louise in his arms, comforting her. The two remaining bridesmaids were paralyzed, gaping in raw fear at their dead companion. Reverend Treece and many of the guests appeared in the doorway. Jay Darr was kneeling next to the unconscious attacker, examining him. A young woman Lanning didn't know detached herself from the crowd at the church entrance and hurried to Jay Darr. Lanning had seen her with Jay earlier; undoubtedly, she was his date or possibly his steady girlfriend.

Simon gently shook Amy, trying to revive her. "Amy," are you all right?"

"Carry her inside and get some water," Lanning suggested.

Simon nodded. He lifted Amy and started up the steps.

Lanning searched the street for any sign of a police officer or a cruiser. There were a dozen or so bystanders nearby, gawking, and a few cars and trucks passed on Diversey, the drivers slowing to observe the spectacle. But there was no sign of the law.

"Look!" one of the female guests suddenly shouted.

Lanning glanced up and saw her pointing down the street to their left. He turned.

Another naked man was squatting on the sidewalk in front of an alley about a block away from the church.

Even as Lanning watched, the man howled and charged a pedestrian, bowling the woman over and sinking his teeth into her neck.

Lanning was about to run to the woman's rescue, when yet a third nude man, howling like crazy, bounded from the alley and joined the second.

What the hell was going on?

Had the whole world gone mad?

Lanning whirled, his stomach muscles tightening, sensing that something was dreadfully, dangerously wrong. He ran up the steps to Jay Darr's side. "We've got to get these people into the church," he urged.

Jay Darr was holding the black-haired woman close, staring at the pedestrians being assaulted. "We should help them," he said, nodding toward the people on the street below. Many of them were running and screaming, fleeing from the pair of lethal killers.

"The cops will probably be here any second," Lanning said. "We've got to get these people in the church and lock the doors. If there's three of these . . . things, there may be more."

Jay looked at Lanning, then at the form at their feet. "You're right." He glanced at the woman he was holding. "Marcy, get all of them inside the church. Hurry!"

Marcy nodded and ran up the steps.

"Did you see this?" Jay asked, crouching.

"See what?" Lanning stooped alongside him.

"Look at his mouth. What's all that white stuff?"

Lanning studied the lips. A bubbly, chalky froth was intermixed with blood from the bridesmaid's throat. "I don't know what it is," he admitted.

"Don't you get that gunk on your lips when you have rabies?" Jay asked.

"I think so," Lanning replied, "but I'm no medical expert. I doubt this bozo had rabies, though."

"Why?"

Lanning pointed at the two seemingly insane men on the avenue below, still attacking pedestrians at random. "Last I heard, rabies was extremely rare in this country. What have we got here, a rabies epidemic? Besides, I don't recall that running around on your hands and feet and howling like a wolf are symptoms of rabies."

In the distance, coming from the west, came the piercing wail of a police siren.

The pair of madmen, now about a block and a half west of the church, also heard the siren. They were straddling a hapless elderly woman, tearing into her soft neck and biting at her face, when they raised their heads, listening. The next instant, they were loping along the sidewalk, heading away from the oncoming siren. They reached the alley from which they'd appeared and vanished into its recesses.

Not three seconds later, the police car roared up Diversey and slammed to a screeching stop, the driver angling the vehicle abreast of the curb and the elderly woman on the sidewalk. Two officers leapt from the cruiser and knelt next to her.

"They'll catch those bastards," Jay said confidently.

"I hope so," Lanning stated hopefully.

Four other victims were sprawled on the ground between the officers and the mouth of the alley. The two officers went from one victim to another, checking their vital signs. They reached the victim nearest the alley and crouched alongside her.

Lanning cupped his hands around his mouth, about to shout a warning to the police officers, alerting them to the proximity of the alley and its occupants.

He was too late.

Howling and snarling, the pair of lunatics erupted from the mouth of the alley, attacking the police officers. The madmen were onto their prey before the officers could draw their service revolvers.

"Damn!" Lanning exclaimed, and bounded down the concrete steps. "We've got to help them!" he shouted over his right shoulder to Jay Darr.

Jay managed only three steps when he heard a gutteral growl behind him and spun.

The bridesmaids's killer had recovered! It was on its hands and knees, its lips curled back to expose its teeth, its wild, bloodshot eyes locked on the man below.

Jay instinctively adopted the Hanging Horse stance, calming his nerves, waiting for the madman to make the first move.

He didn't have long to wait.

The maniac hissed and sprang, his fingers rigid and claw-like, going for his prey's throat.

Jay dodged aside and whirled, bringing his right hand up and around in a Tiger Claw strike, catching the creature on the back of the head before it had landed, and brutally slamming its head into the concrete steps.

There was a loud snapping retort, and the madman crumpled as he struck the concrete, doubling over and flopping down the steps until the body came to rest on the sidewalk below.

Jay started down the steps and caught sight of Lanning at least 20 yards off, running toward the desperate policeman.

"Lanning, wait for me!" Jay shouted, wondering if Lanning could hear him over the traffic on Diversey, the screaming pedestrians, and the howling from the creatures.

Lanning couldn't.

Under the impression that Jay Darr was right on his heels, Lanning darted across Diversey and bore down on the struggling officers. One of them was already out of commission, lying in a pool of blood but vainly endeavoring to regain his footing and aid his partner. The two madmen were concentrating their assault on the lone officer, trying to overwhelm him by sheer force. He was a big, brawny cop, and he was holding his own, but just barely. His massive fists would knock one of his attackers aside, but no sooner was one of them thwarted in its attempt to reach the officer's throat, than the second one would pounce. The officer's revolver was lying next to the curb; he had tried to bring it into play, but one of the creatures had clamped its teeth on his wrist and savagely wrenched his arm, causing the revolver to fly from his grasp.

Lanning closed on the battling threesome. He spotted the service revolver and made for the gun, hoping he could reach it before the officer was killed.

Lanning dove the final yard, scraping his elbows and knees on the cement. He scooped up the service revolver and rose to his knees, leveling the gun at the nearest madman. "Hey! Ugly!"

The creatures, intent on slashing and ripping the policeman, turned, their features bestial, contorted beyond belief. One of them howled and charged.

Lanning let the thing have one in the head, the service revolver bucking in his grip, the blast of the shot deafening his ears.

The thing was caught in the forehead, a small hole appearing in the very center. The back of the head blow out in a spray of flesh, blood, and brain, as it was smashed to the ground by the impact of the slug.

Lanning twisted slightly, aiming at the second one, who came on in a rush, growling and foaming at the mouth.

Lanning hurried his shot.

The thing was struck in the right eye. Its head snapped to the right, and it plowed into the sidewalk not a foot from where Lanning knelt.

Lanning stood slowly, the revolver extended, prepared in case they weren't really dead. He walked from one to the other, turning them over with the toe of his right shoe, confirming they were indeed lifeless. Satisfied, he stepped towards the big police officer to ascertain his condition.

Footsteps pounded on the sidewalk behind him.

Lanning twirled, the service revolver sweeping around, his finger tightening on the trigger, fearing another of the damn things had burst from the alley.

Instead, it was Jay Darr.

Lanning instantly raised the revolver barrel upward and relaxed his trigger finger. "You idiot!" he said angrily. "I almost blew you away!"

"Sorry," Jay apologized. "I was detained."

"Detained?"

"Yeah. The one you knocked out woke up."

Lanning glanced toward the church and saw the madman sprawled once again on the sidewalk. "What happened?"

"I put it out of its misery," Jay answered, and knelt alongside the big cop.

The officer was alive, but his neck was covered in torn flesh and blood. He was gasping for air. His left hand came up and took hold of Jay's jacket. "Did . . . did . . . you get 'em?" he managed to ask, his words almost unintelligible, his throat making horrid sucking sounds as he spoke.

Jay nodded. "We got them."

The big officer smiled. His eyes closed; he shuddered for several seconds, and then lay still.

Lanning walked to the second officer and examined him. "This one has bought the farm, too," he informed Jay.

Jay rose, staring at the dead creatures. "This is insane. What's happening here? I don't understand any of this. Where did these freaks come from?"

Lanning sighed and shook his head. "Your guess is as good as mine. Maybe better."

"Do you think there are any more of them?"

From several blocks off, wafting on the humid, gusting wind, came an eerie, protracted howl.

Lanning listened closely. He could hear more howling, the dreadful baying seeming to be far, far away and arising from several directions at once. Interspersed with the macabre howling was the wailing of sirens.

"Do you hear that?" Jay asked in a shocked whisper.

"I hear it," Lanning affirmed.

Jay looked at Lanning. "What do we do?"

Lanning bent over the officer at his feet and began stripping off the cartridge belt and the holster from the body. "Get the big cop's belt," he directed.

Jay hesitated. "Are you sure it's legal?"

Lanning glanced at Jay, then nodded at the dead things. "Are you serious?"

Jay knelt and removed the big officer's belt.

"Here. Take this." Lanning handed Jay the big cop's gun. "Make sure you reload it."

While Jay reloaded the revolver, Lanning strapped on the other officer's cartridge belt, drew the gun from its leather holster, and made sure it was loaded. "All set," he declared. "Let's get back to the church."

"Shouldn't we wait for other police to arrive?"

Lanning stared down Diversey. Traffic was sparse in both directions, and very few pedestrians remained in the immediate vicinity. "It may be a while before a backup gets here," he replied.

Jay gazed at the nearby alley. "Maybe we should take a look in there and see if there are any more of them."

Lanning snorted derisively. "What was the name of your lady friend?"

Jay was surprised by the question. "You mean Marcy?"

"Yep." Lanning replaced his revolver in its holster. "Do you think it's very smart to leave her alone at a time like this?"

Jay looked at the nearest dead thing, then at the church. "Let's go."

They ran across Diversey and up to the church steps.

"What the hell do they think they're doing?" Lanning demanded.

The wedding guests were flocking from the church and hurrying to their vehicles, parked in a lot to the east of the building.

"They probably want to get home," Jay responded.

"They'd be safer in the church," Lanning said. "Come on!" He led the way up the steps to the church doors.

The press of people exiting the building forced Lanning and Jay to wait several minutes until the entrance cleared.

"Are you going to stay in the church or go home?" Jay asked Lanning while they waited.

Lanning thoughtfully chewed his lower lip. "I get the impression this city is crawling with those things, and my mother's house would afford pitiful protection. I might try and talk her into staying here until we find out what's going on."

"The Brant house is a sturdy brick structure," Jay said, "and I saw a display case containing a lot of rifles in their game room. If we decide to head there, why don't you and your mother come along? There's safety in numbers," he noted.

"I'll talk it over with my mother," Lanning promised.

The entranceway was clear of guests.

Lanning and Jay entered the church, Lanning moving toward his mother who was waiting for him to the right of the doors.

Jay hurried to the front of the church.

The wedding party was gathered near the altar where Simon, Amy, Frederick and Louise were engaged in conversation. Several yards away, the parents of the deceased bridesmaid were being comforted by Reverend Treece, the other bridesmaids, and a half-dozen other guests.

Jay joined the Brants and Simon.

"We heard shooting," Simon said as his brother reached them.

"Lanning killed two more of whatever they are," Jay said. He felt someone touch his left elbow and nervously spun.

Marcy was at his side.

"Calm down, lover," she urged him. "It's just me."

Jay placed his right arm around her waist. "Don't leave me, not even for an instant. We're not out of the woods yet."

"What do you mean?" Louise Brant inquired. Her emotional strain was showing in her wide eyes and perspiring brow.

"Lanning and I heard more of them out there," Jay divulged. "Lots more."

"Dear God!" Louise exclaimed.

Frederick Brant embraced his terrified wife. "Don't worry, honey. The police will take care of them."

"Maybe they will," Jay interjected, "and maybe they won't. The important thing for us to decide is what we'll do next. Do we stay here, or should we try and reach your house?"

Amy Brant, sniffling, cleared her throat. "What do you think we should do?"

"Your house is smaller than this church," Jay answered. "It would be easier to defend if a bunch of those things should come after us." He faced Frederick Brant. "And didn't I see some rifles at your house?"

Frederick nodded. "I was quite the hunter in my youth."

"Have any ammunition for those rifles?" Jay asked.

"Plenty," Frederick assured him.

"Then I vote we go to your place," Jay stated.

"We'll load the rifles, lock the doors and windows, and ride this out. If there really are a lot more of those things, and if the police can't handle them, the government will probably call in the National Guard or the regular Army. We should be able to hear something on the news."

"Do you think any of this is connected with what's going on in New York City?" Simon speculated.

"We may find out when the President gives his address," Amy said.

"Then it's settled," Jay stated. "We make for the Brant house and pray we get there."

Simon pointed at the gun belt around Jay's waist. "Where did you get that?"

Jay patted the revolver. "Lanning and I both got one." He paused. "Speaking of Lanning, it might be a good idea if he came with us."

"Lanning? Isn't he the Interpol agent Simon was telling us about?" Frederick asked.

"He's the one," Jay confirmed. "We all heard about what he did to those terrorists on Simon's flight, and I just saw him in action outside. We need him."

"Then it goes without saying that he comes along," Frederick said.

"I'll tell him," Jay said, and walked off with Marcy.

Simon drew Amy to one side. "Listen. I know you were looking forward to a big church wedding—"

"My parents wanted one more than I did," Amy cut in.

"I suspected as much," Simon stated. "But as things stand now, we're not going to have any wedding at all unless we take matters into our own hands."

"What do you have in mind?" Amy asked him.

"Why don't we have Reverend Treece marry us right this instant? Nothing fancy. A quick ceremony and we're out of here. What do you say?"

Amy pressed against Simon and kissed him on the cheek. "I think it's a great idea."

From somewhere outside of the church, perhaps a block or two away, came another lingering howl.

"Dear Lord!" Amy exclaimed. "They must be all over the place."

"So we don't have any time to lose," Simon declared. He grabbed her right hand and led her over to Reverend Treece. "Excuse me, Reverend."

The minister, in the act of consoling the parents of the murdered bridesmaid, turned. "Yes, Simon? What is it?"

"Amy and I want you to marry us right now," Simon informed him.

"Now? Why not wait until everything calms down?" Reverend Treece proposed. "Then we can have a formal ceremony, exactly as you planned."

"We want it done now," Amy said. "Who knows how long it might be before things calm down?"

"Did I hear correctly?" inquired someone behind them, and Amy's father appeared on her left. "You two want to be married now?"

Amy glanced up at her dad. "That's right. Immediately."

"What's the hurry?" Frederick asked, his tone patronizing. "Your mother and I went to considerable expense to have a proper wedding. We won't mind postponing it for a week or two. Your mother has always dreamed of having her little girl married in fine style. She wants you to have a wedding you'll never forget."

"I won't forget this one, ever," Amy declared.

Frederick smiled and put his hand on her shoulder. "But it would be so much better if you waited," he prompted her.

"I'm not waiting," Amy stubbornly said.

"Not even for us, your own parents?" Frederick

inquired in a low, hurt voice.

"I'm not waiting," Amy obstinately reiterated.

Frederick Brant frowned and sighed. "Very well. If you insist. But I want you to know I think you're making a blunder, one you will regret in the years to come. A wedding should be a supremely special event, a memory you will cherish forever."

"You are positive you want to go through with this?" Reverend Treece asked.

"We're positive," Amy replied.

Simon simply nodded.

Reverend Treece grinned. "As you wish. At least the day won't be a total loss."

"Tell that to Sue," Amy said bitterly, as she and Simon held hands and prepared to become man and wife.

27

It was almost time for the President's nationwide address, and Kramer had instructed him to listen to the speech.

Buddy leaned back in his chair and rubbed his eyes.

What would the President say? The nation had to be told; the government couldn't hide the facts any longer. How would the residents of the infected cities take the news? What steps would the government take to contain the spread of C-666? A quarantine might be effective, but if it failed, if the epidemic continued, what other options were viable short of a complete cure?

The Centers for Disease Control and every other comparable facility in the entire country were working feverishly on the problem. As Kramer had noted though, useful information, hard data they could utilize to combat the plague and counter the rate of infection, was singularly lacking.

The scientists believed the plague began in Egypt.

They had identified Talon and Pritchett as the primary international carriers.

Laboratory studies of victims of C-666 were thwarted at every turn, because all of the researchers monitoring the victims became victims themselves, one of the researchers transforming within 24 hours.

The implications were staggering.

Buddy could readily envision a typical scenario.

Pritchett lands at a major airport and then hails a taxi or rents a car to visit all of his contacts or customers. How many people would Pritchett breathe on or touch during the course of his visit? Dozens? Hundreds? If the disease were transmitted through respiratory spread or physical contact, even an act as casual as a handshake or merely breathing on another person would be sufficient to spread C-666.

The rate of transmission would be incredible.

Buddy idly toyed with some theoretical numbers.

Let's say, he told himself, that Pritchett landed at JFK. Suppose Pritchett touched or breathed on 25 people during the course of his brief visit to New York City, which would be a very conservative estimate.

Now 25 people have C-666, and for the next 24 hours, or whenever they transform, they walk around, going about their daily activities, touching or breathing on another 25 people themselves.

What would happen?

After only 24 hours, 625 people would be carrying the disease.

After 48 hours, 15,625 would have C-666.

And after 72 hours, 390,625 would be infected.

By the end of four days, over 9,700,000 would be affected!

It was no wonder Egypt had fallen in a week.

Buddy recognized his computations were subject to several important variables.

Some of the victims did not transform within 24 hours but took as long as 48, which might slow the rate of transmission somewhat.

Some people might not come in contact with 25 people daily. For others, the figure might even be higher.

And some persons might have a natural resistance to C-666 or possibly be immune. In every epidemic, whether a major disease or a minor one, like the common flu, there were always individuals whose bodies effectually opposed the invasion of their organism. How they did so was often a mystery, but they did it.

Buddy began nervously chewing on his fingernails, as was his habit when under severe stress.

He decided he wouldn't want to be one of those people resistant to C-666.

Could you imagine being the only normal person remaining in a city of ravenous Canines?

28

"He's coming on!" Amy called out excitedly for the benefit of the rest of the people gathered in the Brant living room. Simon sat beside her on the floor in front of the television set. Frederick Brant was seated in his favorite chair with Louise a few feet away in her chair. Jay and Marcy were on the sofa, while James Lanning and his mother, Gloria, were nearby, Gloria in an arm chair, Lanning on the floor.

The trip home from the church had been surprisingly uneventful. They had stuck to the major thoroughfares, avoiding all alleys and back streets where feasible. Reverend Treece had volunteered to wait outside the church for the police to arrive. He had been standing near the dead bridesmaid when they left the parking lot, and he smiled and waved as they departed. The pedestrian and vehicular traffic they passed seemed normal, although lighter than usual. The Brants and Darrs rode in the Brant limousine, while Lanning and Gloria followed in Gloria's sedan. Occasionally, they would hear howling from different areas of the city, and once three police cruisers raced past, sirens wailing and lights flashing.

Now, with the doors bolted and the windows locked, they awaited the Presidential address.

"He looks terrible," Louise commented as the image of the Chief Executive filled the screen.

"My fellow Americans, good evening. It is with a heavy heart that I speak to you tonight," the President began. "Our nation is faced with the gravest crisis in its entire history." He hesitated, his expression downcast. "Up until an hour ago, I was uncertain of what I would say tonight, of how I could convince my fellow citizens of the gravity of the situation. To those already familiar with the facts, no explanation is necessary, but for those living outside of the affected zones, mere words wouldn't be enough. So, you are about to see a short film taken yesterday in New York City. The film will convey, much more eloquently than I ever could, the horror upon us."

The screen went dark for only a second, and then the film came on.

Louise clasped her hands together. "Oh, God, no!"

"It must be the whole damn country," Simon muttered.

The screen showed dozens of the slobbering monstrosities fighting a pitched battle with police and soldiers. The death toll on both sides was enormous. As fast as the police and soldiers would decimate a charging line of feral opponents, another group of attackers would pour from between the buildings to take their place. The gore and bloodshed was appalling.

"Why don't they turn it off?" Louise asked in a frightened tone.

"I guess they're trying to make a point," Simon said.

"What point?" Louise wanted to know.

Simon glanced at Amy's mother. "They're trying to show the folks who haven't seen one of those things how deadly they are, how serious the threat must be or the President wouldn't be making a national address about it."

The film finally ended and was replaced by an obviously worried President. "My friends, the tape you just saw, no matter how shocking it may have been, does not do justice to our plight. I will tell you what has happened and what we are doing about it." He paused. "America is in the grip of a devastating plague."

"Plague? Did he say plague?" Gloria asked.

"This plague is unlike any seen before. It takes perfectly ordinary human beings and changes them, transforms them into what you saw on your screen a moment ago. The plague is spreading very rapidly. Very rapidly indeed. The threat it poses to our national security has prompted us to take extraordinary measures to try and halt its spread. First, the Centers for Disease control, headquartered in Atlanta, is overseeing our scientific efforts to find the cause of the disease and to develop a cure, but I must be honest with you. We do not know what causes the disease, what makes people change into Canines, as they are called."

"DId he say Canines?" Louise asked.

"I will not deceive you," the President was saying. "We are experiencing difficulty isolating the cause and finding a cure. Until we do, and to prevent this plague from destroying our country, I have ordered the following measures implemented:

One. The United States of America will be under martial law until further notice.

Two. Our military forces and the police are empowered to shoot to kill a Canine on sight, without regard to due process of law.

Three. In an effort to contain the spread of this disease, all Affected Zones are placed under immediate quarantine. No one will be permitted to enter or leave these Affected Zones unless on official business. Anyone caught doing so will be shot on sight.

Four. We have learned from our mistakes. Imposing martial law in New York City was not enough to stop the Canines. Consequently, after much deliberation, we have decided to isolate Infected Cities completely, to encircle them with troops and shoot anyone attempting to leave or enter. I repeat. No one, not even the administrative personnel or the police, *no one* will be allowed to leave Infected Cities."

The President stepped to one side and a large wall map appeared to his left. The President picked up a pointer and moved closer to the map.

"It's a map of the U.S.," Louise said.

Facing the camera, the President tapped the wall map with his pointer. "The majority of plague cases have been reported from metropolitan centers, although we have received word of isolated cases from some rural areas. Do you see these blue zones?"

There were about a dozen areas shaded in light blue, and nearly all of them were adjacent to large cities.

"These blue zones are the Affected Zones I was telling you about. The military will establish roadblocks leading in and out of an Affected Zone. All traffic will be stopped and turned back. Aerial surveillance will be constantly maintained around an Affected Zone. Let me make one thing clear. Just because we have designated an area as an Affected Zone, doesn't necessarily mean Canines have been sighted in that area. It means there is a very high probability of the plague spreading to these areas, and we want to contain it before it gets a foothold. Allow me to show you an example."

"I don't understand any of this," Louise commented.

The President tapped the west coast with his pointer. "Do you see this red dot? This red dot is an

Infected City, San Francisco. Do you see the blue area around San Francisco? It's the Affected Zone. It extends from Santa Rosa in the north, to Sacramento in the east, and San Jose in the south. The people within this blue area, this Affected Zone, will not be permitted to leave, but they will be allowed to travel within the confines of the Affected Zone.'' The President frowned and stared at the camera. ''The red dots on the map are all Infected Cities, and until further notice are placed under complete isolation. A security perimeter has been established around each one. If you live in one of these cities, you must not attempt to leave. You will be shot on sight. We have no other recourse.'' He sighed. ''The Infected Cities are San Francisco, Denver, and New York City.'' He hesitated and glanced at the map. ''Oh . . . and there's one more I missed.'' He tapped the middle of the map, near the Great Lakes.

''Please, no!'' Louise suddenly cried.

''The other city,'' the President went on, ''is Chicago.''

29

Buddy was back at his desk after viewing the President's address in Kramer's office. He thought the Chief Executive had done a superb job, given his subject and the limitations of their knowledge concerning the plague. The President had been honest and succinct; his sincerity and understatement should have been enough to deter a mass panic—for a while. The big test would come around one of the Infected Cities when the Canines outnumbered the uninfected populace who then tried to escape the city any way they could.

Buddy picked up the new red file on top of his pile and opened it. Someone must have deposited it while he was watching the President. The title caught his attention—The Quintin Report. Quintin had been the name of one of the scientists seen in the film with the caged Canine. He had transformed into a Canine 48 hours after first coming in contact with it. The thing had been caught in New York City and rushed to the Sanderson Research Center at Southampton, where Quintin worked. This Canine was one of the initial ones sighted, and one of the very few taken alive.

There were only two pages in the report.

One of them contained a synopsis of Quintin's

medical examination, conducted after the Canine was sedated by a massive tranquilizer doze.

Buddy skimmed the page, noting the pertinent details.

The Canine had a constant elevated body temperature of 110.8 degrees.

Both eyes were distended. Every part of the eye was enlarged—the cornea, the pupil, the iris, lens, choroid, retina, sclera, even the optic nerve.

A peculiar rigidity was discovered in several of the major muscles. This rigidity was noticed during the autopsy on the Canine. After it bit the woman holding the plate of raw meat, a security guard had shot it. The stiffness had not been severe enough to impair movement.

Some of the endocrine glands were found to be swollen, and all three sets of salivary glands were engorged.

The big surprise came when the coroner and his crew sawed into the cranial cavity to inspect the Canine's brain. All three layers of membranes enveloping the brain were inflamed. The inflammation was similar to that caused by meningitis. Some sections of the brain were discolored, evidently under attack from a bacteria or virus. The cerebrum was especially affected, and portions of the cortex had actually shriveled. The cerebellum was infected, as were some of the cranial nerves.

Buddy lowered the report.

Now they had some inkling of the specific areas affected by the disease, but they still didn't know whether it was a virus or a bacteria causing all of the damage.

Some of the Canine behavior began to add up, though.

With a constant body temperature of nearly 111, they would literally be burning up. Clothes would only increase their discomfort, make them feel even hotter.

It was no wonder the majority of Canines were naked; they obviously tore off their clothing to seek relief from the heat.

With the evidence of the massive assault on the brain, it tended to explain the Canine's bestial behavior, particularly since the cortex was a target of the disease. The cortex was responsible for setting human beings apart and above the animals. With the cortex disrupted, any man or woman would revert to brute levels of intelligence.

Buddy gnawed on his nails, pondering.

The results of the autopsy might also explain why the Canines traveled on all fours instead of standing erect. The rigidity in the muscles might be a contributing factor, as would the infection of the cerebellum which was responsible for maintaining balance while a person walked or ran. With it out of commission, anyone would experience severe difficulty in attempting to stay upright. The Canines might move about on all fours because it was impossible for them to do otherwise.

Why would the eyes be so distended? To absorb more light? To be more sensitive to movement, enabling the Canines to locate their prey faster?

And what about the endocrine glands? Who could say what the end result would be, what with all of them pumping huge quantities of chemicals into the bloodstream? One thing was for sure. It would drive the body's responses haywire.

Whatever—or whoever—was responsible for designing this plague hadn't missed a trick.

It might turn out to be the disease of the era.

It also might be the last one the human race would ever have to contend with, because after it ran its course there wouldn't be a human race left.

30

"Who wants the 45-70?" Frederick Brant asked.

Everyone was clustered in front of the gun case in the Brant game room. Louise Brant was sniffling; she'd started right after the Presidential address and couldn't seem to stop. Gloria Lanning was also exceedingly distressed but was able to keep a reign on her emotions. Amy was standing next to Simon, Marcy alongside Jay, all four of them subdued and quiet.

Lanning reached for the 45-70. "I'll take it," he told Frederick. "What did you use this for? Elephant?"

"Moose," Frederick replied. He indicated the various trophies mounted on the walls—a large moose head with huge antlers, a ten point mule deer, a black bear, and a snarling cougar. A pool table occupied the middle of the floor, and a rack of cue sticks was located to the right of the gun case. "I made a number of trips to Montana when I was in my twenties," he elaborated. "Back then, I considered hunting to be great sport. But when I reached my thirties, the luster wore off. I can't say if the thrill was gone, or I simply grew tired of hiking all over those mountains in search of the perfect trophy."

Lanning hefted the 45-70. "This baby's a miniature cannon. If I see one of those Canines, I'll put a hole in it the size of my fist."

"There is ample ammunition in the drawers under the gun case," Frederick directed. He turned to the gun case again. "I have five rifles left," he announced. "Two 30-06's, one 270, one 30/30, and a 22. The 30/30 and the 22 are lever actions. The rest are bolt actions."

"The 22 won't be of much use," Lanning commented. "It doesn't have much stopping power." He placed a box of ammo in his pocket.

"At least it's a gun," Marcy said, "and after what happened today, we'll need all the guns we have. I'll take the 22. I used to hunt small game on my grandfather's farm with a 22 when I was younger."

Frederick handed her the rifle. "What about the rest of you?"

"I'll take the 30/30," Jay said.

"Give me one of the 30-06's," Simon stated.

Frederick complied, then turned to the gun case. "For myself, I'll take the other 30-06."

"Hand me the 270," Amy said. She took the gun and bent over to grab a box of shells from the drawer.

Frederick glanced at Louise and Gloria. "I'm afraid, ladies, I've run out of rifles. I never did own a handgun, which means I don't have a firearm for you."

"Jay and I have revolvers they can use," Lanning declared.

Louise Grant shook her head. "No. I don't want a gun."

"But you may need one," Frederick insisted.

"I don't want a gun," Louise said emphatically, sniffling.

"But how will you defend yourself if those Canines should get inside the house?" Frederick asked her.

"I don't want a gun!" Louise screamed, and ran

from the game room.

"My wife is taking this very hard," Frederick said, stating the obvious.

"Do you want me to go after her?" Amy asked, worried for her mother.

"No," Frederick answered. "Perhaps if we leave her alone to think things out, she'll come to grips with this crisis."

Lanning turned toward his mother. "How about you? I know you were never fond of guns, but I'd feel a lot safer if you would take my revolver."

"I don't know . . ." Gloria hedged. "I've never handled a gun before."

"You're never too old to learn a new skill," Lanning quipped. He removed the belt and holster he'd taken from the police officer earlier and gave them to his mother. "Strap this around your waist. I'll give you some lessons in a bit."

Simon cleared his throat. "Speaking of coming to grips with this crisis, shouldn't we hold a conference and decide what our next move should be?"

"Good idea, kid," Lanning concurred, "but let's move to the living room. It's centrally located and we can keep our eyes and ears peeled better than we can in here." The game room was situated in the right wing of the Brant house on the lower floor. Between the game room and the living room was Frederick's den and library, mostly consisting of hundreds of law-related volumes. The spacious living room took up the middle of the ground floor. After the living room, filling the left wing of the house, was a music room containing a grand piano and a harp and a spare bedroom which Jay and Marcy were using during their stay. The kitchen was located at the end of a long hallway extending from the front door. A staircase adjacent to the hallway led up to the second floor, consisting of four bedrooms and two baths.

They began filing from the game room.

"Has anyone checked on how much food we have?" Simon thought to ask.

Before anyone could respond, a piercing shriek echoed through the house.

"Louise!" Frederick shouted.

Lanning was at the head of the procession. He immediately took off, running through the den and into the living room. Each room was connected by a doorway to the next. He paused in the living room, Frederick on his heels.

"Louise!" Frederick yelled again.

Lanning heard a noise coming from the front hallway and raced to the hall.

Something growled to his left.

Lanning whirled, hastily extracting the box of ammunition from his pants pocket. He quickly opened the lid and withdrew one cartridge, then placed the box on the carpet.

Louise Brant was frozen in the front doorway, the door wide open, staring at the thing at her feet.

A Canine!

The thing was crouched on the front porch, not a foot from Louise's shoes, glaring malevolently up at her.

Lanning couldn't get a clear shot, Louise being partially between the Canine and himself. He took a step to the right and dropped to his knees, loading the 45-70.

The Canine's snarling visage was barely visible between Louise's right leg and the front door.

There wasn't time to try for a better position.

Lanning aimed and fired, the big rifle thundering in the restricted confines of the hallway.

The slug penetrated the Canine's left cheek and blew out the side of its head. It twisted to one side, gurgling, and fell to the cement.

"Louise!" Frederick was there, running to his wife and taking her in his arms.

"I just . . . wanted . . . some fresh air," Louise mumbled. She appeared to be in deep shock.

"I'm going to take her to our room," Frederick stated, leading her up the stairs.

Lanning motioned for the others to stay back as he withdrew another round from the box and injected it into the chamber.

Were there any more of the damn things waiting out there?

Lanning stopped to the right of the door and peered outside. Night was descending, the sun sinking below the western horizon. Louise had apparently turned on the front porch light before opening the door. It illuminated the Canine on the porch and a small portion of the yard beyond.

There didn't seem to be any more Canines.

"I'm loaded," Jay announced, coming up to the left side of the doorway, the 30/30 in his hands.

"On the count of three," Lanning instructed him in a hushed voice, "we go out. Ready?"

Jay nodded.

"One . . ."

The Canine on the front porch ceased twitching.

"Two . . ."

Marcy Williams moved closer to Jay, gripping the 22.

"Three!"

Lanning and Jay stepped through the doorway, alertly scanning the yard and the driveway for any hint of motion, their fingers on the triggers of their weapons.

The yard and driveway were quiet.

"Looks like this one was alone," Jay remarked, prodding the Canine with his left foot. "It's as dead as a doornail."

"We've got to move it," Lanning said, "and get it out of sight. It might attract others." He saw Jay out of the corner of his eye, bending over and reaching for the body. "Don't touch it!" Lanning warned him, spinning around.

Jay eyed Lanning quizzically. "What's wrong?"

"The President said this is some kind of plague, right?"

"Yeah . . ."

"So if it's a contagious disease, there must be some way to catch it," Lanning noted. "Maybe all you have to do is touch one of the things and you have it."

Jay straightened, blanching. "I never thought of that," he admitted.

"Just kick it into the shrubbery," Lanning advised. "I'll cover you."

Jay complied, rolling the dead Canine into a row of bushes to the left of the front door, then returned to the porch.

"Let's get inside," Lanning suggested.

They entered the house, and Lanning locked the door. Everyone else, except for Frederick and Louise, was waiting in the hallway.

Lanning faced them. "Before we do anything else," he told them, "let's load up. Our lives may well depend on keeping a loaded firearm near us at all times."

Jay, Marcy and Gloria watched while the others obeyed. Marcy had already loaded the magazine on her 22, and Gloria's revolver had been loaded by Lanning earlier. The hallway filled with the metallic sound of levers being worked and bolts being thrown.

Lanning put three more rounds into the 45-70. He wished the rifle held more, but four was all the magazine could contain. The bullets were too large to allow for additional rounds; each one was two and a half inches in length. If the manufacturers had tried to accomodate just one more round, the rifle would have been too cumbersome to wield accurately. "Okay," he said, "let's move into the living room."

"What about my mom and dad?" Amy asked.

"They should be okay upstairs," Lanning stated. "As far as I know, Canines can't fly."

"Should we post a guard at the front door?" Simon asked.

"We will in a bit," Lanning responded, "but first things first. We've got some serious talking to do." He led them into the living room and stood by the television as they seated themselves. "How are you holding up?" he asked his mother as she walked past him.

Gloria stopped and gazed at her son, her expression troubled. "I feel like I'm living in a nightmare."

Lanning reached out and squeezed her arm. "Hang in there. We'll get through this in one piece. I'll see to it," he promised.

Gloria smiled and took a seat.

Lanning placed the 45-70 on top of the television set. "All of us heard the President," he began. "Chicago is one of the Infected Cities. The military undoubtedly has a wall of troops surrounding the city and will shoot us on sight if we try to leave. On the other hand, by staying in the city we are in constant danger from the Canines."

"How many Canines do you think there are?" Amy asked.

"A lot of them," Lanning replied.

"We couldn't even begin to postulate an accurate estimate," Simon interjected glumly.

Lanning chuckled, trying to alleviate the oppressive atmosphere in the room. "I didn't know you knew so many big words, kid." He grinned. "Now I know why you're a newsman."

"Some newsman," Simon said harshly. "Here I am, smack dab in the middle of the story of the decade, and I may not live long enough to report on it."

"You're in an optimistic mood tonight, aren't

you?" Lanning quipped.

"What are we going to do about our predicament?" Marcy asked. She was on the sofa next to Jay.

"That's the question of the hour," Lanning remarked, sighing.

"We only have two options, as I see it." Jay spoke up. "We remain here and fight the Canines as best we can. Or we could try and escape, try to get out of the city and slip past the security perimeter the President mentioned."

"I say we try and get out of Chicago," Marcy declared. "The longer we stay here, the more Canines we'll have to face."

"What makes you say that?" Gloria asked.

"The Canines are caused by a plague, right?" Marcy reminded her. "The government wouldn't have isolated Chicago from the rest of the country unless they were concerned about the spread of the disease. For all we know, everyone in Chicago could become one of those things."

"Even us?" Gloria asked in a stunned voice.

"Who's to say?" Lanning jumped in, annoyed at Marcy for upsetting his mother. "We don't know how a person contracts this disease. If we don't let the Canines touch us or bite us, we probably won't catch whatever it is."

"You hope," Marcy said.

"So what are we going to do?" Jay demanded. "Stay put or try and escape?"

"If we try to get out of Chicago," Lanning noted, "we'll have to fight our way through most of the city just to reach the military perimeter."

"We could try for Lake Michigan," Marcy recommended. "Maybe we could steal a boat."

"I'm sure the Navy or the Coast Guard would blast us from the water," Lanning stated. "We'd be sitting ducks."

"And what are we here?" Jay asked.

"At least this house affords us some protection," Lanning observed. "With the windows and doors locked, it'll be impossible for them to break in without us hearing them. We have enough fire power to hold them off."

"For how long?" Jay retorted, irritated. He couldn't understand why Lanning was making such a case for staying in the house. The doors and windows wouldn't deter a mass attack by the Canines. Slow them down, perhaps, but in the end, they would overwhelm the occupants. Lanning was a professional. He had to see the weaknesses inherent in remaining in the Brant home. Their best bet would be to locate a better fortified position or flee the city. Jay glanced at Lanning's mother. She was holding her hands in her lap, her fingers entwined, patiently listening to the exchange. Was she the reason Lanning wanted to stay put? Because he knew his mother wouldn't last long out on the streets?

"You can do whatever you want," Lanning said to Jay. "No one is holding you here. If Marcy and you want to leave, go ahead, but I'm sticking."

Jay slowly nodded. "Then we're sticking, too." He detected a flicker of surprise ripple over Lanning's features.

Marcy leaned close to Jay. "What gives, lover? I was under the distinct impression you wanted out of here."

"I did," Jay answered in a quiet tone.

"Then why are we staying?"

"Take a look at Lanning's mother," Jay whispered.

Marcy did and fell silent.

"What about you two?" Lanning said to Amy and Simon. "We haven't heard what you want to do."

"I'm not leaving my parents," Amy stated.

"And I'm not leaving my wife," Simon said.

Lanning rubbed his hands together, smiling.

"Good, good. Now let's set up a guard schedule. Some of us can get some sleep while the others pull guard duty."

"We should guard in pairs," Jay suggested.

"That sounds like a . . ." Lanning began, then stopped.

Clearly discernible, from somewhere in the Brant home, came the clatter of breaking glass.

31

Buddy propped his elbows on his desk and placed his chin in his hands as he read the second page of The Quintin Report. This page, in certain respects, was more interesting than the first.

Evidently, Quintin had recognized the risk he undertook in examining the caged Canine. Apprehensive lest he and his co-workers contract the disease, Quintin had donned a gas mask and compelled his fellow researchers to do likewise. But after several hours spent studying the Canine, they ran out of air for the tanks. Instead of waiting for spare tanks to arrive at the facility, Quintin and his associates opted to continue their investigation without the gas masks, a potentially fatal error. It wasn't known whether the gas masks Quintin utilized, of the type traditionally used by firefighters and the military, were effective in inhibiting the transmission of the plague. Buddy speculated that the gas masks might have hindered the disease; at the very least, the insulated air exchange system between the mask and the tank would have prevented the scientists from contracting the plague through respiratory spread.

Quintin was a dedicated professional who had maintained a journal, a meticulous record of his examination of the Canine. Of special fascination to Buddy, Quintin also monitored his physical condition during the study and logged any abnormalities.

The highlights of Quintin's journal were reproduced on the second page of the report.

Buddy perused the page, noting the progression.

Approximately 18 hours after his initial contact with the caged Canine, Quintin recorded experiencing an unusual itching sensation over his entire body. The itching persisted for some ten minutes before vanishing as inexplicably as it had commenced.

Approximately 20 hours after their examination started, Quintin suffered a severe headache. He described it as the "most agonizing I've ever felt." Fortunately, the headache, like the itching, only lasted about ten minutes before it too disappeared.

The intense headache was followed by a feeling of general malaise throughout his whole body. Quintin complained about the peculiar sluggishness, peeved that it was slowing the pace of his work.

After 21 hours into the examination, Quintin noted an odd stiffness in his lower legs. He also mentioned several bouts of dizziness, but they only persisted for a minute or so each time.

About 22 hours along, Quintin detailed a three degree rise in his body temperature. Simultaneously, he reported an abrupt surge of vitality and strength.

Roughly 23 hours after first entering the chamber housing the caged Canine, Quintin made his final entries. "I'm finding it increasingly difficult to read my own writing. My eyes hurt like the devil and they constantly water. The headache has returned, although not as acutely as before. My mouth continually salivates, as if I'm about to vomit, but I don't feel nauseous. My stomach keeps growling, despite several hearty snacks." The last line was an elongated scrawl, completely unlike any of the other, precise entries. "What the hell am I doing this bullshit for?

Nobody gives a man one way or another! They're all bastards! Every one of them!"

The journal ended.

Buddy stared off into space, reflecting. Thanks to Quintin, they now had some idea of the symptoms a plague sufferer displayed before the actual outbreak, before the transformation. And thanks to the autopsy, they knew which parts of the body were affected. C-666 obviously built up slowly, gradually infecting the host organism until the critical point of transformation was attained. If an antidote could be developed, they could administer it right up to the time of the transformation.

Buddy nibbled on one of his nails.

So they knew a bit more, but they lacked the crucial information required to make significant headway.

Was C-666 a virus or a bacteria?

How was it spread?

And what medication, what substance, if any, could cure it?

32

"That was a window!" Jay exclaimed, rising to his feet.

"It sounded like it came from the basement," Amy added.

Lanning glanced at her. "Basement? I didn't know you had a basement."

"Fully furnished," Amy informed him. "We seldom use it. I made sure all the windows were locked after we came home from church while you were upstairs with my dad."

Lanning picked up the 45-70. "How many windows are down there?"

"Two."

Everyone in the room heard the loud crash of another glass being broken.

"How do we get downstairs?" Lanning asked.

"Follow me," Amy directed. She raised the hem of her wedding dress with her left hand while lugging the 270 in her right and hurried from the living room to the front hallway. "It's that door," she said, pointing at a closed door halfway along the hall.

Frederick Brant, his 30-06 in hand, appeared at the top of the stairs. "What was that noise?"

Lanning looked up. "Breaking glass. It came from

your basement.''

''There's a light switch just inside the basement door,'' Frederick said. ''To the left.''

''Thanks.'' Lanning moved to the door and gripped the knob. He gazed over his shoulder.

Jay was right behind him, Marcy at Jay's elbow. Simon and Amy stood ten feet away, their rifles at their shoulders. Gloria was framed in the living room doorway, the revolver in her right hand, her knuckles pale from gripping it too hard.

Lanning smiled encouragement at his mother. ''Everyone set?'' he asked.

''We'are all set,'' Jay replied.

Lanning tensed, prepared to fling open the door. If there were Canines in the basement, he would need to get the door open and the light on as quickly as possible. ''Here goes,'' he whispered and wrenched the basement door wide open as fast as he could.

He wasn't fast enough.

Canines poured from the basement, howling and snarling and snapping.

The basement door was thrown violently backward by the impact of the first Canine slamming into it, and the door caught Lanning on the right side and hurled him across the hall into the opposite wall. Before he could recover his footing, a Canine was on him, going for his throat. Lanning heard his mother scream as he fell to the floor, his hands clasped on the Canine's neck, striving to hold the demented fiend at bay, to keep those teeth from reaching his skin. The 45-70 had been flung from his grasp.

The crowded hallway became a whirlwind of violence and death, as the Canines closed on their prey in the cramped quarters.

Jay and Marcy fired at the next two Canines. Jay's 30/30 downed the Canine on the spot, but Marcy's 22, as Lanning had predicted, lacked the stopping power necessary to kill instantly. Her target staggered, but didn't stop. It lunged, scrambling over the intervening space and sinking its teeth in her right ankle.

Marcy shrieked in terror and pain, trying to yank her ankle free.

Jay came to her rescue, jamming the barrel of his 30/30 against the Canine's head and pulling the trigger.

The Canine jerked spasmodically as the slug exploded its brain. Its mouth opened, and it flopped to one side.

Jay took hold of Marcy with his left arm, assisting her and propelling her away from the basement door.

Amy and Simon opened up, providing covering fire, and dropping the next two Canines through the door, one of them a teen-aged girl.

The basement was a veritable din of howling and baying as more and more Canines surged up the steps to the hallway.

Frederick Brant began firing from the top of the stairs.

Lanning was still wrestling with the first Canine, their bodies roling and tumbling down the hallway toward the kitchen, away from the main conflict.

Jay and Marcy reached the foot of the stairs. Jay released her and aimed, shooting a charging Canine in the head. He twisted and blasted another one attempting to clamber over the railing.

Marcy's ankle was bleeding profusely. She used the 22 as a cane, hurrying up the stairs, her brown eyes wide in panic.

Jay started backing up the stairs, covering Marcy's retreat. Another Canine tried to climb the railing. Jay's right foot flashed out, flicking between the rails, connecting with the Canine's nose and shattering the cartilage. It fell in a spray of crimson.

Amy and Simon were forced to retreat towards the front door as the Canines filled the hallway. They killed three more and had backed up as far as they could go, when Amy heard a tremendous crash to her left from the music room. She glanced into the room and spotted a Canine shaking itself under one of the windows. The thing must have jumped through the glass!

"Simon!" Amy shouted. "Look!"

Simon risked a hasty glimpse at the music room. Damn! The Canines were outflanking them! Even as he watched, another Canine came through the window and joined the first. Why were so many attacking the Brant house? Was it because they had left all the lights on? "Into the living room!" he yelled.

Howling in unison, a wave of Canines crested around the base of the stairs, cutting Amy and Simon off from the others. Four of the Canines bounded up the stairs after Jay and Marcy. Two of them came toward Simon and Amy and were promptly shot. The rest made for the living room.

And Gloria Lanning.

Simon saw her try to bring the revolver into play, but she was way too slow.

Five Canines piled onto her and dragged her to the floor. She didn't let out a peep as they ripped and slashed with their teeth.

"No!" Simon bellowed. He started to go to her aid, but Amy grabbed his left arm.

"There's nothing we can do," Amy cried.

Simon glanced to his left.

Three Canines were loping across the music room carpet, coming toward the hallway. There were Canines everywhere.

Only one way left!

Simon spun around and threw the front door open.

A solitary Canine was perched on the porch.

Simon shot it between the eyes and gripped Amy's hand. "Come on!"

"I can't leave my parents," she protested, resisting him.

"We've got to," Simon shouted, and forcefully pulled her from the house. He slammed the door closed and felt it shudder as heavy forms collided with the wood.

The front yard was temporarily clear of Canines.

Simon drew Amy to the left, moving behind the shrubbery as they made for the corner of the house. He could see the vehicles parked in the driveway, the limousine and the sedan. If they could only get the keys!

They reached the corner and stopped. Simon cautiously peered around the edge.

Luck was with them. There wasn't a Canine in sight.

"Listen," Amy whispered.

Simon cocked his head. He could hear the sounds of the ongoing struggle in the Brant home. Guns were still blasting, the Canines still howling.

But they weren't alone.

The night was filled with howling coming from every direction, the shrill wailing of sirens, and the popping reports of gunfire.

Chicago was under siege.

Somewhere in the house, a woman screamed.

"That's my mom!" Amy exclaimed and ran past Simon.

"Wait!" Simon raced after her. She was impeded by her wedding dress, and he easily caught up with her. "Will you wait?"

"No!" Amy turned the far corner of the house and halted in midstride.

Simon nearly bumped into her before he saw the reason she had abruptly stopped.

Four Canines were in the backyard, clustered outside of the backdoor, seemingly waiting for someone to make a break for it. They turned at the sight of the two humans and, without any hesitation whatsoever, charged.

Simon raised his 30-06 and fired, the recoil driving the stock into his shoulder.

One of the Canines dropped.

Amy opened up, downing another one.

Simon sighted on a third Canine and squeezed the trigger.

Nothing happened.

In the rush of action, in all the excitement, he had forgotten to reload after expending the five shots in his magazine. He gripped the barrel and held the rifle like a club, bracing himself.

The Canine came on in a drooling, baying rush.

Simon waited until the last possible instant and swung the rifle downward, throwing his shoulders and upper torso into it. The rifle connected, striking the Canine across the face as it leaped for the kill. The Canine buckled and fell to the grass, dazed, trying to regain its footing. Simon drove the rifle down again and again, until the Canine ceased moving. Beside him, Amy's 270 boomed and the fourth Canine fell, twitching.

Amy ran towards the backdoor.

"Wait!" Simon yelled, scrambling to remove the box of ammunition from his pocket and reload the 30-06.

Amy disregarded his shout in her anxiety over her parents. She pulled open the backdoor, heedless of what might be lurking inside, and as she stepped into the house she saw two figures embroiled in combat on the kitchen floor.

It was Lanning and one of the Canines.

Amy tried to aim at the Canine, but they were thrashing and rolling too quickly for her to get a bead.

They tumbled into a cabinet, the Canine bearing the brunt of the impact, and Lanning heaved, pushing himself away from the snarling brute and leaping to his feet.

Amy fired, startling Lanning who was unaware of her presence, her shot true, the slug piercing the Canine's right temple and blowing out its left ear. The thing collapsed in a heap.

Simon burst into the kitchen, the 30-06 reloaded.

Lanning whirled, making for the hallway.

"Wait!" Simon shouted.

Lanning hesitated, glancing over his right shoulder.

"Your mom . . ." Simon blurted.

Lanning stopped, his features paling. His suit was torn and rumpled, his face smudged, and he was breathing hard. "They got my mother?" he asked, shocked.

Simon frowned and nodded. "They're all over the house," he whispered. "Jay and Marcy managed to get upstairs, but there's no way we can reach them."

Lanning unexpectedly began shaking, as if he were having a fit. His fists were clenched, his face reddening, as he turned toward the hallway. "They got my mother!" he hissed between clenched teeth. "They killed my mother!" he bellowed in a livid rage.

"Lanning! Wait!" Simon yelled.

Lanning uttered an inarticulate cry and ran from the kitchen.

33

Jay and Marcy reached the top of the stairs as four Canines barreled up from below.

Frederick Brant, who was standing to the left of the railing, reloading, calmly glanced at Marcy's bleeding right ankle. "Take her to the second door on the left," he directed. "Louise is in there. She can assist in bandaging the wound."

"But . . ." Jay started to object.

"Hurry!" Frederick shoved Jay along and stepped to the center of the stairs. He grinned as he aimed at the approaching furies. The nearest one was only six steps from the top when he fired, the bullet gouging a furrow in the top of the Canine's head and causing it to flip back onto its mates.

In the brief respite before they reorganized, Frederick saw Amy and Simon leave through the front door. Excellent, he told himself. His daughter would escape this madhouse.

The Canines had regrouped and shoved past their dead comrade. They bounded up the stairs, their movements awkward because of their grotesque posture.

Frederick, unruffled, placed his next shot into another Canine's head.

How many more were there? At least there didn't seem to be quite as many emerging from the basement. He glimpsed Jay and Marcy to his left and waved them on.

Jay, astonished at Frederick Brant's evident peace of mind, supported Marcy as they hastened into the bedroom Frederick had indicated. Louise Brant was lying on the bed.

"Louise! Mrs. Brant!" Jay shouted. "We need your help."

Louise sat up and stretched. "Is it time for the wedding already?"

Frederick's 30-06 was booming from the landing.

"Mrs. Brant!" Jay tried again. "Marcy's hurt!"

Louise smiled and stood. "My, that's a pretty dress you're wearing, young woman," she said to Marcy.

"Mrs. Brant . . ."

Louise nodded serenely at Jay. "We mustn't be late. Amy would never forgive us if we're late." She headed for the doorway.

"Mrs. Brant! Don't!"

Louise blissfully ignored Jay and left the room, humming.

"Son of a bitch!" Jay hurried Marcy to the bed. "Wait right here," he ordered as she sat down, grimacing from the pain in her leg.

"I'll be all right," she said bravely.

A strident scream rocked the upstairs hallway.

Jay raced to the doorway.

Frederick Brant was down, a pair of Canines at his throat. Three more were slowly closing on Louise, sensing she was helpless. She was backed against the wall, her hands extended, palms out, in a futile gesture of self-preservation.

Jay brought the 30/30 up and fired, taking out one of the disgusting creatures.

The remaining two jumped Louise, one of them

clamping its jaw on her right wrist, the other jumping higher and locking onto her exposed jugular.

She didn't stand a prayer.

Jay slammed the door shut and leaned the 30/30 against the wall. He crossed to a small vanity and pushed it back to the door, wedging it under the knob.

"This won't hold them back for long," he commented.

"What about Mr. and Mrs. Brant?" Marcy anxiously inquired.

Jay shook his head.

"Do we make a stand here?" Marcy asked, rising and hobbling, using the 22 as a makeshift crutch.

"Not on your life." Jay moved to the window, unlatched the lock and heaved. Fresh, cool air gusted into the bedroom as the window slid up.

"What are you doing?" Marcy nervously asked.

"We're getting out of here," Jay told her.

"But what about Simon and Amy and Lanning and his mother? We can't just leave them."

"We won't do them much good holed up in here," Jay rejoined. "Besides, Lanning was the first one to go down, remember? The last I saw, Simon and Amy were near the front door. Hopefully, they got out. I don't know what happened to Mrs. Lanning."

Marcy hobbled to the window. "It's quite a drop."

"Only two floors," Jay said. "If you hang from my hands, you'll only have to fall about ten feet or so."

"Is that all?"

Jay leaned out the window and looked down. "There are a couple of bushes directly below us. They'll cushion your fall." He pulled back inside. "How's your ankle?"

"Hurts like hell," Marcy admitted, "but I can make it."

Jay peered out the window again, scanning the yard below. He couldn't detect any Canines, but he could hear howling from every direction interspersed with continuous gunshots.

Marcy heard it, too. "Sounds like a war out there."

"It is," he assured her. "Here. Slide over the sill. Keep a strong grip on my arms."

Marcy eased her injured leg out the window. "What about my rifle?"

"I'll drop it after you."

Marcy released the 22, letting it fall to the floor. She carefully clambered out of the window until she was suspended from Jay's arms.

"It's going to hurt like hell when you land," Jay told her. "Try not to make a sound. They may hear you. Are you ready?"

Marcy grit her teeth and nodded.

Jay heard the door rattle as a Canine crashed against it. "I love you," he said, then released her.

Marcy felt the air rush past her, her long hair flying, and then she hit the hard ground, her right leg folding under her, her dress askew, a sharp pang in her right foot prompting her to gnash her teeth and clench her fists in an effort to suppress her impulse to scream. She glanced up and saw Jay was waiting at the window.

Marcy moved to one side, allowing plenty of space for Jay to land.

Jay dropped the 22 into the small bushes, flinching when it clattered, afraid the Canines would hear and come to investigate.

Nothing appeared.

The Canines were actively assaulting the bedroom door.

Jay looked at the door one last time, and as he did he spotted a key chain on a dresser in the far corner.

The keys to the limo?

Jay ran to the dresser, scooped up the keys, put them in his pocket, and returned to the window. He leaned out, held the 30/30 over the bushes, and let the rifle drop, making even more noise than the 22. He paused for an instant, just long enough to permit Marcy to retrieve the 30/30, and then slid over the sill and let go. His legs were jarred by the landing, and he rolled with the impact, letting his mucles absorb the shock. He did two somersaults and came to rest in a sitting position.

Marcy, heedless of her discomfort, scrambled over to him. "Are you all right?"

Jay took the 30/30 from her. "I should be asking you that."

"My ankle and leg hurt," she confessed.

Jay crouched and helped her to move back against the house, behind the slightly flattened shrubs. "Get down," he cautioned her.

Not a moment too soon.

A single Canine was coming toward the house from the direction of the driveway. It stopped in the middle of the lawn, then turned to the left and ran off, crossing into a neighbor's yard and disappearing.

From behind the Brant house came the clamor of gunfire. There were two shots, spaced closely together, then silence. A few seconds later, there was another shot.

"Who do you think that was?" Marcy whispered.

"Could be the neighbors," Jay replied. "Or maybe Simon and Amy got out the back door. If so, we should circle around and pick them up. Come on." He assisted her to her feet.

"I can't move very fast," Marcy said. "I'll slow you down."

'Not if we take the limo," Jay informed her.

They hurried across the front lawn, Marcy limping, Jay's arm around her narrow waist, their eyes constantly on the lookout for Canines. Amazingly enough, they reached the limousine unmolested.

Jay tried the driver's door.

The damn thing was locked!

Jay hastily withdrew the keys from his pocket and tried one in the lock.

No go. The key was too small.

He tried the second key, with no luck.

Marcy, looking for Canines, heard the muffled retort of a firearm coming from inside the Brant home. "Did you hear that?"

Jay, intent on finding the correct key, hadn't been paying attention. "What?"

"I thought I heard a shot from inside the house," Marcy told him.

Jay glanced over his shoulder. He spotted a Canine sprawled on the front porch. What was it doing? Sleeping? "I don't hear anything," he responded, applying his energies to the door.

The fourth key on the chain was the winner.

"Bingo!" he cried as the key turned in the lock.

A Canine howled off to their right.

Jay opened the door and stood aside for Marcy to climb in. She was grimacing as she slid across the seat to the passenger side. Jay jumped inside, slammed the door, and locked it.

"We did it!" he exclaimed, elated. "We're safe—for the moment."

Marcy checked that her car door was secure, then bent over to examine her right ankle. She could feel a wet, sticky substance on her fingers and knew she was still bleeding.

Jay, apprehensively watching her, touched her shoulder. "Is it still bleeding?" he asked.

"Sure is," Marcy replied.

"We need to bandage it," Jay concluded. He glanced around the interior of the huge limousine, but there wasn't anything they could use. "We'll have to rip your dress."

"My dress?" Marcy sat up. "Do you know how much this dress cost?"

"What's more important?" Jay demanded. "Your life or the dumb dress?"

Marcy didn't answer.

Jay leaned over and gripped her expensive blue dress, raising the fabric until he could grasp the hem in both hands. He strained, grunting, and the material parted, enabling him to tear off a wide strip for use as a bandage. "Here." He gave the piece to Marcy. "Can you wrap this tightly around your ankle?"

"No problem," she assured him.

"It will have to do until we can locate a doctor."

Marcy looked out her window at the dark Chicago night. "We're going to find a doctor out there?"

"Either that or a hospital," Jay said. "There has to be a hospital open."

"What about your brother and the others?"

Jay stared at the deceptively tranquil Brant home. "We'll see if we can find a way to drive around to the back of the house. If Simon and Amy got out, we'll head for the nearest hospital and have a doctor take a look at you. Amy was born and raised here. She must know Chicago like the back of her hand."

"What if we don't find them back there?"

"Then I go inside the house and see what happened to them."

"Let's hope it doesn't come to that," Marcy said fearfully.

Jay inserted the key in the ignition and twisted, and the powerful engine cranked over without any difficulty.

"Let me kow if you see one of the Canines," Jay instructed her.

"Haven't you seen enough of them already?" Marcy quipped.

Jay slowly drove down the driveway to the street.

"It's deserted!"

"Not quite." Jay pointed to their left.

A Canine was crossing the street about 20 feet

from the limo.

"It's a woman," Marcy stated, then added an afterthought. "You know, I just realized that about half of those Canines after us inside the house were women. Some of them were even children."

"They were," Jay agreed. "Were. Past tense. Whatever they become after they change, they sure as hell aren't men or women or kids any more. Besides, what difference does it make? Female and juvenile Canines are equally as deadly as the male."

The female they were observing ambled into the darkness and vanished.

"Why did she walk off?" Marcy asked. "She must have heard our car."

"Who knows?" Jay said. "Count your blessings and leave it go at that."

Jay turned right, and at the end of the block he turned right again. At the next intersection, he took one more right. Now he was on West Berenice Avenue. He cruised due east until he reached the home on Berenice which was parallel to, and directly behind, the Brant house on West Grace Street. He stopped the limo and killed the motor.

The house on Berenice was a white frame affair. None of the lights were on.

"I don't like it," Marcy commented.

"I don't, either," Jay concurred, "but I don't have much choice, do I?"

"You have to cut through this yard to reach the Brant property. They could jump you anywhere."

"That's the chance I'll have to take." Jay picked up the 30/30.

Marcy reached over and touched his elbow. "Do you really have to do this?"

"You heard those shots behind the Brant place," Jay reminded her. "Simon and Amy must be in this vicinity. You stay inside the limo with the doors locked. If some Canine's come by, duck down. I'll return as soon as I can," he promised.

Marcy moved closer and kissed him on the lips. "Take care, handsome."

"I will. If you need me, pound on the car horn," Jay advised her.

"Okay."

Jay insured the 30/30 was loaded, smiled at Marcy, and opened his door. He eased out of the limousine and squatted on the asphalt. As gently and quietly as he could, he closed the limo door.

Marcy promptly locked it.

Jay crawled to the curb and paused, listening. The howling of the Canines was filling the city, drowning out all other night sounds. The staccato gunfire was continuing. On this block, though, all was silent. The house in front of him wasn't the only one lacking any signs of habitation; the two homes to the left and the two to the right were all plunged in foreboding gloom. A strong wind was blowing in from the west.

Why was this neighborhood deserted? Had the Canines already been here? Had the people fled? Or were they hiding inside with their lights off so as not to attract the Canines?

Jay rose, keeping low, and ran toward the house. He reached a tree near the corner of the structure and leaned against the rough trunk.

Still nothing from inside the house.

Jay peeked around the tree trunk. The space between this home and the one to his right seemed to be deserted. He took a deep breath and resumed running.

The backyard contained a swing set and a large dog house.

Jay circumvented the swing set and arrived at a low mesh fence separating this yard from the Brant backyard. He flattened at the base of the fence and studied the rear of the Brant home. Every light in the house was still on. No wonder the Canines had assaulted it in force! The lights must have attracted the Canines like a street lamp drew insects. Why hadn't they thought to turn out the lights? Probably because none of them expected to find so many Canines right in the neighborhood. Jay, for one, had erroneously surmised the majority of the Canines were in the inner city.

A solitary shot shattered the night, from the proximity of the Brant home.

Jay rose to his knees. The shot had sounded like the 45-70. Someone was still alive, still battling for life. It could be Simon or Amy. Apparently, he'd been incorrect in believing they had escaped out the back-door. He had to help them.

Something snapped to his left.

Jay whirled.

A pack of four Canines was heading toward him on his side of the fence. Their feral features and unnatural forms were barely visible, but there was no mistaking their strange loping gait.

Had they seen him, or were they patrolling the area for prey? If they were after him, should he return to the limo or make for the Brant home?

His decision was abruptly rendered moot.

The limousine horn suddenly blared.

Jay rose, racing for the limo.

The Canines gave voice to a chorus of howls and angled to intercept him.

Between striving to catch a glimpse of the limousine and keeping an eye on the trailing Canines, he failed to watch the ground in front of him. Consequently, he didn't see the tricycle in time to avoid it.

Jay felt a hard object collide with his shins. He tried to maintain his balance, but his left foot caught in the tricycle and he toppled to the grass. He wrenched his left foot free and scrambled to his knees, raising the 30/30, instinctively knowing the Canines were almost upon him.

He was right.

The nearest was a half-dozen yards away, baying, covering the ground astoundingly fast.

Jay fired, the 30/30 booming, and the first Canine stumbled and went down. He levered in the second round and pulled the trigger, felling the second of the four Canines. The third one yelped as he planted a slug in its head.

But the fourth Canine was on him before he could fire another shot.

Jay brought the stock around, smashing the wood into the Canine's face as the thing leaped at him. His blow knocked the Canine to one side, but it instantly recovered and lunged. Jay swung the barrel end of the rifle in an arc, connecting with the Canine's right temple, dazing it. With a start, he realized it was a woman. Despite what he had told Marcy earlier, he hesitated for a second when the woman gazed into his eyes. In her stunned state, she momentarily appeared to be almost normal, but the illusion was shattered when she shook her head and snarled in rage at her intended victim. She opened her mouth and dove for his legs.

Jay dodged to the right, rolling, coming up with the barrel clutched in his hands. He swung the rifle, the stock whipping into the side of her head and splitting her skull.

The Canine whimpered as it died.

Jay stood, feeling shaky.

The limousine horn was creating a cacophonous racket.

Marcy!

How many Canines were attacking the limousine? The magazine in the 30/30 held six rounds and he had expended half of them in his fight. Three rounds wouldn't be of much help if there were a dozen of more surrounding the limo.

Jay ran around the tree in the front yard and

stopped, gawking, completely perplexed.

No one was assailing the vehicle.

What the hell!

Jay hurried to the driver's door. It was thrown open as he reached it and he slid in, glaring at Marcy. "I thought I told you to use the horn if you were in trouble. What gives?"

Marcy was grinning excitedly. "That second house on the left," she stated, pointing. "She went in there."

"Who went in there? A Canine?"

"No, dummy, a woman! A normal woman like you and me," Marcy exclaimed.

Jay glanced at the dwelling. "The lights aren't on," he noted.

"I know that," Marcy replied, "but I saw her. She had a child with her. They were hurrying, and they cut across the street not more than ten feet in front of the car. I was so shocked, I didn't even think to roll down the window and call to her before she got inside."

"A normal person," Jay said slowly.

"There might be others inside that house," Marcy said. "They can help us. We can band together."

"I don't know . . ." Jay hedged.

"Why not?" Marcy demanded.

"Whoever is in there might take a shot at us. They might not want anyone else near them."

"You're nitpicking," Marcy declared. She looked toward the Brant residence. "Did you see any trace of Simon and Amy?"

"I didn't get there."

"Why not?"

Jay told her.

"Oh." Marcy began rubbing her right leg.

"Is it getting worse?" Jay asked.

"Afraid so."

Jay leaned on the steering wheel, pondering their dilemma. If there were others inside of that house, they might be able to aid Marcy. They might have a first aid kit. Locating Simon was important, but tending to Marcy's wound took precedence.

"Wait here," he said, reaching for the car door.

"What are you doing?"

"Going to check out that house," Jay stated.

"Drive there," Marcy urged him.

"Why? It's not that far."

"We'll be safer in the limousine," Marcy noted. "And if there are people inside, and they see us drive up in the car, they'll know we're not Canines and won't try to shoot us."

Her reasoning made sense. Jay started the limo and cautiously drove to the second house on the left.

"Pull into the driveway," Marcy directed.

Jay complied, then put the gear selector in Park.

The next house over had its lights on, including the porch light. Its picture window had been busted out, and the front door was hanging on one hinge.

"The Canines sure have been through here," Jay observed. He scrutinized the murky residence in front of them. The door and windows appeared to be intact, but that didn't mean a thing. "We could be waltzing into a trap," he said.

Marcy gripped his arm. "Please, Jay. For me. If no one is in there, we'll go back to the Brant's."

"Stay put," Jay ordered. He reloaded the three spent rounds from the box of ammunition in his pocket, then opened his door. "I won't be long."

"Be careful!"

Jay warily walked toward the front door. He detected a motion at an upstairs window, the swaying of a curtain.

Someone *was* inside, and they had seen him.

Jay marched up to the door and tried the knob. Not surprisingly, the front door was locked. He knocked and waited.

Nothing happened.

Impatient, feeling exposed, he knocked again, louder. He counted to ten and raised his fist to pound again.

"Who's out there?" asked someone in a frightened, feminine voice.

"The name's Darr. Jay Darr. My girl friend saw a woman run into this house. Let me in."

"I don't know you," came the reply.

"Look, lady," Jay snapped, "I'm not standing out here all night. Those Canines could show up at any second. We thought you might want some company, that's all." He turned, scanning the street for any hint of the Canines.

With a metallic click, the front door was unlocked and slowly opened a foot or so. "You won't hurt us?" the woman timorously inquired.

Jay could just distinguish her face. "We're not going to hurt you," he said. "How many are there besides yourself?"

"Just my son, Gus. My name is Cora."

"Is this your house?"

"No." Cora opened the door wider. She was a plump woman in her forties, with dark hair and eyes. Her son looked to be in his early teens. "We live three blocks over. Those awful things broke into our house. My husband got us out the back, but I think they got him. It was terrible!"

"I can imagine."

"My friend, Paula, lives here, but she isn't home. I don't know where she could have gone," Cora said.

"Do you know if there is a first aid kit in this house?" Jay asked.

"I think Paula keeps one in the bathroom," Cora replied.

"Would you go get it. My girlfriend, Marcy, is hurt. I need something to bandage her leg. I'll stand guard out here."

"I'll be right back."

"Hurry," Jay prompted her. He waited in the darkness, alert for the Canines.

"Say, mister . . ."

Cora's overweight son, Gus, was standing in the doorway. He was wearing jeans and a T-shirt.

"What?"

"What are those things? The things that got my dad, I mean."

"Didn't you watch the President on television tonight?" Jay asked.

"Nope. My dad said we had better things to do than listen to a dumb political speech."

"It's too bad your dad didn't listen," Jay said.

"They tore him apart," Gus added sorrowfully.

"How do you know?"

"I looked back," Gus said. "My mom didn't, but I did. I saw them . . ." He stopped, unable to continue.

"You don't need to talk about it," Jay said.

A moment later, Cora appeared, bearing a box of bandages and a first aid kit. "Found what you need," she said.

"Okay. Let's get out of here." Jay moved toward the limousine.

Cora and Gus stepped outside. "Where are you going?" Cora inquired anxiously.

"I have to find my brother. After that, we'll search for others like us."

Cora and Gus followed Jay to the limo. "Did you call those horrid things Canines?" she asked.

"That's what the President called them."

"Oh. We didn't watch him. Could you tell us what's going on?"

"Gladly. First, get inside the car where it's safe." Jay opened the driver's door and slid inside. He reached over the seat and unlocked the rear door for Cora and Gus.

"My name is Cora," Cora said to Marcy as they climbed into the vehicle.

"Pleased to meet you," Marcy said, offering her hand.

"Make sure your door is locked," Jay instructed Gus.

Once all the doors were secure, and Marcy was tending to her injured ankle, Jay started the limousine and backed from the driveway. He kept the headlights off to minimize the risk of detection.

"Are we going to check on Simon and Amy?" Marcy asked as she applied some gauze to the bite mark. The pain was subsiding, and the wound wasn't as deep as she had feared.

"We have to go back," Jay said angrily. "We never should have left in the first place."

"We didn't have much choice."

"Would one of you be so kind as to tell me what those things are?" Cora chimed in from the back seat.

Marcy elaborated on the Chief Executive's national address while Jay retraced their route to the Brant home. He braked near the Brant driveway, studying the house. The lights were still on, and there was one Canine still lying on the front porch, but there wasn't any trace of the others. He started up the drive, then slammed on the brakes so hard the entire vehicle lurched.

Marcy had to grab the dashboard for support. "What's the matter?"

"The sedan's gone!"

"What?"

"Lanning's sedan is gone," Jay said.

The driveway was empty.

"Then at least one of them made it out of there," Marcy declared hopefully.

Jay balled his right hand and punched the steering wheel. "Damn!"

"What's wrong, mister?" Gus asked.

"I deserted my brother," Jay answered, infuriated at himself.

"You didn't desert Simon," Marcy said. "You did what you had to do."

Jay glared at her. "I should never have left Simon."

Marcy's intuition sensed the profound inner turmoil Jay was experiencing, and she blamed herself. Jay had fought courageously in the hallway and on the stairs. He had saved her life; in fact, the only reason he had abandoned the Brant home was to protect her skin. If anything happened to Simon, she would be partially to blame. "They can't have gone far," she asserted. "If we hurry, we can catch up with them."

"But we don't know which way they went."

"Pick any direction," Marcy proposed.

"First I've got to check the house."

"What?"

"Maybe only Lanning got out alive. Maybe his mom. I never did see what happened to her." He frowned. "Hold on!"

Jay floored the accelerator. The limousine sped forward, leaving the driveway and gouging ruts in the grass as Jay drove across the lawn to the front door. He braked the limo so that his door was only inches from the front porch.

"I'll come with you," Marcy offered.

"Don't be ridiculous," Jay countered. "Stay put. If something happens to me, get out of here and find a hospital." Before she could respond, he threw his door open and stepped out.

The Canine reclining on the front porch was dead, shot between the eyes.

Jay closed the limo door and bypassed the body. He held the 30/30 in his right hand, ready to fire, and pushed the front door to the Brant house wide open.

Canines were lying all over the place.

"Simon! Amy! Lanning! Can you hear me?"

Silence.

"Simon! Amy! Are you in here?"

No response.

Jay sagged against the jamb. If Simon and Amy were inside, they would have heard him. They must have escaped with Lanning or Lanning's mother, or both. He was about to return to the limousine when another thought occurred to him. What if they were injured, too weak to cry for help? The least he could do was scour the premises for his own peace of mind.

The driver's door suddenly flew open. "Jay! The driveway!" Marcy shouted.

A pack of Canines was coming up the drive at full speed.

They must have heard him yelling. Enraged, Jay snapped off a shot at the pack. He jumped over the dead Canine and into the limousine.

"It's them!" Cora screeched. "It's them!"

"Get us out of here, mister!" Gus wailed.

Jay gunned the motor and took off, circling across the lawn to the driveway. He deliberately attempted to run down several of the Canines, but they easily dodged the huge vehicle. They bayed and snarled as he left them behind, tearing down the driveway and making a tight left turn.

"We're losing them," Cora called out.

Jay pushed the speedometer up to 70. Three, four, five blocks flashed past in rapid succession. "Where's the nearest hospital?" he asked, glancing over his shoulder at Cora.

"There are several downtown," Cora answered. "The Veterans Hospital, Passavant, and Wesley Hospital."

"But which one is the closest?"

"The Chicago State Hospital. They would have doctors there," Cora replied.

"Which way is it?"

"We have to turn around," Cora stated. "It's back the other way."

"Look out!" Gus suddenly screamed.

Jay, twisted in his seat to catch a glimpse of Cora,

perceived their situation too late.

The limousine was almost upon an intersection. Speeding toward the same intersection was a blue van.

Jay jammed on the brakes, hoping he could avert a collision. The limousine swerved sideways, the tires smoking, the brake drums squealing in protest. The limousine's rear end whipped around and into the path of the hurtling blue van.

"Dear God!" Cora shrieked.

Jay was jarred violently by the impact. His body became airborne, his head smashing into the windshield. A bright light flooded his consciousness. Intense agony lanced his cranium and something moist and sticky seeped over his eyes. He was only dimly aware of a peculiar crunching noise and of being tossed end over end. The world spun before his eyes and his head crashed against a hard object. He could vaguely hear someone calling his name. A sharp spasm rocked his left side. He shook his head, trying to dispel his wooziness, to no avail.

Marcy!

Where was Marcy?

Jay exerted a supreme effort to rouse his garbled senses. His eyelids fluttered, and for a fleeting instant he swore he saw stars high overhead.

Then he passed out.

34

Lanning stopped five feet from the kitchen. The hallway beyond the basement door and the area near the front door was crawling with Canines. None of them had spotted him—yet. He saw the 45-70 on the floor, slightly behind the basement door, and boldly stalked over to the rifle and picked it up. A cold rage blazed in his soul, an acute hatred of these slobbering, demented misfits. The bastards had killed his mother! The one person left in this cruel world who really and truly loved him, who unselfishly cared for him with her whole heart, had been murdered by these pricks.

And they were going to pay.

Lanning stepped into plain sight from behind the basement door.

One of the Canines spotted him, howled, and charged.

Lanning casually aimed and fired, the 45-70 blasting and bucking.

The Canine's head exploded in a crimson spray, showering the wall with red dots and chunks of flesh.

Without missing a beat, Lanning sighted on another Canine and shot it in the chest. The thing was propelled backwards several feet to collapse in a gurgling, twitching heap.

Another Canine was emerging from the living room.

Lanning took three steps forward and planted a bullet in its mouth, the rear of its cranium imitating a miniature volcano. Lanning levered his fourth and final round into the chamber.

Something growled to his left.

A Canine was perched on the stairs, on a level with Lanning's head. The thing pressed its face against the railing and attempted to bite at him through the slats.

Lanning brutally rammed the barrel of the 45-70 into the Canine's nose and pulled the trigger. The middle of its face crumbled in upon itself and the thing dropped in its tracks.

Two more Canines came out of the living room.

"Lanning! Here!"

Lanning glanced over his shoulder and saw Simon and Amy a yard behind him.

"It's loaded," Simon yelled, and tossed the 30-06.

Lanning dropped the 45-70 and caught the 30-06 in one smooth, fluid motion. He whirled, sighted, and put a slug in one of the two attacking Canines as they rounded the base of the stairs. The second managed to get within a foot of Lanning's leg before he shot it through the top of its head.

His jaw clenched, his lips a thin line, Lanning advanced along the hallway. As rapidly as he could work the bolt, he fired, killing yet another coming from the living room and one from the music room. He came abreast of the living room and stopped, virtually paralyzed by the grisly scene on the living room floor.

A pair of Canines, one male and one female, were feasting on the remains of his mother. They had literally ripped her to shreds. Her arms were detached from her torso, one of them lying near the television, the other, bearing evidence of teeth marks, near her feet. Her dress had been torn asunder, and the Canines were feeding on her abdomen. They looked up as Lanning appeared. One of them, the female, had a section of intestine in her mouth, the other a layer of skin. Both snarled and hissed at this intruder who dared to interrupt their meal.

Lanning lost control. He plugged the male and went to shoot the female, but the gun was empty. Instead, in a livid frenzy, he gripped the barrel of the 30-06 and closed on the female as she came toward him. He swung, the heavy stock plowing into her mouth and crushing her front teeth. She staggered and endeavored to back away, but he wouldn't allow it. He went after her, swinging the rifle again and again and again, connecting each time, pulverizing her face and head as she slumped to the carpet. Even after she was down, Lanning didn't let up. He swung, over and over, oblivious to his surroundings, unaware her head had caved in. Only when her face and head were pulp did he finally desist, breathing heavily.

But he still wasn't through.

Spotting the revolver he'd given his mother on the floor, he walked over and retrieved the handgun. The 30-06 fell from his fingers as he moved to the hallway. More! he told himself. There had to be more!

There were.

Four more were hurrying down the stairs, their mouths covered with blood, one of them a small girl not more than eight.

Lanning knew they had been eating someone upstairs, and his wrath mounted. With deliberate precision, he aimed the service revolver. As he had done countless times on the firing range when employed by the F.B.I. and later Interpol, he focused on the target and pulled the trigger. Again. And again. He continued pulling the trigger until someone took hold of his arms and forcefully lowered his hands.

"They're dead," someone was saying. "They're

all dead. You can stop shooting. Your gun's empty."

Lanning slowly regained his composure. He became cognizant of the dead creatures littering the stairs, one of them not six inches from his toes.

"Can you understand me?" Simon was asking.

Lanning nodded.

"You were out of it," Simon said. "You kept pulling the trigger long after your gun was empty."

Lanning wearily leaned against the railing. "Any more?" he mumbled.

"Doesn't appear to be," Simon replied, "but there are bound to be more soon. We'd better get while the getting is good."

Lanning numbly nodded. His mother was gone! Who cared about anything else?

Simon recovered the 30-06 and returned to Lanning's side. "I'll check upstairs," he volunteered.

"I'm coming with you," Amy announced, joining them.

"Stay with Lanning," Simon suggested. "He looks wasted. I'll be right back." He ran up the stairs before she could object. At the top of the stairs he remembered to reload the 30-06. As he was inserting the cartridges into the magazine, he spied Amy's father and mother. Both were dead, lying not far from the stairs, and both had been partially consumed. Frederick's face was gone except for his left eye and half of his nose. Louise was totally unrecognizable. Simon looked down the stairs at Amy. There was no way he would let her see this. "Make sure your rifle is loaded," he instructed her to keep her busy.

Amy nodded.

Lanning was sagging against the railing, his features pale, his eyes glazed.

Simon hurried down the hall and checked each of the bedrooms. They were empty. In the second room on the left, he found a vanity on the floor near the door.

Where were Jay and Marcy?

Simon inspected the bedrooms on the other side of the stairs with similar results, then hastened to the top of the stairs. "Any sign of more Canines?" he asked.

Amy shook her head. "I peeked down into the basement. There aren't any more down there."

Simon saw Frederick's 30-06 lying in the hall. He scooped the rifle up and started down the stairs.

Amy's eyes locked on the extra rifle. She gulped and gazed upstairs. "Are they . . . ?" She couldn't finish the question.

"I don't want you going up there," Simon stated by way of confirmation.

Amy's eyes misted over. "Oh, no," she said weakly. "I knew it. I just knew it."

Simon reached her and laid Frederick's 30-06 on the stairs between two Canine bodies. "Listen," he began, afraid he would have another vegetable on his hands if she didn't snap out of it, "we can't stay here. More Canines are bound to show up. I couldn't find a trace of Jay and Marcy, but I know they ran upstairs during the fight. They must have climbed out a window. We've got to get the hell out of here, too. Where are your clothes? You can't run around in that wedding dress for the rest of your life."

Amy was making a valiant effort, struggling to remain calm, telling herself she wouldn't break, not now, not when Simon needed her assistance. "My clothes? They're up in my room."

"I'll go get you some," Simon offered. He ran upstairs to her room, fetched a pair of pants, blouse, and her sneakers, and went back down. "Here." He handed the articles to Amy. "Change. I'm going to get more ammunition." He took off for the game room and stuffed his pockets with ammunition for the 45-70, Amy's 270, and the 30-06's. By the time he returned to the front hallway, Amy had changed outfits.

"Can I help?" Lanning asked.

"Are you sure you're up to it?"

"Try me."

"Okay. Grab that 30-06 on the stairs, there, and get your 45-70," Simon directed.

Lanning complied, moving very slowly, still not in full command of his faculties. He couldn't stop thinking about his mother, about what they had done to her.

"Where would I find the keys to your limousine?" Simon asked Amy.

"They could be in the car," she responded, "or my father might . . ." she sobbed once, then continued . . . "might have them."

Simon walked to the front door and eased it open. The lawn was clear of Canines, except for the one he'd shot earlier on the front porch. He glanced toward the driveway and couldn't believe his eyes. "It's gone," he exclaimed.

"What's gone?" Amy moved up beside him.

"The limo is gone."

"But who would have taken it?"

"It had to be Jay and Marcy."

"They took off and left us?" Amy asked. "Why?"

"I don't know," Simon confessed.

Lanning came up to them, the 45-70 in his right hand, the 30-06 in his left. The revolver was tucked under his belt. "I didn't peg your brother for the cowardly type, kid."

Simon glanced at Lanning. "You recovered fast."

"I'm a trained professional, remember?" Lanning said and snickered.

"What are we going to do now?" Amy asked.

"We'll take my mom's buggy," Lanning stated. "I have the keys."

"Okay. Let's make a run for it," Simon said. "I'll keep you covered."

"Let's not be hasty," Lanning said. He loaded the 45-70 from the box of shells in his own pocket. "I'd best load this sucker, too," he declared, indicating the 30-06.

"Here." Simon extracted a box of ammunition.

"Thanks." Lanning loaded the 30-06 and slung the rifle over his shoulder. He gave the box back to Simon. "Now we're all set."

The trio raced from the house to the sedan.

Without warning, a lone Canine leaped into view at the front of the sedan.

Lanning's reaction was instantaneous. The 45-70 thundered, and the Canine, struck in the neck, was thrown backwards. It flopped on the ground for several seconds, then lay still.

Simon watched for other marauders, while Lanning climbed in behind the wheel and Amy settled in the center of the front seat.

"Get in, kid," Lanning called.

Simon jumped in next to Amy and closed and locked the door.

"What now?" Amy wanted to know.

"We'll cruise the neighborhood and hope we find Jay and his girlfriend," Lanning proposed.

"After that?"

"Beats me, gorgeous. We're playing this one by ear." Lanning started the blue sedan and drove out to the street. "Which way, kid?"

"Try a left," Simon advised.

Lanning bore to the left, traveling with the headlights out.

"Try the radio," Amy suggested. "We might hear something important."

Lanning did as she recommended, but very few stations were still on the air. He twisted the dial, hoping to locate a newscast, and finally did.

". . . not attempt to leave the city," an announcer was saying. "We repeat—do not attempt to leave the city. We have reports of thousands of people trying to break through the military lines ringing Chicago. The military is shooting anyone, whether it be man, woman, or child, who comes within a hundred yards of their perimeter. All residents of Chicago are being warned to stay in their homes and lock the doors, or to get to one of the emergency shelters. In a moment we will supply a list of those shelters, but first this update on the Canines.''

There was a pause, and a different announcer came on. ''The Police Department reports the Canines are all over the city. Higher concentrations have been reported in the northwest and the southwest, but the entire city is overrun. The government still has not advised us on how the plague is being spread, but if someone you know has been bitten by a Canine, you are urged to get him to a hospital. Do not try to call the police. They are swamped and lack the manpower to respond to all the emergency calls they've already received. Barricades have been erected around the hospitals and certain key areas. These barricades are being manned by the Police Department and volunteers. These areas and shelters are your best bet. We have word of Canines going door to door in some neighborhoods, seeking victims. There is no official estimate of the number of Canines in the city, but a source close to the mayor says there are at least several hundred thousand, and that number is increasing. The city administration has not released an official fatality count as of yet. Now here's Ross with a list of those shelters.''

''Maybe we should head for a shelter,'' Amy recommended.

''If you can get your family to one of these shelters,'' the announcer said, ''please do so. You will be under police protection and receive medical treatment if it is required. The first shelter on my list is the Chicago Public Library. Here are the others: City Hall, the Federal Building, the Newberry Library and the Washington Square area, the Chicago Natural History Museum, Mercy Hospital, Michael Reese Hospital, Wesley Memorial Hospital, Passavant Hospital, and the Veterans Hospital. The Civic Opera House, at last word, was also safe. Most of these shelters are located in the same general area because the Police Department can not stretch itself too thin. The Police Commissioner urges all citizens to try and reach one of these shelters . . ."

Lanning lowered the volume on the radio. "What do you guys think? Should we try for one of the shelters?"

"We'd be safer there," Amy said.

"It seems like our best bet," Simon concurred.

"Are you going to turn on the headlights?" Amy asked.

"No," Lanning said. "Lights might attract the Canines." He slowed as he reached an intersection, verified no one was coming from the other direction, and drove on. "Which shelter should be try for?"

"All of them he listed are southeast of us," Amy reported.

"So which way do I go?" Lanning asked.

The sedan neared another intersection. Amy leaned forward, trying to read the signs. "I can't see," she remarked.

Lanning flicked on the lights, braking to a complete stop.

"That's Cicero," Amy said, identifying the intersection. "You want to take a right."

Lanning turned.

"There's other cars," Simon exclaimed happily.

Other vehicles were traveling in both directions, many of them exceeding the speed limit. Only a few traveled without lights.

Lanning kept the sedan's lights on. He didn't want to become involved in an accident because another driver didn't spot the sedan.

"Where are they all going?" Simon wondered.

"Who knows? I'd imagine most of them are running around like a chicken with its head chopped off," Lanning commented. "Panic is the name of the game right about now."

A Canine suddenly darted into the traffic about 50 yards in front of the sedan.

A large truck up ahead intentionally swerved, its huge tires crushing the Canine, leaving a gory mess on the highway in its wake.

"Good for him!" Simon shouted.

Lanning allowed his taut nerves to relax a bit. If they could reach one of those shelters, they'd have a fair chance of riding this thing out. At least they could take a breather, which they all could use.

"Look for the intersection with Chicago Avenue," Amy advised, "and take a left. Chicago should take us to where we want to go."

Lanning carefully noted the signs as they passed several intersections. Finally, after about three and a half miles, he found the junction they were looking for and took a left. The traffic volume increased considerably, the majority of the vehicles heading for the downtown area.

"I feel safer already," Amy announced.

"I wonder why we haven't seen more Canines," Simon said.

"Maybe they know they'd get squished like that one we saw," Amy said.

"Or there aren't as many in this area," Lanning added. He turned up the radio.

". . . even remaining in your homes is now considered to be unsafe. Locking the doors and windows will not stop the Canines," the announcer was saying.

"Tell us about it," Amy cracked.

". . . If you have a vehicle, try and reach one of

the shelters we mentioned just moments ago. If you do not have a vehicle, you should not try to reach the shelters on foot, as you are especially vulnerable on foot. Most of the phone lines are still operative. Contact a friend and car pool to a shelter if necessary.'' The announcer paused. ''We have this bulletin just in to the newsroom. Two more cities have been added to the list of Infected Cities and have been placed under a total quarantine. Those cities are Philadelphia and Los Angeles.''

''Philadelphia? That's where Marcy is from,'' Amy remarked.

''Where can she and Jay be?'' Simon asked apprehensively.

''Jay can take care of himself,'' Lanning said.

''. . . the list of Affected Zones is growing each hour. Here is the latest . . .''

Lanning turned the radio off. They rode in silence for five minutes.

''Hey, what's that?'' Simon inquired in an excited tone.

A police car was parked 30 yards ahead in the middle of a crowded intersection. An officer was perched on top of the cruiser, directing traffic with the aid of a flashlight.

''I've never been so happy to see a policeman in my life,'' Amy said.

Lanning had to slow to a crawl until they were through the intersection. Once beyond it, he still wasn't able to go much faster than 25 miles per hour because of the dense traffic.

''Which shelter should we go to?'' Simon asked Amy.

''Any one.''

They passed the Moody Bible Institute and reached the junction with LaSalle. Half of the traffic was continuing on ahead, while the rest swung to the left. Lanning wanted to go straight, but he was caught in the wrong lane and forced to bear to the left.

"We're near Washington Square," Amy stated.

"That's one of the safe areas," Simon noted.

Several police officers were controlling the traffic flow up ahead, diverting cars to designated parking areas. Lanning rolled down his window as he drew alongside one of the officers.

"Hello, officer."

She was too busy to acknowledge his greeting. "Take a right here," the patrolman directed. "Go two blocks and take another right. You should find a parking space in the vicinity of the YMCA. You'll have to walk to Washington Square from there."

"Will do," Lanning said. "Have you see many Canines in this area?"

The policeman frowned. "Earlier we saw a few, but we took care of them. I hear it's real bad west of here."

"Believe me," Lanning told her, "you wouldn't want to be caught dead out there."

35

Where was he?

Why did his head hurt so much?

He attempted to concentrate, but the effort produced a wave of dizziness.

What had happened? His memory was fuzzy. He'd been having a nightmare. He remembered that much. A terrible nightmare about people eating other people. Funny, how dreams and nightmares could be so vivid sometimes. He recalled Simon being in the nightmare, and a man named Lanning and Marcy . . .

Marcy!

Jay abruptly became fully alert, recollecting every vivid detail—the wedding, the President's speech, the Canines, and the ensuing battle at the Brant house. They had escaped in the limousine and were heading for a hospital when . . . they crashed!

Jay opened his eyes, momentarily disoriented. He was on his back, his body at an awkward angle, and something heavy was lying on his legs. He could see stars far above him, and a cool breeze was blowing on his face.

"Marcy?" he mumbled. "Marcy?"

There was no answer.

Jay raised his right hand and felt his head. There

was a nasty gash on the top, and his hair was matted with dried blood. A large, tender welt was located behind his right ear. His temples were throbbing, his skull pounding, and the pain was intense.

What had he hit? The windshield and what else?

He started to move his left arm and stopped as a piercing, lancing pain racked his chest.

What the hell! Had he broken or fractured his ribs?

Jay strained, elevating his head to get his bearings.

The limousine was overturned, resting on its roof. All of the windows were shattered, and the rear end was crushed, resembling an accordion. About ten yards from the tail of the limousine was the blue van, upright, its front caved in, at least a third of the vehicle a total wreck.

Jay struggled up onto his elbows, ignoring the agony in his left side. He was lying half-in, half-out of the car.

What was on his legs?

Jay grit his teeth and managed to attain a sitting position. He bent forward, reaching out, trying to touch whatever was pinning him down. His fingers barely brushed against a soft material. He placed his palms on the ground and heaved, striving to pull his legs free.

Someone whimpered.

Jay tensed and looked around, searching for the source.

A naked man was standing not more than five yards off, observing Jay's actions.

Jay looked for anything he could use as a weapon, but nothing was handy.

The stranger whined and stumbled toward the limousine. His hands were cradling his head.

Jay frantically tugged on his legs and was able to extricate his right foot. His left leg was still wedged inside the limousine when the naked man reached him.

"Help me," the stranger said in a plaintive voice. "Please."

At this range, Jay could see the man's eyes were watering and his mouth was salivating.

"Please," the man repeated. "Can you help me? My head hurts. I feel lousy. And I'm so damn hot! What's happening to me?"

"I'll help you," Jay promised, "if you'll give me a hand getting up."

The stranger was weaving. "I can't take much more of this. Oh, God!" He staggered off into the night.

Jay breathed a sigh of relief. Was that what happened to you right before you became a Canine? What if it had *been* a Canine? He redoubled his efforts, finally sliding his left foot out from whatever was restraining him.

Where was Marcy?

Jay twisted and poked his head inside the limousine. The nearest streetlight wasn't much help; he could distinguish few details in the Stygian gloom. He carefully probed with his hands and made contact with the object responsible for weighing him down.

It was a body.

Dear Lord, no!

Jay ran his fingers over the still form until he located the armpits. He grabbed them and slowly drew the body towards him.

"Marcy?"

Her head appeared first, and he sobbed when he saw the quantity of blood dampening her long black tresses. He tugged, gingerly removing her from the limousine. When he had her safely on the ground, he held her head in his lap and took stock of her visible injuries.

Marcy was in bad shape. In addition to the deep wound on the top of her cranium, her left cheek was swollen, her lips were bloody and puffy, her right arm had been torn open from the shoulder to the elbow, and her right leg was bruised and swollen from the ankle to the knee.

Jay gently caressed her right cheek. "Marcy?" he said softly.

She groaned, but didn't come out of it.

Jay tried to peer into the back seat of the limo, hunting for Cora and her son, Gus. He could dimly perceive a body near the rear window, but he couldn't determine whose it was.

Were they dead? The back seat had borne the brunt of the impact, and the van must have been doing close to 90 when the two vehicles collided.

Jay went to lay Marcy down so he could check on Cora and Gus. He hoped Cora was alive since she knew where the nearest hospital was located. What was it she had said right before the crash? They had to go back the way they had come? Which meant the hospital must be to the west or northwest since they were bearing due east at the time.

The dark was rent by a howl, not far away, on the opposite side of the limousine.

Jay hesitated, listening. What if the Canine was coming toward the limousine?

Another howl echoed after the first. And a third. The volume was louder than before.

It was a whole pack, and they were traveling in this general direction!

Jay had a choice to make. He could stay and hope the pack passed them by. Or he could stay and try to fight them off if they discovered Marcy and himself—but what could he do against an entire pack unarmed?

Where the hell was the 30/30?"

Jay looked into the limousine but failed to detect the rifle.

There was a chorus of howls now, and they were much, much closer.

Someone in the rear of the limousine moaned.

Jay hastily lifted Marcy into his arms and stood, keeping his head down, below the limousine. He spied a house to his right, approximately 60 yards away.

From inside the vehicle came a weak voice. "Is anyone there?" It was Cora.

Jay leaned down. "Don't move! Keep quiet! I'll be back as soon as I can." He turned and ran towards the house.

"Wait!" Cora called out after him. "Don't leave us!"

From the sound of the baying, the pack was almost upon the limousine.

Jay reached the sidewalk and spotted a tree up ahead. He angled toward it and ran behind the wide trunk for cover.

Howling like starving wolves, a pack of ten Canines appeared in the intersection.

The pack approached the van first, growling and sniffing. Unable to clamber inside, they turned their collective attention to the limousine.

Please, Jay prayed, please don't let them find Cora and the boy! Please let her keep her mouth shut!

One of the Canines poked its head into the limousine.

Cora's scream could be heard for miles.

In an instant, the pack swarmed onto the overturned limousine, cramming in through the broken windows. A lot of snarling and snapping mingled with Cora's terrified shrieking and babbling. Her final cry was her death cry, and it carried to Jay Darr's ears and stabbed into his very soul.

"Hellllllppppp me!"

Jay stumbled away from the tree, heading for the house he'd seen. He felt sick to his stomach and suppressed an impulse to puke. He crossed a driveway and staggered across a yard until he was brought up short by another tree. Holding Marcy tightly, he bypassed the tree and moved toward the side of the house. If he used the front door, the Canines at the intersection might spot him. He couldn't see any lights on inside the house, a two story building covered with aluminum siding, as he walked around to the back.

Would the door be locked?

Jay was becoming light-headed when he finally stepped up to the backdoor.

It was slightly ajar.

Cautiously, Jay eased the door all the way open and slid inside with Marcy. He patiently waited until his eyes adjusted to the murky interior, then he closed and locked the door. His left side was a fount of sheer torment as he moved along a hallway, scarcely noticing the rooms he passed. He reached the front door and fumbled with the lock.

There was a flight of stairs to his right.

Jay had to force his unwilling legs to cooperate as he climbed the stairs to the second floor. Marcy seemed like she weighed the proverbial ton.

Jay shuffled along a hallway and turned into the first room he found, a bedroom. He took several halting steps and collapsed on the bed with Marcy at his side.

Why couldn't he think straight?

How could this happen?

First, he abandoned his own brother. And now, a woman and her son were dead because he had failed them, had let them down when they desperately needed his help.

It was all his fault.

Jay endeavored to rise, but his body refused. He sank back down, relishing the soft, pliant feel to the bed, the beckoning warmth and tranquility. His eyes began to close in blissful slumber.

Sleep.

He needed sleep.

Hours and hours of it.

After a good rest, he'd get Marcy out of the house and find a hospital.

What was that?

Jay tried to resist his urge to sleep. He had heard something, a slight noise nearby. If it was a Canine, he was as good as gone. There was no way he could fight them, not in his condition.

With a reluctant sigh, Jay slipped into dreamland.

At the same instant, a throaty growl filled the bedroom.

36

"I never expected to find so many people."

"The more the merrier, Amy," Lanning quipped.

Amy, Simon and Lanning were approaching the barricades erected around Washington Square and the Newberry Library. The barricades were constructed of anything and everything the Police Department could find to suit their purpose—primarily sandbags, several buses to fill in the gaps, and even a collection of sturdy furniture at some points. Police officers and volunteer civilians were manning the top of the barricade, armed with M-16's, shotguns, and rifles. A gap had been left in the middle of the southern barricade to permit entry and allow for an exit. Four burly cops were stationed at the opening.

"Names?" one of the police officers demanded as the trio stopped at the entrance.

"Amy Brant," Amy answered. "This is my husband, Simon . . ."

"Right," the officer noted, "Simon Brant." He was writing their names on a clipboard.

"No," Amy corrected him, "Simon Darr."

The officer stared at Simon. "I thought she said she's your wife."

"She is," Simon confirmed.

"And what's your last name?" the police officer asked.

"Simon Darr."

"So why did she say her name is Amy Brant?"

"What difference does their name make?" Lanning interjected. "They were just married today. The girl isn't accustomed to using her married name yet."

The cop glanced at Lanning. "And what's your name, buddy?"

"Darr Brant."

The officer frowned. "Are you some kind of smartass?"

"No." Lanning grinned. "I'm an Interpol agent."

"And I'm Santa Claus," the police officer retorted, and his companions laughed.

Lanning stepped up to the officer with the clipboard. "I want to speak with your superior officer."

"Oh, you do, huh?" The cop chuckled. "Don't hold your breath."

Lanning's eyes narrowed and his voice lowered. "My name is James Lanning, and I *am* an Interpol agent. I would like to talk with your superior about trying to get a call through to Interpol. I have spent the greater part of the afternoon and the evening killing Canines, and in the process I lost someone I cared for very much. I'm not in the mood to be trifled with. I want to see your superior, and I mean right now."

Amy was amused by the officers' reactions. They glanced at one another, then at Lanning, patently perplexed.

"If you're an Interpol agent," the officer with the clipboard spoke up, "what are you doing in Chicago?"

"I told my travel agent I wanted some excitement during my vacation this year," Lanning replied, "and she recommended your fair city." He fished in his jacket pocket and removed his identification. "See for yourself."

The police officer with the clipboard examined Lanning's I.D. "I'll be damned! This joker is with Interpol."

"Talk about being at the wrong place at the wrong time," one of the other officers commented.

"Don't I know it," Lanning agreed.

"We have a command post in the library," the officer with the clipboard explained. He pointed at one of his friends. "Bob here will take you around to it, and you can see about your call."

"Thank you," Lanning said sincerely.

One of the other officers scanned the rifles they held. "We can use those guns on the barricades. When the Canines finally decide to launch an all-out attack, we'll need every gun we can muster."

"Do you really think they will?" Simon inquired anxiously.

"It's bound to happen," the cop remarked. "Sooner or later they'll run out of their food source in the suburbs and concentrate on the inner city."

"Food source," Simon repeated, the implications upsetting him.

"Follow me," Bob directed, walking through the opening in the barricade.

Amy glanced around before following Lanning and Simon, noting the dozens and dozens of people flocking toward the barricade. She derived some comfort from the presence of so many other people. As many as there were outside of the barricade, they were a drop in the bucket compared to the incredible number crammed into Washington Square. Amy had never seen so many people in Washington Square at the same time. Most of them were engaged in conversation, a few were sleeping, and nearly all of them were carrying weapons, everything from a hatchet to a high-powered rifle.

Bob led them across the Square, threading his way

between the packed refugees.

A ring of fully armed police officers encircled the Newberry Library, six of them stationed at the entrance. They parted to allow Bob and his party to enter.

"Wait here," Bob directed and walked off.

A large area had been cleared for use as the command post. One officer was seated behind a desk with four phones. A group of officers were gathered in front of a makeshift bulletin board. Tacked to the bulletin board was a giant map of Chicago and its environs with different colored pins stuck in the map at certain points.

Bob approached another officer and conversed with him for a minute, then both returned to Lanning and his friends.

"This is Captain Fry," Bob said, introducing his superior. "He can help you."

Captain Fry was a tall, rugged man with brown hair and green eyes. He extended his hand toward Lanning. "I undertand you're an Interpol agent?"

Lanning shook hands, nodding. "That's right." He handed his identification to Captain Fry.

"How may I help you?" Captain Fry inquired as he studied Lanning's I.D. card.

"If it's okay with you," Lanning explained, "I'd like to use one of your phones. I want to try and contact my headquarters."

Captain Fry motioned to the desk with the four phones. "You're welcome to use one of our lines, just don't keep it tied up too long. We're merely a subsidiary command post. The main command center is located in City Hall. They're constantly calling us with updates on Canine activity, and we appraise them of any new information we receive. We're also in touch with several other subsidiary command posts, so please keep your call as brief as possible."

"I will," Lanning assured the officer. He nodded at

the huge map. "Is that your monitoring map?"

Captain Fry frowned. "Yes. We've divided the city up into quadrants. A blue pin is a shelter. White pins indicate areas where Canine activity hasn't been reported as of yet. Yellow pins stand for areas where the Canines have been reported but haven't taken over the whole neighborhood—yet. Red pins are for neighborhoods or sections of the city under complete Canine control."

Amy stared at the map. There were only two white pins on the map, and they were both in the extreme southeastern corner of the city. The yellow pins filled a seven to ten miles radius surrounding the inner city. Beyond that, the map was a virtual sea of red pins. Even as she watched, four more red pins were added to the map in place of yellow pins.

"You seem to be losing the war," Lanning observed.

Captain Fry sighed. "We're doing the best we can. Although the city itself is under a quarantine, the phone lines to the outside world are still functional. Our command center at City Hall is in constant contact with the government. They warned us to be prepared for the worst, that this plague spreads fast, but we had no idea it would spread this fast. No wonder Egypt and Paris and those other places fell so rapidly."

"Egypt and Paris?" Lanning repeated.

"I guess you haven't heard the latest," Captain Fry said. "The government has released some more information on the plague since the President's address. Apparently, this thing got started in Egypt, and Paris was one of the first Euorpean cities affected."

"No wonder I haven't been able to get through to Interpol," Lanning declared.

"You're still welcome to try again," Captain Fry said.

"Thank you," Lanning responded. "I think I'll try

the London Bureau. They're still operational."

"Maybe not for much longer," Captain Fry said. "We heard that the plague has spread to London, too."

"Which phone can I use?"

Captain Fry led Lanning over to the desk with the phones.

Amy walked to a nearby chair and sat down. Egypt! Captain Fry had said Egypt. She thought of Professor Crenshaw and wondered if the Canines had gotten him. Possibly not. The Valley of the Dog People was located far from any urban center. Maybe the Canines hadn't . . .

Valley of the Dog People!

Canines!

Think, Amy, think! she told herself. What was it Professor Crenshaw had said about the Dog People? They had conquered an Egyptian city and defeated Prince Hiros when he was sent against them. She vividly remembered the striking hieroglyphics on the tunnel wall, the hieroglyphics depicting men and women running on all fours. And she recalled the gold coffin of Prince Hiros, shaped as if the Prince were down on his hands and knees. Was there a link? Were the Dog People of antiquity the same as the rampaging Canines? What else had Crenshaw said? Something about some scientists being worried over the possibility of a virus or bacteria being released from an ancient tomb or from exposure to a mummy. Was it possible? Was that what had happened? Dazed, she reviewed all of Crenshaw's words. The Dog People had been destroyed by a mighty magician, and the hieroglyphics on the tunnel wall had said fire dust was used. What in the world was fire dust?

A hand fell on her left shoulder, startling her. Simon was standing alongside the chair. "Are you all right?" he asked. "You look a bit pale."

Amy glanced up at him. "I don't rightly know."

"What is it? What's the matter?"

"It's impossible," Amy muttered. "It can't be."

"What can't be?" Simon pressed her.

Amy stared into his eyes. "Do you remember the tomb we excavated in Egypt?"

"Of course. Why?"

"Did you take a good look at the tunnel? Did you see the heiroglyphics on the walls?"

"Sure," Simon answered. "When Abdel was bringing me down to you."

"Don't you recall anything peculiar about those hieroglyphics?"

"A lot of them were strange," Simon stated. "The figures weren't standing up, they were . . ." He stopped, flabbergasted.

"And what did you say when you saw the coffin?" Amy reminded him.

"I said it looked like he was imitating a dog," Simon replied slowly.

Amy nodded.

Simon gaped at the map. "Do you think there's a connection?"

"There has to be," Amy said. "It can't be just a coincidence."

"Even if there is a connection," Simon noted, "how does it help us? So what if the Canines were around thousands of years ago?"

"Something stopped them way back then," Amy elaborated, "and it might stop them again."

"But we don't know what stopped them before."

"I may have a clue," Amy declared.

Lanning approached them, muttering under his breath. "Damn snotty operators," he snapped when he reached them. "She told me all of the overseas lines are tied up and I would have to wait. I told her this was a priority call, but she still said I would have to wait my turn." He paused. "I wonder if they're allowing overseas calls to go through, or if she was just stonewalling."

"Do you think we can call another state?" Amy asked him.

Lanning shrugged. "Why?"

"I need to reach the Centers for Disease Control in Atlanta."

"What? Why?"

"Didn't the President say that the Centers for Disease Control is trying to find a cure for the plague?"

Lanning thought about it for a moment. "Yes, he did. So what? Why must you call them?"

Amy told Lanning about the Valley of the Dog People, Prince Hiros, the hieroglyphics, everything. When she was done, he looked at her, then at the map, then back at her again.

"Son of a bitch!" Lanning exclaimed.

"Do you think there may be a link between the Dog People and the Canines?" Simon asked.

For an answer, Lanning grabbed Amy's right hand and hauled her over to the desk. He scooped up one of the receivers and dialed O.

A squeaky voice came on the line after four rings. "Operator. May I help you?"

"Operator," Lanning said, "I need to place a call to the Centers for Disease Control in Atlanta, please. This is an emergency."

37

Buddy was returning to his desk from the bathroom when the intercom buzzed. "Yes, Ms. Krepps?"

"Mr. Kramer called while you were out," his secretary informed him. "He said he wants you in his office, right away."

'Thank you." Buddy hurried to Kramer's office and opened the door without knocking. He stopped, stunned by the sight before him.

Kramer was down on his hands and knees on the floor.

For a fleeting instant, Buddy believed Kramer had transformed.

Kramer looked up and smiled. "Close the door," he ordered. "I don't want anyone to see me." He stood, brushing the lint from his suit.

Buddy closed the office door. "What were you doing?"

"Practicing," Kramer replied. "Have a seat."

"Practicing what?" Buddy asked as he sat down.

Kramer moved to his own chair, grinning self-consciously. "I was practicing moving the way the Canines do," he explained.

"So you'll be ready if the plague strikes Atlanta?"

"No." Kramer chuckled. "I was impressed by the

speed they can attain, running the way they do on their hands and feet, all bent over. I wanted to see how they do it. It's really not too difficult, but it kills your back."

"Is that why you wanted to see me?"

Kramer lifted a brown file from his desk. "This is why I wanted to see you." He tossed the file across the desk.

"What is it?" Buddy asked as he picked up the file.

Kramer smiled broadly. "It's the breakthrough we've been waiting for. Our analysis of the Canine blood Quintin removed before he died is complete. C-666 is a bacteria. The medium of transmission is both respiratory spread and close contact. Read the report. I'll wait."

Buddy eagerly opened the file and scanned the three pages inside. He had already suspected C-666 might be a bacteria from the way it attached itself to certain cells in the body, which was a characteristic bacterial trait. Preferential attachment, as it was called, accounted for why some bacteria concentrated on specific parts of the body, like the ears, nose and throat, but left the rest of the body unscathed. C-666 was one of the higher bacteria, the type which appeared as multicellular groups instead of single cells. In size and shape, C-666 could be classified as one of the spirilla bacteria, those which resembled a snake, but in most other respects, C-666 was exceptionally unique.

Several paragraphs in the report were devoted to a comparison of C-666 to hydrophobia, or rabies, although rabies was a virus and not caused by bacteria. Like rabies, C-666, once it had penetrated the body via the lungs or a casual handshake, traveled to the brain. Like rabies, C-666 only affected certain muscles. Like rabies, C-666 developed into an excitation phase characterized by extreme aggression, causing the victims to attack others without reason. Unlike rabies, so far as the scientists knew, C-666 did not eventually kill its victims.

Autopsies on Quintin and his associates had confirmed the medium of transmission as respiratory spread or casual contact. Combined with Quintin's journal and the results of other studies, particularly those conducted by French medical experts, transmission parameters were established. The minimum time frame between exposure and transformation was established approximately 24 hours. The maximum time frame was 48 hours.

Buddy skimmed the final page of the report, then glanced over at Kramer. "Still no word on a possible cure, I see."

Kramer sighed. "Not yet. The bacteria has not reacted to any of the traditional drugs, not even to our cure-all, penicillin. The lab people are trying every substance conceivable. Sooner or later, we'll find the right drug, either an antibiotic or chemotherapeutic agent. *Something* has to work. There has to be a way to fight this thing."

"Let's hope you're right," Buddy remarked.

Kramer's intercom buzzed, and he pressed a button on a speaker-amplifier. "Yes?"

"Mr. Kramer, I have a call on line four you might want to take."

"Who is it?"

"I don't know, sir."

"Did they ask for me?"

"No. sir."

"Tell them I'm busy and I'll call them back," Kramer directed.

"Sir, Mr. Ortlund said he thought you should take it. He said it might be important."

Buddy recognized the voice as belonging to one of the front receptionists. Ortlund currently worked in Public Relations, supplying news releases to the media and fielding queries from the general public.

"All right, I'll take it," Kramer said. He depressed the appropriate button for line four. "This is Tom Kramer. May I help you?"

A woman came on the line, her voice sounding faint, as if she were calling long distance. "Mr. Kramer? My name is Amy Brant. They told me you were the person I should contact."

"Yes, Ms. Brant, what may I do for you?" Kramer wondered why Ortlund had passed this call on to him.

"It's about the plague," Amy Brant said.

"What about it, Ms. Brant?"

"Call me Amy," the caller stated. "I think . . ." Her voice suddenly was drowned out by loud, crackling static. When the static finally faded, there was only silence on the line.

"Ms. Brant? Are you still there?" Kramer asked.

"Yes, I'm here," came the response.

"I'm afraid we have a bad connection," Kramer told her. "Where are you calling from?"

"Chicago."

Both Kramer and Buddy sat forward in their chairs.

"Chicago? Chicago is an Infected City. How are things there?" Kramer asked.

More static disrupted the line.

"Amy? Amy? Are you there?"

"I'm still here. I'd better make this short. The police need to use this line. I think I know where the plague came from. It started in Egypt."

Kramer looked at Buddy and frowned. "We already know that, Amy."

"Then you know about Professor Crenshaw?"

Kramer's brow furrowed. "Who is Professor Crenshaw?"

"He was working at an excavation site in Egypt. I was his assistant. We were uncovering a tomb in the Valley of the Dog People," Amy explained, then paused. "I'm afraid he may be dead by now."

"What does all of this have to do with the plague?"

"Don't you see? We may have unwittingly unleashed this plague. We found a tomb containing the mummy of an Egyptian prince. This prince was killed in a battle with the Dog People. The tunnel walls of the tomb were covered with hieroglyphics depicting men and women down on all fours, just like the Canines. Even the coffin of the prince was in the shape of a man on all fours. Please, you've got to believe me!"

"Calm down, Amy," Kramer said. "Will you hold on for just a second?"

"Okay," Amy replied, "but hurry. Like I said, the police need to use this phone."

"I'll be right back," Kramer promised. He pressed a button on the speaker-amplifier so Amy couldn't overhear his comments. "What do you think?" he asked Buddy.

"She sounds sincere to me," Buddy said.

"She could just be an emotional crackpot," Kramer speculated. "We've received all kinds of crank calls since the President's speech."

"She knows the plague began in Egypt," Buddy noted.

"Anyone could have figured that out from the newscasts," Kramer countered.

"What about the tomb business? Could we run a check on that Professor Crenshaw she mentioned?"

"We could wind up wasting a lot of time and money on false information," Kramer said. He depressed the speaker-amplifier button again. "Amy?"

"I'm here."

"I'm going to return you to Mr. Ortlund. He'll take down all the information we need. We'll—"

"You don't believe me!" Amy practically screamed, cutting him short.

"I didn't say that," Kramer said.

"I know you don't," Amy stated. "Please, you

must believe me! There really is a tomb and a mummy. The Dog People really existed. You must believe me!"

Buddy was impressed by the woman's evident earnestness.

"Please, calm down," Kramer was saying. "You must understand our position. We must verify the facts you give us. Tell me, where are you at in Chicago. At home?"

"No," Amy said, her tone strained. "I'm at one of the shelters, at the Newberry Library."

"Is there a number where we can reach you?" Kramer asked.

"You can reach me through the command post here," Amy answered, "but you're only losing precious time. Oh, why won't you believe me?"

They could hear the woman sobbing in frustration.

"Amy . . ." Kramer began.

"Listen," Amy interrupted, "there's one thing you must believe."

"What's that?"

"I may know how to stop the Canines," Amy said.

"What?"

"I may know how to stop the Canines," Amy repeated. "The hieroglyphics on the tunnel wall told us how the ancient Egyptians defeated the Dog People. The same thing may work on the Canines."

Kramer and Buddy exchanged glances.

"What if she's telling the truth?" Buddy asked.

"Who's that?" Amy demanded, hearing the voice in the background.

"A friend," Kramer said. "Do you mean to tell us you may know of a cure for the plague?"

"That's what I've been trying to tell you," Amy cried.

"What is it?"

The static returned.

"What is the cure?" Kramer reiterated when the static ceased.

"I was with the Professor when he read the hieroglyphics," Amy stated, her voice breaking up, her words punctuated by intermittent static.

"What is the cure?" Kramer pressed her.

"He . . ." More static squelched her words ". . . was a magician who . . . used . . . know what . . . eans."

"Amy!" Kramer exclaimed. The connection is breaking up. We still don't know what the cure is. What is the cure?"

"I . . . hear . . . me . . ."

"Amy!" Kramer shouted.

The line abruptly went dead.

38

Bright sunlight on his face awakened Jay.

He sluggishly opened his eyes, wondering where he was. The events of the preceding night flooded over his consciousness, and he sat up with a start. He was still on the bed, Marcy asleep at his side. The sunlight was streaming in through the bedroom window. He shook his head, trying to clear the cobwebs.

It was daylight.

Jay raised his arm and checked his watch.

Almost 11:00 o'clock!

Jay began to slide from the bed, his feet almost touching the carpeted floor, when an ominous growl rumbled from nearby. He froze, expecting an attack.

A Canine must be in the room!

The growl sounded again.

Jay slowly moved his head until he could see the bedroom doorway.

A large Doberman Pinscher, weighing at least 50 pounds, its smooth coat pitch black, was lying across the threshold, eyeing Jay suspiciously.

Jay started to rise.

The Doberman stood and snarled, baring its formidable fangs.

''Whoa, there, big fella,'' he said in a quiet tone,

"I'm not going to hurt you. I'm your friend."

The Doberman cocked its head, studying the human.

"I won't harm you," Jay stressed. "We should be friends. Our enemy is outside." He cautiously extended his left hand.

The Doberman carefully moved forward until it could smell the hand, sniffed it for several seconds, then sat down.

"Does this mean I can stand up?" Jay asked. He eased himself from the bed and straightened up, leery of making any sudden moves.

The Doberman watched him.

"Are you hungry?" Jay asked, hoping his voice would soothe the animal, would reassure it he wasn't a foe. "I know I'm hungry. How would you like it if I went downstairs and fixed us something to eat?"

The Doberman merely watched.

Jay slowly walked around to Marcy and knelt over her. He gently shook her, endeavoring to rouse her.

Marcy opened her eyes, spotted his worried features, and grinned. "Hi, handsome," she greeted him, her voice a whisper.

"How are you feeling?" Jay anxiously asked.

"Like a ton of bricks fell on my head," Marcy said. "I feel so weak."

"Don't move," Jay cautioned. He inspected her from head to toe. The top of her head was all swollen, and her top lip had been split in the middle. Her right arm had stopped bleeding, but there was a wicked wound from her elbow to her shoulder. The Canine bite on her right ankle was inflamed, as was her right leg.

"What's the prognosis, doc?" she joked when his examination was finished.

"I've got to get you to a hospital," Jay told her. "You must be in a lot of pain."

"It's bad," Marcy admitted, "but the itching is

worse."

"The itching?"

"Yeah, my whole body itches. Maybe you'd like to scratch it for me?" she suggested playfully.

Jay tenderly stroked her forehead. "I want you to lie still and get more rest. I'm going downstairs to find some food and see if the Canines have left the area."

"Where are we?"

"I don't rightly know," Jay admitted. "I carried you to a house I saw from the road."

"Where are Cora and Gus?"

Jay's teeth clenched, and he averted his gaze. "The Canines got them."

"Oh, sorry I brought it up," Marcy said, detecting his anguish.

"Now don't move. If you need anything, holler. Dobby and I will come on the run."

"Dobby?"

Jay pointed at the dog. "A Doberman Pinscher. It appears to be friendly. The owners must have deserted it when they split."

"Be careful," Marcy said.

Jay leaned down and kissed her on the forehead. "You try and get some more sleep." He crossed to the doorway, the Doberman on his heels. Together, they went down the stairs to the front door. Jay checked that it was still locked, then walked into an adjacent living room with yellow drapes covering a huge picture window. He stepped to the drapes and peeked outside.

The van and the overturned limousine were still in the intersection, but there was no sign of the Canines, nor anyone else for that matter. The world beyond the picture window was completely devoid of life.

Jay turned and moved along the hallway of the modestly furnished home to the kitchen. He found the refrigerator and opened it.

"Well, look at this," he said to the dog. "We

won't starve. There's enough food here to last us for weeks."

Jay sorted through the kitchen cupboards and located a dozen cans of dog food.

"This must be yours, right?" He held one of the cans aloft.

The Doberman whined expectantly.

Jay couldn't find a dog bowl anywhere on the floor, so he reoved a china bowl from one of the cupboards, found a can opener in one of the drawers, and proceeded to feed the ravenous Doberman.

"There you go, Dobby," he said as the dog wolfed down the food.

Jay tossed the empty can in the trash and walked to the back door. He peered outside, confirming the backyard was also clear of Canines. Satisfied the house was temporarily secure, he went about preparing a hearty meal of eggs, bacon, and toast. After pouring some milk into a glass, he lugged the meal upstairs to the bedroom.

Marcy stirred and opened her eyes as he entered.

"Chow time," Jay said.

"I don't know if I can," Marcy said.

"What's the matter? You don't like my cooking anymore?"

"I just don't feel very hungry," Marcy elaborated.

Jay sat on the bed next to her. "You've got to eat something and keep up your strength until we can reach a hospital."

"I hope we reach one soon. My headache is getting worse."

"This food will help," Jay said. He placed the plate and the glass of milk on a nightstand.

"I'm really not hungry."

"Try come of this." Jay heaped a metal spoon with scrambled eggs and lowered the spoon to her mouth. "Please."

Marcy allowed herself to be fed. Her mouth and

jaw ached terribly, forcing her to chew slowly. Jay patiently bore with her until she indicated she was full by raising her left hand to her mouth to prevent him from continuing.

"Are you sure you've had enough?" Jay asked.

"I'm positive," Marcy replied. "Besides, I don't feel too well. I feel sick in my stomach. Where's the bathroom?"

Jay put the spoon on the nightstand and rose. "I'll carry you there. You shouldn't put any weight on that right leg of yours."

Marcy inadvertently grimaced as he lifted her into his strong arms.

"Sorry if I hurt you," Jay apologized.

"It's not your fault. Just breathing hurts me."

Jay left the bedroom and searched the upstairs until he found a tidy bathroom two doors down the hall.

"Set me on the toilet," Marcy instructed. "I'll call you if I need you."

Jay sat her down. "All right, but first . . ." He opened the medicine cabinet above the bathroom sink.

"What are you looking for?"

"This." Jay removed a first aid kit from the cabinet.

"Let me take care of my business first," Marcy said, "and then you can take care of me."

"Call if you need me," Jay said as he walked to the door.

"I think I can potty on my own," Marcy said, her grin lopsided because of her puffy lips.

Jay closed the bathroom door and waited in the hallway, taking stock of his own body. His left side was hurting, but the pain was not as intense as the night before. His other injuries were insignificant compared to Marcy's. He couldn't afford to slack off now. Reaching a hospital as quickly as possible was imperative.

The Doberman padded up the stairs and joined him.

Jay reached down and patted the dog's head. The Doberman would come in handy, providing added protection for Marcy in case of trouble. He decided to take the dog with them when they departed.

Were the Canines as active during the day as they were at night? If not, and if he could obtain a vehicle, they'd better get to a hospital by nightfall. He tapped on the bathroom door. "Marcy?"

"What?"

"I'm going downstairs to use the phone to see if I can get directions to the nearest hospital. I won't be long."

"Take your time."

Jay stared at the Doberman. "Stay!" he ordered and was surprised when the dog obeyed. He hurried down the stairs to the living room, where he had noticed a phone on an end table. He eagerly grabbed the receiver and raised it to his ear.

The phone was dead.

Jay frowned and replaced the receiver. Damn it all! Were they the only ones remaining in the city? He crossed to the television set and turned it on, hoping to find some news. The screen filled with the image of an announcer.

". . . advise you to get to one of the emergency shelters before it is too late. Again, the Police Commissioner has announced that they will be unable to handle emergency calls. Every man and woman on the force is being used to defend the inner city. The Canines have taken over two-thirds of Chicago. Reports of Canine activity have tapered off since daylight, but they are still abroad, and all citizens should take appropriate precautions."

A map of Chicago appeared on the screen.

"Take a good look at this map," the announcer advised. "The points circled in white are the shelters where food and medical treatment are available."

Jay scanned the map. All of the shelters were in the inner city area. He wasn't certain of the location of the house they were in, but he did know the inner city would be to the southeast. Good. At least he knew which way to head. Now all he required was a car or truck to get them to one of the shelters. Optimistic, he switched the television off and hastened upstairs to the bathroom.

The Doberman was lying on the floor next to the bathroom door.

"Good dog." He knocked on the door. "Marcy?"

The door swung open and Marcy staggered into his arms.

"I just saw a newcast on the TV," he informed her. "They've set up emergency shelters, and we should try to reach one. You need medical attention."

Marcy wearily laid her right cheek on his shoulder. "Whatever you say, lover, but not right now."

"Why not? The sooner the better."

Marcy gazed up into his eyes. "I feel lousy, Jay. Real lousy. Let me take a nap for an hour or so, and then we'll leave."

"I'd feel better if we left right now," Jay said.

Marcy sagged against him. "Okay. But you'll have to carry me until we find a car, because I can't manage more than a few steps on my own. What happens if the Canines come after us while you're toting me?"

Jay frowned, unhappy with her logical reasoning. She had a point. He certainly wouldn't be able to defend them while bearing her. "I could leave you in here with Dobby while I scour this neighborhood for a car," he suggested.

"I'd rather you stay with me. Don't leave me. I don't want to be alone. I'm so tired and stiff and hot. All I need is a nap and I'll be okay."

"Some rest would do you some good," Jay agreed, "and while you're sleeping, I'll fix myself some breakfast."

"Sounds great to me."

Jay lifted Marcy and returned her to the bed.

Marcy sighed contentedly. "This bed is so soft. Too bad I'm not in the mood." She winked at him.

Jay chuckled. "Has anyone ever told you that you have a one-track mind?"

"Everybody."

Jay opened the first aid kit and meticulously cleaned Marcy's wounds and applied ointment to her cuts and lacerations and the Canine bite. By the time his ministrations were done, she had fallen asleep. He leaned down and tenderly kissed her on her forehead. "Sleep tight, beautiful," he whispered. Before leaving the bedroom, he crossed to the window and checked it was latched. He paused in the doorway and affectionately admired her sleeping form. Lord, but she had guts! She was holding up well, considering the circumstances. He'd never suspected she possessed such an incredible inner reservoir of strength and courage. He only hoped he could perform as well when put to the test.

With the Doberman trailing along, Jay quietly closed the bedroom door and walked downstairs to the kitchen. His stomach was growling. He cooked a pan full of bacon and eggs, then carted the pan and a fork into the living room where he could keep an eye on the front door, the hallway and the stairs. Nothing would be able to approach Marcy without him spotting it. He sighed as he sat down in a comfortable easy chair.

Where were Simon and Amy? They must have escaped from the Brant house alive. Where would they go? To one of the emergency shelters, probably. He resolved to check each and every shelter after obtaining medical treatment for Marcy.

The Doberman lay at his feet as Jay heartily dug into his meal. The scrambled eggs and crisp bacon tasted delicious, and in short order he polished off the contents of the pan. There was a warm sensation in his tummy when he placed the pan on the floor and reclined in the easy chair.

It was amazing how a little food could perk up the old spirits.

Jay stretched, being careful not to agitate his left side, and drowsily closed his eyes. A quick cat nap might be just the thing. After he woke up, he'd hunt for a vehicle and get the hell out of here before . . .

He awoke with a start, sensing something was very, very wrong. The living room, which mere moments ago had been illuminated by brilliant sunlight, was csat in shadows.

What time was it?

Jay consulted his watch, his eyes widening in alarm.

It was 7:10. He must have slept through the afternoon and early evening. Jay heaved himself up, disregarding the twinge in his left side.

Damn his stupidity! The Canines would be out in force soon.

Jay started for the stairs, then froze as a low growl came from the direction of the kitchen.

Where was the Doberman?

He hurried down the hall and found the Doberman standing near the backdoor, its fangs bared, its short hairs bristling.

Something was on the other side of the door.

Jay could hear scratching coming from the outside. A window was inset in the top third of the door, and he cautiously peered over the lower rim.

A trio of Canines was crouched on the other side of the door, one of them pawing at the wood, a boy of only six or seven years of age.

Jay backed away from the door. Did the Canines know there were people inside the house, or had they only heard the Doberman? Would they go away after a while?

"Here, boy," he whispered to the dog. "Come with me."

The Doberman reluctantly turned from the door and followed Jay down the hallway to the living room.

Jay paused at the foot of the stairs. There might be more Canines out front, but he risked being detected if he peered through the drapes. His best bet would be to go upstairs and remain in the bedroom with Marcy and the dog until the Canines departed.

The Doberman suddenly whirled, facing the picture window, snarling.

"Quiet!" Jay hissed. "They'll hear you!"

They already had.

With a tremendous crash, the picture window caved inwards, showering glass and Canines all over the carpet. Five of them had charged the window in a concerted rush. For a moment, they were entangled in the drapes, but the next instant, they were free, two of them closing on the Doberman while the other three headed for the human.

There was no time to find a weapon.

Jay instinctively adopted the Horse Riding stance, his right hand forming into a Leopard fist.

The first Canine was three feet off when it launched its body into the air.

Jay swung, driving his fist into the Canine's nose. The blow shattered its cartilage and dropped it to the floor. Jay assumed a left forward stance, drew his right foot up, and executed a thrusting side kick to the Canine's face, sending it sprawling.

The second and third Canines were on him before he could react. One of them hit low, at the knees. The other one plowed into his chest, the impact driving him backwards in the wall.

Jay felt teeth sink into his left shin as he toppled against the wall. His hands encircled the neck of the Canine clinging to his chest as he lashed out with his right foot, knocking aside the Canine grasping his legs.

The Doberman had dispatched one of its opponents and was ripping into its second foe.

The Canine in Jay's grasp struggled to break loose, snarling and snapping at Jay's arms.

The two Canines Jay had kicked were up and bearing down on him again.

Jay could feel and smell the Canine's fetid breath, the saliva spattering on his face and arms. Nauseated by the proximity of the Canine's contorted, bestial features and its rank odor, Jay frantically spun around, whipping the Canine in a tight circle and releasing the monstrosity directly into the path of the other two.

His strategy worked.

All three collided and tumbled in a writhing heap onto the carpet.

Jay was on them before they could scramble to their feet. He caught one of them under the chin with his left foot. Blood erupted from the Canine's mouth as it fell to the floor. His right hand plunged downward, his first two fingers held rigid and straight in the traditional snake strike, and he drove his fingers into the distended left eye of the second Canine. It wailed and jerked away, but not before he planted his right foot in the throat, crushing the larynx. The Canine gagged and gasped, dropping onto its face.

The third one was on its feet, lunging at the human's legs, its mouth opened wide, its lips coated with white froth.

Jay barely side-stepped his attacker and pivoted, his left leg flicking out as the Canine turned. His foot slammed into the creature's right temple, slowing it down. Jay whirled, automatically performing a spin kick. Once. Twice. Three times he struck the Canine in the head, and on the third spin kick the thing fell.

Jay assumed the Cat stance, bracing for another assault.

The Doberman had killed its second adversary,

but had sustained a long slash in its right side in the process.

The five initial attackers were out of commission.

Jay moved to the stairs. Now was the time to get Marcy out of the house, while there was a temporary lull in the fighting. They could slip out a ground floor window and take the Doberman with them. Once outside, they could locate a vehicle and drive to a shelter.

The Doberman suddenly snarled.

Jay was halfway up the stairs when the second wave of howling Canines burst into the living room, cresting over the sill of the ruined picture window and jostling one another in their fervid fury to seek new prey.

The Doberman went down, battling to the last, submerged under the weight of six savage Canines.

Jay took two steps down the stairs, intending to aid the dog, but stopped, realizing it would be useless, even as the baying pack rounded the base of the stairs and started up.

He had to get to Marcy.

Jay backed up the stairs, knowing he wouldn't be able to reach the top before they caught up with him.

He was right.

The Canines, forced to bound up the stairs two at a time for lack of sufficient space, overtook their quarry when he was only one step from the upstairs hallway and mere yards from the bedroom door.

Balanced precariously on the stairs, Jay snap kicked the first pair in the face. Stunned, they lost their footing and toppled down the stairs, blocking the pursuit of the others behind them. In the few precious seconds afforded by the tangle on the stairs, Jay ran to the bedroom door, jerked it open, entered, and closed it, throwing his shoulder against the door to hold them back.

"Marcy!" he shouted. "Wake up!"

A heavy body barreled into the other side of the

door, shaking it, jarring Jay's shoulder. He kept his right hand on the doorknob, holding it closed.

"Marcy, it's the Canines!"

The pack plowed into the door, trying to force it open.

Jay was thankful the Canines weren't smart enough to remember how to use a doorknob, but sooner or later, doorknob or no doorknob, they would break the door down through sheer force of numbers.

"Marcy!"

Why hadn't she answered him? Surely she couldn't sleep with all of this racket?

There was a feral growl to his rear.

Jay glanced over his shoulder, fearing a Canine had somehow managed to gain entry to the bedroom.

One had.

She was squatting on the bed, stark naked, her brown eyes bulging and watering, her mouth covered with foamy froth, her swollen lips twisted in a vicious snarl.

"Marcy?"

Shocked to the core of his being, unwilling to accept the credence of his own vision, mentally dazed and emotionally devastated, Jay released the doorknob and took several steps toward the figure on the bed.

"Marcy? Is that you?"

The Canine on the bed seemed to recoil slightly at the sound of his voice. It cocked its head, scrutinizing him intently.

"Marcy, it's me. Jay."

The bedroom door vibrated from the continued assault of the pack.

Jay took another step toward her.

"Marcy, it's Jay. Jay. You remember me, don't you?"

Outside in the hallway, one of the Canines howled

at the top of its lungs.

"I love you."

The figure on the bed responded to the howl from the hall, answering the cry, throwing back its head and baying, reveling in its primeval glory.

Jay simply stood there as the Canine on the bed sprang at his throat and the bedroom door went down under the weight of the frenzied pack.

39

"Are the phones still dead?" Amy asked as Lanning approached Simon and her in Washington Square.

The Interpol agent nodded. "It's been about twenty-four hours now, and they're still down. There's no telling when, or even if, we'll get them back again. Captain Fry doubts we will. The police still have their car radios and their walkie-talkies, but the range is too limited to do us much good. Sorry, gorgeous, I tried my best."

Amy wearily leaned on her 270. "I know you did, and I appreciate it. I was so close to telling them about the fire dust. I'm sure they couldn't understand me because of all the static."

Lanning hefted his 45-70 and stared at Simon. "Hey, what's with you, kid? I know we're in a tight spot, but there's no need for you to look like death warmed over. What gives?"

Simon glanced at Lanning. "I was thinking about Jay and Marcy. What could have happened to them?"

"They're probably at one of the other shelters," Lanning replied.

"You really think so?"

"You told me that your brother is a martial arts instructor," Lanning stated. "He can take care of himself. We'll find him when this is all over."

"Who the hell are you kidding?" Amy rudely demanded.

"I'm not trying to kid anyone," Lanning said.

"Then be realistic," Amy retorted, the accumulated strain from all of the events since her aborted wedding beginning to show. "Chicago is one of the Infected Cities, remember? We're under a quarantine. There's no way out. There's nothing we can do except sit here and wait for the Canines to wipe us out!" Her voice rose, drawing the attention of some of the nearby refugees.

Simon placed his hand on her shoulder. "Calm down. We'll get out of this in one piece. I promise."

Amy started to say something, to loudly rebuke him, but changed her mind and turned away, instead. She had to control herself. There was no use in taking out all of her anger and frustration on Simon and Lanning. She gazed up at the police officers and the civilian volunteers manning the barricades.

"She has a point, kid," Lanning said to Simon, motioning toward the west barricade wall about 20 yards away.

"We can't give up hope," Simon said.

"We can't delude ourselves, either," Lanning remarked. "Captain Fry told me the Canines are massing to the west of us. He believes tonight will be the night. The police have erected roadblocks and other barricades at strategic points. They plan to try and prevent the Canines from crossing the Chicago River to our west and south, and holding them back to the north. But let's be realistic, like Amy said. The number of Canines in the city, according to police estimates, is somewhere between one and two million. There's no way a few thousand police are going to hold them back."

"One or two million?" Simon repeated, astonished.

"That's right," Lanning affirmed.

Amy glanced at Lanning. "So what do we do? Stay here and wait for them to attack?"

"What else can we do?"

"I don't know," Amy admitted.

"Look on the bright side," Lanning suggested.

Amy snickered. "What bright side?"

"Think of how educational this experience is," Lanning said, smirking. "Now you know exactly how Jim Bowie and Davy Crockett must have felt at the Alamo."

Simon shook his head. "How can you joke at a time like this?"

"Lighten up, kid," Lanning recommended. "Don't let this get to you or you won't be of any help when the big crunch comes."

Amy tilted her head and looked at the stars overhead. What a way to spend a honeymoon! She wished she could suddenly wake up in her bed and discover this was all a terrible nightmare.

Suddenly, from off in the distance to the west, came the muted blast of gunfire. A chorus of howls seemed to arise from every direction.

"This is it," Lanning declared.

"Do we stay here or help man the barricades?" Simon asked nervously.

Lanning was studying their situation. They possessed five guns between them—Amy's 270, Simon's 30-06, his own 45-70 and the service revolver tucked under his belt. In addition to the 45-70 and the revolver, Lanning also carried the spare 30-06, the one Frederick had used, slung over his left shoulder. Five measly guns against a veritable horde. Not exactly the greatest of odds.

"What should we do?" Simon anxiously inquired. "You're the expert in these matters."

"We'll do whatever you say," Amy added.

Lanning scanned the barricades. "The way I read

it is this. The police roadblocks and barricades at the Chicago River won't do more than temporarily slow down the Canines. Most likely, they'll attack this shelter from the west and the north, meaning the east is where we should head if Washington Square falls. So lets get closer to the eastern wall of the barricade."

They pushed their way toward the designated wall.

The howling was growing louder, closing in on Washington Square from the west and north.

"You're a genius," Simon commented to Lanning.

"Not quite," Lanning said. "Besides common sense, I'm a firm believer in self-preservation."

There was a commotion on top of the western barricade of Washington Square. Voices were uplifted in alarm, and the police officers and civilians with rifles opened fire. Inside the barricades, the crammed refugees stirred restlessly.

Lanning, Amy and Simon continued moving closer to the eastern barricade. Lanning noted the eastern barricade, unlike the southern wall, lacked an opening in its center. If the Canines breached the defenses and remaining in Washington Square became untenable, they would need to climb over the sandbags and other debris used in the construction of the barricade to effect their escape.

A number of police officers appeared at the north end of the Square, coming from the Newberry Library, with Captain Fry in the lead. They clambered to the top of the western wall.

"Why didn't Fry stay in the Library?" Simon asked. "It would be considerably easier to defend than this place."

"Like any good captain," Lanning said, "Captain Fry is going to go down with his ship."

"I'm sorry I asked," Simon rejoined.

The firing from the western barricade increased in volume. Some of the men and women stationed on the southern wall also began shooting.

Lanning frowned. He could hear massive gunfire from the north as well, and he didn't like it one bit. The Canines might not adhere to his prediction; they might surround the Library and the Square first, and then launch an overwhelming attack.

Sure enough, the firing along the top of the southern barricade was spreading.

"I don't know how to tell you this," Lanning admitted to the other two, "but I may have committed a slight tactical boo-boo."

"What do you mean?" Amy asked.

Some of the riflemen on the eastern barricade entered the fray, their guns booming.

"Follow me," Lanning ordered. "Hurry!" He ran toward the center of Washington Square, Simon and Amy right behind him.

"I don't get it," Simon said. "One minute you say we'll be safer to the east, and the next you're taking us back the way we came. What's going on?"

Lanning glanced over his right shoulder. "The Canines are smarter than I thought. From the sound of things, I expect they'll completely encircle us and then attack. We won't be able to escape to the east."

"Then how will we get out?" Simon demanded.

Lanning stopped and stared at each of them in turn. "We won't. There's no place left to go."

By now, the gunfire and the howling had reached a raucous crescendo.

"Get to the middle of the Square," Lanning yelled.

All around them, the refugees were bracing for the onslaught. Those with firearms or other weapons waited expectantly, while many of the small children, and not a few of the adults, were bawling. A large number stood with their eyes closed and their hands clasped together in prayer.

Lanning guided Simon and Amy through the multitude to the middle of Washington Square.

The roar of the M-16's, shotguns and rifles was almost deafening.

The refugees had lit a dozen or so fires in the Square, scores of lanterns and lamps providing additional illumination. The police also had erected generator-powered spotlights at strategic points along the top of the barricade. All served their purpose admirably, enabling the refugees to clearly see the first of the Canines to attain the top of the barricade.

"Look!" someone shouted.

Lanning had already seen it. A solitary Canine had scrambled to the top of the western barricade. It was immediately shot for its troubles, but Lanning knew it wouldn't be the last one to reach the top.

Simon took Amy's right hand and leaned over so his lips were next to her ear. "No matter what happens," he told her, "I want you know I'll always love you."

Amy swallowed hard and nodded. "And I want you to know how sorry I am."

"Sorry for what?"

"For causing all of this," she replied.

"How do you figure that?"

Amy gazed at the barricades, her eyes misting. "I know there is a link between these Canines and the Dog People. I just know it! And I know the Canines wouldn't be here if Professor Crenshaw and I hadn't opened the tomb of Prince Hiros." She paused. "I'm to blame for all of this. Indirectly or not, I'm responsible.,"

"That's ridiculous," Simon argued. "How were you to know? How many tombs were opened in the past with nothing like this ever occurring? You can't blame yourself."

"Yes, I can," Amy countered, "and I do."

"Now isn't the proper time for guilt trips," Simon stated.

"I know." Amy nodded. "Now's our time to

die."

"Don't talk like that!" Simon said harshly.

"I can't help it," Amy replied. "I have this . . . feeling."

Simon kissed her on the lips, savoring the sweet taste of her mouth and the lingering fragrance of her perfume. "We're not going to die," he told her when he broke the kiss.

Amy didn't comment.

A woman nearby screamed.

Several Canines were on top of the western barricade. They, like their predecessor, were promptly gunned down, but no sooner were they riddled with bullets than others appeared to take their place.

Lanning surveyed the barricades, assessing their predicament. From the frenzied pace of the firing, he deduced the militia was hard pressed to prevent the marauders from reaching the top of the barricades. There must be thousands upon thousands of Canines on the other side of those barricades.

It wouldn't be long.

Lanning faced Simon and offered his right hand.

Simon, surprised by the unexpected gesture, arched his eyebrows. "What's this for?"

"Are you going to shake or not?" Lanning demanded.

Simon shook. "What's this for?" he reiterated.

"I'm saying good-bye," Lanning explained.

"Not you, too," Simon snapped.

"It's been nice knowing you, kid. For what it's worth, I kind of thought we had the makings of a wonderful friendship. Too bad it's been nipped in the bud," Lanning said, a tinge of regret in his tone.

"We're not dead yet," Simon shouted.

"I wouldn't give odds on how long we'll last," Lanning yelled back.

"You've got to have faith," Simon declared.

Lanning grinned. "Sorry, kid, but I'm afraid I'm running a little low in that department."

"Dear God!" a man near Lanning exclaimed. "They're over!"

Lanning spun around.

The Canines had successfully breached the top of the western barricade, slaying a score of riflemen in the process. Without hesitation, the Canines leaped from the top of the barricade into the refugees below.

Pandemonium ensued.

The refugees were initially able to kill the Canines as soon as they landed on the ground, but as more and more poured over the western barricade in seemingly endless numbers, the refugees were compelled to grapple with their foes in primitive life or death struggles.

Lanning saw Simon raise his 30-06 and sight on the western barricade. He reached out and lowered the barrel of Simon's rifle before he could fire. "Don't waste the round. Save it for when we'll really need it."

"When will that be?"

"When you can see the white foam on their mouths," Lanning answered.

The scene below the western wall was absolute bedlam, and there were now more Canines on top of the western barricade than humans. They had also scaled the southern barricade and were engaged in a pitched battle with the forces protecting the shelter.

Lanning raised the 45-70 to his shoulder. So this was how it was going to end—torn apart by a bunch of crazies with a fido complex! What a rotten way to cash in your chips! He would have much preferred to pass on while enjoying sex with the woman he loved. It might cause her to become celibate, but at least he would go out with a smile on his face.

As things stood now, he probably wouldn't have a face left to smile with.

As the number of Canines in Washington Square increased dramatically, the efforts of the refugees to save themselves and their loved ones took on frantic overtones. Some of them, in their haste to shoot a Canine, would miss and strike a fellow refugee instead. If a Canine grabbed a young child, the unarmed mother would throwh herself on the Canine in an attempt to rescue her offspring. One big man, armed only with a sword, was doing a tremendous job of hacking the creatures into several pieces.

Canines were now surging over the western and southern barricades.

A burly black one appeared ten yards in front of Lanning, grappling with a policewoman.

Lanning aimed at the Canine's head, biding his time, waiting for an opening. It came when the policewoman kneed the Canine in the groin and pushed herself free of its grasp. The 45-70 thundered, and the Canine was wrenched backwards by the impact.

Three more became visible in the milling crowd, each of them struggling with a refugee. All over Washington Square, people and Canines were dying brutally, some of the people going utterly berserk when confronted by a charging Canine.

Lanning shot another, then hastily reloaded the two spend rounds.

Simon was watching their southern flank, while Amy concentrated on the east and the north.

Lanning grinned, an incongruous expression in the sea of turmoil. He was pleased he was going to die in such excellent company. Somehow, the companionship made his impending death much easier to accept.

Simon's 30-06 blasted, and a Canine coming from the south had the back of its head blown out. It had once been a young boy.

The number of refugees was falling drastically. Those able to move were backing toward the middle of the Square. Some had used up their ammunition and were wielding their rifles effectively as clubs, bludegoning their foes to death.

Some Canines had ascended the eastern wall and were endeavoring to eliminate the few defenders remaining on the barricade.

Simon spotted another one, its teeth locked on the leg of a child, a terrified boy of ten or so. He carefully aimed and fired. The petrified child screeched as Canine blood splattered all over his face.

The refugees in the center of Washington Square were slowly being forced into a compact mass by the oncoming creatures. Unable to shoot for fear of striking another refugee, many had given up shooting and were fighting the Canines hand-to-hand.

Simon wasn't about to stop firing the 30-06. He tended to disregard his personal safety, concentrating instead on any Canines in Amy's vicinity, focusing on any and all threats to Amy's life.

The howling in Washington Square had become louder than the gunfire.

Simon saw a Canine bearing down on Amy, drool coating its mouth and chin. He instantly shot the thing, inadvertently shivering as he did, his body breaking out in goose bumps.

"Help me!" an elderly woman screamed.

A Canine was on her back, biting at her neck.

Simon let it have one in the head.

The barricades surrounding Washington Square were devoid of any human defense. Unchecked, the Canines were having a field day, clawing and maiming at will.

A female Canine with red hair was only six feet from Amy before Simon spotted it. He snapped off a shot, the slug penetrating the Canine's left eye, boring through her brain and exploding out the back of her head, dyeing her hair an even darker red.

Two Canines burst through the crowd and charged Simon, viciously howling.

Simon aimed and pulled the trigger, braced for the recoil of the rifle and the sight of one of the Canines toppling to the turf. But the 30-06 didn't recoil, and the two Canines kept coming.

The rifle was empty!

Lanning suddenly stepped between Simon and the Canines, the 45-70 tight against his right shoulder. The big gun discharged, and the Canine on the right reacted as if it had smashed into a solid brick wall, stopping in midstride and falling to the ground. The 45-70 boomed again, and the other Canine lost the top of its head in a crimson geyser.

Simon hastily reloaded the 30-06.

Lanning stepped up close to Simon, his mouth only inches from Simon's left ear. "Listen, kid, before I forget, you might want to save two bullets."

"For what?"

"What do you think? Do you want Amy eaten by the Canines? Do you want to be eaten by them?"

Simon looked at Lanning, shocked by the suggestion. "I don't know if I could!"

"You don't have much time to make up your mind," Lanning said and whirled, shooting a Canine coming up on them from their left.

Simon, his mind spinning, watched Lanning reload the 45-70.

On all sides, the battle was nearing its climax. Washington Square was a gory, gruesome tableau; corpses littered the Square, while those still alive fought with an intense fury to remain alive. The Square was a virtual whirlwind of shooting and bashing, biting and slashing, but the Canines, by virtue of their superior numbers, were winning.

A ragged line of six Canines bore down on the center of the Square, coming from the west.

Simon, about to shoot one of them, hesitated when Lanning blocked his line of fire.

The Interpol agent was laughing. Calmly, coldly,

he strode toward the six Canines, the 45-70 held loosely in his hands.

What the hell was he doing? Simon started to follow Lanning, but suddenly held up, torn between his conflicting urge to assist Lanning and stay near Amy.

Lanning seemed to be challening the Canines, to actually want them to get closer. He waited until they were ten yards off and shot a husky male. With a practiced, smooth motion he levered another round into the chamber.

At eight yards he downed a second one.

Simon couldn't comprehend Lanning's peculiar behavior. He was acting as if he were on a firing range instead of being caught up in a tumultuous melee.

At six yards Lanning downed a third one.

Shoot faster! Simon mentally screamed.

At four yards Lanning blew the face off a fourth foe.

The two remaining Canines closed in, howling.

Simon saw Lanning sweep the stock of his rifle around and smash one of them in the right eye, even as he dodged around the last one.

The one struck in the eye recovered quickly, lunging for Lanning's legs.

"Lanning!" Simon shouted in alarm.

The agent was way ahead of him. Lanning twisted aside, his right hand dropping to his belt and flashing up and out, the service revolver clutched in his fingers. He cackled as he shot the Canine near his legs and laughed louder as he gunned down the last of the original six.

Amy shot a Canine coming from the south. "What's the matter with Lanning?" she yelled.

Lanning contemptuously kicked the dead Canine near his legs in the face, then strolled over to Simon and Amy, an odd grin on his lips.

"What's the matter with you?" Simon demanded.

"Are you trying to get yourself killed?"

Lanning gestured at the lethal bedlam surrounding them. "We're dead, anyway. Besides, I owe these bastards for what they did to my mother. Not to mention the fact they ruined my vacation." He chuckled at his sense of humor.

Simon glanced around.

None of the Canines were in their immediate proximity.

Lanning was reloading the 45-70 and the service revolver. He was even whistling while he worked.

"Here they come!" Amy abruptly yelled.

Canines were loping toward the few humans still on their feet in the middle of the Square. Attacking from every direction, the demented demons launched their final assault on the pathetically few still capable of opposing them.

Lanning took a step forward. "Come on! Come and get it, you miserable sons of bitches!"

Simon and Amy exchanged tender looks.

"I love you!" Simon shouted.

"And I love you!" Amy replied.

Further words were useless. The Canines were upon them!

Lanning bore the brunt of the initial onslaught, firing the 45-70 as fast as he could. Four Canines in almost as many seconds felt a searing, excruciating pain as a heavy slug rent their bodies from one end to the other, and they collapsed in twitching heaps on the ground. Lanning discarded the 45-70 and unslung Frederick's 30-06 from his left shoulder.

Simon and Amy opened fire, supporting Lanning, shooting as rapidly as their limited experience allowed, but for every Canine shot, two more instantly took its place.

Lanning emptied the 30-06, a ring of dead or dying creatures at his feet, and drew the service revolver, firing at another one.

Ten yards away, a big black man wearing a tan suit and wielding a large knife, went down under a snapping mass.

Simon and Amy had expended the rounds in their rifles, but there wasn't time to reload.

The Canines were on them in a savage rush.

Amy shrieked as a Canine clamped onto her left leg, biting deep and drawing blood. She futilely struck at it with her 270.

Simon lunged to her rescue, slamming the stock of his 30-06 onto the Canine's head and splitting its cranium.

The thing released Amy and sagged to the ground.

Another one barrled into Amy from behind, knocking her to her knees and ripping her left shoulder open.

Simon tried to aid her, but he was rammed from the left side and knocked onto his face. He frantically twisted, feeling teeth dig into the back of his neck. The Canine was straddling his legs and hips, preventing him from rising.

Suddenly, Lanning was there, a bloodstained Lanning, his suit torn, the jacket hanging in strips, the empty service revolver in his right fist. He laughed as he pounded the Canine on the head again and again, forcing the thing to leap to one side, but Lanning went after it, refusing to give it a chance, pounding again and again and again until it dropped, its forehead a pulpy, quivering mass.

Simon rose unsteadily to his hands and knees. Blood was flowing from his neck wound, pouring down his back and sides, dribbling down his jaw to his chin. He glimpsed three Canines as they plowed into Lanning, still game, fighting them to the last.

Amy was wrestling with a snarling Canine, her hands on its throat, striving to stop it from tearing her open with its fangs.

Simon started to rise to help them, when a heavy

form crashed into his right side and he was flung to the ground. His head connected with a hard object. Before he could regain his footing, a Canine was on him, its teeth tearing into his right shoulder. Simon tried to shove it away and stand, but a wave of vertigo overcame him and he sank down again, flat on his back. He was only dimly aware of a snarling visage inches from his face, and then everything became jumbled. He thought he heard a strange sound, a loud whoop-whoop-whoop, filling the air above him, accompanied by the sustained chatter of automatic weapons fire. For a fleeting second his vision cleared, and he could have sworn he saw a military helicopter hovering overhead, a man in a green uniform manning a huge machine gun on the side of the craft and firing down at the ground—firing and firing and firing.

Simon's consciousness started to slip away, and his final thoughts were of the woman he loved.

Amy, oh, Amy!

40

He was standing in a tunnel, alone and slightly frightened, and he could see a light at the end of the tunnel, far, far away.

Where was he?

He moved toward the light, but it seemed like it took an eternity to reach it.

He was back.

He knew it.

A soft voice told him his time had not yet come.

His eyelids trembled and opened, and for a moment the bright overhead lights stung his eyes.

"He's awake," someone said.

"I'll get the doctor," stated another.

He wanted to open his mouth and speak, but he felt so terribly weak.

A kindly, elderly face appeared above him, examining him. "He's still not out of the woods, yet," the elderly man commented. "The next stage is crucial. Have Nurse Toner keep a close eye on him."

He tried to move his tongue, but his mouth wouldn't cooperate. What had happened to his body? He was so very tired. He had never been so tired in his entire life.

He fell asleep.

The next he knew, his eyes opened, squinting at the glare of the lights, and he could feel his limbs. He tentatively touched his teeth with his tongue and found his mouth functioning again. "Is anyone there?" he asked.

Somone gasped. A pretty woman in white loomed above him. "Damn! You scared me to death, Mr. Darr. I was reading a book. Don't move. I'm going to get the others." She disappeared.

He swallowed, his mouth and throat feeling dry and raw. Straining, he managed to turn his head to the right. With a start, he realizing he was lying on a bed in a hospital room. There were two more beds in a row with his own, but he couldn't see the faces of the occupants.

The elderly doctor entered the room, smiling broadly. "At last! Can you talk, Simon? How do you feel?" The doctor stopped at the side of the bed and felt his forehead. "How do you feel?" he repeated.

Simon licked his lips. "I feel weak," he croaked, "and thirsty."

"That's to be expected, after what you went through. Your temperature has broke, and that's the sign we've been waiting for."

A nurse entered the room.

The doctor glanced at her. "Would you fetch a glass of water for Mr. Darr, please?" He smiled at Simon. "I'm Dr. Adams, by the way. I've been watching over you the past three weeks."

Simon's mouth dropped. "Three weeks!"

"That's right," Dr. Adams confirmed.

"Where am I?"

"At the Centers for Disease Control in Atlanta, Georgia," Dr. Adams replied.

"Georgia? How did I get here from Chicago? Where is . . ." Simon began, but stopped at the sight of the nurse bearing the glass of water.

Dr. Adams took the glass from the nurse and

handed it to Simon. "Don't gulp it," he directed.

Simon gingerly held the cool glass in his right hand, afraid he would drop it, then slowly raised the glass to his lips and sipped. The refreshing liquid revitalized him, soothing his parched mouth and throat. He sighed contentedly when he finished the glass and gave it back to the doctor.

"I would imagine you have a lot of questions," Dr. Adams said, setting the glass on a nearby stand. "I'll answer as many as I can."

"My wife," Simon said, almost choking on the words, suppressing an impulse to cry. "Amy Brant . . . sorry . . . Amy Darr. Do you have any idea what happened to her? Or my brother Jay? Or . . ."

Before Dr. Adams could respond, someone else spoke up from one of the other beds. "Will you keep it down over there, kid! I'm trying to catch up on my beauty sleep."

"Lanning? Is that you?" Simon exclaimed in delight, attempting to rise.

"Hold still a moment," Dr. Adams ordered. He reached down and pressed a button on the side of the bed. With a muted whine, the upper half of the hospital bed elevated until Simon was in a sitting position. "I don't know about your brother, but as for Amy . . ."

"Amy!" Simon inadvertently shouted, relief washing over him.

Amy was in the bed next to his, sound asleep. Beyond her, Lanning was sitting up in the third bed, his body swathed in bandages, looking ludicrous in a light blue hospital gown.

"Glad to see you finally joined us," Lanning said. "I think your woman was growing bored with my company."

Simon gawked at Amy. "Is she all right?"

"She's fine," Dr. Adams assured him. "Would you like me to wake her?"

"I'll do it," Lanning interjected. "Hey! Bone freak! Prince Charming is awake!"

Amy's eyes fluttered and opened. She gazed at Lanning, puzzled, not fully alert.

"I know I'm adorable," Lanning told her, "but you should be looking the other way."

Confused, Amy complied. Her eyes widened when she saw Simon. "Simon!" She glanced at the doctor. "Is he going to be okay?"

Dr. Adams nodded. "He's out of it."

Amy started to slide from the bed.

"Don't even think it," Dr. Adams declared. "You will stay in your bed until I tell you otherwise."

"It isn't fair," Amy said, pouting.

"I don't understand," Simon interrupted. "The last thing I can remember is Washington Square and the Canines. What happened?"

Dr. Adams looked at Amy. "Do you want to tell him, or should I?"

"Be my guest," Amy said.

Dr. Adams leaned on Simon's bed. "I don't have all the facts, mind you, but most of them. If you want all the details, you should talk to Buddy Snyder. He can fill in the gaps. He should be around to see you presently. He's taken a personal interest in your case."

"Don't forget to tell him he snores in his sleep," Lanning commented. "It sounds like he's sawing steel bars."

Dr. Adams grinned. "Do you remember Amy making a phone call from Chicago to the Centers for Disease Control?"

Simon nodded.

"Well, she impressed Mr. Snyder and a Mr. Kramer with her sincerity. They believed her when she told them about a tomb in Egypt and a mummy, and . . ." He paused, looking at Amy. "What was it you said they were called again?"

''The Dog People.''

''Ahhh, yes. Anyway, Mr. Snyder and Mr. Kramer decided they wanted to talk to her. She had told them she was calling from Chicago, from a library there, I believe. It took them hours to prevail on their superiors to agree to sending in a military force to retrieve her. By the time the commandos arrived in their helicopters, there was a full-fledged battle going on. They literally plucked the three of you from the jaws of death. I understand they were only going to rescue Amy, but she refused to leave unless they brought you along.''

''And don't forget me,'' Lanning chimed in.

''It was horrible,'' Amy said, taking up the narrative. ''Both you and Lanning were unconscious. There were only two or three other people alive when the helicopters swooped in and started firing. I don't know what type of machine guns they used, but they mowed the Canines down in droves. It seemed like the firing never would end. They dropped smoke bombs all around us, and one of the helicopters landed. I couldn't believe it when one of the soldiers walked up to me, pointing a gun at my chest and wearing a gas mask of some sort, and asked if I knew an Amy Brant.'' She giggled. ''I was so nervous when I called here, I forgot to use my married name.''

''To make a long story short,'' Dr. Adams continued, ''so that you can get your rest, the three of you were airlifted to Atlanta. You were placed in quarantine. Amy told Mr. Snyder about the Egyptians and the Dog People and the fire dust a magician used to wipe them out. Every researcher was put on the case, trying to discover what fire dust could have been. Prominent Egyptologists were consulted, and they narrowed the possibilities down to three or four minerals and compounds, finally deciding on sulphur.''

''Sulphur?'' Simon repeated.

"That's right," Dr. Adams affirmed. "Some people call it brimstone. As you know, we use sulphur in things like matches and gunpowder, also in medicine. Sulphur is an electronegative mineral used by the body for promoting the secretion of bile and for helping the liver absorb minerals. Some people like to call sulphur the beauty mineral, because the body needs it for healthy hair, skin and fingernails. It has the opposite affect on Canines, however. Kills them. The military concocted a mild sulphuric mist and sprayed it over the Infected Cities. The mist might make a normal person slightly sick, but produces severe, fatal reactions in the Canines."

"Did you use the mist on us?" Simon asked.

"No," Dr. Adams said, frowning. "The three of you were infected with the Canine bacteria, but you hadn't transformed yet. So the chemists developed an experimental sulphur-based antidote, and you three were our first guinea pigs. The antidote eradicated the Canine bacteria, but unfortunately they miscalculated and made your doses too strong. Any mineral, if consumed in excess, can act as a toxin on the body. For the past three weeks we've been doing our best to keep you alive, Simon. Most of the sulphur has been removed from your system, and you'll be good as new in a week or so. You were the last one to recover. Mr. Lanning woke up about ten days ago, and Amy revived six days ago."

"And I won't become a Canine?" Simon inquired anxiously.

Dr. Adams smiled. "I assure you that you won't become a Canine. You'll enjoy a normal life and probably live to a ripe, old age."

Simon stared at the ceiling. Thank you, Lord, for sparing us, he silently prayed. For the first time in many years, he had to admit he felt religious.

Dr. Adams headed toward the door. "Now I want all of you to get some rest. That includes you, Mr.

Lanning. The nurses tell me you're giving them a hard time."

"Me?" Lanning countered innocently. "What did I do?"

Dr. Adams paused at the door. "Let me put it this way. Your hands aren't buffalo."

"What's that supposed to mean?"

"It means your hands shouldn't be roaming where they've been roaming," Dr. Adams said. He looked at Amy. "Try and get more sleep, and don't keep Simon awake. He needs all the rest he can get at this point." He glanced at Simon. "We'll continue your intravenous feeding for a few days, until you get your strength back. Now get some sleep."

Dr. Adams departed, the nurse on his heels.

Amy caught Simon's eye. "Do you know how worried I've been? I was afraid you weren't going to make it, darling. I've wanted to touch you and smother you with kisses."

"Ohhhhhh," Lanning groaned, "I think I'm going to be sick!"

"Why don't you?" Simon asked Amy. "I don't see any intravenous tubes sticking in your arm."

Amy grinned as she clambered from her bed. The tiled floor was cold on the bottom of her feet as she quietly padded over to Simon's bed. She stared into his eyes, her own watering. "I love you so very much," she said gently.

"And I love you, Mrs. Darr," Simon stated.

Amy bent over and passionately kissed him on the lips. Her mouth opened and their tongues entwined.

Simon savored the sweet taste of his wife, thrilled at being alive, at being able to love and be loved. He mentally resolved to never waste another precious second of life again. Life was meant for living! He couldn't imagine anything grander than simply being able to breathe fresh air, to observe the radiant splendor of a setting sun, to have the love of a wonderful woman like Amy, or to have a friend like Lanning.

Lanning!

From the third bed in the room, a mischievous voice addressed the room at large, directing a question to no one in particular.

"Why is it you never have a camera when you need one? They didn't tell me this room is rated Triple X!"

41

Buddy Snyder was seated at his desk, idly gazing out the window. His brow was furrowed, and he was biting his fingernails. He was troubled, and he didn't like it, because by all rights, he should be elated.

An effective antidote to C-666 had been developed.

The military had destroyed the Canines in the Infected Cities and all isolated cases in rural areas had been tracked down and promptly dealt with.

NATO forces had eliminated the Canines in Europe and Africa, using American supplied sulphuric mist. The antidote had been mass produced with huge quantities shipped overseas.

The Canine threat was effectively at an end.

So why was he still troubled?

Two reasons, actually. Both of them hinged on the TV show he had seen last night, Gladys' religious program featuring her favorite TV evangelist. This evangelist, predictably, claimed the Canine epidemic was the divine wrath of God descending on mankind for its wickedness. He went on to talk about Satan and how the Devil was deceiving the majority of mankind with his sophist distortions of the divine Word. And then he mentioned what he called "the mark of the beast,'' or the mark of Satan.

Buddy could vividly recall the evangelist's next words.

''Let him who has ears, hear! I quote from Revelation, Chapter 13, Verse 18,'' the evangelist had said. '' 'Here is wisdom. Let him that hath understanding count the number of the beast: for it is the number of a man; and his number is six hundred threescore and six.' '' The evangelist had paused and glared into the camera. ''That is the number of Satan! Six hundred and sixty-six!''

Buddy frowned.

666.

It was a coincidence, he told himself. It had to be. So what if the Centers for Disease Control had assigned the identification code number C-666 to the Canine plague? It didn't mean a thing. He would have passed it off as a fluke, if it wasn't for the second reason he was disturbed.

The antidote to C-666 was common, ordinary sulphur, the mineral used in matches.

The mineral also known by the name of brimstone.

Which meant that C-666 was, in essence, destroyed by fire and brimstone.

Buddy looked up at the azure sky.

It *had* to be a coincidence.

It had to be!

Buddy's scientifically oriented mind wouldn't allow him to accept any other explanation.

But just in case, he promised himself, he was going to begin attending church again after years of neglect.

He glanced at his desk, surprised to see a dispatch lying on top of his Incoming box. How did that get there? Someone must have deposited the message while he was ruminating. He picked it up and read the one page report.

So. It seemed the Canine epidemic wasn't completely eradicated. Word of a few Canine sightings had been received from Istanbul, Madrid, and Amsterdam. The authorities in each city maintained all the Canines had been slain, but to be safe, they were advising travelers to avoid those cities until further notice.

The intercom buzzed.

"Yes?"

"It's your wife, on line two," Ms. Krepps said.

Buddy groaned and lifted the receiver. "Yes, Gladys?"

"You should be ashamed of yourself." Gladys tore into him. "You just don't care what the neighbors think, do you?"

"Gladys," Buddy sighed wearily, "what are you talking about?"

"The grass," she snapped indignantly.

"What about it?"

"Have you taken a good look at our lawn lately?"

"Well, no," Buddy confessed, "I have—"

"You bet you haven't!" Gladys cut him off. "You've been too busy at work to bother mowing our lawn. Now look at it. The grass is so tall you can't even see my flamingos. When were you expecting to get around to cutting it—next year?"

"I've been real bu—"

"Don't give me that excuse. I've heard the news. That silly Canine business is over. So how come you're spending so much time at work? Why aren't you staying at home with me like you should?"

"I . . ."

"Don't try to sweet talk me!" Gladys exclaimed. "I know why you're doing it. It's just an excuse for you to get out of doing your chores. Honestly, I don't know why I bother putting up with you. Mother's right. You're a lazy bum. All you care about is your job." Gladys paused and sniffed. "I don't know if I can take much more of your abuse. I need a rest, a vacation. I think I'll go and visit mother."

"That's an excellent idea."

"See how you like it with me gone," Gladys continued, oblivious to his comment. "See how you like doing your own washing and cleaning and iron . . ." She abruptly stopped. "What did you just say?"

"I said it's an excellent idea," Buddy repeated, "going to visit your mother." He paused as inspiration struck. "In fact, I'll go you one better."

"What do you mean?" Gladys asked, confused.

"I really am busy at work," Buddy stressed, "and I can't get away for weeks, maybe months. But how would you like it if I agreed to foot the bill for a trip to Europe for two, for you and your mom?"

Gladys snickered. "Yeah, sure."

"I'm serious," Buddy assured her.

"You are? I didn't think you liked my mother."

"We've had our disagreements," Buddy tactfully admitted, "but I know how close you two are. You haven't had a real vacation in three years. Wouldn't you like to go to Europe?"

"Of course."

"And don't you think your mom would like to go?"

"You know she would."

"So why not go? You said that you need a vacation."

"It would be fun," Gladys said excitedly.

"Sure it would. Why don't you call your mother right now?" Buddy suggested. "If she agrees, and all goes well, you can be on your way inside of twenty-four hours."

"I can't believe it! Europe!"

"Believe it," Buddy said.

"But where would we go?" Gladys asked.

"Any place you want," Buddy replied. "It's on

me."

"Say!" Gladys exclaimed. "I just had a idea."

"What's that?" Buddy asked innocently.

"You know how my mother has always wanted to go see the city where they have all those paintings," Gladys said. "The one where they have all those works by Rembrandt and Van Gogh. You know what an art buff my mom is."

"She certainly is," Buddy agreed.

"What's the name of that city?" Gladys asked.

"I think it's Amsterdam," Buddy answered.

"That's it! Amsterdam!" Gladys laughed happily. "You really wouldn't mind if we spent two weeks in Amsterdam?"

"Gladys, dearest," Buddy said sweetly, "I won't mind. You two stay as long as you want."